THE LIGHT FALLS

THE KILLIAN BLADE SERIES

STELLA BRIE

Cover Design: Covers by Jules

Editing: Kaye Kemp Book Polishing

❀ Created with Vellum

Playlist

"I Hope ur Miserable until ur Dead" - Nessa Barrett

"Shatter Me" – Lindsey Stirling (feat. Lzzy Hale)

"Hiding in the Crowd" – Molly Kate Kestner & Night Panda

"Stand By You" – Rachel Platten

"Hate You + Love You" – Cheat Codes (feat. AJ Mitchell)

"Just Breathe" – Pearl Jam

"Rise Up" – Imagine Dragons

"Top of the World" – The Score

"Inside Out" - Zedd, Griff

"Princesses Don't Cry" - Carys

"Take Over" – Hidden Citizens (feat. Ruelle)

"Who Are You" – Svrcina

"Feel Invincible" – Skillet

"Man or Monster" – Sam Tinnesz + Zayde Wolf

"White Flag" – Daughtry

"Little Fight Left" – Tommee Profitt, Fleurie & Jung Youth

"Revolution" - The Score

AUTHOR'S NOTE

This book is a Why Choose romance, which means the heroine does not have to choose between male interests. The book is a spin-off from The Killian Blade Series and includes fictional characters and places introduced in that world with little additional explanation or backstory.

Please take care of yourself and read at your own discretion. Recommended for 18+ due to mature content.

DEDICATION

Killian Blade Series fans—you inspire me to write more. Thanks for following me on this journey.

CHAPTER ONE

<u>MERI</u>

Doubt and fear creep into the silence to press against me, their wicked mouths whispering the cruel truth of my inadequacy for this role. *Pretender. Imposter.* The words hit home. Solandis should be standing here. As Princess of the Light Fae, she grew up in this world. It's hers by birthright. Too bad she doesn't want it.

A harsh laugh escapes. Technically, I wasn't even born. A sadistic sorceress seeking revenge created me out of essence and the darkest of magics. Yet here I stand instead of my aunt, the princess, all because I am her sister Nyssa's "daughter." Fate has a nasty sense of humor.

Without the chatter of others, the negative voices in my head grow louder every minute I'm alone. My neck becomes clammy. Desperate to escape, I cross the bedroom to the mirror, hoping the image I saw earlier will silence my insecurities.

The reflection wears my features, but not the ones I'm used

to seeing. Magic has transformed average into stylish perfection. Familiar platinum hair falls perfectly and softly around my face and down my back while turquoise eyes, framed by impossibly long dark lashes, sparkle and look almost otherworldly. A wry smile twists my mouth. Too bad the glamour can't hide the fear and uncertainty swirling in their depths.

Maybe this dress will draw their eyes away from the emotional chaos bubbling beneath the surface. It's certainly a statement in itself. Custom made by the royal seamstress, my coronation gown is a masterpiece of Fae magic and talent. The plunging strapless neckline and semi-sheer bodice skims my body in a way that defies gravity until it meets the full skirt at my waist. Made of a beautiful champagne-gold silk, the voluminous fabric is heavily embroidered with platinum roses, the exact shade of my hair, that bloom when faery light shines on them. It should be heavy, but magic has made it so airy and light, it feels like I'm not wearing anything at all. The true wow factor, though, is the matching cape with its over-the-top poofy half-sleeves and billowing fabric that cascades behind me as if a gentle breeze is moving through its folds.

The woman in the mirror looks like a queen, but she is a beautiful fraud. A nobody playing dress up. All my life, I lived in the Underworld with very little power to call my own. Yet here I am, full of magic, in the Light Fae Kingdom, about to accept the crown and vow to be their queen. This is a fairytale dream, right? Why does it feel like it's not? Panic engulfs me, and my trembling hands clench the delicate fabric.

"Scared?" a sarcastic voice mocks, then Cormal appears beside me in the mirror, looking devastatingly handsome as usual. His tall, dark frame the perfect complement to my petite fairness. A fairytale couple like Cinderella and her prince, except neither of us could convincingly play the role.

The scent of his masculinity, along with a hint of the Underworld, fills the air, making me ache... for him and my home.

One sniff and a familiar longing fills me, sliding low, until I'm craving the unattainable. Unfortunately, it's been like this since the moment we met, but it's one-sided and pointless, and I'm so tired of it.

Angry, I grind my teeth and glare at him. "Nobody invited you."

Bright blue eyes sweep down my dress before returning to stare at me in challenge. His mouth quirks up. "Admit it. You missed me."

Looking away from eyes that see too much, I shift my attention to the formal suit he's wearing and raise an eyebrow. Custom made, the black tailcoat jacket, embroidered with the same platinum pattern of my dress on the chest and sleeves, falls elegantly from his broad shoulders to his knees. The full-bloom roses should look ultra-feminine, but if anything, they only emphasize his masculinity. As does the all-black ensemble underneath. A seemingly effortless look, but everything Cormal does is intentional.

My gaze lingers on the pattern sewn into his clothes and a part of me is thrilled he went to so much trouble to match my dress. But I can't help but wonder why? Ever since I stabbed him with the knife and told him to get out of my life, he's been unpredictable and moody. Almost like he cares.

Damn him. The thought just pisses me off.

I return my gaze to the mirror and give him my most haughty look. "Outsiders are not allowed to attend the coronation ceremony. Don't you have a criminal kingdom to run?" With now-steady hands, I smooth the tiny wrinkles I'd made in the delicate skirt.

The air between us is thick with unspoken words and needs that never get fulfilled. We stand so close, yet we've never been further apart. I pause. The thought is terrifying. Maybe this is the beginning of the end. The point in time when I save myself instead of wishing he would step up and do it.

His voice is raspy when he finally replies. "Rules rarely apply to me."

True. He sets his own rules. I'd ask how he got in here, but I've yet to discover a place he couldn't enter.

"What do you want?"

The smallest of smirks appears. "It isn't what I want. I'm here to help you—escape, of course. I figured you would lose your resolve... right about now." He turns toward me. "I don't think you have time to change, but honestly, I quite like this look on you. Beautiful. Sophisticated. Almost a queen." A blunt finger glides across the tops of my breasts, making me inhale sharply. "Don't worry, I'll send someone to get your things later."

For a split second, hurt blooms, stealing my breath, but blinding fury soon eclipses it. My magic flares in response, and I jab a finger into his chest. "All my life I've looked for you to save me, but not anymore. I have my own magic now, and once I'm queen, I'll have true power." Sparks fly from the tip, piercing his skin, and his mouth twists in a wince. "Now, get out of my way so I can go get my crown."

A gleam appears in his eyes as he tilts his head in consideration. After a second, he extends his elbow. "Allow me to escort you."

I stare at the muscular, elegantly clad arm. Even angry, I'm tempted to take it and draw on his strength, but I can't. I won't.

Gathering up my dress, I sweep past him and stride into the hall, only to stop abruptly when I see it's empty. The guards Solandis tasked with escorting me to the coronation are gone.

Furious, I pivot to face Cormal. "Where are the guards?"

He steps to my side and smoothly places my hand in the crook of his arm. "I dismissed them." Without waiting for my consent, he moves forward.

The hall is a blur of white marble and delicate gold accents as we walk. Confusion joins my anger. I'm never standing on solid ground with him.

Does he believe I can do this or not?

I heave a disgusted sigh. This habit of examining his every word and expression will be tough to break. All my life I've looked to him for... everything. Approval, security, confidence, and even love. No more. Determined to move on, I take a step away from him.

With a fierce look, he stops me. "Once you accept the crown, you'll have a target on your back. Don't try to navigate the politics or court intrigue by yourself. Rely on Solandis. She grew up in this world," he orders me, a note of worry in his voice. "The captain owed me a favor, and I asked him to assign his most trusted soldiers to be your personal guard. He's also going to assign someone to you for defensive training. Keep your guard up at all times. Trust nobody." In a rare sign of agitation, he thrusts a hand through his wavy black hair. "I'll check in on you regularly. Be careful."

A sliver of gratitude rolls across my shoulders, but I take a deep breath and shrug it off. "Don't worry. I learned my lesson long ago. The only people I trust are family—Callyx, Arden, and Solandis. They've never let me down."

His mouth hardens when the words hit him, but I refuse to flinch, not when the past sits between us like an immovable object.

I turn to face the imposing doors at the end of the hall. Twenty feet tall and made of gold, each of the engraved doors tells the origin of the Fae, the cleaving of the land and people into light and dark, and the brilliant rise of the light Fae. It's a powerful reminder to all who enter of their heritage.

For me, those doors symbolize the future, not the past. The next chapter of my life. One where I'm powerful, not weak. A world full of magic and filled with Fae like me. No sorceress, demons, or criminals allowed unless I give them permission. I glance at Cormal one last time.

He bends down to whisper harshly in my ear. "You have everything you need to be queen, but you're going to have to fight like hell to stay in power. Don't let anyone take your crown from you." Straightening, he releases me and steps into the shadows.

A shiver runs down my spine as his voice echoes inside me. I want to dismiss the warning, but Cormal's damn good at strategy. He sees and anticipates more than most. It's how he stays on top of the largest criminal empire in any realm. King of a bloodthirsty and brutal hill.

After a moment, I lift my chin, turn to the doors, and wave my hand.

They soundlessly glide open to reveal a cavernous room specifically designed to serve the light Fae court. Tall, golden columns rise fifty feet in the air to the gilded ceiling, giving the room its grandeur. Instead of chandeliers, magic spheres bathe the room in a golden glow. Tiny decorative swirls and filigree mirrors grace the walls on both sides of the room, but they pale in comparison to the magnificence of the back wall. Gold climbing vines cover the entire surface from floor to ceiling. Nestled within the delicate arms and branches, brilliant flowers made of colorful jewels wink in the light. High above, a massive sun shines fairy light down on the entire scene. It's an utterly breathtaking homage to the land.

My gaze moves from the room to the light Fae court. Dressed in their finest attire, they flank the center path, all eyes locked on me. I smile but none return the gesture. It's as if they're frozen. Not a whisper of sound or movement breaks the absolute stillness of the room.

My nerves flare, but I clamp down on them. Deliberately blurring their faces, I search for Solandis. I don't have to look very long.

Elegantly regal in a royal purple gown that clings to her every curve, she moves to the center of the room, and with a serene smile gracing her face, beckons me forward.

Releasing my breath, I enter the coronation hall. The second my foot crosses the threshold, the smell of spring surrounds me. Honeysuckle, newly grown grass, and a bouquet of blooming flowers fill the air, and I automatically breathe in their enticing scents. Buzzing bees and the melodic sound of a nearby stream instantly soothes my racing heart. And when the warmth of the sun hits my bare shoulders, it makes me want to raise my face to the sky to bask in its glory. The land is present here, welcoming every light Fae who enters those doors... including me. I belong here. The overwhelming doubt and fear I've felt all day eases to a dull roar.

When I reach Solandis, I drop into a low curtsy to pay my respects. Until I'm crowned, she is the highest-ranking royal Fae in the room, even if she refuses to accept the position of queen. I've begged her to reconsider so many times, but she insists the power is calling for me. And whether Vargas is alive or not—and she truly believes he is—it's her destiny to follow a different path.

When I rise, Solandis gestures for me to proceed down the center of the path.

Every step carries me toward the wooden throne on the dais. Pure white and made of wood, there are no decorative ornaments or color to distract from its appearance, only the faintest impression of a crown imprinted on the back. The ancient throne magically appears for every coronation. Fae believe the enchanted wood is carved from a sacred tree in the Wilds. A mystical forest that thrives between the light and dark where few dare to venture, except, of course, the Wild Hunt, who calls it home.

With a practiced move, I sweep my dress into my hands and carefully navigate the three steps, then turn to face the crowd.

Solandis moves to my right. This is it. One quiet deep breath in, and I sit on the throne.

The collective stillness of the room deepens as everyone watches for the slightest hint of rejection. When nothing happens, I release the breath I've been holding and nod at Solandis.

She holds her hands up high, and a crown appears in them. For the briefest of moments, she pauses, and sadness crosses her face.

Nyssa. She must be thinking of her coronation. Solandis did the same for her sister that she now does for me. Nyssa's daughter.

A dip of her chin has me holding my hands out. This is the second test. If the crown rejects me, it will simply disappear. When I envisioned this moment, my hands were trembling, and the Fae were sneering with disdain. But to my tremendous relief, they're completely steady, and the faces around me are emotionless.

Solandis lays the crown in my hands.

I'm surprised to see it's almost an exact replica of the wall behind the throne. A circle of intricate gold branches intertwined with delicate-looking jeweled flowers, but unlike the wall, these are all diamonds. Similar to the throne, the crown is ancient and filled with the magic of the land.

For a minute or two, it does nothing. I continue to hold it high. Either I'm the queen it wants or I'm not. There's nothing more I can do. I wait for it to decide.

The Fae push closer. Signs of emotion appear—the lift of an eyebrow, a slight tilt of a head, a spark of glee, and, of course, the dreaded half smirk.

I continue to wait.

Moments later, the branches begin to move. Thorns appear. One extends to prick my finger. It absorbs my blood, and the crown begins to glow.

The tiniest tremble shakes my hands when I realize it's truly happening.

Straightening on the throne, I carefully place the crown on my head. The bright golden light encompassing the crown spreads to cover my entire body. Power, sharp and piercing like a live wire, begins to flow in my veins, bringing me knowledge of the kingdom. The way it looks, smells, tastes, and sounds. Power races to each corner of the land, mapping boundaries in my mind.

The exhaustiveness of the information is almost overwhelming, and my back arches from the strain. Digging my hands into the arms of the hard chair, I continue to ride out the wave, refusing to let one sound leave my lips. Pain is nothing. I have Leandra, the sorceress and my illustrious guardian, to thank for those lessons.

Invisible threads tie me to the Light Fae Kingdom. The gossamer strands feed information back to me as they sweep across the kingdom. Once I'm firmly tethered to the land and its people, the power whispers my new name in my ear, then settles to a low hum.

One final act.

Searing heat and pain streak across my forehead. Thankfully, Solandis prepared me for this part, although it's more than I anticipated. A scream threatens to emerge, but I clench my teeth to hold it in. The crown, and its power, will live inside me, but my forehead will bear its brand as a sign of my status to the light Fae and those who have sworn fealty to this kingdom.

Just when I don't think I can bear it any longer, the crown disappears along with the pain. A cool breeze sweeps over my brow, drying the beads of sweat. Stunned, I sit for a minute, trying to comprehend the magnitude of what I am now, but the knowledge of the land and its people is so vast it's like a deep, dark hole inside me. When I envisioned being queen, I thought only of the aristocratic light Fae in front of me and the lands surrounding the castle. The reality is almost immeasurable, and the weight of it settles like a mantle on my shoulders.

Clamping down on the panic edging into my emotions, I release the arms of the chair and stand. All visible emotions are immediately erased. As one, the crowd moves into a deep curtsy or bow to pay their respects. My eyes dart to Solandis, and she, too, sweeps into a curtsy. With a wave, I motion for them to rise.

Solandis turns to the crowd. "Queen Merindah, ruler of the light Fae, with dominion over the land and its people. May The Keepers bless her!" Solandis' words ring out.

"May The Keepers bless Queen Merindah," the crowd repeats.

CHAPTER TWO

<u>MERI</u>

Movement above causes me to look up, where I find two balconies practically hidden from the rest of the room by the massive pillars, standing on each side. Castle staff, like the royal seamstress and maids who helped me get ready today, fill every inch of space. Unlike the stoic lords and ladies, these faces are filled with emotions. I smile and nod at them. Several seem surprised by my actions, looking at each other first, before letting their lips curve in return.

Bright blue eyes lock with mine. Cormal stands proudly amongst the masses. He didn't leave. I almost smile.

As I hold his stare, he bends at the waist, bowing deeply.

I quickly glance around to see if anyone is looking at him, but all eyes are on me.

My eyes move back to Cormal, and he gives me a slow wink.

Arrogant asshole.

The handsome Fae guard at his side says something to him, and he turns away to engage in conversation. When the guard pats Cormal on the back, my eyes narrow. Very few are given the privilege of touching him. They must know each other well.

Tearing my eyes from the two of them, I return my gaze to the blank faces in front of me. My new court. Stunning perfection in every line and feature. While their expressions show nothing but mild curiosity, hatred burns in more than one pair of eyes.

Get in line, I silently scoff. Thanks to the sorceress's utter disregard for others and the distasteful tasks she often assigned to me, the list of people I've pissed off is long and a hell of a lot more dangerous than the individuals standing here.

Their hatred worries Solandis, though. She canvassed the highest-ranking lords and ladies of the light Fae last week to ascertain my support. Several stated their willingness to reserve judgement and give me time to prove myself, but she is concerned they are too set in their ways to be trusted. Nyssa took the crown with a divided court, but she knew how to maneuver around them.

Maybe I'm a bit worried. My teeth clench at the honesty in this statement. Their intentions are unknown, and judgement is nothing but a sword hanging over my head. When I screw up—and I will—it will fall across my neck. At least the hatred they're showing me right now is familiar and honest.

I brush off the worry and observe the people in the hall.

While the males might be dressed similarly to Cormal, the elaborate decoration on their clothing borders the absurd. Outlandishly adorned with jewels, feathers, and precious metals, their bright suits make them look like peacocks arrogantly strutting across the floor.

For the females, this is a brutally fierce competition. Formal gowns with intricate designs and layers of luxurious material are but tools to showcase them and their power. Faery lights twinkle among layers of tulle and painted skirts, wind gently blows their hair and fluffs their skirts, fire cascades in thin rivers down long locks, and jewels, each more extravagant than the next, actually twinkle in the magical light. It's so elaborate, I can't even take it all in.

The excessive power used to enhance their fashion is extremely indulgent and mind boggling. According to Solandis, the ability to display continuous magic is proof of the vast magical reserves available to them and their status in the light Fae society.

Forcing a smile, I address the crowd. "Thank you all for attending. This is traditionally the moment when I'm supposed to give you specific promises for our future, but there is still much for me to learn about what the light Fae truly need. Instead, I offer you the following: I promise to do everything in my power to increase my knowledge and make informed decisions. I promise to protect the land and its people against any threats, and most of all, I promise to serve the needs of the kingdom." It's a simple statement of my intentions without going overboard on promises that will bite me back later.

Nobody claps or says a word, but that's not a surprise, and honestly, it doesn't matter. I'm not trying to win their approval tonight. As light Fae, their fealty is to me and the crown. My goal was to make my first statement as their queen.

Solandis loops her arm with mine in a show of solidarity. "Well done. Now, for the hard part." She leads us off the dais to greet the couple standing nearby. "Lord Camon, High Fae of Spring, and his lovely mate, Brina."

Tall and arrogantly handsome like most aristocratic Fae, Lord Camon has rich brown hair and bright green eyes the color of new grass, but surprisingly, his dark green court attire, while stylish, is quite subdued.

His petite mate, on the other hand, is spectacular and unique compared to those I see around us, and I'm not talking about her clothing. At around five feet tall, Lady Brina has long, dark blue hair, contrasting light blue eyes, luminescent scales on her temples, and luscious curves. Her gown is so form-fitting, it looks painted on. Absolutely stunning. He certainly 'mated' up.

Lord Camon bows stiffly, but his partner flows gracefully into a curtsy.

"Queen Merindah, it's lovely to meet you," she assures me. Her eyes dart briefly to her husband, then return to me.

Lord Camon is the highest-ranking spring Fae and, according to Solandis, the most vocal opponent of my coronation.

"It's a pleasure to meet you both. Lord Camon and Lady Brina," I reply firmly, although I can't help wondering why he's so opposed to me ruling.

The crowd around us audibly inhales, and Lord Camon's mouth compresses in fury. Lady Brina freezes.

Confused, I raise an eyebrow to Solandis.

She leans down and whispers in my ear. "Brina is a Water Fae. As a Lesser Fae, she cannot use the title of Lady."

Shit. I remember Solandis telling me about the Lesser Fae, but I expected them to be creatures with sharp teeth, animalistic features, and such. I inwardly groan at how much there is to learn, but hopefully, now that the coronation is over, I can focus.

"Please forgive me. You're so gorgeous, my brain went blank for a second. Maybe I should just call you Beautiful Brina," I jokingly plead. My first introduction and I'm already apologizing.

Her light eyes study me for a second before she graces me with a small smile. "Of course, Your Majesty." She steps closer to Lord Camon, and he automatically puts his arm around her waist.

It's obvious she doesn't believe me.

Tactfully retreating, Solandis moves us along to the next person. "Lady Demira of Summer."

A tall, blond woman with sharp cheekbones and purple eyes dips into a curtsy. "Queen Merindah." When she rises, she eyes me with disdain. "It's beneath the Queen to speak to the Lesser Fae. They exist to serve us and should only be addressed in that capacity, unless, of course, you're a High Fae with special privileges."

Out of the corner of my eye, I see Lord Camon swivel around in fury, and while I don't blame him, I don't need this scene to escalate. "Lady Demira of Summer," I repeat, scrambling for something to say... summer. "Any relation to Lord Theron?"

A sour look crosses her face. "He's my father's child." She doesn't elaborate further. Another person who doesn't meet with her approval.

With a purposely confused look, I clarify. "Theron's your half-brother?"

She fails to realize I just called him by his first name. "I don't claim him as a relative." Her eyes dart to the Fae around us who give her approving smiles. "He's an indiscretion from my father's past."

Indiscretion. Unbelievable. Theron is the result of a mated match, and therefore, a very legitimate heir to summer.

I dart a mischievous glance at Solandis. "Isn't Lord Theron part of your immediate family?"

Solandis' blue eyes coldly assess the Fae in front of her. "I absolutely claim Lord Theron as family. Come, Queen Merindah, let's find you more... suitable company." With a toss of her head, she turns her back to Demira in an elegant, but deliberate, snub.

The crowd follows Solandis' cue and turn their backs on the Fae they heartily approved of just minutes ago. Lady Demira looks stricken for a second, then her eyes narrow hatefully on me.

Another fan. To be fair, we were never going to be friends anyway, not with the way she feels about Theron. I can't help but look back at Lord Camon, but he's already moving away.

How am I supposed to turn him into an ally? Not only does he oppose me as queen, but he's also actively working to reduce my power within the council. The laws for the light Fae are introduced and voted on by the lords and ladies who rule within the council. Right now, as queen, I can veto any law. He seeks to take that power away.

We approach the next group, and Solandis introduces them. We make small talk for a few minutes, then move on. It's all so civilized and restrained compared to the riotous hedonistic parties we give in the Underworld. The quietness of the room alone is driving me insane. After another hour of meet and greet, faces and names start to blur together, and my patience is nearly gone. Tired of listening to snide comments and thinly veiled insults, I need to escape for a few minutes and breathe less hate-filled air.

I scan the walls along the side of the room, looking for a discreet exit, but I don't see a single door. Surely this room has more doors than just the two at the entrance. A glint of red stops me in my tracks, and I crane my neck to get a better look.

It's him.

Standing alone, he's almost blocked from my view by a large pillar, but his hair is a beacon he can't hide. The auburn top layer flares red under the golden lights, giving it the look of fire, while the black strands underneath resemble the soot left in its wake.

Excusing myself, I slowly make my way to his side of the room. The last thing I want to do is trigger old memories by rushing toward him. The bland mask he's wearing says casual and relaxed, but looking closer, I see the tic in his chiseled jaw and tightness in the corners of his golden eyes.

Dressed in black and the deepest of reds, Rivan's attire is similar to Cormal's, but the decorative pattern on his jacket is only displayed on one side. When I get closer, I notice the pattern is the same as my dress. A deliberate sign from Cormal to identify one of his chosen protectors? Or a silent sign of support from Rivan himself?

"Rivan," I exclaim, reaching out to grab his hand.

Stiffening, he pulls it quickly behind his back and bows. "Your Majesty." When he stands, his gold eyes automatically lock on my forehead, and he flinches.

Stricken, I stare at my friend. Why did I not realize the crown would bring up bad memories? Nyssa's attacks were brutal. I should know. I was there for one of the worst.

My guardian sent me to Rivan for a rune. Nyssa went into a rage. When he heard her coming down the hall, he hid me in his closet. For hours, all I could hear was her screaming, but not a sound came from Rivan. Once it was quiet, I snuck out and found him on the floor, his skin brutally shredded until there was almost nothing left. I begged him to regenerate, but he refused. Regeneration would incinerate all his runes, leaving him too vulnerable to her in the interim. Giving in, I stayed and nursed him for three days until his magic could heal him enough to take care of himself.

Now I wear the same crown on my forehead.

Deliberately keeping my voice low, I ask, "Is everything okay?"

His eyes dart to the nearby crowd, and he gives a subtle shake of his head.

"I'm not Nyssa, Rivan. I won't ever abuse you," I inform him, taking his hand in mine and giving it a squeeze. "You're my friend."

He scrutinizes my face.

I hold his gaze, letting him see my sincerity.

After several minutes, a cautious smile appears.

"Guess she's Nyssa's daughter after all, even likes the same toy," an obnoxious voice jeers from behind me. "If I ask nicely, can I watch you torture him?"

Rivan steps back a foot, and my temper flares. Jerking around, I crook my finger and magically yank the owner of the voice to the front of the crowd. There's little to distinguish him from the rest of the Fae men here. Black hair, brown eyes, and the usual handsome features, only his are twisted with rage and hatred.

Solandis moves to my side and lays a hand on my arm, silently telling me to exercise caution.

"What is your name?"

"Lord Faris. Your… Majesty," he replies in a mocking tone.

Breathing in deeply to control my magic, I focus on the arrogant prick standing in front of me. "Rivan is a good friend of mine. Is there a reason you're insulting him?"

"I insult him because he's the enemy. At least that was something Nyssa understood. *Friend*," he spits back at me. "He killed my brother, and his kind killed my father. He deserves far worse than mere insults, but the treaty prevents me from killing him. If the only weapon left to me are words, then I shall use them to make him bleed." The dark-haired Fae defiantly folds his arms and sneers at me.

I blink at the idea of Rivan killing anyone, much less being called out as the enemy of the light Fae.

"Perhaps Queen Merindah is unaware of our history, particularly the Fire Fae Rebellion," a strong, masculine voice interjects.

The crowd parts to let a tall, handsome blond couple step into the center of the circle. After they bow and curtsy, dark eyes flash to mine.

All my attention snaps to the man in front of me. Insanely

gorgeous, even by Fae standards, his deep purple eyes make every womanly part of me stand up and shout hello. Tall, with broad shoulders, massive biceps, and barely tamed long, thick blond hair, he easily overshadows most of the other men here. Tingles spread throughout my body, but thankfully, the anger coursing in my veins, and the woman at his side, douses the heat of desire.

Clearing my throat, I wait for him to continue, but he doesn't say a word. Puzzled, I dart a quick glance at Solandis, but the microscopic frown on her forehead tells me she doesn't know him.

Several men and women sway toward to the couple in a way that makes me narrow my eyes. In the Underworld, nymphs, lust demons, and incubi are just a few of the creatures who can drive a person insane with lust. People around them often act in a similar manner. Could this couple's Fae magic be sexual in nature? Maybe, but neither of them is looking at anyone but me.

Impatient for answers, I raise an eyebrow. "What were you saying about a Fire Rebellion?"

Surprise flits across their faces.

The woman smiles. "Forgive us, Your Majesty. We were only trying to help explain why you may not be aware of Rivan's… status. Let us start over." She pats the arm she's holding, and her companion relaxes. "I'm Lady Allandra, of the Autumn Court. This is my brother, Lord Lorn."

Her brother, that's a relief. My eyes catch a flare of amusement in the depths of his eyes, and my mouth twitches, but I don't dare smile right now.

"Queen Merindah," he states, the low timbre of his voice sending a shiver of desire down my spine.

"Lady Allandra. Lord Lorn," I repeat, acknowledging their status. Her mentioning the Autumn Court was a surprise. It is my understanding that very few of the light Fae claim allegiance with autumn or winter.

Solandis squeezes my arm, then addresses the crowd. "Yesterday, you were ready to call the Wild Hunt to prevent her from taking the throne. Now that everything is settled, let's give *Queen* Merindah time to learn everything she needs to know." With the reminder of my new position of power, the crowd quickly disperses.

Lady Allandra smiles sheepishly at us both and disappears into the crowd, tugging Lord Lorn with her.

Lord Faris, who first spoke out against Rivan, is the last to leave. And the zealous glint in his eyes tells me he's not done tormenting my friend.

Once we're alone, I swivel around to apologize to Rivan, but he's already slipping out of the room. "Damn it."

Solandis leans down to murmur in my ear. "I know he helped capture Nyssa, but I didn't know you were friends. We need to talk about his past and the reason he's here." A weary sigh escapes her lips. "There is so much to learn. Not just about the Fire Fae Rebellion, but, well… everything. It's going to take time. But I will tell you Rivan's story tomorrow. In the meantime, stay away from him." Her hand goes up when I immediately start to protest. "You need all the facts first."

I slowly nod in agreement.

She flashes me a wry smile. "There are only a few more council members to meet." With those words, she drags me across the room to introduce another Fae.

Pretending to listen to their conversation, I paste the requisite smile on my face. Inside, my thoughts are swirling. How can Rivan be a sworn enemy of the light Fae?

CHAPTER THREE

<u>CORMAL</u>

Captivating. Fierce.

Hidden on the balcony, I can stare without her knowing. She stirs the blood in me like no other. An addiction so strong it takes everything I have in me to treat her with the detached coolness I decided upon so long ago. Seeing her become queen is exciting but watching her grow into the power she was always meant to have will be exhilarating.

No stranger to pain, the control she portrays during the coronation immediately impresses the crowd. Not that the arrogant pricks would ever show such emotion, but the Fae respect strength in all its forms, and her ability to handle the power coursing through her beautiful body without a whimper was the purest sign of the steel inside her.

Meri is one of the strongest people I know, a true survivor. If only she believed it, too. The verbal abuse that bitch of a sorceress rained down on her all her life warped her foundations. But Meri is growing. She might not see it, but I do. It's more apparent after she spends time with Solandis or Arden, their innate confidence a boost to her own. Only when she is by herself do her crippling insecurities and doubts weigh her down.

Her turquoise eyes meet mine in surprise.

I bow deeply to show my respect for her new position.

She looks around to see if anyone is paying attention to me. When her gaze returns, I deliberately wink.

"I heard Solandis was worried she would bolt, but Meri marched in here like she was already wearing the crown," Vargas remarks with a questioning glance in my direction. Flicking his gaze back to Meri, he glows with pride when she stands to address her people.

Vargas stands beside me, looking every inch the Fae he portrays. It's not an illusion. When Vargas was searching the dead for a body, he came upon Kaius and took his body as his own. Both Fae and demon, and "damn good looking," he told me Kaius fit the criteria. Given that Solandis was staying with Meri in the Light Fae Kingdom, he thought looking like a Fae would allow him to follow her without detection.

It wasn't until later that he realized Kaius was also a powerful chameleon, meaning he had the ability to temporarily change his appearance and DNA to other races. Now Vargas has the power to transform, although he's only used this Fae appearance and his old demon one.

I shrug lazily. "My presence is enough to spark a fire in her, and I was happy to be of assistance." An image of her turquoise eyes dancing with fury and desire makes me my body twitch in response. The passionate combination drives me crazy. "I'm assuming Solandis didn't recognize the new you?"

A soft smile plays on Vargas' lips. "She paused when I arrived to escort her earlier." One shoulder lifts negligently, but I can see how much the slight gesture meant to him. "Her senses are pretty honed. She doesn't know yet, or I'd be catching hell, but it won't take her too long." Anticipation coats his voice.

My lips compress, but I don't dare smile. "Did you find a team you can trust?"

Vargas watches Solandis loop her arm through Meri's. "Surprisingly, the royal guards swear their fealty to the crown, not the ruler. I don't agree with the premise, but for now, it works in our favor. Meri wears the crown, so they will protect her and her family with their lives, which includes Solandis. I've handpicked a team of six to be their personal guards. The rest will serve throughout the castle."

"Good," I state with satisfaction. "I'll add additional wards to their rooms, and Rivan's, before I leave tonight."

A quick scan finds the phoenix, standing alone on the other side of the hall with his eyes fixed on everyone but Meri. Carefully hiding his interest and familiarity with the new queen, he keeps his focus on the crowd, waiting for them to use their magic against him.

A familiar anger rises. Anyone looking at him now wouldn't know he was once a legendary warrior, but living under the boot of your enemy for thousands of years will crush you until there is nothing but a shell. It galls me to think of the terms he agreed to in order to protect his people, but a new queen means he can negotiate new terms.

The coup sparked something in him, and with Nyssa gone, there is little to prevent Rivan from finding his way back to himself. The bonds he accepted long ago are beginning to chafe.

Unfortunately, I suspect he won't even try to negotiate unless he knows his people are safe. Maybe I can help. I send a quick text to a hellhound who owes me a favor and one to Lucifer. The mutt can find almost anyone, and since Lucifer owes Rivan a favor, maybe he'd be willing to loan us Callyx for the search as well. After all, he's Lucifer's best spy. Between the three of us, we should be able to find Rivan's people, then help him get out of his contract.

Vargas crosses his arms and grunts.

With a frown, I follow his line of sight to where a handsome red-haired Fae is whispering in Solandis' ear.

"Have you uncovered anything about the Fae whose body you've claimed?"

Without taking his eyes off the couple below, he spits out. "No."

Strong hands grip the railing tightly, probably to stop himself from leaping over the balcony and removing that idiot Fae's head.

I glance at my watch. "I've got to go. Stay on top of her security. Also, Meri needs someone to train her on how to use magic in a fight. Can you set that up?"

Solandis moves on from the flirty Fae, and Vargas releases his grip. With a slight nod, he agrees to get it set up, and I clap him on the back.

The sight I stole from an old seer long ago shows me the many paths in front of us. Too many. A frustrated sigh escapes. For now, all I can do is ward their rooms from anyone who wishes them harm. And for Meri, the sorceress Leandra, is at the top of that list. I plan to add something extra to the wards just for her.

Putting Meri into The Pit violated our pact and weakened Leandra's hold on Meri. Today, the ties disintegrated into nothing the moment Meri was crowned queen. Without the protection of our agreement, Leandra has nothing to stand between her and the overwhelming number of enemies who want her dead. But they'll have to stand in line. She's mine. Our pact prevented me from going after her then, but hunting season is now open.

CHAPTER FOUR

<u>MERI</u>

Solandis finally gives the signal to leave, and a loud sigh of relief escapes me. An expressive eyebrow arches high on her aristocratic forehead.

"After all I've done," she says haughtily, but the laughter she's holding back spills out into the room before she can finish the sentence. "You're going to make a very different queen than my sister. Nyssa loved the parties and court intrigue." Her mouth turns down. "Let's go. Tomorrow begins the real work."

It's strange to hear Solandis talk about Nyssa. On one hand, she knows her beloved sister did so many unforgivable things and killed so many people, including her mate, Vargas. And she hates her—for all of it.

Yet, there's a lifetime of sisterhood, thousands of years where their relationship meant everything to her. Those memories and feelings slip out when she least expects it. And she grieves for her sister.

I might have nothing but loathing for Nyssa, but I have all the love for Solandis. Whatever she needs to do to heal from all of this, I'm here for her.

The two of us exit the coronation hall and find guards waiting for us. Led by the man I saw Cormal speaking with earlier, there are six more standing at attention nearby. He spins into an elaborate bow.

Up close, he's extremely good-looking. Tall with rich chestnut brown hair slightly longer than his chin and light green eyes that pop against his tanned complexion.

Solandis inhales sharply, her deep turquoise eyes fixed on the man, but she says nothing.

My hand drifts to the hidden knife on my thigh, unsure what to think about her reaction. When she continues to stare but makes no move to pull from her deep well of power, I decide it's only the one man who has her undivided attention.

"Are you our escort?"

Observant green eyes return Solandis' intense stare for several seconds before he snaps his gaze to mine. "Queen Merindah. We're your personal guards. The seven of us will be responsible for the safety of you and your family. I thought it best to introduce you to the team tonight."

Pivoting to face the men, he points to the first one, a tall male with white hair and icy purple eyes. "Laken."

He motions for the next two to step forward. Good-looking, identical twins with golden blond hair and sparkling deep blue eyes. "Galen and Garren."

A serious-looking Fae with auburn hair and chocolate brown eyes steps forward. "Ansel," he says, introducing himself.

He's followed by a tall, well-built Fae with amber eyes and black hair who sort of reminds me of Rivan. "Tiernan."

Lastly, a young Fae with brown eyes and green hair, named Kian, quietly introduces himself.

It's a damn good day to be queen.

Every single one of them is hot, but the twin sandwich, my weakness, almost makes me whimper. Reminding myself to act like a queen, I smile and clasp my hands together. "It's nice to meet you."

This is normally when I'd sashay over to them and run my hands across a few chests, but I'm almost positive that is not proper royal behavior, which is why I am clenching my hands into fists. Unsure of what else to do or say, I look at Solandis.

"And your name?" she demands, throwing a haughty look at the leader.

His voice is husky when he answers, "Kaius." Green eyes sweep over Solandis with clear intent.

Maybe it's a good day to be a princess too. With a choking cough, I loop my arm through Solandis' and gesture for them to lead the way.

I glance up at her. "What's on the agenda for tomorrow?"

It takes her a moment to find her voice. "The council always meets the day after the coronation to walk the new queen through the current initiatives and to establish protocols. It's a long day, but necessary to get you up to speed."

We reach her door first. "I'll be ready. Thank you, Solandis. For everything. I couldn't have done this without you. And I promise, I'll do everything in my power to make you proud of me." The knot in my throat almost prevents me from getting it all out. All my life, I wished for a family. She is so much more than I could have dreamed up.

She gathers me in her arms and places a kiss on my forehead. "I'm already so proud of you." Her fingers sweep my hair behind my ear. "No more promises, either. To anyone. The Fae like nothing better than to twist your words to benefit themselves, and a promise gives them the foundation to enforce it."

When I nod, she smiles. "Goodnight, dear."

Kaius stations Garren in front of Solandis' door before

motioning us forward. Her room is in the same wing as mine, just down the hall.

Ansel opens the door, checks the room, then gives the signal to indicate it's safe.

"Thank you," I tell him, walking into the same room I stormed out of prior to the ceremony. Startled, I turn in a circle. All the chaos is gone. There's not one ribbon, needle, or swath of fabric on any surface. It's absolutely immaculate. A huge perk I never even thought about until now.

A glint of gold catches my eye, and I swivel to face the same mirror I desperately ran to earlier. Except this time, I don't have to imagine being queen. An exact depiction of the crown itself delicately wraps across my forehead like a brand or a golden tattoo. Light Fae who have sworn fealty to this kingdom will see it. Outsiders will see nothing at all.

I peer closer. My doubts and fears are still there. I thought they would go away, but they haven't. Maybe only time will erase them.

"Excuse me, Your Majesty," a raspy voice says behind me. "If you're going to stare at yourself all night, I can come back later."

Whirling, my power immediately rises, becoming a shield around me. "Eris!" I exclaim with my hand on my chest. "You startled me. What do you need?"

The tiny brownie scoffs and walks through the shield like it's nothing. "I'm here to help you out of your dress, of course."

Did she roll her eyes? And how did she get through the shield? Bemused, I stare down at the tiny woman. She's probably seen a lot of strange things in this palace. Solandis said she's at least four thousand years old, but she doesn't look it. Not one wrinkle mars her smooth, nutmeg brown skin.

I drop the useless shield. "Thank you." Bending my knees, I start to lean toward her, but stop when she immediately backs up and glares at me. "Now what?"

"I'm a Brownie," she says, as if stating the obvious. When I continue to look confused, she scoffs. Seconds later, she's undoing the clasp of the cloak around my throat. "You don't need to bend down. With just a thought, I can be anywhere. Not even shields can keep me out." She snickers. "Hold still and let me do the work."

A minute later, dressed in a white silk pajama set, I slide into bed. Under her orders, of course. I press my lips tightly together, knowing she'll scold me if I laugh. "Thank you, Eris. Would you mind handing me my phone?" Expecting her to go to my duffle, she reaches into the nightstand and pulls out the device.

Hmm. Looks like everything has been unpacked and put away.

"If you need me, call my name. No need to shout it, though. I'm not hard of hearing," she tartly informs me. Without another word, she douses all the lights except the one by the bed and disappears.

That's when I feel it. Power. Unlike any other.

"Cormal?" I murmur his name in the dark, but there is no response.

Casting my magic takes a minute, but it finally pours into the room. It slides along every inch, processing information and feeding it back to me. Cormal was here after the coronation. His magic is in the wards. He must have reinforced them. Obviously, he doesn't believe I have enough power to take care of myself. I want to be angry with him, but instead, I'm relieved. I feel safe knowing he has taken care of it.

So far, I'm liking this queen business. Custom dresses, gold crowns, delicious guards, someone to clean my room and tuck me in at night... I feel coddled. Sinking down into the fluffiest pillows, I pick up my phone.

Arden warned me it might not work well here, but I see several text messages waiting for me.

Arden: Congratulations! All Hail Queen Meri! Or should I call you Queen Merindah? I heard you looked beautiful, and you were amazing, not flinching once during the ceremony. A good move to gain their respect.

Arden: I remember when I was preparing for the Gathering of the Light. Solandis warned me not to show any pain. Looks like she gave you the same advice. Text or call when you get a minute.

Arden: And let me know when I can come visit.

Arden: Did you meet Kaius?

How did she know about Kaius? I swear more people know what's going on here than I do. As queen, I should know first, right? Maybe she spoke to Solandis, then sent the text. Nope. Time stamp says her messages were sent earlier tonight. The only person Kaius spoke to at the ceremony was Cormal. Arden and Cormal don't exactly get along, so why would he send her a message about me? Obviously, we need to have a little chat.

Meri: Queen Meri works for me. ;-) I'm just happy the crown didn't reject me.

Meri: Who told you? Tell me you're not becoming friends with Cormal? Seriously. I'm begging.

Meri: Met Kaius. He introduced my new guards. 6 hotties incl. twins. I'm not even kidding. Twins. Groan. Will send a pic. #tryingtoactlikeaqueen

Meri: I'll ask Solandis about visiting. She knows more than I do about this rabbit hole I've fallen into…

The second text is from Callyx. I smile.

> Callyx: Why the hell would you want to leave the Underworld for the Fae? They're vicious little fuckers on a good day.

> Callyx: Congrats on your new crown. Don't forget about us lowly peons, okay? I miss you. And Solandis.

> Callyx: Lucifer's sending me on a mission. Text when you get a chance and watch your back.

> Meri: It smells better here. And everyone is so beautiful. No more foul-smelling, ugly ass demons catcalling me. Plus, they gave me a gold crown and hot guards. What can I say? I'm easily bribed. Be careful. Miss you too.

The third text is from an unknown number.

> Unknown: Congratulations. What I have created, I can destroy.

I sit straight up in bed and stare down at the phone. Fear skips down my spine and beads of sweat break out on my brow. When I reach up to swipe them away, the glowing tips of my fingers light up the bed. Magic. I'm not defenseless anymore. She thinks she can threaten me. At the thought, my fingers curl into a fist.

Closing my eyes, I search for the bond between Leandra and me, the one she used to track and control me all my life. It's time I sent a message back—a magical hit to remind her of my new powers. But when I reach for the thread, it isn't there.

Did it move? With a frown, I continue to search my body for the tiniest of threads with her signature. I find nothing. It's gone.

For over nine hundred years, I've felt her inside me like a spider in its web, watching and waiting to deliver its poison. She must have felt it the moment the bond broke. No wonder she sent a text. With a smile on my face, I pick up the phone.

> Queen Merindah: Leandra, you evil bitch. Bring it on. I've got a huge score to settle and a hell of a lot of power at my disposal. Look for the gold palace, I'll be the one wearing the crown.

My hands are shaking when I lower the phone, but damn, it felt so good. All those years I bit my tongue, holding back the words I wanted to spew at her. Free. Free. Free. I am free. If she thinks she can destroy me, let her try. The magic in my fingers becomes a ball of power in my hand. I'll be waiting, and I've got a hell of a lot of anger to get rid of.

CHAPTER FIVE

<u>MERI</u>

Bright light shines directly on my closed eyes. With a groan, I turn my face in the other direction, but there is no escape. Blinking, I lift my lids a fraction and see the sun shining through the window. My hands automatically reach for the covers, but the only thing under my hands is… rough and dense like wool? Confused, I sit up and glance around me. Why am I on my bedroom floor?

With a huge yawn, I stand and look longingly at the comfy bed. Once I'm awake though, I can't go back to sleep. What time is it? I look at the nightstand, but my phone isn't on it. Grinning, I raise my hand and a second later, my phone lies in my palm. Using magic feels weird. Awesome, but weird. My first thought is to look for the phone not make it come to me.

I walk over to the mirror and admire the crown on my forehead. Queen Meri. Queen Merindah. Besides the magic, it's still hard to fathom that I'm a queen. How long will it take to sink in? A year? A hundred years? Will I find a mate and give birth to princes and princesses? A big snort escapes, and I slap a hand across my nose and mouth.

Dirt flies to the ground in front of me. I lift my arm up to eye the cuff of my sleeve where black smudges the edges and skims the back of my hand. What in the world? I bend down to scoop up the dirt and freeze when I see the same dirt covering my feet. There's only one explanation.

Fuck! The nightmares must be getting stronger. Instead of waking up in a cold sweat, they're trapping me in the dark. Where did I go? And more importantly, how did I get back? Did the guard, Ansel, follow me and bring me back to my room when he saw what was happening?

Heat flares on my cheeks when I think about it. What must he think of me? A queen who sleepwalks because she can't control her demons. Should I talk to him about it? Or Kaius? I cover my face to escape the evidence staring back at me. Shit.

A brisk knock at the door startles me.

"Your Majesty, Eris told me breakfast will be here in ten minutes," Ansel's quiet voice informs me. "Princess Solandis will be joining you."

Scrambling out of my top, I immediately run to the closet. It's completely full of clothes. Row upon row of tops, pants, dresses, shoes, jewelry, and everything else. I choke out a strangled laugh. There's even a stand with at least ten pairs of sunglasses on it. But it all looks so, so… fancy. Where the hell are the jeans or leggings?

Spotting a dresser, I pull open a drawer and find underwear. Bingo. I grab a pair. Yanking open the next one, I see it's full of bras. I grab one and slam it closed. My luck runs out when I open the third and fourth drawers. More lingerie. The kind you wear for someone special. I can't help but reach out to run a finger over the delicate lace but stop when I see the dirt.

Another knock at the door. Panicking, I look around, trying

to find something to wear and catch sight of a wild woman in the mirror at the back of the closet. The crown shines brightly in the dim closet. I take a deep breath in, hold it, then let it out. I do this two more times.

You're a queen with magic. Use it.

Waving my hand, I clean every speck of dirt off me, brush my hair and teeth, and put some make-up on so I don't look so pale. Another wave, and I'm wearing my favorite lounge set.

When I turn around, Eris is standing in the entrance to the closet. "You're not wearing that to the council meeting, are you?" A grin accompanies her dry remark.

"Good morning, Eris," I greet her in return. "And no, I don't know what to wear, so I thought I'd be comfortable until I could ask Solandis." When she sniffs, I quickly add to my statement. "And you, of course."

She immediately straightens to her full height of two feet. "I'll pull together a few outfits. You and Solandis can decide which one is best suited for the first council meeting." With those words, she starts zipping around the closet.

Strolling into the bedroom, I notice Solandis is on the balcony sipping her usual coffee. A flick of my wrist and sunglasses cover my eyes.

I bend down and place a kiss on her cheek. "Good morning." Sliding into the chair on her right, I pluck the napkin off the plate in front of me and place it in my lap. "Mmm. This looks delicious. So many advantages to being queen."

Instead of laughing, Solandis looks sad. "Having someone make breakfast for you isn't a perk of being queen. It's a simple, kind gesture."

Shaking my head, I smile softly and remind her, "Not everyone can afford food. People go without every day. And I ate. Not this fancy, but I usually found something." Too busy running my demonic guardian's errands to do more than satisfy the rumblings of hunger.

Anger crosses her face. "You deserved more. And if I ever get my hands on the sorceress, she'll pay for treating you so badly." An eyebrow twitches. "Don't look so worried. Her power isn't even half of mine, and under this gorgeous exterior is a ruthless Fae. I can handle her."

The flowers and plants in the large stone vase behind her instantly turn black and crumble. I blink.

She swivels to follow my gaze and chuckles. "Oops." A wave of her elegant hand and everything inside comes roaring back to life. "Moving on. How did you sleep?"

The berry I'm chewing gets stuck in my throat. After coughing a few times, I finally swallow it down. "Good. Can't remember most of it." That's the truth. "Eris is pulling some outfits for the council meeting."

Solandis eyes my current clothes with disdain. "Oh, good. I wasn't sure if you were intending to start a new trend or already rebelling against the aristocracy." Pink manicured nails pinch the perfect pleat on her black pants as if to emphasize the need to dress well.

After taking a few more bites of breakfast, I push the plate away. My stomach is nervous enough without over stuffing it with food.

Solandis peers over the balcony. "We need to talk about Rivan."

I glance below and see him walking in the garden. Dressed in black pants and a sleeveless black t-shirt, he looks much more comfortable than he did last night. The cut curve of his biceps is impressive. And when the sun's rays touch him, his burnished skin gleams under the runes inked on its smooth surface.

Mmm, is there drool on my chin?

Unable to stop staring, I can't help but notice that he is stopping every couple of feet to sweep the dirt with his boot.

What in the world is he doing?

He suddenly turns and looks directly at me.

Heat flares in my cheeks as I return his smoldering look, but I'm unable to look away.

"Oh dear," Solandis murmurs beside me. "Are you sure you want to hear about the Fire Fae Rebellion right now?"

I swing my gaze guiltily back to her and away from the temptation below. "Yes, I do. Rivan's... my friend, and I can't help him if I don't know what's going on."

She winces. "The rebellion took place almost three thousand years ago, not long after Nyssa took the throne. Led by the phoenix, the Fire Fae rebelled against the Dark and Light Fae Kingdoms. Phoenix, Salamanders, Embers, Fire Drakes, Fire-birds, and several other Lesser Fae races make up the Fire Fae. Instead of living in one of the two kingdoms, most of the Fire Fae lived together in a fairly inhospitable land, filled with volcanoes, barren earth, and scorching heat, that straddled the two kingdoms."

With an elegant lift of her shoulder, she continues. "They wanted the rights to the land and the ability to govern themselves, so they declared their independence. The Dark Fae King, Denir, and Nyssa sent several delegations to negotiate with them, but they refused to grant them what they wanted most. So, they declared war."

Her turquoise eyes are dark with devastating memories. "The light and dark greatly underestimated what it would take to fight in a land filled with nothing but fire and dirt. And they failed to recognize the huge military advantage the phoenix brought to the table. How do you defeat a lightning-fast enemy who can repeatedly die and regenerate?"

She motions toward Rivan, who is still strolling through the garden. "Rivan's father, Brixton, led the rebellion, and Rivan led the phoenix army. He might not look like it now, but he's one of the most feared warriors in this kingdom. A fierce fighter and brilliant strategist, he commanded the entire Fire Fae army, but his biggest advantage was the elite squad he wielded with precision. His small band of lethal warriors were responsible for killing most of the Fae commanders, and because of Rivan, the phoenix killed more Fae than all the rest of the fire units combined."

Speechless, I turn my head back to the man walking alone. It's hard to picture him as the fierce warrior and leader Solandis is describing to me. He feels broken and adrift.

"How did they lose?"

"We took their children," she murmurs in a strained voice. "When the rulers realized they couldn't win without sustaining huge losses, they paid a group of witches to locate the hiding places of the women and children. The women were killed, and the children were held prisoner."

My eyes widen in horror at the idea of using children as leverage. "What the fuck?" It's absolutely incomprehensible to me. Even in the Underworld, we had lines. Standards.

Her eyes are intent when they look at me. "The Fae will do anything to preserve their way of life. The tactic served a dual purpose. It immediately ended the Fire Fae Rebellion and served as a powerful reminder to other Lesser Fae of the consequences of fighting for their independence."

My voice is hoarse when I ask, "What happened to the children?"

She tilts her head to the garden. "Rivan. He made a bargain. In exchange for the lives of the elite phoenix squad, including his own, the children would be released to their families." Her lips turn down. "The rulers agreed to the bargain with one caveat. Rivan would watch the execution of his squad, but to ensure future generations didn't rise up, Rivan would remain a prisoner here for the rest of his life. He agreed."

Bitterness coats my mouth. "A prisoner forced to live with the enemy who can't even kill himself to escape. I can't begin to imagine the hell he's endured at the hands of the light Fae. No wonder he wears so many runes of protection."

And Nyssa was the worst one of all, although I don't say those words out loud. His flinch at the sight of my crown says it all.

Solandis reaches out and grasps my hand. "I fell in love with a demon, and I had to choose between him and my kingdom. For me, it was an easy choice. Not for a second did I think about staying. But I wasn't queen, and my powers weren't dependent on the kingdom." She shakes her head sadly. "Fae will never condone a relationship between the two of you, not even one of friendship. I'm sorry."

The worried look on Solandis' face prompts me to respond. "Thank you. I know it wasn't easy telling me. The last thing I want to do is cause Rivan more pain, and our friendship would only put an even larger target on his back," I assure her. "Let's go inside and find an outfit for me to wear to the council meeting."

I know what it's like to spend hundreds of years with one abuser. Thousands of years is too great a sacrifice. I can't imagine being the target of unending hate day in and day out for the rest of my immortal life.

The number of people who mean something to me are so few, I wouldn't even need to use all ten of my fingers to count them. Leaving a friend to endure this kind of humiliation and torture isn't in me, not even if it was Cormal. There must be something I can do to help Rivan. But what?

CHAPTER SIX

<u>MERI</u>

Pain pools at the balls of my feet. The black stilettos with four-inch heels that looked so incredibly sexy when Eris brought them out are freaking killing me. How in the hell do women strut through life wearing these things? Don't get me wrong, the additional height is an adrenalin shot for a shorty like me who's barely over five feet, but I can't take another second of this torture.

Solandis eyes my pinched face and leans down to fuss with my mauve-colored silk blouse. "Magic, darling. Use it." With a wink, she straightens and smooths a hand down her hip.

Of course. Feeling stupid, I swirl a finger toward my feet and it's as if I'm suddenly walking on clouds. When the pain disperses, I sigh in relief. "Thank you."

She starts to say something but eyes the two guards waiting for us and decides against it.

I know what she's going to say, but it's like my brain can't comprehend the enormity of the change inside me. Understandable, I guess.

When I was young, I had zero magic. None. But it's not an uncommon occurrence for some supernatural children. Magic often comes with maturity. I waited and waited. My days were filled with pacifying Leandra, hiding from whoever she wronged, and generally surviving the Underworld without magic.

Just as I was about to turn ninety-four, well past the age of maturity, I suddenly gained the ability to mimic others' powers. Ecstatic, I went around borrowing powers from everyone I met. But when I tried to use them later, they were gone. My magic had a huge limitation—I could only use those powers when I was around the person I was mimicking. It felt like a trick.

But the cruelest joke… it didn't work on everyone, especially not the one I needed protection from the most. The sorceress seemed to be immune to my every attempt.

For almost nine hundred and ninety-three years of my life, I couldn't count on magic. Everything had to be done the hard way, the human way. There were no shortcuts for me. Bitterness ate at me for the longest time until I learned to work the system and get what I wanted without magic.

If I needed something done, a simple mention of Leandra's or Cormal's name, and people jumped through hoops for me. Necessities like food, clothes, or a bottle of wine, I either bargained for or stole them. Cormal's men taught me how to fight dirty and defend myself against the predators I encountered in the Underworld.

Three months ago, I inherited more magic than I ever dreamed of getting. Last night, I gained the power to rule. Three months and one day compared to nine hundred and ninety-three years. No wonder my brain can't remember I have magic. The only time it seems effortless is when I get angry.

Solandis has been working with me, but as someone who

never had to learn magic, it's tough for her to understand why it doesn't flow so easily for me.

My chest begins to buzz, and my magic spikes. With every step, it grows worse. Pressing my hand to my chest, I stop and try to breathe it away.

"Something's wrong. I think I'm having a magical heart attack. Is there such a thing?" It sounds weird to say out loud. There's no pain, only an incredible pressure and a massive amount of adrenaline.

Solandis grasps each side of my head with her hands and forces my gaze up to meet hers. "It's the power. When you get close to a large group of light Fae, your power will spike. It serves many purposes—a warning system, an impenetrable shield, an additional pool of power. For example, if you were to go to war, the spike would be enormous, giving you access to deep reserves of power to use against your enemies or shield your army." Her cool hand wipes the hair back from my face. "I'm so sorry, darling. I didn't think to warn you. As royalty, I got used to it long ago. Can you control it?"

I hold my hand out. It's steady. All the weird stuff is happening inside me, but it's not showing on the outside. "Yes."

She releases me and moves back to my side.

At my nod, the guard rushes ahead to open the oak doors.

"Thank you, Garren," I say, my voice strained with tension.

Deep blue eyes flick to me in surprise, but the emotion is quickly wiped from his face. Am I not supposed to address them? I'll have to ask one of them later.

Light wood beams cross the high arched ceiling, mimicking the floor beneath my feet. Fae line the white wooden pews on each side of the room. Solandis enters first and steps into the last pew. When I walk in, they stand and pay their respects. Per Solandis' instructions, I walk to the front of the room and take a seat in the gold chair. Solandis, along with the rest of the council, follows my cue and sits.

Council meetings begin with roll call. The list of names goes by too fast to catch more than a few of them, but a voice answers "present" for each one. Wonderful. Looks like everyone's here for our first day together.

Next, the minutes from the last meeting are read aloud. While the official-looking Fae in uniform drones on and on, I look around the room. Most of the Fae, backs ramrod straight as if there is a stick shoved up their backsides, barely acknowledge my existence.

That's okay. It gives me a chance to study them while I try to remember their names. Hmph. I didn't realize it last night, but there are only two women on the entire council. Solandis and a woman with red hair whom I've never met. I wonder why? Are the seats passed down from one lord to the next until there are no more lords in the family? I was always under the impression that the light Fae were matriarchal. Another question to ask Solandis.

Angry brown eyes glare at me from the second row, and my magic surges. I remember him. Rivan's nemesis, Lord Faris. I return his stare with an angry one of my own. There's so much I could do to the little weasel. His eyes drop from mine, and I smile.

A broad grin with bright perfect teeth catches my full attention. It's him. Lord Lorn. I didn't realize he was on the council. *Mmm.* Or what a nice smile he has. His eyes dart to Lord Faris, then return to me. He winks in approval. The corners of my mouth turn up. At least there is one friendly, exceedingly handsome face in here.

Dressed in a sharp grey suit with a dark purple shirt that matches his eyes, he looks every inch a Fae Lord. But instead of the reserved demeanor that seems to be the hallmark of the rest of them, he exudes a sexy warmth. Approachable. And it only makes him more enticing.

Silence reigns, and I hurriedly look around. A gentleman in

the top row is getting up. Lord Camon. Today the surly Fae is dressed in a crisp navy suit with a green tie. For the High Fae of Spring, he is certainly a somber man.

Once on the floor, he addresses the council. "We have several items on the agenda today. Lord Keir, what is the status of our trade with the Elves?"

An extremely tall gentleman wearing a brown suit stands. "There is no update. King Elwen is completely mad and refuses to let anyone into the light Elven lands. Prince Fallon has stepped down. All trade is halted."

Camon looks resigned. "Keep trying. Hopefully, the situation resolves itself soon."

I lean forward. "What do the Elves provide for us?"

A pained expression crosses Camon's face, but he nods at Keir to answer.

"Mainly metals like gold, silver, and copper that fuel our new solar panels, electrical grid, and other technical inventions. It's how we've been able to power the city of Meira. Using electricity instead of magic allows us to store more magic in our reserves. Metals appear to be the most stable in these applications, although we are experimenting with new nano technology. To a lesser degree, we also import weapons from them. Elves are masters at crafting the finest of swords, arrows, and other items," Keir explains in a rather snide voice.

"Is there a reason we can't get the supplies from the dark Elves?" I ask the question, knowing their prejudice likely holds them back.

Solandis said the light Fae like to follow rules and process and abhor the wild lawlessness of the dark Fae. Dark Elves are likely worse. Personally, I don't get it. We didn't have light and dark in the Underworld, only a million shades of grey.

The collective inhale from both Camon and Keir answers my question.

"It's out of the question," Camon states stiffly. He turns back to Keir and waves a hand for him to sit.

Irritated with them both, I smile broadly. "Have you used all your resources?"

Exasperated, Camon swivels sharply to face me. "Of course, Your Majesty. I'm happy to walk you through all our initiatives in more detail after the council meeting. For now, let's move on with the agenda."

Ignoring Camon, I turn to Solandis. "Has anyone reached out to you regarding this matter?"

Laughter shines in Solandis' eyes, but she's careful not to let it slip into her voice. "No, I don't believe I've received a request from Lord Keir, but I'm happy to reach out to Prince Fallon to ask for his assistance in this matter."

Camon frowns and swivels to face his fellow council member. "Keir, we discussed this weeks ago. Our supplies are dangerously low. Work with Princess Solandis to get this resolved quickly. Understood?"

Keir compresses his lips together, but a sharp dip of his chin signals his reluctant agreement. Looks like I'm not the only one the council doesn't like.

Lord Camon flashes me an impatient look. "Do I have your permission to move on, Your Majesty?"

Over the next hour, Camon leads several discussions on relevant government topics, such as the expansion of the nearby city, new housing development requests, the installment of a new water system, and the budget. It's incredibly boring, but I listen intently, trying to understand what the people need and how we're going to provide it to them. It's also extremely complex and over my head. Honestly, I'm glad there's a council to deal with most of these items.

Lord Camon hesitates for a second, but then pushes forward. "The last item on the agenda is the topic of local representation for Lesser Fae. This is the first step in giving them their rights, and it will help establish trust between us. If we allow them to have more of a voice in their cities and the laws that are passed, we will achieve our initiatives faster and more economically. Creating a relationship with a local leader will only benefit us. Not only does it give us a single point person for negotiations and trade, but it also gives the Lesser Fae some confidence that their voices are being heard. We discussed this in length the last time I brought up this agenda item. I'm calling for a vote."

Council members give their aye or nay. A majority of them vote against the proposal. Solandis votes in favor of it. Lord Camon calls the outcome before the vote even gets to me. Since I haven't read the proposal, I don't mind. This time.

With a fierce frown, he ends the meeting quickly, and everyone immediately scatters. Except for Solandis, the other woman on the council, and me.

"Your Majesty. I'm Lady Estrella," the red-haired woman states firmly, introducing herself. "Solandis." In a surprising move, she leans forward and gives her a quick hug.

My eyebrows flash upward, and the woman laughs.

"Solandis and I have been friends since we were in the cradle," Estrella informs me. "I'm sorry I couldn't attend the coronation last night. The journey took longer than I expected."

Solandis tilts her head and studies her friend. "Is everything okay?"

Estrella glances uneasily at me, but Solandis' firm nod reassures her. "The fire drakes are causing a bit of trouble, but we're negotiating with them. I was hoping Lord Camon's proposal to give the Lesser Fae local positions was going to pass. It would go a long way to establishing some trust between us."

Interesting. Solandis mentioned the fire drakes earlier when she was talking about the Fire Fae Rebellion.

"Estrella lives in the disputed land previously occupied by the phoenix. After the rebellion, her father, Lord Carlen, was given the right to govern the land, but he passed away. Lady Estrella now resides over it," Solandis explains with a frown. "Do you think they're gearing up for another rebellion?"

"No. Without the Phoenix, I don't think they have enough of an army at their disposal for an outright rebellion. But they're blocking trade routes, stealing livestock, and causing general mayhem," she admits with a sigh. "Maybe we can ask Camon who his greatest opponents are and work to overcome some of their objections? We can't be the only territory dealing with Lesser Fae issues."

Solandis agrees. "The council is old and set in its ways. Maybe we can work from behind the scenes. Their mates might be of better use. A ladies' luncheon. I can position it as an opportunity to meet the queen."

"Brilliant," Estrella remarks.

"Why are there so few ladies on the council?" I ask while I have them both here.

Estrella raises a single eyebrow toward Solandis.

"Nyssa," Solandis inserts quietly. "She didn't like most women. Over the years, she harassed and belittled the female council members until most of them handed the reins over to the men. The only two she allowed to remain is Estrella and me."

"Maybe it's time we changed the ratio," I murmur. "Let's also use the luncheon to see if any of the women would like to rejoin the council."

CHAPTER SEVEN

<u>MERI</u>

I've been dying to see the Fae capital, Meira, for years. We heard so many rumors in the Underworld about the technologically advanced city, but few have visited. Cormal and Leandra are the only ones I know who have seen it. Apparently, you need a special invitation from an aristocratic Fae, or the queen, to enter its gates. Good thing I've got that covered.

Built over the last thousand years, it's a living tribute to the inventions and advances the light Fae have made to their society. The evolution is quite similar to the modernization the human world went through during their industrial revolution.

The city is the perfect blend of science and magic. Sophisticated advances in Fae living with absolutely no smog, dirt, or crime. The light Fae have found ways to enjoy technology without experiencing the glitches of the past that used to happen whenever someone tried to implement human technology in a magical realm.

With Solandis occupied planning the luncheon, I decide to visit the city alone. I haven't been anywhere without her since I arrived, so it feels really weird to leave her behind, but this is my new life. I can't expect Solandis to stay forever. She believes Vargas will come back to her, and at some point, she'll want to leave and be with him.

Kaius assigns three guards to go with me—Ansel, Laken, and Kian. Hmm. An auburn, blond, and brunette. It's like getting Neapolitan ice cream. All the flavors. I grin. Even if I can't flirt like I used to, I can still appreciate the fine view.

Laken holds the back door of a black SUV open for me. I slide in, and he follows. We discussed going via portal, but I haven't been in a car in a long time, so I opted for this mode of transportation. I immediately roll the window all the way down, but Laken mutters something about security. With a sigh, I roll it back up.

Cars were one of the first things the Fae brought here from the human world. Getting them to work was a challenge, but the Fae came up with a solution. Instead of gas, they run on a combination of magic and a complex organic-based fuel. When they completed the project, they realized they could do so much more. It sparked the age of technological advancement, and the city of Meira was born. Besides a place to showcase their inventions, Meira provides a working environment for learning and testing new ideas. The city also has the light Fae's first higher education school dedicated to the sciences.

I never went to school. Most Underworld children don't. Cormal, a huge proponent of educating oneself, would bring in tutors for anyone who wanted to learn, no matter their age. I took advantage of it whenever Leandra gave me some freedom.

As we crest the next hill, the city comes into view. It's so amazing; I'm almost speechless. Perched on the edge of a large river, it's an amalgamation of nature and architecture—a huge white, gold, and green masterpiece. Buildings made of the purest white stone scale to impossible heights, some capped with a golden spire or dome. A waterfall flows from the center of the tallest building to a large pool at the bottom, where birds and other creatures can be seen flying and swimming around in it. There's nothing flat about the city. Everything is built at different levels to emphasize the grandeur and scale of the modern white cityscape. There's so much to see I can't take it in with just one look.

Beautiful trees, meticulous lawns, and flowers are everywhere, softening the rather austere facades glinting in the bright noon sun. But the nature isn't just decorative. It has a purpose. Each of the plants was chosen for specific reasons. Whether it's the chemicals they release, the food or shelter they provide to the animals that live in the city, or as a way to harness the sun for energy. We pass by a building with plants meticulously stacked in between the stones. I must look puzzled, because Laken informs me they are air plants used to help purify the air.

Nature is at the forefront in a lot of the architectural designs too. Instead of linear or structured bridges, most of them have curved, fluid lines like those found in nature. Instead of city lights designed like steel posts, the Fae have used nature to disguise the electricity. Planted in the ground, lights are displayed in the shape of trees and bushes.

The city is spotless. No trash, graffiti, or dirt anywhere. Rolling down the window again, I ignore Laken to breathe in the city air. Flowers, plants, and food are the only things I smell. Nothing rank or obnoxious like most cities. It's quite remarkable.

My stomach grumbles. We've been driving around for a while, and breakfast was hours ago. "Can we find a place to eat?"

Unease crosses Ansel's face, but he agrees and orders the driver to a restaurant in a quiet part of the city.

"This is where the aristocratic Fae live. Most of them have already met you, so they won't be pushing to get closer." He checks his weapons, then signals to Kian to step out of the vehicle and scout the area.

When Kian waves two fingers, Laken opens the door and helps me out. The three guards immediately place me in the center and usher us into the restaurant. Similar to the city, it has a modernistic décor that's mainly done in shades of white and tan, with wood accents to give it a feeling of warmth. The massive wall of windows in the front brings in a ton of light and lets the diners enjoy a view of the city outside.

A stylish young Fae stops us when we enter. With a slight sneer in his voice, he positions himself in front of my guards. "Do you have a reservation?"

Ansel subtly shifts another inch or two to let him get a better glimpse of me.

The Fae's eyes immediately widen when he sees the crown. "Welcome, Your Majesty." He gives a decisive nod. "Right. Reservations aren't necessary. If you'll follow me." Pivoting sharply on his heel, he quickly leads our little group across the room to a private booth in the back.

Glimpsing the other diners through the gaps in the guards, I watch everyone's head swivel when I pass. Whispering follows us the entire way.

Fine crystal wine glasses, gold silverware, and the purest white linen napkins grace the table. Dismayed, I hesitantly slide in, and as soon as the host is gone, I immediately stand.

"Ansel, can you ask him if we can order food to go? I'm not feeling... like..."

This is so uncomfortable. I don't want to eat in a fancy restaurant by myself. Food is food.

Someone steps up to the guards, but they close ranks, so I'm unable to see who it is. When I hear the smooth, warm voice, it sends familiar shivers down my spine.

"We'd like to invite Queen Merindah to join us at our table," Lord Lorn's deep voice informs the guards. "As you can see, it is only my sister and me."

Ansel immediately shakes his head, but I put a hand on his back.

"I'd like that very much. Thank you so much for inviting me," I state clearly and loudly, forcing the guards to shift to the side.

Kian clears his throat and points to the table in the middle of the room. "It's not a secure location. Perhaps they would like to join you here, Your Majesty."

With a wide grin, I look at Lord Lorn and raise an eyebrow. "Would you and Lady Allandra like to join me?"

He's still impeccably dressed in the same suit he wore to the council meeting earlier, and he looks even better up close.

"We would be delighted to dine with you," Lorn accepts with a sardonic smile. "Please excuse me while I fetch my sister."

When he turns to leave, I can't help but look. Yep, the back is almost as good as the front, but it's missing his best feature. That gorgeous smile.

Lady Allandra stands and takes Lorn's arm, her elegance and femininity a perfect match to his dominant masculinity.

Cormal and I looked like that standing side-by-side in the mirror yesterday. My brow furrows, and I shove the irritating thought away.

In a lavender silk dress, Allandra exudes the same aristocratic sophistication as Lorn. It's easy to see they're accustomed to their higher station in life. Power, beauty, wealth. The epitome of the upper echelons of the Fae. I don't hold it against them, but I am envious of their innate confidence.

"Thank you so much for inviting us, Your Majesty," Allandra states with an almost teasing lilt in her voice.

"Thank you for accepting, and please call me Meri," I urge

them both, motioning for them to sit across from me as I take my seat.

I can't believe I just invited strangers to eat with me. Was it the thought of eating by myself in this fancy restaurant or the idea of dining with Lord Lorn that made me speak up?

Allandra slides in first, followed by Lorn.

Recalling the way she managed the situation last night, I can't help but be grateful for her tact in dealing with the Faris and Rivan situation. "It's good to see you under better circumstances."

Her cheeks grow pink. "Everyone knows you didn't grow up in the Light Fae Kingdom. Why would someone in the Underworld have any knowledge of one of our little rebellions? It's not even the first or last time the Lesser Fae demanded more." Her elegant shoulder lifts.

Little rebellion? I wonder why she's downplaying it. Or is this how most of the Fae think about that time in history?

Lorn flashes an exasperated look at his sister. "It really shouldn't even be called a rebellion. Based on what we heard, it was a brutal war."

Quicker than I can follow, he picks up the wine menu. "Do you have a preference?" Dark eyes flick to me in question.

Well, the answer used to be "cheap," but I doubt he would understand. "I'm not picky. Please feel free to choose whichever one you like." It's not like I have the first clue on how to choose a "good" wine.

Lorn's comment about the rebellion eases my irritation with his sister. My gaze shifts back to Allandra, who's now staring at the table. "Your dress is beautiful. Where did you get it?"

A funny look crosses her face. "It was made for me, of course. Don't you have a royal seamstress?" She eyes the black pants and silk blouse I'm wearing. "One of my favorite things to do is sketch new outfits for Kenaris, my seamstress, to make. I could design a few for you if you like?"

Insult, or is she just passionate about design? Hard to tell. "Thank you for the kind offer, but my closet is full of clothes I haven't even worn yet." More clothes than I've owned my entire life.

Our server sets a tasting in front of Lorn for him to approve first, then pours us each a glass.

"Thank you." I smile at him, and he stiffly bows before he walks away.

Lorn picks up his glass and lifts it to the center of the table. "To our new Queen Merindah." When he sees my raised eyebrow, he amends his statement. "Queen Meri."

Feeling silly, I clink my glass with theirs and take a sip. Grapefruit, green apple, and peach assault my tongue.

"It's wonderfully refreshing." And potent. I need food. "What's good here?" Hmm. Several things on the menu look delicious.

Silence. I look up.

Lorn flashes a wry smile. "We've never been here, but I hear the salmon is good." He closes his menu. "That's what I'm going to order. Allandra?"

With a shudder, she closes her menu. "Salad, of course." Her nose wrinkles. "I can't stand the thought of eating meat or any other animal."

The server comes up to the table. "May I take your order, Your Majesty?"

"The spring chicken with seasonal vegetables," I tell him as I hand him the menu.

"Very good. Lady Allandra?"

There's a look of speculation on her face when I glance over at her. It vanishes almost instantly. "Beet salad with champagne vinaigrette."

Lorn picks up her menu, adds it to his, then hands them to the server. "Salmon with coconut rice." Placing his forearms on the edge of the table, he leans in closer. "What did you think of the council meeting earlier?"

I take a tiny sip of wine. "There are too many men and not enough women."

Surprise flits across his face, then he chuckles. "True. Would you like me to step down and let my sister take my place?" His eyes gleam with approval and a hint of desire.

"Don't be absurd," Allandra inserts. "He's only kidding, Your… Queen Meri." Narrowed eyes flash with irritation. "Why would I be interested in politics?"

Not wishing to start an argument between the two of them, I interject with a better answer to his question. "There's a lot to learn, but I'm looking forward to learning more about what the people need." That sounded queenly enough, right? And non-committal?

The tiniest smirk appears on the corner of his mouth, telling me my neutrality wasn't very convincing. My eyes drift to the rest of his strong, handsome face and firm lips.

"Ahem," the waiter says, holding my plate in front of me.

Embarrassed, I lean back to let him set it down, then dive in. "Mmm. This is delicious. How's your salmon?" When I look up, Lorn's staring at me with an inscrutable look on his face. "Lorn?"

His sister darts a glance at him.

He grins. "Sorry, I was lost in thought. What was the question?"

My eyes drop to his potent smile.

"I simply asked if your food was good." The husky timbre of my voice makes him lean forward.

"Sweet with a hint of spice. Exactly how I like it."

Allandra drops her fork. "Sorry." Her eyes skip between the two of us. "We would love for you to come to our party tomorrow evening. It's just a small get together at the house. Nothing too fancy. You're welcome to bring Princess Solandis with you." She pastes a pleading look on her face and bats her eyelashes. "Please. I'll send all the details to the palace."

I laugh and recite my number. "Just text me. I'd love to come, but I'll have to check with Solandis to see if there's anything on my calendar first."

Lorn puts the number into his phone, then leans back in his seat with a satisfied smile. "Wonderful. We look forward to having you in our home."

One last bite and I place my fork at the five o'clock mark on the plate. Solandis told me it signals I'm finished with my meal.

"Everything was delicious."

The server, who's been standing by, immediately removes our plates.

Uncertain whether I have any money, I look at Ansel who bends down to whisper in my ear that all bills are sent directly to the palace.

Relieved, I stand and wait for them to join me. "Thank you both for a lovely meal. If I can attend the party, I'll let you know."

Ansel signals to Kian and Laken, and the three men usher me out the door and into the vehicle. I glance back and wave at Allandra and Lorn, who are standing on the sidewalk staring at the SUV. I've been invited to a party. I don't even try to hold back my grin.

When we arrive at the palace, Ansel quickly dismisses the other two guards and escorts me back to my room.

"A word, Your Majesty." He clasps his hands behind his back and stares down at me. "Forgive me for bringing you this news, but I'm from the Autumn Court, and I wouldn't feel right if I withheld it from you. Lord Lorn and Lady Allandra were banished from light Fae court by Queen Nyssa." His chocolate brown eyes study me for a second. "I'm not sure why, but I thought you should know."

The giddy feeling inside me pops like a balloon. On one

hand, it's Nyssa, so the banishment could be a point in their favor. But as queen, I can't just go with my gut anymore.

"Thank you, Ansel. I appreciate you looking out for me. I'll look into the situation."

He bows and opens the door to my room. Once it's all clear, he leaves me alone.

Plopping down on my bed, I swirl my finger to remove the beautiful but torturous shoes and wiggle my toes. Thanks to the magic, my feet feel pretty good, but I'm still not a huge fan of sky-high heels. They look fierce, and I'm sure I looked good wearing them, but I think we can achieve the look with an inch or two less.

My phone pings with a text, and I grin until I realize it isn't Lorn. It's Cormal.

> Cormal: Heard you were sleepwalking last night. Ask Rivan for a rune. It's too dangerous for you to be walking around unaware of your surroundings. Don't fight me on this one.

> Meri: Are you seriously spying on me? Get a life. I'm completely surrounded by guards. There's no need to bother Rivan.

> Cormal: Where was your guard when you were out in the garden last night?

There was dirt covering my feet and hands this morning. How did I get outside without the guard noticing? Did my magic take me out there? That's kind of a scary thought.

> Meri: I'll think about it.

> Cormal: I don't have time to visit, but if you don't ask Rivan for the rune, I'll come do it myself when you're sleeping.

He would too. The bastard.

Meri: Fine. I'll get it.

Cormal: Send me a picture when it's done.

Asshole is too used to getting his own way. He says *jump* and fifty men immediately comply. Completely ignoring the fact that I caved… again… I toss the phone down on the bed and cover my eyes with my arm. Wine always makes me sleepy. Maybe a little nap will help.

CHAPTER EIGHT

MERI

Dressed in simple pants and a tunic, Solandis walks into the room a couple of hours later. With a yawn, I stretch. My nap was heaven. All the stress of the coronation and the council meeting disappeared for a while.

"What would you like for dinner, darling?" Her turquoise eyes soften when they see me lying on the bed. "I heard you went into the city and had lunch with Lord Lorn and Lady Allandra. How was it?" Her tone is nonchalant, but I can see the way she's watching me.

After stretching, I stand and straighten the wrinkles in my clothes with a little magic. "The city is magnificent. I didn't get to see everything, but I'm seriously impressed. It completely lives up to its reputation."

Picking up the brush from the vanity table, I run it through my hair. I could have used magic to comb it, but I don't want her to see how he impacts me. "Lunch was delightful. We've been invited to a party at their house tomorrow night. Do we have anything planned?"

Surprisingly, Solandis' cheeks grow pink. "I think I have a date." She drops into a chair as if she's still in shock over it. "After I met Vargas, I never thought of dating anyone else. And even now, I can barely stand to think about it. I know he's going to find a way back to me, but what if it's a thousand years from now? What if I'm meant to have more than one man in my life? Look at Arden. She has five and loves them all."

I squat down in front of her and take her hands in mine. "You must feel pretty strongly about this person if you agreed to a date."

Excitement fills her eyes. "The moment I met him, something sparked between us. With Vargas, a seer friend told me he was my destined mate. I was prepared to meet him. Kaius is unknown and exciting. In some ways, he's completely different from Vargas. Refined, sophisticated. More like the men I dated in my youth. But in other ways, he's very similar. A warrior with an air of danger that leaves no doubt of his fighting capabilities." She shivers and wiggles her eyebrows.

Kai's. They were exchanging pretty intense looks last night so I'm not surprised. I laugh. "You definitely have a type." As I say the words, I can't help but wonder about my type. Sex and flirting aside, the only man I've ever felt anything for is Cormal. What does that say about me? Only the ruthless and heartless need to apply? Maybe I need to try dating someone warm and sexy with a great smile who isn't carrying around a ton of dark baggage.

She groans. "I do. I love when they're fierce and protective." Her hands slip from mine, and she stands. "Enough. What would you like me to order us for dinner?"

Still full from earlier, I scrunch up my nose. "I wouldn't mind dessert, but no more food."

Eris arrives a few minutes later with a light vegetable pasta for Solandis and Neapolitan ice cream for me. We sit on the patio to eat.

"What do you know about Lorn and Allandra?" I ask, flipping the spoon upside down to savor every bite.

A tiny line appears between her brows. "Nothing really. Their parents used to spend a lot of time at court when I was young. I was fascinated by them. It's always interesting when a light Fae calls the Autumn or Winter Courts home, because there are so very few of them. Most are born to spring, summer, or nature, but there are a few who come from the other territories. Honestly, I can't recall ever meeting Lorn or Allandra. Why? Did something happen at your lunch?"

I shake my head. "No, lunch was nice. Ansel, the auburn-haired guard, is from the Autumn Court. He said Nyssa banned Lorn and Allandra from this court. Do you know why she would take such a drastic step?"

She pauses with her fork in the air. "Honestly? It could have been anything. Nyssa ruled with an iron fist. I'll ask around, but if it was really bad, I would have heard about it."

Biting the inside of my cheek, I think about it. How much does the past really matter? I wouldn't want someone looking at all the bad stuff I did in the past and using it to judge me now. Did I do it? Yes. And I don't regret most of it. I did what I had to do to survive, but there are some really bad things I've done that I do regret.

"Is it okay if I go to the party alone?" I ask, not wanting to commit some faux pas I'm not even aware exists.

Solandis puts down her fork and reaches across for my hand. "You are the queen, Meri. It's entirely your decision. People will want to be close to you for many reasons. It's up to you to make sure they're the right ones. The Light Fae Kingdom can be more ruthless than the Underworld, not because they are stronger or have more magic, but because they are masters at hiding their real intentions."

She waves an elegant hand, and our empty dishes disappear. "Use caution around them until they've proven themselves. It's up to them to earn your trust, not the other way around." Bending down, she places a kiss on my forehead. "The luncheon is scheduled for the end of the week. You have defensive training tomorrow morning. Kaius mentioned the name earlier, but I confess, I was a bit distracted."

I chuckle. "Good night, Aunt Solandis." I absolutely love calling her my aunt, but I only do it in private.

And I totally forgot to ask her if she had a chance to talk to Fallon. It can wait, though.

Eris pops into the room behind me, and I jump. She immediately picks up my shoes and lays out clean pajamas.

While she's busy, I quietly order a second bowl of Neapolitan ice cream. When I enter my bedroom, she's fluffing the pillows on the bed.

"Thank you, Eris. I appreciate it."

She lifts her chin and eyes me closely. "Good night, Your Majesty. Try not to spend too much time in the garden tonight."

Maybe Eris and Cormal are related. They both know everything that's going on. "Good night, Eris. Don't forget your ice cream." I point to the one I ordered for her.

She pauses and stares at the bowl for a second. Then she snatches the ice cream off the table and disappears.

Laughing, I change into the pair of silk shorts with a matching camisole she put out for me and slide into bed.

Ping. A message flashes on the lock screen.

Cormal: Did you ask Rivan about the rune?

Meri: Did you have a lot of magic when you were born?

Cormal: ...

I sigh. He's waiting for me to answer, but two can play that game.

Meri: …

Cormal: I didn't have magic when I was born.

He didn't have magic. I dismiss the idea immediately. Maybe he was one of the ones who didn't get it until he matured.

Meri: Right.

Cormal: I was born human.

My mouth drops completely open. I've never heard of someone changing from human to supernatural unless they are bitten by a vampire or a shifter, and while Cormal might bite, he doesn't have fangs. Human. The word bounces around in my head while I try to picture him without the power that clings to him like a second skin, but I simply can't.

Even if he didn't have magic, I doubt he's ever been weak or defenseless. Not only is he entirely too arrogant, but I've seen him physically fight. I bite my lip as the image of him shirtless in the ring pops into my mind. It was brutal and sexy at the same time.

Meri: Why didn't you tell me? I wouldn't have felt so alone.

Cormal: Because you would have wanted to hear the whole sordid story.

Meri: True. I've always wanted to know more about you, but I'm finally realizing need and want are two completely different things. I don't need to know. It's late. I'm going to bed. I'll ask Rivan for the rune tomorrow.

Cormal: …

But nothing ever comes across and the dots disappear. Same old Cormal with a slight twist. Human. The dynamic man I know who wields power so effortlessly started life without a drop of magic. Maybe that's why he's so prickly and secretive.

With a sigh, I close my eyes and follow the threads inside me. While we were in the city, I felt the tiniest pull on a string. I don't know what it means, though. When I look, none of the gossamer threads tying me to the kingdom are vibrating. If I follow one, it leads to a black hole. Solandis explained that the black hole will eventually fill with information.

An image of Lorn's brilliant smile is the last thing I see as I fall asleep.

Cool air brushes against me. Groggy, I can tell I've been asleep for a while. Without opening my eyes, I reach for the sheet, but it's gone. And the bed is moving beneath me.

Tearing open my eyes, Rivan's golden gaze is the first thing I see.

He shifts me in his arms. "You're okay. I've got you. You were sleepwalking in the garden again. If I put you down, you'll get dirty."

I immediately scan the area around us, but all I see are the same flowers and manicured bushes I stare down at from my balcony.

"How did I get past the guard?"

His shoulder moves in a slight shrug. "My guess is magic, but I'm not a hundred percent sure. You were in the garden when I came out for… some fresh air."

My hand is pressed against his chest. Under my palm, his heart is rapidly beating, and his skin has a thin layer of sweat on it. It could be from carrying me, but I doubt it.

"Nightmares?"

"Memories," he replies curtly. "The guard is likely standing outside your door. Do you want me to fly you up to the balcony?"

I wonder what his wings look like.

Before I can stop myself, my hand slides up from his hip to brush against his back.

He stops and stares down at me with narrowed eyes. "Don't. I..." The cords on his neck stand out when he swallows hard. "Her nails... shredding my back... it's too close tonight." His intense gaze drifts to the mark on my forehead, then darts away.

I immediately remove my hand from his back. Eyes tearing, I whisper, "I'm sorry." With a tiny swirl of my finger, a thin knit cap hides the crown on my forehead.

The tension in his body eases. "Which way back?"

Not wanting to leave him, I blurt out Cormal's request. "Cormal wants me to get a rune to prevent this from happening again. He doesn't like how vulnerable and unaware it leaves me. Is there a rune that can help? Would you mind?" I bite my lip nervously while I wait for his answer.

He studies me for several seconds before slowly nodding. "A rune would ward against the sleepwalking, but it won't stop whatever is causing it to happen."

Thinking of what is likely causing this behavior makes me shudder, but I can't continue to sleepwalk. Not only is the garden dark and perfect for an ambush, but my behavior isn't very queenly, either.

"I understand. I want the rune. Do you think you can stand my company a little while longer?"

A bittersweet smile appears on his pouty lips. "The tools are in my room." He pivots and heads toward a small balcony on the left. "Hold on." His lean, muscular arms tighten as large, red-gold wings emerge from his back.

My breath catches in my throat, not in fear, but in awe. They look downy soft in the light cascading down from his room. I ache to touch them, but I don't dare. Instead, I greedily let my eyes feast on their glory. What happens to them when he regenerates?

"My entire body, including my wings, is engulfed in faery fire until I'm reborn in the same form," he answers, apprehension lining his voice. "Why?"

My eyes widen, and I feel my cheeks burn with embarrassment. "I didn't realize I asked the question out loud. Sorry. You're the only Phoenix I know." As soon as the words are out of my mouth, I want to cut off my tongue. "Fuck. I'm sorry. Again. I only wondered because I don't know anything about your race or any other light Fae race beyond the aristocrats in this court. I grew up in the Underworld, remember?" Worriedly, I stare up at him and wait for him to either dump me on the ground or accept my apology.

Instead of answering, his wings flap hard a couple of times, and we fly up to the balcony. He removes the arm from under my knees but continues to hold me until my feet touch the ground. Once I'm steady, he pulls his other arm from behind my back.

"Stay here. Let me get something for your feet," he orders me.

My brow furrows, and I glance down. Just like yesterday morning, my feet are covered in dirt. I whip up my hands and see they're caked too.

"Both times, you seemed to be searching for something in the dirt," he informs me, an inquisitive light in his eyes. "You didn't wake last night."

He'd taken me back to my room last night. My embarrassment deepens, and I groan.

"Thank you. I didn't even know I was sleepwalking until I saw the dirt in the mirror."

While he's getting me supplies, I ask the question that's been bugging me all day. "What were you doing in the garden this morning?" It looked like he was hiding something. He mumbles something, but I can't hear him. "Wait. Were you hiding my footprints?"

"Nobody saw you last night but me," he explains. "I didn't think you would want anyone to know."

Bending down, he sets two large stone bowls full of water on the floor. He kneels and lathers his hands, then picks up my foot and places it in the water.

I immediately put a hand out to stop him. "Please. I'm embarrassed enough. I can use magic to clean my feet."

Without answering, he picks up my foot and starts to wash it. Strong fingers press firmly into my arch, and I practically melt into the floor. "Mmm. That feels incredible." My words come out with a breathless sigh. A low heat begins to burn inside me.

Trying to keep my mind off how good his hands feel, I stare down at his bent head. Legendary warrior. His arms and legs have nice muscular tone, but the rest of him is lean. Too lean. It's hard to picture. Solandis wouldn't exaggerate, though, and out of everyone here, she knows what it truly means to give someone that label. My heart hurts for how much he's endured for his people. Too much.

He lifts my foot out and places it down on his hard thigh, where he has a towel waiting to dry it off.

Not once does he look up.

After both feet are done, he stands and reaches for my hands. Strong, soapy hands scrub the dirt off, sliding in between my fingers and up my arm until every inch is clean. He leans down and grabs the other bowl and motions for me to rinse them off.

When I'm done, he hands me a towel and takes both bowls into the bathroom. I hear water running for several minutes, then he comes out drying his hands.

His gaze skims my body. "Where do you want this rune? It shouldn't be in a conspicuous place or people will question its purpose."

My hand goes to the place behind my ear where Rivan

tattooed a rune on me when I was younger. I don't know why I never questioned Leandra when she sent me here, but all these years later, I can't help but wonder about its purpose.

"What did she ask you to do?"

His shoulders drop, but after a deep breath, he tells me, "First, you need to know... The sorceress asked Nyssa for a favor, and she granted it. When I protested, Nyssa ordered me to do it. I had no choice."

The words fill me with dread.

Rivan's voice is almost hoarse with anguish when he continues, "Someone gave you power. Leandra wanted me to remove it or bind it, but I couldn't. The best I could do was limit it."

Shocked, I stare at him. The only power I've ever had was the ability to mimic others' magic, but it was so limited, it was almost useless. It only worked on certain people and left me as soon as they weren't near. I didn't dare count on it to save me. And no matter how hard I tried, it never worked on Leandra. The person I needed to escape from the most.

"You... know what it's like to be vulnerable to those around you. I needed power and magic to protect myself from Leandra and all the other predators in the Underworld. I don't understand how you could do that to me," I say, anguish filling my voice. "I... I can't stand the sight of you right now."

Stumbling, I turn around in a circle, trying to find the door. I need to get out of here. The urge to hurl magic and abuse at him is practically choking me. Why didn't he ever tell me? There. I focus on the door and place one foot in front of the other.

He takes a step toward me, but I throw out a hand to stop him.

With a sigh, he rakes his hand through his hair, pulling hard at the strands. "When you arrived that day, you were under some kind of memory spell. I don't know what happened, but whatever it was, I think it scared Leandra."

That's why I don't remember much. I grasp the cold knob

and throw open the door. Stalking out of the room with clenched fists and teeth, I walk until I see nothing but barely lit empty hallways. Then, I release the dam holding everything inside. Magic bursts out of me, flying in every direction, as does the scream that's been building the entire time.

CHAPTER NINE

ights are blown out. Walls are bowed. Pillars are warped and barely standing. The hallway is in shambles. On my hands and knees, I slide one foot under me, then the other, and stand. Lightheaded from using that much magic, I sway while I stare at the damage I've done.

All these years, I could have been using magic, and she took that away from me. Not only to make me defenseless to her, but to the entire world. Yeah, I survived, but damn, it was close sometimes. And if it hadn't been for Callyx and Cormal, I wouldn't have survived her last act. I slam the door before those memories can get out. Of all the things she's ever done, two stand out as the worst. The Pit and this heinous act. If it's the last thing I do, I will find a way to destroy her.

A long whistle has me whirling to face the person behind me. One of my guards, Tiernan, stands there with a look of appreciation on his face.

Heat crawls up my neck and face. "How do I fix it?"

He blinks. "Do you have any juice left?"

I lift a shoulder. "I don't know." Stumbling over to a pillar, I place my hand on it and close my eyes. *Please work.* Spiraling down into my core, I dredge up a pool of magic and push it into the stone under my palm. When the marble moves, I open my eyes and watch the pillar return to its former state.

Lethargic, I drag myself another few feet and slap my hand onto the stone. This time, I have to go deeper to get the magic, but somehow, I find enough to fix it.

My knees give out and meet the floor. Hard. I wince.

"I'll have to come back in the morning. Would you mind helping me to my room?" Lids slide to half-mast. I'm going to pass out soon, and I don't want to do it in front of a stranger, even if he is my guard.

Strong arms pick me up and carry me for the second time that night. My head bobs back as I look up at him. I'm dying to close my eyes, but I can't, so I take the time to study him. There's something about him that has my instincts on high alert.

"You remind me of Rivan. Are you a Fire Fae too?"

Yellow eyes blink slowly. "My mother was a fire drake. Father a lord. I only claim one side of my heritage, though. There's nowhere to go if you're a Fire Fae. As a Fae lord's son, I could rise through the ranks and become a guard." A slight tinge of bitterness seeps into his tone.

Fire drake. I knew it. "Does Kaius know?"

He jerks his chin. "I haven't said anything. Why? Are you going to tell him?" Under me, I feel his arms tense.

Unsure, I think about it. If I say something, will that get him kicked out of the guards? I've seen the hatred the light Fae have for Rivan. The only thing holding them back are the terms of Rivan's agreement. Tiernan would have no protection against retaliation.

And then there's me. Everyone knows Nyssa is my "mother," but nobody here in the palace knows the truth except Solandis—that I was actually created from essence taken from both the light Fae queen and… the dark Fae king. I've never been a hypocrite, and I refuse to start now, but I also need to be cautious.

There might be one way to ensure his loyalty. "Would you swear an oath to me?" I nibble the inside of my cheek while I wait for his answer.

His brow lowers. "I've already sworn an oath."

"To the crown, not to me," I remind him. Solandis told me the guards will protect the crown.

He stops and stares down at me. "How do I know you're worthy of my oath?"

"How do I know you aren't a spy for the fire drakes causing trouble at the border, or an assassin waiting to kill me?" I counter, lifting my chin. It sounds ridiculous to even say it out loud, especially when he is carrying me, but Cormal taught me to never underestimate the timing of a good strategic move. He could be biding his time for some reason.

With an exasperated sigh, he reluctantly nods. "I give you my oath. I promise to protect you, not just the crown." With those words, he starts moving again.

"Thank you," I murmur. Exhaustion is weighing me down, but I'm still too uneasy to shut my eyes around him. Thankfully, I see the door to my room coming up on the left. Garren is standing guard outside of it. "Put me down here."

Hesitating, he glances at me, then at the guard.

"I would rather not have to explain why you're carrying me in the middle of the night," I whisper furiously. "I'll make it, but if I can't, I'll call out to Garren."

He carefully props me up against the wall. "This should help steady you."

Leaning heavily against the marble, I shuffle forward a few

steps. My body sways, and I hear him curse behind me. With a wave of my hand, I motion for him to get back. "Garren!"

The yummy twin immediately jumps and peers down the hall. Sword drawn; he cautiously approaches until he realizes it's me. With a flick of his wrist, the sword disappears, and his arms go around me. Just in time, too, as my knees give out again.

With me in his arms, he swings around to look down the hallway. When he doesn't see anything alarming, he turns his attention back to me. "What happened? Do I need to sound the alarm?" Without waiting for my reply, he strides quickly to my room.

He smells delicious, like peppermint. "Just a small burnout," I wearily inform him. "I'll be fine with some rest."

"I have to tell Kaius about this incident. It's protocol," he tells me, a flash of sympathy in his eyes. The door swings open, and he sets me down on the bed in my room. "Do you want me to call Eris?"

Barely able to keep my eyes open, I shake my head. "No. I'll be fine. Thank you for your help." My words are stiff, but I need him to leave immediately. The second the door clicks shut; I let the darkness sweep me under.

Minutes later, I hear Eris' voice.

"According to the schedule, you're supposed to go to training this morning. Are you going, or do you want me to send a note and cancel?" Eris asks in her usual brisk manner.

Groggy, I lift my head in confusion and realize the sun is shining. When I move to sit up, I can't help the groan that escapes. Every muscle in my body hurts.

"I'm not sure I can go today." I wonder what will happen if I just lie here? Can a queen take a day off? An image of the wrecked hallway pops into my mind, and I just want to bury my head in the pillows.

Eris lays down workout clothes. "Well, if you're not sure, maybe you should go down there and try first."

Her no-nonsense tone makes me cringe. Staggering up from the bed, I push one foot into the leggings she laid out, then the other. Once I've rolled them on, I exchange my shirt for the sports bra and cropped top. For the first time in days, I feel like I can breathe in the clothes I'm wearing.

Eris points to the chair and motions for me to sit. She quickly braids my hair back, then bends down to put my socks on.

"Eris." I groan. "Stop. There is no reason for you to put my shoes on. Surely, you have more important things to do?"

She taps my head. "Do you think I don't know burnout when I see it?" A humph sound comes from her throat. "You can't hide anything from me. Might as well not even try. Now, sit still and let me get these on you."

Giving in, I close my eyes and try to muster up the energy I'm going to need for training today. This is worse than any hangover I've ever had. And that's saying a lot.

She pats my leg. "There. All done." Her hand grabs mine and places a glass in it. "Drink. It will put you right as rain."

Skeptical, I open my eyes to peer into the glass. "Arrgh. No." I try to hand it back to her, but she refuses to take it. "Fine." Pinching my nose, I throw back the orange drink like it's cheap tequila. It takes a minute for me to swallow the thick substance, but I finally get it down.

Eris nods approvingly, takes the glass, and disappears.

Instead of using magic, I use the human way to brush my teeth. As long as it gets done, it doesn't matter to me.

Feeling like death, I walk gingerly over to the door and open it to find Ansel waiting for me.

He gives me a sympathetic look and offers his arm, but I decline. This time, he gives me an approving nod.

Ignoring his gesture, I start walking.

He quickly catches up and guides me down several hallways until we reach a large indoor training room. The fifteen-minute walk gives Eris' potion time to start working, and I'm feeling less like dying by the time we walk in.

Nobody even looks our way. Guards are sparring with each other on mats and in rings; their grunts and colorful curses loud in the quiet room. The air is heavy with the smell of sweat and testosterone, and I can't help but take in a deep, appreciative smell. It's the same no matter what realm. Muscles moving, bodies pushed to the limit, sweat running in rivulets over hard abs. Tingles spread throughout my body, making all the secret places perk up. Good thing I'm wearing a sports bra and a shirt.

Looking further back, I see an entire wall covered with weapons. Knives, swords, axes, spears, staffs, and whatever the rest of it is. Weapons aren't really my forte. I bet Arden could name and use every single one of them. I grin. And she could fight better than the guards currently practicing in the corner.

There are very few women in the room. It's not surprising, since Nyssa didn't like having them around her. What is surprising... nobody is using magic. I wonder why?

Five minutes turn to ten, and I'm starting to get irritated. Where the hell is Ansel? I search the group at the far end of the room, but not one of them has auburn hair. This is ridiculous. I could have stayed in bed. I glance at my phone. Fifteen minutes have gone by. If I knew my way back to my room, I'd leave, but I don't.

Stalking in the same direction Ansel took earlier, the entire room begins to notice a woman is in the room and training grinds to a halt. One of the males lets out a long whistle. I glance in his direction, ready to flip him off, but the mark of the crown on my forehead shuts him up quick.

Someone shouts, "Shit! Queen Merindah!"

I pivot toward the voice and see a knife flying toward me. My head swivels looking for cover, but there isn't any. All I can do is duck at the last minute and hope it misses me. Shifting to the balls of my feet, I wait, ready to dive or squat, but in the end, I don't have to do anything at all.

A large, masculine hand reaches out and catches it in mid-air. With a flick, he sends it into the nearest target, embedding it all the way to the hilt. The entire hall sighs in relief. Except him.

Similar to most Fae, he's tall, maybe even one of the tallest I've seen, but that's where the similarities end. There's nothing urbane or polished about this man. He's sharp edges and darkness. A huge, lightning-fast predator sums up my first impression, and those aren't even his most interesting traits. Dark complected with thick black hair to his shoulders, he has scars, lots of them, and not the barely seen, almost transparent scars most supernaturals get from battle. These are brutal, like massive claws carved deep furrows into his skin.

He doesn't seem to like me, either. Feet planted wide, arms crossed, he is staring at me with pure contempt. His animosity is almost smothering.

Leery, I eye the dark, massive Fae who's obviously not my biggest fan, and my irritation rises. What's his issue? He didn't have to stick his hand out and save me. I would have found a way to avoid the damn knife. Besides, I'm immortal. Most knives won't kill me. Except the one.

Damn it. Ansel is going on my shit list… when I find him. "Thank you. I appreciate your help. If you'll excuse me, I was just looking for my guard."

"Ansel's busy," he informs me in a rough, gravelly voice that matches his unpleasant demeanor. "You're training with me today."

The hell I am. "I appreciate the offer, but I'm done with training today. If I can just get someone to escort me back to my room, that would be wonderful."

Silence reigns around me. Not one guard steps forward to volunteer. I wait. Nope. None. I knew I should have stayed in bed. My gut is never wrong. If it says it's going to be a shit day, it is. *Fuck it.* I will walk around the hallways until I find a member of the staff to help me.

Before I've taken one step, he's standing directly in front of me.

I blink. "Excuse me." I step to the side, but he immediately blocks me. Furious, I place my hands on my hips and get up in his face. "Get out of my way."

He leans down until our noses are almost touching. "Make me." Steel-grey eyes gleam with challenge, but I just roll my eyes. "If you want to leave, you'll have to go through me." The smallest half-smirk appears on his face.

What is it about the Fae and their bullshit microscopic expressions? I mean, seriously. Would it kill them to have a full-blown reaction? Pivoting quickly from side to side, I watch him follow my every move, but not one muscle twitches in response. With a wink, I slip by and take off running toward the pole in the middle of the room. Just as my hand grabs it, he appears in front of me.

I grin, swing around the pole, and slide right between his legs. I jump up on the other side and take off again.

He reaches out to grab me, but I sidestep through two guards. When he follows, I jump back to the main path and run straight for the ring in front of me. Diving between the ropes, I flip up to a standing position, then take a running leap to the top rope and somersault to the ground on the other side.

I take two steps forward and slam into the mat face first. *Ow.* Instead of letting it faze me, I wait for him to ease up. When he does, I throw my elbow into his windpipe and slither out of his arms. A meaty fist catches my ankle, and I flip over and kick him in the head with the heel of the other foot.

He growls. "Enough."

Suddenly, I'm frozen. Unable to do anything but breathe, I glare up at the asshole.

Grey eyes study me intently. "Not once did you use your magic. Ansel told me you wouldn't be able to train because you were experiencing burnout, but you didn't even try. Not one spark to avoid the knife or me."

It didn't occur to me to reach for my magic. I don't know if there's anything left after last night, but he's right. Not once did I try to use it. Instead, I resorted to the tactics I've used my whole life. Running, evading, defending.

He hauls me to my feet. For several minutes, he stares into me, trying to see the magic underneath. "You're almost empty. That must have been some tantrum. Try not to have another one before our next training session. I won't take it easy on you just because you're a queen."

Ansel appears to the left of him, along with Kaius. "So, you'll train her?"

A muscle ticks in his jaw, but he answers. "She needs to replenish her magic. Bring her back in two days. I'll train her." He strides away.

Free to move again, I flip all three of them off and stalk out of the room, Ansel and Kaius following close behind. "No. Absolutely not. I'm not training with that neanderthal. It's not happening."

Kaius laughs. "I originally picked someone else, but they suddenly became unavailable. Dead, actually. Something I'm not upset about anymore. Besides me, he's the best fighter here, but I can't teach you how to wield your magic. He can. Give him a chance."

I think about the vow I made last night to do everything possible to kill Leandra. She excels at magic. If I'm to have a fighting chance, I need someone brutal to teach me.

"Fine. I'll do it."

CHAPTER TEN

<u>MERI</u>

Someone fixed the hallway. But who? I doubt a fire drake would have the kind of magic it would take to restore it. Solandis isn't aware it happened. Maybe the staff took care of it. Embarrassed but relieved, I swing into my room and stop when I see the very regal Princess of the Light Fae in the tiniest black velvet dress.

I let loose a long whistle.

"Is this too much for a first date?" She turns to me with her lip between her teeth. Reaching down, she tugs at the bottom hem. "I feel like I'm all boobs and legs in this dress."

Not used to seeing my supremely confident aunt looking unsure of herself, I plop down in the chair behind her and look more closely at the dress. "It depends on your goal. This screams sex. Nothing wrong with that objective. But if you also want to get to know Kaius, I suggest something a little… more."

"You're right," she admits with a sparkle in her eye. "This is completely a second date dress." Her melodic laugh fills the room.

Crossing over to the rack of clothes she must have brought with her, she whips through them until she finds a deep turquoise silk slip dress. In a blink, she's standing in front of the mirror, turning side-to-side to look at it from all angles.

The color matches her eyes perfectly. Held up by tiny straps, the maxi dress follows every curve of her body. It's sexy without being obvious. Until she turns around. Backless, the dress plunges until it hits her butt.

Her confident smile is back. "This is the dress."

"It certainly covers all the bases. Kaius isn't going to know what hit him," I choke out. "Where are you going tonight?"

She lifts a shoulder. "No idea." Whirling around, she grabs my hand and pulls me into my closet. "I'm sure you haven't even thought about what to wear to the party tonight, have you?"

I wince. "Lorn said it was casual."

She laughs. "Casual means something less than court attire." With her manicured hand, she flips through the dresses in the closet until she finds six or seven that fit her criteria. "It's your turn."

She puts them on the rack, then holds them up one at a time for me to view.

I immediately veto the red. Nod yes to the black one. I'm tempted by the dark purple because it matches his eyes, but it's kind of obvious. I like the gold one with the sheer netting. I nix the pretty mauve one because I wore that color the last time I saw him. But when she holds up a strapless navy dress with delicate silver flowers on it, I know that's the look I want for tonight.

"I want to try that one on first," I tell her.

Her eyes narrow, and a second later, I'm wearing the dress. "Kaius told me about the burnout. I couldn't believe it. You barely use magic. What happened?"

My finger automatically goes to the place behind my ear where the rune used to be. I tell her what Leandra did.

She stiffens in disbelief. "I knew it. Your ability to mimic was always odd to me. I felt like I was missing something." Her head shakes back and forth. "How could she have left you practically defenseless your entire life? It's inconceivable."

"I truly think she despised me because I didn't give her the revenge she wanted against her lover." My voice is soft as I state the truth I've carried around for so long. "She talked about him all the time, and it wasn't all hate."

Solandis' elegant fingers grip my chin. "No, she should have taken it out on him. Never on you. She has no excuse for the way she treated you." Her blue eyes implore me to believe her.

Avoiding her gaze, I move over to the mirror to look at the navy dress gracing my body. Strapless and fitted, it skims my body to a mid-calf length, giving me the appearance of height. Over the silk skirt is a sheer overlay with exquisite silver flowers embroidered on it. A high slit on the right keeps it from being too cutesy. "Sophisticated, romantic, and not too sexy. It's perfect."

Solandis squeezes my bare shoulders. "You look fabulous." She places a kiss on my cheek. "I need to go finish getting ready. Are you going to be okay tonight by yourself?"

I nod with a confidence I don't quite feel. "Absolutely."

When I head out an hour later, I see Kaius and Solandis leaving in another SUV. She looks positively radiant and maybe a tiny bit nervous. Even with her height and heels, he tops her by at least another three inches. He's protectively leaning over her, his arm a barrier to the outside world.

I smile wistfully, wanting someone who acts like that around me.

Shaking it off, I glance from Laken's ice white locks to Tiernan's messy dark hair. Salt and pepper. Not quite as good as the Neapolitan from the other day, but two is better than one. A snicker escapes, but I cover it up by clearing my throat a few times. Flirting is as natural as breathing, but with the guards off limits, I've resorted to bad humor and ice cream.

Stepping into the portal, we arrive in seconds and are immediately greeted by our hosts.

After a quick curtsy, Lady Allandra takes my hands in hers and air kisses my cheeks. "Queen Meri. Stunning and elegant. Thank you for coming. Please make yourself at home."

Lord Lorn flicks his dark purple eyes to his sister and a warm look passes between them. "Queen Meri. Absolutely dazzling." Placing his mouth by my ear, firm lips graze my cheeks with a light kiss. "Go. Have fun. I'll find you later."

Being this close to him for the first time is quite intoxicating. I breathe in his raw masculinity, along with the distinctive smell of bergamot, vanilla, and a woodsy scent. He even smells luxurious.

"Hmm, perhaps. Unless I run off with the handsome Fae in the corner."

I pull myself away from temptation and saunter into the house. Every few feet, I make it a point to stop and have a quick chat with the male guests. Or at least the handsome ones. Once I've made it to the other end of the room, I pick up a glass of champagne and strike a pose. The high slit parts at the very top of my thigh, leaving my entire leg exposed, and I nonchalantly slide my eyes in Lorn's direction.

Amusement. Not lust or possessiveness. His eyes skim down my leg, and a gleam of appreciation appears, but not for long.

That's a first. Either I misread the signs, or he's taken. I'm usually pretty good at reading attraction, but my game is off here.

I look around the room. Side glances and whispers tell me I'm the subject of their discussion. Lovely. I'll mingle for an hour, then leave. Conscious of my new status, I paste a smile on my face and walk over to a small group of people.

To my delight, they're scientists. After my quick tour the other day, I have all kinds of questions about the city and their latest experiments.

"Meira is brilliant. I love how seamlessly everything blends with the nature around it. What do you have planned next?"

My plan to leave disintegrates pretty quickly. After speaking with that group for a while, I make my way to the next. They all belong to a theatre group, and their play is opening in a week. It's a romantic comedy about mistaken identity.

"It sounds hilarious. I'll definitely have to come watch it."

My stomach rumbles, and I realize I haven't eaten anything since I got here. Making my way to the buffet, I fill a plate with an assortment of delicious-looking hors d'oeuvres, fruit, and the most perfect mini chocolate cake I've ever seen.

I look around for a place to sit and eat, but there doesn't seem to be an available spot. The buzz about my presence hasn't died down either. Not wanting to eat with everyone staring at me, I bite my lip and wonder if I should just put my plate down.

Tiernan subtly taps my arm and dips his head toward the stairs, where a few people are heading up with plates in hand. Smiling my thanks, I nod and follow him up. Laken takes the rear.

When we emerge, we're on a rooftop with the city surrounding us. Enchanted, I grab a seat at the table nearest the wall in order to see the view.

It's not long before several ladies grab the rest of the seats around me. Giving them a polite smile, I do my best to ignore them and dive into my food. It tastes even better than it looks. If I wasn't a queen, I'd go back for seconds in a heartbeat.

All that's left is the itty bitty chocolate cake.

One of the ladies leans toward me. "Are you going to announce your ladies-in-waiting soon?"

As one, the rest of the group turns to look at me with expectant smiles.

Solandis hasn't mentioned anything about it, but I don't say that to them. "I'll confer with Solandis and determine the proper way to proceed." I also fully intend to tell her that I don't want any ladies attending to me.

One of the blonds heaves a dramatic sigh and looks around at her friends. "Nyssa didn't have any ladies either. I swear. Nobody wants to uphold our traditions anymore."

"What other changes do you plan on making?" a sophisticated woman in red asks with a slight sneer on her face.

Uneasy with her tone and the conversation, I shift until I'm facing her. "I'm sorry. I didn't get your name. I'm Meri. Queen Meri to my friends. Queen Merindah to strangers…"

I don't continue, but by the compressed lips around me, they've gotten the hint. It's rude to not introduce yourself, then proceed to make snide comments to my face.

Lorn strides onto the rooftop and saves them from my irritation. "Asena will begin singing in five minutes. Seats are filling up quickly." He stops at our table, and several ladies immediately stand to press up against him. With careful moves, he extricates himself from their grasping hands and sends them off with a promise to see them later.

Determined to eat my dessert, I pick up the fork by my plate and hover over the miniature cake. It's so beautiful, I can't stand the thought of cutting into it.

"Queen Meri? Are you coming?" Lorn asks from the end of the table. "Asena will love having the queen watch her performance." He turns and waves the last of the guests downstairs.

"I'll be there in just a minute," I tell him. "I'm going to savor the view and my dessert for a few more minutes."

He walks over and takes a seat next to me. "I'll wait with you." When I start to protest, he waves a negligent hand. "I never pass up a chance to sit up here. This is my favorite place in the house." He sweeps his blond hair over his shoulder and props his chin in his hand.

I trace my eyes over his strong, masculine features. There is nothing delicate about this man. "Meira is truly a masterpiece. I met a few of the scientists earlier and had an enlightening conversation with them about what it takes to maintain the city. They also spoke about some of their current experiments. I honestly didn't want to leave them to mingle with the next group, although I'm glad I did," I say enthusiastically before telling him about the theatre group.

He's staring at me in fascination. "You're truly excited, aren't you?"

"Of course," I say, with a confused frown. "I'm interested in everything happening in the kingdom, whether it's the latest Fae hit singer, a play, or the challenges we're facing with our low metal supply."

He doesn't say anything, but I see the wheels turning in his head.

I put the fork down and turn to him. "I know the Fae are known for their intense magnetism, but you seem to have an extra dose of it. Females and males almost fall over themselves trying to be near you. Why?"

The corners of his mouth turn down. "Honestly, I didn't think you noticed. You seem oddly immune to it, something I enjoy immensely."

I throw my head back and laugh. "I'm not oblivious, trust me, but I don't feel an unnatural pull toward you."

His gorgeous smile appears. "So, you're saying you like me?"

"Answer my question, and I'll answer yours," I tell him, wanting to see if he'll trust me with the truth.

With his other hand, he reaches for the cake on my plate. "I've always had the ability to inspire desire in others. My guess is an ancestor nobody talks about, but the Fae like to hide their indiscretions." He places the cake against my lips. "There's no need to cut it. You can have it all with one bite."

I hold his stare and open my mouth. He feeds the cake to me, then trails one finger along my lips.

Rich, decadent chocolate cake with chocolate orange frosting. The flavors explode in my mouth, and I moan. It's mind-blowingly good. Suddenly, warmth rushes through my body and hits my core, making me gasp.

"What's in this cake?"

His eyes darken to the deepest purple, and he leans over and whispers in my ear, "Faery dust. Just a touch to liven the party."

Faery dust. I've always wanted to try it, but it was too expensive. A nice buzz settles around me, almost like I've downed a half a bottle of wine in two minutes.

"Mmm, it's lovely."

His shoulders relax. "It is, isn't it? We should go down and join the rest of the guests." He holds out his hands to help me stand. "Would you go to dinner with me tomorrow night? Just the two of us. No sister or guests to distract us?"

Inside, I squeal, but on the outside, I force myself to pause. "One condition. No games. I've had enough of men running hot one second and cold the next." Cormal's blue eyes and sardonic smile pop in my head. "Deal?"

He flips my hand around in his and brings it to his mouth for a feather-light kiss. "Deal. If you liked the cake, you'll love Asena. Come on."

CHAPTER ELEVEN

<u>MERI</u>

The sun rises in three hours, but who can sleep after a night like this one? My blood is still pumping with excitement. Like a fairytale, I drank, ate, and danced my fill. It was marvelous. Asena's music plays on repeat in my head, making me hum and twirl while I walk. Lorn was right. Her voice was intoxicating, although the dessert continues to hold first place with me.

Allandra and Lorn know the most interesting people—scientists, musicians, actors, authors, and artists. All creative and smart influencers who live in Meira. Not one stuffy individual in the bunch. The only council member in attendance was Lorn.

The image of his broad smile and mischievous smirk makes me smile. Suave. Sophisticated. One of the aristocratic Fae, yet so different from the rest. Easily mingling with guests all night, he exuded a magnetic charm none could resist. Fae are typically self-serving. Not him. In conversations, Lorn's focus was completely on the other person and their words.

I've never met anyone like him. He's so real compared to the rest of the Fae that I almost feel like I can be myself around him. Only Solandis' earlier words of caution hold me back.

I'm still smiling when I round the corner of the garden and see Rivan. Anger flares for a brief second but deflates the longer I watch him.

Dressed in casual loose pants and a sleeveless shirt, his head is down and shoulders bent, as if the weight of the world is on his back. And fuck. I know that feeling so well. When your decisions are dictated by the whims of others, you live in a dark tunnel with no end in sight. Everything weighs on you, and there is no hope of lightening the load. Nyssa might be gone, but Rivan is tied to this court by the agreement he made long ago.

"Rivan," I call out softly into the night, quickly conjuring a thin scarf to wrap around my head to hide my crown. "Don't you ever sleep?"

He immediately tenses. "Meri. Sorry, Queen Meri." After a short bow, he moves to the side of the path as if to let me pass. "The night carries... too many memories," he reluctantly answers. Avoiding my gaze, he stares over my shoulder, unwilling to let me see his pain.

It breaks my heart into a million pieces. How do I fix someone so completely broken?

"I'm sorry."

His eyes slide to mine in disbelief.

"I'm angry you didn't tell me, but perhaps it's better I didn't know until the bond was broken and the rune gone. It would have driven me crazy to know she had limited my only power."

"I'm truly sorry. I know what it's like to have no control," he says sadly. "I wish I had told you sooner. Can you forgive me?" Gold eyes stare at me with a glimmer of hope in them.

"I already have," I murmur. "And I still want a rune to prevent me from sleepwalking. If you're willing to do it?" I bite my lip, hoping this will help bridge the gap between us.

The corner of his mouth turns up. "Of course. When do you want to get together?"

"How about now?" The thought of trying to sleep makes me shudder.

A knowing look enters his eyes, and he tentatively holds his hand out for me to take. "I have no other plans."

I firmly grip his hand with mine. It's smooth and strong.

"Should I change first?"

His grip tightens as if he can't stand the thought of me leaving even to change clothes. "It depends. Where do you want the rune?"

My nose scrunches up while I think about it. "I don't want anyone to ask about it."

Behind my neck doesn't work because it would be seen when I pull my hair up. Same goes for the rest of me.

"The thought of putting it behind my ear makes me cringe, but most other places won't work. Even my feet are visible." I lift my foot to show him the strappy sandal that doesn't hide much, and the slit in my dress opens, exposing my entire leg. "See?"

Bright eyes turn molten gold, but he immediately looks away. "How about the inside of your hip?"

When we reach the area below his balcony, he unfolds his wings and holds out his arms.

My heart stutters.

He's magnificent.

The other night I couldn't see the full picture like I do now. Full red-gold wings extend from the ground to several feet above his head and out to each side. Encased in a magical glow, they radiate power and strength. And even as lean as he is right now, I can start to envision the warrior he used to be.

His eyebrow rises, and he gives me a quizzical look.

Blushing profusely, I step forward and let his warm arms wrap around me. We land on the balcony moments later.

"Flying must be incredible. How far can you travel?"

He turns away. "Flying is pure freedom. There's nothing tying me to the world below. I used to be able to travel for miles, but it's like a muscle. When you don't use it much, it becomes weaker." With a wave of his hand, he gestures to the chaise in the corner by the fireplace. "Lie down and remove any clothing from the spot where you want the rune. We can put it inside your hip or on the outside. Your choice. I'll get the supplies."

If I put the rune on the inside of my hip, I'll have to look at it when I dress or undress. Maybe outside is best. Mind made up, I cross over to the chaise, lie on my side, and pull the slit up until it exposes my outer hip.

Rivan pulls up a nearby stool and sets his supplies on the floor beside it. A twirl of his finger and a ball of faery light appears above my hip to help him see. After he sits, he shifts forward and runs his finger in a small circle on my hip.

I suck in a small breath at the sensation of Rivan's touch on my bare skin.

"Here?"

Unable to speak, I nod.

He bends down to pick up a small notebook and piece of charcoal. With quick fingers, he draws three lines that look like a stick figure waving hi. "This is the Algiz rune. It provides protection and defense. At its core, it attracts positive forces and defends against negative ones." With a flick of his wrist, he turns the notebook toward me. "What do you think?"

I shrug. "Whatever you believe is best."

Flipping it back around, he studies it for a second, then gives a firm nod. With the charcoal in hand, he lightly sketches the design on my outer hip. "Algiz is powerful, so it doesn't need to be big. Take a look."

Angling my hip toward me, I lean up and look at the faint lines. They're even smaller than I imagined, and any fears of someone noticing vanishes.

"Perfect."

Lying back down, I watch while he rummages around in his supplies for a second.

Brow furrowed, he carefully pulls out a small needle and a jar of black ink. "Hold this." He places the ink in my hand. "I'm going to do the rune first. Once it's complete, we can add a flower or something to disguise it further, if you want."

Intrigued with the idea of adding something beautiful to the powerful rune, I nod enthusiastically. "I like that idea. Would it need to be black, too?"

He pauses. "No. The rune doesn't have to be black, either. I can tattoo it in another color if you want?"

"What are my options?"

He takes the black ink from me and bends over to pick up a small tray with several bottles in it. "Besides black... red, blue, green, pink, orange, or white."

I'm not sure how much I want it to stand out. "What does white look like?"

Pink stains his tanned cheekbones. "I have one, but it's on the inside of my hip. White isn't as noticeable on my darker skin. Do you want to see it?"

Intrigued, I nod. He pulls down the right side of his pants really, really low and I can't help but lick my lips. *Hello Adonis belt.* Just when I think I'm going to see everything he has to offer, a small white rune appears, and the reveal ends.

Swallowing the groan in my throat, I force myself to study the rune. One line goes up and down. The other looks sort of like an angular S or a lightning bolt.

He clears his throat. "Do you see it? The white color isn't noticeable until you get closer. I think it will be perfect for a rune you want to keep incognito."

Is his rune incognito? "What does it mean?"

Rivan stiffens. "It's a combination of two symbols: Isa and Sowula. The single straight line represents a frozen heart, and the bolt represents the power of the sun to overcome darkness."

Maybe I'm not asking the right question. I'm getting a rune to help with nightmares. "What does it do for you?"

The muscles of his jaw become rigid. "Gives me strength in the face of adversity. I tattooed it on me after Sima was murdered by Nyssa."

I'd heard about Sima from Arden. One of the five MacAllister witches who was destined to survive the massacre. Unfortunately, she had not been the one prophesied to carry on their lineage, but she had met Rivan along the way and had fallen in love.

Without thinking, I lace my fingers in his. "Arden shared the MacAllister history with me. Sima must have been very brave to set out on her own, knowing she was leaving nothing but death behind her." My thumb makes small soothing circles on his hand. "I'm sorry for your loss. If you ever want to talk about her, I'd love to hear it."

Fingers grip mine tightly for a couple of minutes. "Maybe. One day." Slipping his hand from mine, he pulls up his pants. "What color?"

"White. And maybe you can add a daisy to it," I answer, putting my head back down on my left arm. There are several of them in the garden, and I can't think of anything better than to have Rivan add something that reminds me of him.

Sitting on the stool, he gets his tools and the white ink and sets them up on a small tray on the chaise. He leans over my hip and begins.

Warmth from his body covers me, and the cocoon makes me feel safe. "Where did you learn to do this?"

"My mother taught me. She was born a daughter of Avalon. The Fae who lived on the sacred island for thousands of years developed different magic than those born in the Land of the Fae. She could infuse runes with her power," he murmurs, never looking up from his task.

Avalon disappeared long before I was born. "How old are you?"

The corners of his mouth twitches, and he stops what he's doing. Silent for a moment, I can almost see him counting in his head. Suddenly, a devastated look crosses his face.

"Four thousand one hundred and thirty-three years old." He picks up his tools and resumes his task.

Damn, damn, damn. I mentally smack myself on the head.

The rebellion was almost three thousand years ago, which means he's spent most of his very long life here. A prisoner, enduring a seemingly endless sentence. A wave of sadness washes over me. Am I ever going to get this friendship right? It feels like I keep making mistakes with him.

Heaving a disgusted sigh, I lay my hand lightly on his shoulder. "Sorry, old man." The words slip out, and my eyes widen in horror. When he turns to look at me incredulously, I bust out laughing and groaning at the same time.

"Sorry. Sorry. I don't know what's wrong with me. Leandra did drop me on my head a few times when I was little."

Rusty laughter erupts from his throat, and he's forced to put down his tools. When it stops a minute later, he flashes me a blinding smile.

"I don't know why I'm laughing. That was so wrong." His words make him pause. "Maybe that's why. You forget the reason I'm here." Lean hands wave at the walls around us. "It makes me forget, too."

Still a tiny bit embarrassed, I shrug. "I see you as my friend, and since I don't have many of those, I refuse to treat you any differently. I'm one hundred—no, make that two hundred—percent positive I'll stick my foot in my mouth a million times.

Please consider this my upfront and universal apology. I hope you'll forgive me every single time."

A soft smile lingers on his lips. "Friends, huh? Those are pretty scarce around here." He picks up his tools. "I'm almost done." Seconds go by. "Okay. What do you think?"

Leaning up, I twist sideways to look at my hip. The three branches at the top of the rune all have daisies on them. It looks like a mini bouquet. "I love it. Thank you."

With a firm nod, he collects his tools and puts them back into the box at his feet. Swallowing hard, he spears me with an intense look.

"Friends. I'm a little rusty and given how old I am…" Silence. "I'm sure I've forgotten how to be a good one. We may have to forgive each other."

A slow grin spreads across my face. "Deal."

CHAPTER TWELVE

CORMAL

Dusty weapons line the shelves of the forgotten storage room. Most would dismiss them as old or useless, but my gut is telling me there are a few valuable items in here. Feeling a particularly strong pull behind me, I ignore it to concentrate on the two men in front of me.

"I don't like it. Coincidence means the odds were in someone else's favor," I say furiously. "The guard we chose to train Meri is suddenly dead. Likely from a deliberate act, even if we can't prove it."

Kaius runs a hand over his head but jerks it away quickly. A sheepish grin crosses his face when he sees my raised eyebrow.

"Still not used to having a head full of hair. When this is done, it's getting buzzed." Crossing his arms, he stares at me. "I've checked everything. Twice. Whoever did it can move through shadows. I sure as hell didn't do it. I thought you had taken him out for some reason. Or sent Callyx to do it."

95

My mouth hardens. "Shadow walking is not a common ability, but it's not rare either. Narrowing it down to one person is near impossible."

Rivan steps forward. "Who's going to train her now? I'd offer to do it, but it's been so damn long, I'm not sure I remember how to hold a sword."

Kaius claps him on the shoulder. "She needs to learn how to fight and wield magic. Together. All the years she spent with very little magic have made her think like a human." One corner of his lip curls up in a sneer. "If she doesn't learn how to use the immense power at her disposal, someone will waltz in here and challenge her for the crown. And win."

"We're not going to let that happen, are we?" I interject. "Tell me about this replacement you found."

Kaius' mouth stretches into a feral grin. "I'd like to see them try to kill this one. He wouldn't even have to wake up to take them out."

Uneasy, I shift my weight between my feet to prevent myself from pacing. I completely trust Kaius' judgement when it comes to finding a fighter.

"He can take out a small army. What else?"

"His name is Madoc. Captain says he's been here a while but can't recall how long," he recalls. "Big, lethal. Scars everywhere. Aristocratic Fae. Doesn't talk much."

Fae rarely scar. "What kind of scars?"

He thinks about it for a second. "I'd guess demon." An evil grin appears.

Ignoring Kaius' sense of pride that a fellow demon did that much damage to a Fae, I turn to Rivan. "You've been here a while. Ever seen a Fae guard with scars?"

Rivan straightens. "Never. I don't like it."

"Neither do I."

"We don't have another option," Kaius insists. "Most of the guards are soldiers, not warriors. Meri needs a warrior.

Someone who will ignore the fact that she's queen and force her to defend herself. This is our man. Until he does something I don't like, he's it."

We don't have a choice. With a reluctant nod, I agree. "For now, we'll go with him. In the meantime, I'll try to dig up more information on his background." I turn to Rivan. "See if you can also find out anything from the staff."

"I will," he replies firmly. "Before I forget, I tattooed a rune on Meri last night to prevent her from sleepwalking. Just to make sure, I'll continue to keep an eye out for her." His lips curl.

Eyeing Rivan's faint smile, I want to laugh. Looks like Meri's charm is working perfectly.

"Good. One thing off my list. Took long enough."

He winces. "We had a hiccup. Meri asked about the old rune behind her ear."

Satisfaction sings in my veins. *It's about damn time.*

Rivan continues, "She wasn't happy to learn the sorceress limited her only power. Or my role in it. Thankfully, she chose to forgive me." He points to me. "By the way, the rune is gone. She should gain full use of that power soon, along with the memory of how she gained it in the first place."

Anticipation curls in my gut. It can't come soon enough. "I'll handle it." I sigh. "Unfortunately, I haven't been quite as successful as you. Unless Leandra decides to show up, we won't find her."

Both Rivan and Kaius scowl.

"The wily bitch made a deal with Evren that can't be undone." My teeth are clenched as I spit out the information. I'm not angry with Evren, but I hate the fact that Leandra found a loophole. "Finding her will have to go on the back burner for now."

Rivan's expression changes to confusion. "How does Evren know Leandra?"

When Lucifer asked for a list of the fastest flyers, Rivan

was at the top of my list, and he jumped at the chance to leave his gilded prison for a few days. He met Evren and helped her save the world. Something very few people know. "She offered the amulet as payment to anyone who could bring her solid information on the Druids. Of course, Leandra took her up on it."

"Maybe we can bait her into appearing," Rivan murmurs, a calculated look on his face. "Is there something she wants? Besides Meri?"

"The dark Fae king's head on a silver platter," I say with a chuckle. "But for some reason, she needs Meri to get her revenge, and I'm not sure why." A frustrated sigh slips. "It's a puzzle I've been trying to solve for hundreds of years, with no luck."

Frustration beats at me. It feels like the fucking answer is right in front of my face, but I'm blind to it, and that gives Leandra too much of an edge over us. She's cunning and plays to win. My hands were tied by the pact I made to save Meri's life, but those restraints are gone. I'm more than capable of taking her down if she would just show herself.

"One more thing," Kaius interrupts my train of thought. "Lord Camon. I passed by him last night when I was taking Solandis out on a date, and the strangest look appeared on his face. As if he knew me. Can you find out if there is any connection between Kaius and Camon? I need to know in case he approaches me."

Lord Camon. What would a half demon, half Fae have in common with the High Fae of Spring? The intrigue of such a pairing has my gut singing.

"I'll look into it."

Rivan glances around. "I'll find us a better place to meet next time."

Although I nod my head in agreement, I can't help but think fortune favored this location. A hilt with a ruby the size of a chicken egg winks at me from the corner. "Why don't you go first? Then Kaius. I want to check in with Meri before I leave."

Rivan eases the door open and disappears.

Kaius gives me a knowing look. "Don't take all of it." He steps into the shadows and is gone.

With a half-smile, I slip the short sword into my coat, then turn toward the item in the back that has been calling to me since I arrived. I hover my hand over the pile of weapons, but their energy is cold. Quietly shifting them out of the way, I continue to dig until it appears. Practically pulsing with life, the carved brown box whispers to me.

Holding my palm over it, I pick up a benign power. Neither good nor bad, the power simply exists, waiting for someone to use it. I inch the lid up to peer inside. Two golden scarabs sit side-by-side. One with diamonds for eyes, the second with onyx. Interesting. But why is it calling to me? Sliding the box into my pocket, I slip into the shadows.

IN A TAILORED lightweight cream wool dress, Meri is the epitome of a queen. Stylish, poised, and elegant from her chignon to the tips of her peep toe pumps. My eyes trace every curve and line of her body. Her confidence is growing. It's in the way she carries herself… chin up, shoulders back, more purpose in her stride.

With a casualness I don't feel, I prop myself up against the wall. "You look good in those clothes. Way better than the rags you used to wear." I push the words out, keeping to the role I adopted long ago. "Off to do your queenly duties?"

She swivels around with a small ball of magic in her hand. When she sees it's me, she holds it for a solid minute before slowly extinguishing it. Normally, there would be a smirk on her face at the thought of reducing me to ash, but it's strangely absent.

"Cormal," she says with an irritated sigh. "I've got a luncheon to go to in five minutes. What do you want?"

Curious about the reason for her mood, I decide to probe a bit. "Did you get the rune?"

A soft smile crosses her face. "I did. Rivan did a beautiful job. I'd show it to you, but I'm already dressed."

Hmm. The possibilities.

I chuckle. "I can come back later to see it."

Where would she have put it? Somewhere hidden. Is that the reason for the sweet smile on her lips or something else?

"I won't be here later," she says breathlessly. "Lorn's taking me to dinner."

The nonchalant façade instantly evaporates. "Who the fuck is Lorn?" My tone is hard, and she rolls her eyes.

"Lord Lorn, from the Autumn Court. He and Allandra, his sister, had a wonderful party at his house last night," she blithely informs me. "He hand fed me the most delicious dessert and asked me on a date."

An image of a suave Fae feeding chocolate-dipped strawberries to Meri crosses my mind, and I slam my teeth together.

She walks over and taps me on the chest. "Do you remember the rune behind my ear? The one Rivan gave me a few hundred years ago."

Unable to trust my voice, I nod.

"Did you know its purpose?" she asks pointedly.

Treading carefully across the quicksand under my feet, I consider how to answer her question. "I did. She told me after it was done. You were there. Don't you remember?"

Her brow furrows. "No."

Someone knocks on the door. "Queen Meri, are you ready to go?"

"We'll talk soon," I murmur. Staring into her turquoise eyes, I see the questions in her eyes, but I can't tell her what she wants to hear. She has to remember the past on her own. "Go to your luncheon." Hating the fact that she's going on a romantic date with someone else, I bend down to kiss her on the cheek, but she turns her head, and the quick kiss lands on her lips.

Inhaling sharply, I stare down at the mouth I've been avoiding for so long. Her plump bottom lip disappears in between her teeth, and I lose all sense of reason. My lips capture hers and feast like the starving man I am. For hundreds of years, I've dreamed of nothing but tasting these lips again and again until my kiss is imprinted into her very bones.

She jerks her head back. "What the hell are you doing?" The whispered words fall between us. "Never mind. I don't want to know. Take a long look at these lips. Think about how good they feel under yours, then stand by and watch while I offer them to Lorn later tonight." With a toss of her head, she strides out the door.

Taking back what's mine, I silently snarl. That's what I'm doing.

Harshly exhaling the breath I've been holding, a sliver of satisfaction burns through me. She may not remember the past, but tonight, she'll feel my lips on hers, not his. With a grim smile, I step into the shadow behind me. The guard will have to wait. Lord Lorn just moved to the top of my list. How have I not heard of him?

More importantly, how do I get rid of him?

CHAPTER THIRTEEN

<u>MERI</u>

Slightly puffy lips and a tinge of pink on my cheekbones. Nothing that can't be attributed to makeup. Relieved, I run a trembling finger under my lip to erase the slight smear and step away from the mirror. Shoving the kiss to the back of my mind, I smile and enter the sitting room.

"Please excuse me. I'm running a little late today."

Solandis narrows her eyes but says nothing, only motions to the seat beside her.

I swear that woman has the intuition of a seer. "Did I miss anything?"

The blond from last night is sitting across from me. "I was telling Solandis about the party. It was spectacular, wasn't it? Asena is a magnificent performer." A predatory smile graces her lips. "Too bad it was ruined by your refusal to talk about ladies-in-waiting."

Irritated with her snarky attitude, I look at her in confusion.

"I don't recall meeting you last night, but there were so many people in attendance. What is your name?"

Her cheekbones flush with embarrassment. "We didn't formally meet, but I spoke to you on the rooftop."

"Ah, that explains it. I don't speak to strangers about my business," I say lightly, looking around the room. "Besides Solandis, I know Lady Estrella." The red-haired lady winks and bows her head. "And, of course, Lady Allandra."

Allandra is sitting on the chair next to me with a cup of tea in her hand. She smiles at the other ladies.

"Why don't you introduce yourself, and the other ladies," I suggest to the blond.

Silence. She jerks to her feet and goes around the room, introducing the ladies. When she gets done, she turns to me. "Lady Brilla of the Spring Court."

I smile. "It's nice to meet you, Lady Brilla. Any relation to Lord Camon?"

A haughty expression settles on her face. "My brother."

Well, that certainly explains her hostility. "I see. Tell me, why would you want to be a lady-in-waiting when you could join the council? Is the latter too much for you?"

She rears back. "The council? That's my brother's role."

I glance at Solandis. "Is there a rule that says only one family member may join the council?"

Solandis laughs. "No. We do limit the number of available seats for each family, but that's to ensure order is maintained. There are currently six open seats." She darts a look at Lady Brilla. "We only accept members who are smart and interested in improving our kingdom."

The sound of a teacup hitting the table is loud. "Oops, sorry. I'm just a bit excited." A petite, dark-haired lady bobs her head. "Lady Fiora of Summer, Your Majesty. I'm interested in joining the council."

She stares at me earnestly while she pleads her case. "I

attended the technology school in Meira, and I have a lot of ideas that can improve our way of life. How do I apply for the position?"

"Is there a specific protocol?" I ask Solandis.

"You only need the backing of a current council member," she replies. Turning to Fiora, she smiles. "Why don't we chat over lunch, and if I like what I hear, I'll recommend your placement."

Lady Brilla immediately stands. "I'd also like to apply for a council member position."

Lady Estrella steps forward. "Sit next to me at lunch, and we'll discuss it."

Scanning the rest of the ladies, I see a couple of others who look like they're thinking about it. "Assuming Lady Fiora and Lady Brilla get sponsored, there are only four remaining seats. If you're interested, sit next to Solandis or Estrella at lunch and tell them about yourself."

Solandis motions to one of the brownies standing nearby. The tiny Fae immediately enlists help to replace the long dining table with round ones.

Divide and conquer.

"I refuse to have any ladies-in-waiting," I inform the rest of them. Angry, they glance knowingly at each other. "However, I do need a social team. Three ladies to help me plan events at the palace, decide which outside events to attend, and organize my time."

I stand and move to one of the tables. "Those who wish to apply for one of the three positions, please join me at my table. For those remaining, let me know if there's a specific skill or area that interests you. I'll do everything I can to help you find a place to help too." I hold my breath while I wait to see if anyone takes me up on my offer. Surprisingly, all the seats at my table fill up.

The rest of the luncheon goes by quickly. All six council

member seats are filled by smart, interesting women, including Fiora and Brilla. Lady Allandra, Lady Tanith, and Lady Sylva join my social team. Lady Tanith helps the remaining ladies schedule appointments so I can figure out the best fit for them.

"Do you have an outfit to wear for tonight?" Lady Allandra asks me. "Lorn told me he was taking you to dinner and a show." Her eyes skim the business-like dress I'm wearing. "I could help you pick out something?"

Unused to letting anyone outside my trusted circle into my bedroom, I hesitate for a second, but when I glimpse the hopeful look in her lavender eyes, I give in. "Sure, that would be lovely. Thank you. Let me say goodbye to Solandis."

Estrella and Solandis are in deep discussion when I come over. "Is everything okay?"

"It's perfect," Estrella replies excitedly. "We were able to choose candidates who are both qualified and open to finding solutions for the Lesser Fae issues we face. And we now have nine women on the council, including yourself. We haven't had those kinds of numbers in ages."

The anxiousness I've been carrying all day eases. When I put the crown on my head, I became determined and focused for the first time in my life. I want to be a good queen for the light Fae. One they can be confident will have their best interests at heart. For someone who never thought in terms of good and evil or light and dark, it's a huge adjustment.

Solandis gives me a brief hug. "You were perfect, my dear." She looks at both of us and gives a dry laugh. "I can't wait to attend the next council meeting."

I can't wait to see Lord Camon's face when his sister shows up. "When is it?"

"Next week," Estrella inserts.

Glad we've got a few days to prepare, I nod. "Well, I'm going to get ready for my date tonight. I'll see you later."

"Have fun, darling," Solandis calls out.

I walk over to Allandra and link my arm with hers. "Let's go find an outfit."

Tiernan is on guard this afternoon and walks us back to my room.

Allandra leans in and whispers, "Is he a Fire Fae?"

Leaning away, I answer clearly. "Tiernan is my personal guard, and his allegiance is to me."

She shakes her head. "You mean his allegiance is to the crown."

On the verge of correcting her, I stop. Sometimes it's better to keep your secrets close. "This is my room." When she goes to walk in, I stop her. "Tiernan will check it first."

She scoffs. "I highly doubt anyone is hiding in your room."

I ignore her and wait for Tiernan's signal. "It's clear. The closet is to the left. I'll ask Eris to get us some drinks."

She steps in and winces. "What type of wards are these?"

"I don't know. Why?"

"There's a darkness to them," she murmurs. "Sorry. They make me feel a little claustrophobic. Would you mind opening the window?"

With a flick of my finger, the doors to the balcony open and the room floods with light. "Better?"

Her face is still looking pinched, but she nods and heads into the closet. Following her in, I watch while she runs a hand across the hanging clothes.

"Simply gorgeous." She picks up a pair of sunglasses and tries them on. "What do you think?" Not waiting for my reply, she moves on to the dresses.

"Lorn's taking you to a show at the theatre, then to an incredible restaurant for a late dinner," she informs me. Swiftly sifting through the dresses, she pulls several and hands them to me. "Let's start with those and see if any of them work."

Back in the bedroom, I look over each one as I hang them on the rack. There's a soft pink silk dress with a pleated skirt. A baby blue halter neck dress. The third one is a yellow silk dress with spaghetti straps. I check the other two dresses in my arms —lavender and light green. Every single dress is pastel and would look gorgeous on someone like her.

"Which one will you try on first?" she asks excitedly.

I turn around and find Eris setting drinks down on the table. "Thank you, Eris."

With an imperceptible wave of my hand, I place a piece of smoke chocolate in front of her. The way she tilts her head to study the candy tells me she's never had any. I'm not surprised. It's a specialty candy only made in the Underworld. An envy demon family makes it. They use smoke to infuse wonderous flavors, like black truffle honey, dark chocolate ganache with clea chilis—the hottest peppers anywhere—or vintage AB cabernet which includes the finest reserve blood. They have specialty chocolates for every race. Wonder what they offer for Fae? Faery dust?

I wave a hand over my body and try on the blue halter neck dress. Unused to seeing the color on me, I swivel to the mirror. It completely washes me out. Not wasting another second, I switch it out for the pink silk dress.

"Wait. Did you not like the blue?" she asks, a tiny line between her eyes.

"It looked terrible on me. If you want the dress, you can have it," I reply, switching the pink for the lavender. "None of these are going to work. Pastel colors really aren't my style. Most of them wash me out."

She immediately looks down at her hands. "Sorry. I guess I didn't realize. Lorn is a romantic, and I want you to look perfect."

Taking in a deep breath, I find my patience and force a smile. "The closet is full of clothes. I'm sure we can find one romantic dress that works for him and me." I grab her hand and pull her back to the dress section.

I grab a short skater dress with spaghetti straps in a dark green. "How about this one?"

She laughs. "That's not the least bit romantic. There." She grabs a maxi dress in white with colorful flowers on it. "Beautiful. Romantic."

"Too daytime," I say, rejecting the dress. The red dress I vetoed for the party catches my eye. "This one."

Her nose wrinkles, but I completely ignore her and put it on.

It fits like a dream. Strapless with layers of sheer material that flow from my chest to my knees in an asymmetrical high-low pattern. What makes the dress interesting and sexy is the ombre color and movement of the dress. The burgundy top lightens to a red, and when you walk, the fabric flows around you, making the dress look like a living flame. Or the tips of Rivan's wings.

I take it off and place it on the rack. "You're right. This is too much," I concede, unwilling to examine why I don't want to wear it for Lorn. Quickly exchanging it for a short, strapless fuchsia dress with delicate beading laid in a horizontal pattern, I twirl in front of her. "What do you think?"

In the mirror, we both smile at the same time.

"It's perfect. Pair it with silver heels," she orders me. The corners of her mouth turn down. "You're the first person Lorn's asked out here. He's so charismatic. Sometimes I worry he'll find someone who won't want me around, and I'll be all alone."

"He would never leave you," I assure her. "Besides, even if he found someone, I know he would make sure they accepted you, too."

Her lavender eyes find mine. "You're right. I'm being silly." Spinning around, she heads toward the door. "Have fun tonight!"

Her step falters the tiniest bit when she opens the door and sees Tiernan on the other side, but she slides around him and into the hall.

"Bye," I call out softly, shutting the door behind her.

I can't quite figure her out. Mercurial one moment, calm elegance the next. I sigh. Maybe she's like me, a little mixed up and trying to find her way.

Or a lot mixed up, especially after that kiss earlier. I rub my lips lightly, still able to feel the intense kiss. Cormal had to have felt something when he kissed me. But what? I've been insanely attracted to him for years. I was so sure he would eventually give in to the mountain of sexual tension between us, but he never did. So, why now? I know it's not because I have a date. In the past, I tried everything to make him jealous, including flaunting my dates in his face. He'd flash an amused smirk and walk off.

Cormal's intuition is extraordinary. Maybe he senses that I'm ready to move on and find something real. Preferably with someone who isn't surrounded by secrets and lies.

CHAPTER FOURTEEN

<u>MERI</u>

Kaius assigns four guards to go on the date. I beg him to reconsider, but he coolly informs me that until I'm prepared to defend myself and my guards, this will be the protocol for all my dates. The mulish expression on his face tells me I'm not going to be able to sway his mind.

With a frustrated sigh, I give in and text Lorn to let him know I'll be bringing four men on our date. What if he thinks this is too much trouble for a date? I nervously chew the inside of my cheek, waiting for his reply.

> Lorn: At least they won't be competing for your attention.

I grin. Perfect answer.

> Meri: Leaving now.

Tiernan and Laken go through the portal first. When Ansel receives the signal, I step through with Garren and him. The first person I see is Lorn wearing his signature smile, which immediately makes me smile too.

He strides forward and bends down to give me a kiss on the cheek. "You look stunning, Queen Meri."

Mmm, you smell delicious, Lorn.

Dressed in a sharp navy suit with a baby-blue button-down that emphasizes his broad shoulders and height, Lorn looks suave and sophisticated.

My magic spikes with the large crowd, and it's all I can do to breathe through it.

"Thank you," I say breathlessly. "Would you mind calling me Meri on our date? When you add the queen, it sounds so formal."

A delighted smile appears. "It would be my pleasure, Meri." He picks up my hand and tucks me into his side. "The crowd's a crush tonight. Word must have gotten out that you were attending. It's probably a good thing you brought extra guards with you. Stay close, and I'll make sure nobody bothers you."

With my petite frame protected by him, and the four guards surrounding us, we easily get through the crowd in plenty of time. Our plush, gold velvet seats are in a box overlooking the entire theatre. Lorn pulls my chair out for me to sit first.

"These seats are incredible. We can see everything from here."

I look across at the other boxes and see several individuals staring at us. Guess the view goes both ways.

Lorn's mouth twists into a wry smile. "My original tickets were for two seats in the middle." He gestures to the main seating area below us. "Ansel felt it would be too hard to protect you in a sea of individuals." He places his mouth near my ear. "This is your box."

The low timbre of his voice in my ear makes me shiver. I

turn and find my lips only a couple inches from his. "Thank you for being so understanding about the security. Honestly, it feels odd to have someone watching over me."

A line appears between his brows. "Who took care of you before you became queen? Your father?"

"I did," I say with an amused smile. "Although having a guardian who most people feared was an advantage I made sure to flaunt." Not just Leandra, but Cormal too. But his role in my life is entirely too difficult to explain.

Lorn looks appalled. "Where was your father?"

I nonchalantly shrug. "Who knows?"

He studies my face. "Do you know who he is, or is it a mystery?"

The lights in the theatre flicker, startling me. "What's going on?"

He gives me a strange look. "It's a signal to find your seats." His mouth opens, then closes. Shifting in his seat, he leans close to me. "Have you never been to a show?"

I shake my head. "I didn't have a lot of spare time. My guardian kept me busy running errands." When I crook my finger, he leans closer. "And we didn't have money for luxuries." Or for food and basic necessities, but I made it through, and look where I'm at now. In my own luxury box at a fancy theatre.

For the first time, he has a serious look in his eyes. "That I understand. After our parents died, Allandra and I struggled for a long time. We finally came here and petitioned Queen Nyssa for reparations. She gave us the inheritance we were owed. Things became better, but we never forgot what it was to be hungry."

Reeling from his announcement, I open my mouth to question him, but the lights dim, and the curtain opens. A brownie riding a dog comes out on stage and captures everyone's attention.

Except mine. Reparations? The fact that both his parents

died certainly points in that direction, but how were they wronged? Could this be the reason Nyssa banned them?

Lorn reaches over and takes my hand in his.

The simple gesture temporarily silences the barrage of questions in my head. Bemused, I stare down at our linked hands until he nudges me. When I glance in his direction, he raises an eyebrow. I give him a reassuring smile and turn my attention to the show.

The play is surprisingly funny, and if it were anywhere else besides here, it would have the audience roaring with laughter. This audience awards them with a few subdued chuckles, but that's about it. Although, I do see a lot of expressions on those faces below.

Lorn's deep chuckle is addicting. It does such delicious things to my imagination that it's all I can do to sit here and platonically hold his hand. One day, I want to hear it when we're naked in bed. Close to my ear.

He stands. "Intermission."

I look around and see other people getting up. "What do we do during intermission?"

Lifting a shoulder, he pulls me up and tucks my body close to his. "Eat, drink, mingle." Using his finger, he swipes a curl off my cheek. "Hopefully not for too long."

The last part is muttered and makes me laugh. "Let's be quick."

As soon as we step outside the curtain, guards surround us, and Lorn's arm tightens around me. A giddy feeling bubbles up inside me. Is it wrong to like this so much? All my life, I've wanted someone to protect me. Lorn is the type of man who would protect any woman in his company. It feels damn good to be that person tonight.

We mingle for fifteen minutes, then head back to the box. Whispers follow behind us, but I can't tell if it's because we're together or if it's just me. Fidgeting a little, my hand flutters to smooth my skirt.

"Don't let them get to you," he murmurs. "Boredom is their enemy, and they'll do everything to avoid it."

Nodding several times, I paste on a smile and look up at him with gratitude. "Thank you. I'm used to people whispering behind my back, but it's usually because my guardian did something to warrant their derision. This is all me, and it's nerve-wracking."

A group of ladies nearby catches my eye. They're whispering and staring, but their eyes are following Lorn, not me.

"Well, maybe it's not all about me."

He throws a mock glare my way, but not once does he look in their direction. "Be nice. They can't help themselves. I'm charming, incredibly good-looking, and a Fae lord. They tell me I'm a catch."

Laughter spills out of my mouth and into the theatre lobby. Heads turn in disbelief and disdain. Their message is clear. Fae do not show this much emotion, especially not in public.

His eyes widen, then fill with a mischievous glint.

"Don't look at me like that," I order him. "Or I won't be able to hold back."

With a sad shake of his head, he quickly leads me back to the box. "You're not helping my ego, you know. What is everyone going to think when the queen is laughing at me on our first date?" His eyes trace my lips, and they tingle in anticipation.

"With you," I correct him. "And they would take my place in a heartbeat."

"I'm enjoying my date with you," he states firmly. "Now, if you can behave yourself during the second act, I'll surprise you after dinner with an utterly delicious dessert."

The lights dim, and my mind is so busy imagining dessert, I can barely pay attention to the rest of the play.

"Are you ready?" Lorn asks, standing beside me with his palm out.

"Definitely," I tell him, my voice husky.

Lorn and the guards get us through the crowd and to the street pretty quickly.

"The restaurant isn't far."

We're passing by an alley when I hear a child crying. I immediately stop. "Do you hear that?" Pushing against Lorn, I try to gain some distance to listen, but he immediately pushes me behind him. "Ansel. Can you please check it out?"

Wind in the shape of a miniature tornado appears in Ansel's left hand, and a sword in the other. He nods at Tiernan, who throws a light above the alley. Holding his palms up, fire flames instantly. Ansel shouts an order at Laken. Ice forms in the back of the alley, slowly coating every inch. It moves forward in an attempt to drive the person out of hiding.

Garren motions for me to follow, but I refuse. With a fierce frown, he moves into position behind me.

Wailing pierces the air, and I push against Lorn. "It sounds like a child." I move to the side, but he steps in front of me. "We need to help."

"A lot of things can sound like children in this world. It's a tactic they use to lure innocents into their lair. Wait," he says harshly.

"Fine, but I want to see what's happening," I tell him.

He shuffles a couple of inches to the right.

Ansel walks three feet into the alley and stops behind a pot full of flowers. He swings his sword forward to point at something on the ground. "Get up."

Small in stature, the boy slowly stands up. "Please don't kill me. I've been sent to deliver a message." His head twists unnaturally until he's staring right at me. "Tell the sorceress to return what she stole, or he will unmake her abomination."

"Who's sending the message?" I ask, dread filling my stomach.

"His Majesty, the Dark Fae King, Denir," he says reverently.

Laughter spills out of me. My mother tried to kill me. Dear old Dad is threatening to unmake me. Wow. Talk about winning the parent lottery pool.

"Nobody knows where she is, but tell him, if he can find her, I'll deliver a message." Not that one, of course. I have one of my own.

His brow creases in confusion, but he inclines his head toward me. "I'll pass on the message, Your Majesty." Snapping his fingers, he takes a step to his right and drops into the shadow beside him.

My message will probably get him killed, but there's nothing I can do. Leandra is exceptional at hiding, but if it's important enough, he'll find her. Either way, it helps me.

Ansel's eyes flick from one corner of the alley to the other. "I don't like the look of those shadows on the wall. It's time to go, Your Majesty." Walking backward, he keeps his sword ready. "Garren, open the portal."

Lorn turns around to face me. His eyes are full of questions, but he simply pulls me into his arms and gives me a tight hug. "Thank you for a wonderfully surprising evening. I haven't laughed this much in a long time. I'm sorry we didn't get to the dessert I promised you, but if you like, I can bring it by tomorrow?"

Here I thought he meant a different type of dessert.

"I have training in the morning, but come by in the afternoon," I reply, standing on tiptoe to kiss his cheek and inhale his scent again. "Thank you for taking me to my first show."

Ansel pulls me from him and ushers me into the portal.

When I look back, Lorn's staring into the alley.

The second my foot touches the marble floors of the palace,

Ansel leaves to find Kaius, and Tiernan escorts me back to my room.

Safely in my suite, I pick up my phone.

Meri: What did Leandra steal from the dark Fae king?

Cormal: …

"Tell me what happened," he demands, stepping from the shadow in the corner of my room. Gripping my shoulders, he scans me from head to toe.

"I'm fine. That's not true. I'm pissed I didn't get to finish my date with Lorn," I snarl. "But other than that, fine."

An incredulous look crosses his face.

Knowing he's getting annoyed; I roll my eyes and spill every single detail.

"Sending messengers into enemy territory. Pretty extreme. I can't help but wonder what in the hell Leandra stole from him," I muse. "Besides the essence she took to make me, of course." The words bounce around in my head.

"Something he desperately wants returned," Cormal murmurs softly. "I'm going to look into a few things. I'll get back to you. In the meantime, start your training. We need you at full power." He swoops down and places a hard kiss on my lips.

And he's gone. Again. Since when did we start kissing each other goodbye? My lips tingle, and I rub them together as I try to convince myself that it wasn't the kiss I wanted tonight. I fall back on the bed with a scowl. Even with the creepy messenger, it was a damn good first date, and Lorn's kiss would have been spectacular.

CHAPTER FIFTEEN

MERI

Chaos and fear plague my dreams. Flashes of scenes and people cycle rapidly in my mind, but every time I try to hold on to an image, it slips away. Emotions bombard me. Magic, power, anger, fear. When I wake, pixies are hammering in my brain, and the scowl I wore to bed is the same one on my face this morning.

Solandis strides gracefully on to the balcony where I'm sitting with a strong cup of coffee. "Oh, dear. You look dreadful. What's the matter?"

Where to start… With the messenger, Cormal's new habit of kissing me, or the nightmares? Not ready to discuss the first two, I keep it simple.

"Bad dreams," I reply with a sigh. "What do you have on the agenda today?"

A fan appears in her hand, and she waves it across her face. "Fallon and I have a call to discuss the metal supply situation.

I need an answer for the next council meeting." She flashes me a grin. "Tonight, Kaius is taking me on a midnight picnic to look at the stars. A good choice for our third date. Very romantic. And I have the absolute perfect little number to wear. He's going to melt when he sees it on me. I do hope he's picked out an isolated spot." Her turquoise eyes gleam with intent.

Chuckling, I raise my coffee cup to her. "He has no chance whatsoever." Third date? I must have missed one somewhere. "Do you think you made the right decision to move forward with Kaius?"

Cormal's kiss weighs heavily on my mind. Part of me wants to just move on from our co-dependent relationship, but I can't help wondering if I'll have regrets.

She places an elegant hand on her chest. "None. I feel it in here. I was like this with Vargas too. Although it was tougher with him. A demon mated to a royal Fae. A fairytale for me, and a nightmare for everyone else. Nyssa and I fought for weeks, but I refused to deny him. It took her a long time to speak to me again, but it's hard to argue with fate."

Her shoulder lifts in a dismissive shrug. "I'm sure the aristocratic Fae will look down on Kaius for being a guard, but at least he is Fae. Until Vargas returns, I want to stay here with you, and I couldn't do it if Kaius was a demon." With a smile, she leans over and pecks my cheek. "I've got to go. Have fun with the trainer."

Training today. At this rate, there's going to be a permanent scowl on my face. "Wait. If I wanted to find out what happened in another part of the palace, who would be able to tell me?"

She stops and gives me a questioning glance, but when I refuse to elaborate, she answers. "Eris. She either knows the answer or can find it for you. Brownies pretty much run this place. Is that all?"

I nod my thanks. When she's gone, I call for Eris.

Should I just blurt out my question or see if she knows anything first?

"Some of us have important things to do today," Eris says, impatiently crossing her arms and tapping her tiny foot. "What can I do for you, Your Majesty?"

Eris has to be the absolute snarkiest person in the entire kingdom.

"I may have lost my temper a few nights ago," I admit with an embarrassed smile. "Do you happen to know who fixed the hallway?" Sucking my lip between my teeth, I nervously wait for her to answer.

Mahogany brown eyes shoot me a strange look. "Your friend. Cleaned everything up and erased all your magic."

"Rivan?"

Her eyes practically pop out of her head when I say his name. She shakes her head. "No, the other one. Dark hair, dark magic."

There's only one with dark hair and magic. "Cormal?"

She jerks her chin. "That's the one. Anything else?"

By the time I finish shaking my head, she's gone. Cormal. Great. He always knows. Did he save me from embarrassment? Abso-fucking-lutely, and I might be the teensiest, tiniest bit grateful. Not that I'll tell him. One of us would have to be dying for me to admit it.

My phone chimes, and at the same time, there's a knock on my door. Five minutes until we leave. Scrambling around, I find a workout outfit in the closet and dress with a wave of my hand. After tossing my hair into a ponytail, I brush my teeth. The old-fashioned way. I can't help it. I've been trying to use magic more and more, but not for this. For some reason, if I don't see it happening, my teeth don't feel clean.

When I open the door five minutes later, Ansel is standing guard. "Ready?"

Instead of the training room, he drops me off in the

dungeon. Pitch black. Dripping water and a dank, musty smell. Sounds of animals scurrying nearby. The stench of death.

"Hell no," I mutter, throwing a ball of light into the air. It immediately gets extinguished, but not before I spot a torch on the wall. Pissed off, I throw a fireball at it. It lights.

A dark giant detaches itself from the wall, and a deluge of water immediately puts out the burning torch.

Angry, I fist my hands, then raise them sky high. Fire roars from the floor to the ceiling, exposing every inch of this place. Along with Madoc.

"What in the hell is wrong with you? Training doesn't give you the right to carry out whatever sadistic fantasies are rolling around in that brain of yours. I'm leaving."

He snorts. "You think your enemies are going to attack you in the training room with soft mats to cushion your fall?" His big body brushes up against mine and he yanks my hands down. The fire dies, leaving us alone in the dark. "The best-case scenario is they kill you. Immediately. But there are worse things than dying. Trust me, I know. What happens if they kidnap and dump you in a dungeon like this one or some other equally hideous place? A queen has powerful enemies. You need to be able to think on your feet and conquer anything they throw at you."

My clammy skin reminds me of what happens when you piss off the enemy. "Been there, done that. Barely survived The Pit, and I damn sure didn't get a t-shirt out of the deal."

"How did you get out?" he whispers in my ear.

Thump, thump, thump. My heart starts racing. Whispers in the dark mean they're close. Different time. Different place. Focus. Breathing shallowly, I tell him what he wants to hear. "Someone saved me." Two, actually, but who's counting?

"Why didn't you save yourself?" The rough timbre of his voice scrapes along my nerves.

"Like an idiot, I fought. Over and over," I spit out, angry with his arrogant questions. "With no magic to call on, it was useless. Do you know what it's like to be at the mercy of monsters? Fighting off my flimsy attempts amused them. I was nothing but a toy for them to play with or break as they pleased."

A derisive chuckle comes from the left. "Monsters? What is The Pit?"

Voice raw with memories, I answer. "It's a literal hole in the ground filled with the soulless. Once, they were something—human, demon, Fae, whatever—but because of their depravity, they lost their soul. When they died, they couldn't move on, not even to Tartarus. Nameless. Faceless. They exist in The Pit. Monsters who drink from the well of evil and feed off their victims' terror."

Fear coats my skin. Panicking, I double over and place my hands on my knees. My chest is tight, and I can't breathe.

Fuck. You're a queen, dammit. With power. Do something.

Shoving the hopeless emotions down deep, I suck in a deep breath and listen for his location. The only sounds I hear are those of the dungeon. Where did he go? A minute ago, he was to my left. I do a half-turn and fire to the right. I see him for the briefest second, but that's all I need. I fire over and over in that direction. Left, middle, right.

Air moves behind me, and I pivot to fire in that direction. He's gone in a blink. I throw ice on the floor, hoping to slow him down, but he turns it to water instantly. Pulling stones from the walls, I toss them in groups across the room, hoping one will hit its target.

A foot whips out and sweeps me off my feet.

Pain radiates up my side, but it's minor. Cold concrete against my cheek brings the memories roaring back. Trying to stand, I put my hand down and encounter a slimy texture, similar to the monsters in The Pit, and a switch flips. I immediately cower with my hands over my head.

Harsh sounds fill the air. Distant words I can't understand. Arms band around me, and I flinch.

We cross from the darkness into the sun-drenched garden. He sits in the grass with me in his arms. Grabbing a handful of dirt, he rubs it on my arm and shoulder. Over and over, he smears it on me until I'm completely covered. Barely cognizant, I don't have the strength to protest.

The land seeps into my skin, then slides deeper. It wakes the strands inside me, and they begin to pulse with the magic of the kingdom. A babbling brook blocks past memories of my screams. Bright sun eclipses the darkness that traps me. Sweet honey coats my tongue, erasing the taste of blood.

The past recedes, and I come back to the present.

I glare into his steel-grey eyes, expecting to see remorse, but there is nothing but blankness.

"I hate you."

He gives me an approving nod. "Good. It's a start. Hate gives you strength. Enemies give zero fucks and no mercy. You can expect the same from me." Without stumbling, he rises from sitting to standing with me in his arms, then puts me down. "I'll see you tomorrow."

Barely able to hold myself upright, I watch him disappear from sight.

CHAPTER SIXTEEN

MERI

Dirt covers me on the outside, but it's the leftover grit of the memories that has me itching and desperate to scrub my skin. I look up, but there are no balconies near this spot, and the garden gives me no clue. It all looks the same to me. Weary, I trudge toward the palace, hoping to find my way back to my room, preferably without someone seeing me.

Upon entering, I look up and down the hall. Two oak doors about halfway down the corridor look kind of familiar. I walk over and twist the handle to peek inside, and to my relief, it's the room where we hold our council meetings. I'm not too far from my room. Quietly closing the door, I pivot and run straight into someone.

Firm hands grip my shoulders. "Meri. I mean, Queen Meri." Rivan's concerned voice is music to my ears. "What happened to you?"

"It's a long story. I need to get to my room and take a long, hot shower. Would you mind escorting me?" I plead, looking up at him.

Red rims the outer circles of Rivan's gold eyes and a rune on his shoulder starts glowing. "Did someone attack you?"

"No, he barely touched me," I tell him, a strangled laugh falling from my lips. "I did most of this to myself. My mind got the better of me in training." Dirt flakes off my arm and falls to the ground. "I know I can use magic to clean myself, but it won't... I won't... I need to scrub every inch of my skin." Desperation makes my voice rise as I try to explain without elaborating on why I won't feel clean without actual soap and water.

Rivan's head tilts to the side while he gives me a considering look. "I understand. Come with me." He quickly looks around, then grabs my hand and takes off.

My nails lengthen with the need to scratch until there's nothing left. Dirt. Slime. Memories. Too weary to ask where we're going, I follow, trusting he will help me.

Heading out the door, he pulls me into the garden. Red-gold wings appear, and his arms wrap tightly around me. Before I can take a breath to ask where he's taking me, we're in the sky. Wind whistles by us. I turn my face into his neck, seeking protection from it but also a little comfort. He smells of sun and earth.

Ten minutes later, we're landing. Wings disappear, revealing a cave in the side of a mountain. Swiveling around, I stare out into the valley below. Forest covers the land for miles. The palace is nowhere to be seen.

"You're not going to get into trouble for leaving, are you?" I ask, worrying my bottom lip. "And we have to tell Kaius, or he'll think I've been kidnapped." I don't even know the rules where Rivan's concerned. Can he leave? For how long? Am I the one who grants him permission, or does he have to go to the council?

A large thumb gently pulls my lip out from my teeth. "Stop worrying. I'm on a short leash, but I can leave the palace without asking for permission. I only need to ask if I'm going to be away for days." He leans in close. "Although sometimes I… forget and just disappear for a while." Taking a step back, he nervously watches for my reaction.

My jaw drops open. "Do you really think I care if you go? Or that I'd purposely hurt you for revealing your secret? If so, take me back. Right now. I mean it." Tears come to my eyes. Already emotional from training, his reaction takes me back to the edge. "I never want to see that look on your face. And to see it directed at me… it kills me."

I'll never understand how someone can deliberately abuse another. It's an anathema to me. Yet it happens every day. In hovels, palaces, and every place between.

"Nyssa and Leandra raged against everything outside of their control. Tied to them, our existence allowed them to assert absolute authority over someone who couldn't fight back. A convenient punching bag capable of withstanding their tantrums and the power they wielded."

Tentatively reaching for his hand, I link my pinky with his. "I can barely manage magic or assert authority, and I have zero desire to control everything around me." His eyes are locked on me. "I'm not weak, though. Lately, I've started to understand I'm stronger than Leandra. Not because of the power I have now, but the lack of it all those years. I realize I'm not afraid to fail or lose or fight against the odds." Even in The Pit, without any magic, I fought. I'd forgotten that until today.

When others hear about the abuse, they wonder why you didn't "just leave" or "get help." How? Who? Where do you find the miraculous strength to fight for yourself? I didn't even have the courage to try. Without magic, where would I go? The Underworld is a dangerous place. Even if I left it and went somewhere else, Leandra would have found me. Persuaded me to come back. It wasn't until Arden entered my life that I began to dream of something more. Defying Leandra landed me in The Pit. Getting saved showed me how many people cared, which gave me the courage to leave her. Maybe Rivan needs the same.

I link another finger with his. "You lost everything and endured the worst of Nyssa's punishments. If you think about it, you're mentally stronger than your previous self, and more than Nyssa could ever hope to be. When you helped Arden, you defiantly stood from the ashes and risked everything to show Nyssa you weren't afraid to fail or lose. Thousands of years after the war, you fought.

"It's my turn to fight for you. I will do everything in my power to champion your freedom," I promise him. A Fae's promise is a tangible thing, binding the person to their words, but I mean every word.

Rivan blanches. "Don't. It will never happen. They asked for my sacrifice, and I agreed. The treaty ties me to the light Fae without a time limit. Forever." He thrusts a hand through his hair. "It's treason to even talk about it." Turning on his heel, he yanks his fingers free and stalks into the cave.

My promise offers him the one thing that terrifies him— hope. With the seed planted, I follow him inside.

"There," he says angrily, pointing his finger.

Lit sconces show a pool in the middle of the cavern with steam rising from it.

"A hot spring?"

Leandra found us a shack in the middle of a forest once that had a thermal spring nearby. Pure heaven. One of the few winters I didn't freeze.

Shucking my shoes and socks, I dip a toe into the water. It's almost too hot. Perfect. I strip off my shirt and see Rivan whip around to face the wall.

Once my clothes are gone, I step onto the small ledge inside the pool. "Is it deep?" I peer down. but the water is dark.

"Maybe four feet deep," he replies, his voice rough.

With a small jump, I land in the middle of the pool. Water comes to my chest. Warmth surrounds me, but it barely penetrates the dirt covering me. Grimacing, my focus returns to the reason we're here.

Sinking lower to cover the important bits, I call out to Rivan. "I'm decent."

Palm out, I create a bar of soap and scrub every inch of my body. Dirt begins to flake off and pink skin appears, but I don't stop when the first layer is gone. I need to purge my skin of all the slime and residue from the floor and my memory. I do it again.

On my third round, a tanned hand takes the bar from me. "Let me get your back."

Running a finger over the palm of my hand, I realize the slime is gone. I turn and lift my hair. "Thank you."

Warm, soapy hands wash my neck, and all over my back. Strong fingers dig into knotted muscles in a hypnotizing pattern, easing the anxiety built up inside until all that's left is a languorous feeling with a hint of sensual need.

"I'll wash your hair," he rasps, placing a hand on the back of my neck. The husky note in his voice tells me he's aware of the tension rising between us. "I'm going to lean you back and wet it first."

Wrapped in the hazy warmth of the cocoon he's created, I simply nod.

He tilts me back until I'm almost floating, then scoops water over my head.

Glancing up at him, I can't help but ask about his past. "Where did you learn to do this?"

A distant smile curls his lips. "In another time." He turns his eyes toward me, but instead of stopping at my face, they continue south, where my breasts have risen above the water. Barely breathing, I let him look his fill at the crests with their hard nipples.

His eyes turn a burnished gold, and he swallows. Strong cheekbones flush with desire, and the hand on the back of my neck tightens. His breath becomes ragged, and he moves closer.

Seeing his reaction amps up my own. Heat curls up inside me, making me ache, and I arch my back, offering him more. "Rivan."

At the sound of my husky voice, his eyes jerk back to mine, then rise higher. To the crown on my head. He shakes his head, instantly denying us both.

"You can stand up while I wash your hair. Just keep your head tilted back, so the soap doesn't go in your eyes."

My eyes try to catch his, but he avoids my gaze. With a sigh, I stand. At least with my back to him, I can't remind him of Nyssa. Hands work and massage the shampoo into the depths of my hair. Swirling and shaping, he carefully washes every strand as if he has all day to make sure it's clean. Why didn't anyone ever tell me how good it felt to have someone else wash your hair? It takes everything I have to smother the groan on my lips.

"Did you wash Sima's hair?" My voice is soft when I ask, hoping he won't think I'm prying or that I'm jealous. She died twelve hundred years ago. I want to know about this woman he loved so much.

He never pauses. "I did. It was practically the only time she left it down." He chuckles. "She called it a nuisance, because it was so long, but I refused to let her cut it."

"How did you meet?"

Lean fingers comb through the strands, carefully detangling the knots. "At a market. I was buying ink. She was haggling with a vendor for meat. I thought he was charging her more because she was a witch, and I stepped in to help. The man saw me and immediately lowered the price. Happy, I turned around, expecting her thanks, and she roasted me. Told me I took all the fun out of buying, and she didn't want it anymore. Stalked off."

I laugh. "She loved the haggling."

"I didn't know it at the time, but her ability to haggle with the vendors had earned their respect. If she could get them down lower than their intended price, they would reward her with little extras," he states quietly. "Lean back, and I'll rinse your hair."

Putting my arm across my breasts, I do as he asks. "What did you do?"

Water cascades down the back of my head. "I paid for the meat and chased after her. Told her I hadn't had a decent meal in weeks and asked if she would cook for me. Guess I looked skinny because she agreed. I went home with her and never left." He clears his throat. "All done."

Standing up, I turn toward him, careful to keep most of my body below the waterline. "Thank you. For washing my hair and telling me about Sima. She sounds feisty and wonderfully sweet."

Face to face, the tension between us returns. I can't help but look at the body only inches from mine. Muscular, but too lean, almost hollow in a few places. With Nyssa gone, he's started to fill out the last few months, but it will take time to gain his former strength. Runes cover his arms and part of one pec. Symbols run close together, creating a stunning piece of art. Underneath, tanned skin shimmers like burnished amber in the firelight. My fingers tingle with the need to touch him.

"She was," he says gruffly. "I'll turn around so you can get out. We need to return."

With a sigh, I step out of the little pool and dry myself with the wave of a hand. Quickly making new clothes, a scarf for my head, and shoes, I get dressed. "Done." While he gets out, I focus on burning the clothes on the ground and using the wind to chase out the smoke and ashes.

He walks up beside me and hooks his pinky around mine. "Ready?"

How does something so little mean so much? Some of my words must have made it through. With a soft smile, I nod.

Minutes later, we're standing awkwardly at my bedroom door trying to figure out what to say to each other when Galen comes around the corner, red faced and swearing. "Queen Meri." He looks from me to Rivan. "Rivan."

I raise one eyebrow. "Is everything okay?"

"We've been looking for you. Kaius is furious we didn't escort you back from training. I promise. We tried, but we couldn't find you." The words rush out of his mouth. "He ordered me to stay here and wait for you. But I know he's going to want to know you're back." Conflicted, he stares at me, waiting for me to tell him what he should do.

Rivan holds up a hand. "I'll escort her. Do you know where he was going?"

"The training room to find Madoc," he says with a sigh of relief.

"I'm sorry I worried you. All of you. I should have told someone where I was going," I say, patting his arm. I did think about it, but promptly forgot again. "Stay here. We'll find Kaius."

Rivan and I head toward the training room. We're only a few hallways away when I hear Lord Faris' loud voice. I wince and glance at Rivan. "Go. I'll be fine."

He stubbornly shakes his head.

"It will be worse if you stay."

We turn the corner and see Lord Faris standing in the middle of the hall talking to Lord Camon. Farther down, I see Kaius' tall build. "There's Kaius. I'll hurry and catch up. Go."

With a growl, he pivots on his heel and storms off.

Just as I get close to the two lords, Faris calls out to me. "Queen Merindah. I need a moment of your time. It's important."

Lord Camon immediately excuses himself and heads down the hallway.

Not wanting to ruin my good mood, I pause and smile at the little weasel. "Lord Faris. I'm so sorry, but I'm in a bit of a hurry. Please reach out to Lady Tanith. She's managing my calendar and will schedule you an appointment. Thanks so much."

"But…" he stutters.

With a little wave in his direction, I hurry away. The hallway is now empty. *Damn.* Picking up my feet, I rush to the end and stop. *Right or left?* I hear Kaius' angry voice to my right. When I turn the corner, I see Lord Camon shove Kaius up against the wall. Unsure what to do, I quickly step behind a pillar.

"What are you doing in this form? There are wanted posters with this face on them everywhere. Do you want to get caught?" Camon asks Kaius furiously. "If you go down, Brina does too. You know that, right? I'll bury you before I let your actions take her away from me."

Kaius snarls at him. "I'm working a new angle. Don't worry."

"I don't believe this. You're putting everything in jeopardy. Do you even think before you do things?" Camon's voice echoes loudly in the marble hall. "It's like you never learn."

"I don't answer to you," Kaius sneers.

"No, you report to Fisk," Camon says, wiping his hand over his face. "Have you completed the new assignment?"

Kaius shoots him an arrogant look.

Camon abruptly straightens, anger riding hard on his face. "Are you at least going to see Brina?" Arms crossed, he stands there waiting for Kaius to respond, but when he doesn't, Camon stalks away. "Fuck you, Kaius."

When he's gone, Kaius picks up his phone. "We've got a problem."

Tiptoeing back around the corner, I slowly walk back to my bedroom. Kian is now standing with Galen at my door. "I missed him. Would you mind letting him know I'm back?"

Galen dips his chin and opens the door. "Don't worry. We'll take care of it."

The second the door clicks shut, I pull my phone out of my pocket.

> Meri: Do you trust Kaius?

A couple minutes pass. While I wait for him to reply, I write down everything I heard.

> Cormal: Yes. Why?

> Meri: Lord Camon thinks he's hiding something. Asked about a man named Fisk. Talked about his form. Wrote it all down. Will text it to you.

After sending the conversation to him, I wait for his reply.

> Cormal: I'm going to check this out. If you need anything, you can trust Kaius, Solandis, or Rivan. No one else. I'll text you in a couple of days.

> Meri: Be careful.

Cormal trusts very few people, but he trusts this Fae. It makes me wonder who Kaius is to Cormal. One of his men? Then I remember he's not the only one who knows him.

Tapping on my phone, I scroll through the messages from Arden. There. She asked if I'd met Kaius. I bite my lip and consider texting her to find out who he is, but if Cormal is investigating, I don't want to jeopardize anything.

A gold box with a pretty bow sits on the table in my sitting area. Picking it up, I lift the lid and find a note written with strong masculine strokes. Under the note is a beautiful chocolate with a pink marble glaze and a pair of sunglasses.

Meri –

Sorry I missed you. I was hoping I'd see the look on your face when you tasted this truffle. If you're free, I'd love to see you tomorrow night. There's an event at the botanical gardens with a display of plants known for their affinity to the dark. Let me know.

Lorn

P.S. The sunglasses are from Allandra, the little thief, along with her apology for accidentally taking them. Can you forgive her?

I tap the sunglasses with my nail. Odd, I didn't notice them on her when she left. With a shrug, I send Lorn a quick message.

> Meri: I'll savor the chocolate. And yes, I'd love to go to the gardens. Let me know the time, and I'll meet you there. I'll be the woman with four men in tow. Tell your sister not to worry about it. Night.

With a smile on my face, I tuck the note in my nightstand and get ready for bed. What a horrendously awful, yet weirdly wonderful day.

CHAPTER SEVENTEEN

<u>CORMAL</u>

Whispers in the wind tell of the destruction that happened here long ago. Secrets, broken pacts, life, and death. Singed stones weep with white and black blood. The innocent and the guilty. A dark massacre with few survivors. Where a keep once stood, only rubble remains. Opening my eyes, I slice my palm and spill my blood on the highest mound. A willing exchange of power for the knowledge given.

Lord Lorn did an admirable job of covering up the past. Long lives get boring and the Fae love to gossip, but few know anything about Lord Lorn and Lady Allandra beyond the most superficial of facts such as their wealth, cultural habits, and how well they fit into society. What I found more interesting was what they didn't say.

I'm an extremely private man, but if you ask a hundred people what they know about me, you'll get at least fifty different answers. There will be a few common answers such as king of supernatural criminals, lives in the Underworld, and maybe a basic physical description such as dark hair and blue eyes. Business associates would describe me in colder terms—ruthless, demanding, driven. Those closest to me would be able to offer up the more intimate details of my life and personality. I'm sure Meri's description would be long and colorful... and full of my character flaws. I chuckle at the thought.

Every Fae I spoke to about Lorn or Allandra had the exact same information, as if they were nuggets meticulously shared to make them comfortable and accepting of the relatively unknown pair. Everyone except Solandis. Surprisingly, she didn't know them, but did know their parents—Lord Basilus and Lady Kyra of the Autumn Court. They visited Solandis' parents at the palace quite often when she was younger. Basilus was her father's cousin, and the two couples got along well. She last saw them when they attended Nyssa's coronation.

With that additional information, I questioned others much older than Solandis, yet none could recall Basilus and Kyra. On a race that prides itself on longevity, the past is rarely forgotten. How can two people have disappeared so thoroughly from history?

Autumn Court lies in dark Fae territory. Taking a chance, I decided to visit and ask my sources if they knew anything about Basilus and Kyra. One remembered the couple and pointed me to their former residence. According to the same source, twenty-eight hundred years ago, they left the Autumn Court to live on new land Queen Nyssa had granted to them after the Fire Fae Rebellion.

Their Autumn Court home was a substantial, but beautiful, limestone house in the city. The exterior told the story of its abandonment, but even with the missing roof tiles, broken windows, and overgrown vegetation, you could see it had been a grand home.

Impulsively, I slipped into the house and found something interesting. The entire lower level had been modernized to some degree. Furnishings were dusty, but fashionably current. Walls and windows were intact. Bedrooms were completely livable. Someone recently occupied the house.

Upstairs was an entirely different story. Decay had set in. Crumbling wood and plaster were everywhere. This part of the home hadn't seen visitors in a very long time.

Squatters, maybe. Finding nothing to indicate who had lived there more recently, I followed the trail to the land Basilus and Kyra inherited from Nyssa.

In order to find Rivan's family, I've been researching the Fire Fae Rebellion. When the Fire Fae surrendered, they were forced to give up their land. Denir, King of the Dark Fae, and Nyssa, Queen of the Light Fae, split it in half. Nyssa gave her half to two of her most trusted lords. Denir decided to mine the volcanic land on his half for diamonds and the precious obsidian favored by the dark Fae.

The book never mentions the name of the two light Fae lords who inherited the land. When I arrived, I discovered one half was given to Lord Carlen and Lady Aoine. He died in a skirmish with the dark Fae a thousand years ago. His daughter, Lady Estrella, now runs the estate.

Not one of the light Fae I spoke to had ever heard of Lord Basilus or his family, but there are two sides to every war. Betting on the enemy, I followed a group of fire drakes last night. After several rounds in the ring with their leader, they told me about the abandoned keep destroyed almost twenty-six hundred years ago and gave me directions to its location. When I pressed them for more information, they disappeared into the sky.

Home to Lord Basilus, Lady Kyra, their daughter, Lady Allandra, and eventually, a son, Lord Lorn. I sweep the rubble under my feet while I sift through the information given to me by the aether.

Two hundred years after Lord Basilus and his family moved here, the massive keep was destroyed. The wind told of secrets and broken pacts. Blood and ash cover the stones. The scene of a great massacre with very few survivors.

Ringing breaks the silence.

"We have a problem."

While I'm listening to Kaius' confrontation with Lord Camon, Meri texts me to question Kaius' integrity and relay the same conversation.

"Meri overheard it all. Keep her safe, and I'll get answers," I assure him. "Camon has ties to the Water Fae through his mate, Brina. I'll start searching in her hometown first."

Hanging up, I consider the ground beneath my feet. When I set out to investigate Lord Lorn, I didn't expect to find myself in the desolate land once inhabited by the Fire Fae. I've ended up with more questions than answers, and nothing has told me whether Lorn can be trusted.

AFTER MAKING several calls and stopping to pick up a few of my men, we step out of a portal on the outskirts of a small light Fae city called Seva. Home to a large population of Water Fae, the port city serves as a transportation hub for goods and services heading inland. I nod to Sika, a blue-haired Selkie-and-nymph hybrid who happens to resemble his father, and he disappears ahead of us.

Once he leaves, Ren, a merman I saved from an unscrupulous demon, and Kavi, a Chaos demon who serves as one of my guards, follow me to Brina's house. Or at least the one she grew up in.

Made of bleached stone sanded smooth from the thousands of years of salt water and wind, the weathered house is huge. On a bluff overlooking the sea below, its size and prominence tells me her family holds significant status among the Water Fae. Like the aristocratic light Fae, the Lesser Fae have tiers to their society. Obviously, Brina's family belongs to the upper echelons.

Workers slip in and out of the house, tending to the gardens or heading into town. We watch the busy household for a couple of hours but see nothing out of the ordinary. Tapping Kavi on the shoulder, we disappear into the shadows and enter the house. Once inside, he guards my back while I search for information.

A little finder's spell, and my magic hums. The layout of the house appears in my mind, along with a beacon to guide me where I need to go. With Kavi on my heels, we head down a flight of stairs, then out the back of the house. Fifty feet from the house, we take more steps down into an old cellar filled with stored goods. Passing through the shelving, we head to the very back.

The beacon passes through the stone wall, and without hesitation, we follow. On the other side, we find rooms and tunnels filled with people. Motioning for Kavi to stay, I slip from one shadow to the next, listening to bits of conversation along the way. On the far side of the room is a large map on the wall. I move to the corner to get a better view.

It's a map of the Light Fae Kingdom. Lines are strung with string, various color dots are distributed throughout the map, along with a few stars. My gut sinks. It's a war map with cities, supply routes, soldiers, and strongholds.

The purple stars scattered across the kingdom aren't tagged, but when I see five at Meri's palace and a couple dozen in the nearby city of Meira, my guess is they are spies.

While I stand in the shadows and memorize the map, a

group of very familiar fire drakes stride in from a side tunnel. They clasp forearms with an older looking man on the other side of the room.

"Fisk."

My interest switches from the map to the man. Fisk. Reeks of power. Medium stature. Stocky. Dark blue hair indicates he's Water Fae, and the aged appearance to his face tells me he's old. Very old. Unlike light Fae, Lesser Fae do age, but the process takes thousands of years. This is the leader Camon mentioned to Kaius.

"How's the heckling going?" Fisk asks the fire drakes with a harsh laugh.

The leader, who I fought in the ring last night, shrugs. "My sources say Estrella will ask the council for an intervention soon. We'll handle it. More importantly, when are you going to give us a real mission?"

Fisk makes a note on a pad at his elbow. "I'll let my man in the palace know." He tosses down the pencil. "You have one of the most important missions right now. Drawing the eye of the council. It looks like you're succeeding, too. Well done." Fisk runs his hand against the scruff on his chin. When the fire drakes continue to stand there, he turns light blue eyes toward the leader.

Face whitening, the fire drake quickly makes a motion to the rest of his team to move out.

When they're gone, the old man chuckles, then stills. He casually scans the people around him. Light blue eyes pass where I'm hidden in the shadows, never stopping, but the sight of his eyes makes my gut tighten.

Son of a bitch.

He's a myth. A cirein-croin. No wonder the fire drake almost shit his pants. Staring down a legendary sea monster that can give a kraken a run for his money would make the fiercest Fire Fae flee. I thought they were extinct. Bet a lot of others did too.

This operation is heavily funded and well planned. By him? I would bet this is his house, which makes him Brina's family. Not likely her father, but someone a bit further back. This is a big stand for a creature that has chosen to remain hidden and "extinct" for the last few thousand years.

Lord Camon strides into the room and up to the man. "Fisk."

With a broad smile, Fisk turns and pulls the High Fae into a tight hug. "Camon. Where's that granddaughter of mine?"

Camon's face is tight. "At home. She wanted to come, but in her condition, I won't let her travel. Besides, this is family business, and until we know for sure, I would rather wait to tell her."

Fisk steps back to lean on the desk. "What is it?"

"Kaius is at the palace," he tells him. "But there's something strange going on. He refused to answer any of my questions about the new assignment or when he was going to visit Brina. Nothing. We may have our differences, but she's his twin sister. The first thing they've always done is see each other after a long absence."

Camon paces back and forth. "And to make matters worse, he's still wearing the light Fae form from his last job. It's only a matter of time before the wanted posters make their way to the capital." He stops to look at Fisk. "I need you to call him home."

Fisk slumps forward with a devastated look on his face. "It's not Kaius. A chameleon can only hold a form for a limited time. Maybe three or four months. It's been over six since he did that last job."

Well, that's a handy piece of news Kaius should know.

Camon's face whitens. "Who the hell is it? And where's Kaius?"

"Dead. My grandson is dead," Fisk whispers, his eyes turning from light blue to white. "If a chameleon dies in another form, he doesn't revert to his original."

"Fuck. Brina's going to be devastated, and she's so damn

delicate right now," Camon says, slamming his hand on the desk. He looks at the man in front of him. "Damn, I'm sorry, Fisk. I know how much you loved him."

Part demon, part cirein-croin, and who knows what else. No wonder Kaius ended up as a chameleon. It's so rare, I could barely believe it when Vargas told me about his new "body." Hell, he's going to be over the fucking moon at this piece of news.

A loud commotion in one of the nearby hallways makes them both jump. Fisk turns and grips Camon's arm tightly. "Not a word about Kaius. Not to anyone. Not even Brina. Let me figure out what to do."

Camon nods, his eyes going to the doorway nearest to them. A fierce man with flaming red hair and a warrior's build strides into the room.

I narrow my eyes trying to place where I know him.

"Caught a damn spy following me here. Can you believe the fucking nerve? Dog has a death wish," he roars, throwing the animal into the middle of the room.

Fuck me. It's the hellhound I sent to find Rivan's family. I study the red-haired man. That's why he looks familiar. Rivan's family looks pretty damn alive to me. I wonder if there are more of them.

Unfortunately, the only person who can tell me has been outed as a spy.

Fisk reaches out a hand to grab the animal, and the hellhound immediately turns his body into an inferno. "He's a fucking hellhound? This got worse in a hurry. Probably a mercenary, but they only contract for the Underworld. Who did you piss off now?"

The phoenix plants his fists on his hips. "I don't think now is the time to get jealous. If you weren't such a recluse, I'm sure you'd have your own Underworld spy following you."

My mind races, trying to figure out how to get Tarquin, the

hellhound, Red, Kavi, and myself out of here without incurring the wrath of a Phoenix, a High Fae, and a mythological cireincroin. I scan the space around Tarquin and see a small shadow under his belly.

Suddenly, a large explosion rocks the hallway. Turning quickly, Brixton and Fisk rush toward the entrance.

Callyx appears across from me. "Go!" he mouths silently.

Gritting my teeth, I glare at Meri's cousin. He's going to gloat over this for years.

Callyx throws me an incredulous look and motions for me to get moving.

Flipping him off, I yank Tarquin through the shadow under his belly to the one I'm standing in, but it isn't big enough to house us both.

"You're going to need to change for me to get us out of here," I murmur.

Camon's head turns in our direction, and I grip the hellhound by the neck and take us through the wall to the other side. An uproar has me swiveling to see who's behind us. *Fucking infernos.* It's an entire squad of Phoenix. One immediately conjures a large ball of fire, and I jump into the shadow with Tarquin and coast to the wall where I left Kavi.

"We've got men on both sides," Kavi quietly informs me when I arrive. "What do you want to do, boss?"

I thrust the hellhound into Kavi's arms. "For some reason, he can't change. Let me see if I can get a hold of Ren." Shoving my cuff up, I touch a rune on my wrist. "Ren. We need a big diversion. Something to pull at least a hundred men from behind the house. What do you see—"

Callyx appears in the shadow next to us. "We need to get out of here. Now."

"Hold on, Ren," I tell the merman. "No shit. I'm working on a plan."

"No time. The only way we're getting out of here with our

heads still attached is if we are the enemy," he calmly says, cutting me off with a shit-eating grin. "Fae remember. But not like any Fae here." In a blink, he wraps the shadows around us and we suddenly turn into four men with varying ranges of blue and green hair. Water Fae.

He glamoured the shadows. I'm impressed, dammit, but hell if I'll admit it to him. If I still had the ability to steal powers, that would be at the top of my list.

We stroll out of the cellar. Once we're out of sight from the house, we cruise the shadow stream to where I left Ren and grab him. Fleeing, we get to the spot where we stepped out of the portal earlier. Sika's waiting for us.

Muttering obscenities to myself, I turn to Callyx and hold out my hand. "Thank you. We probably wouldn't have made it without losing a man or two."

"Don't worry, I'll be sure to remind you in the future," he jokingly says, shaking my hand. His expression turns serious. "I've been following Brixton for days. They're planning one hell of a coup. A lot of men and firepower. More than they had at the Fire Fae Rebellion. I have to report to Lucifer but expect me at the palace soon."

Callyx steps in close with a fierce expression on his face. "My family is in that palace. Don't let anything happen to them. Do whatever it takes to protect them."

I flash a grim smile. "I plan to."

He creates a red portal under his feet and disappears.

What a day. Vargas choosing Kaius' body just gave us one hell of an advantage. It tipped the enemy into unknowingly revealing themselves and their plans. Unfortunately, our enemy now knows Kaius is a fake, putting a huge target on his back.

I shake my head. They're damn good. There hasn't been a whisper of a coup. By the time we would have realized what was happening, the Light Fae Kingdom would be burning to the ground.

CHAPTER EIGHTEEN

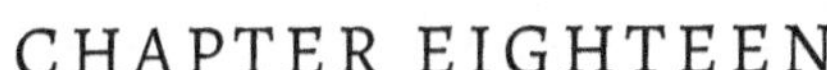

CORMAL

Lucifer's office is brightly lit by the faux sun shining into it. An idea he stole from me. Originally dark and gloomy, and filled with body parts, he recently updated it to something that pleases him instead of his predecessor, the Devil.

Striding into Lucifer's office with Tarquin in my arms, I set him gently down on the carpet. "He can't change for some reason."

Lucifer's brows come together in a fierce frown. "It's terror. What happened?" Hands scarred from sword nicks reach out to the hellhound, palms glowing bright red. Placing them on his body, frozen muscles begin to thaw, the hound stretches out, then slowly transforms into a man with black shaggy hair and red eyes.

"Same mission I told you about last week. He was looking

for the Phoenix," I say with a perplexed look on my face. "He found one. Brixton, Rivan's father."

"Callyx told me," Lucifer admits with a frown. "Tarquin, what happened?"

Tarquin scowls. "He caught me. I refused to answer. He tortured me to death." When we look puzzled, he throws his hands up. "Hello. Phoenix. He kills you. Resurrects you. Kills you. Resurrects you. Worst fucking torture I've ever been through. Almost broke me." In the depths of his eyes, the truth of his ordeal lies in the terror still lingering in their depths.

"How did he catch you?" I ask him.

"Apparently, Phoenix can sense powers. He essentially sniffed me out," he reveals, to my astonishment. "When I wouldn't answer his questions, he tortured me. After about the fifth time, my body transformed into my hellhound state and locked up. He decided to take me to Fisk."

Rivan never said a word about this ability. With a grimace, I hold out a hand to help him up. "Sorry. Wasn't aware of that, but the good news is he brought you back. Could have left you permanently deceased. And we wouldn't have known he was a part of this coup until it was too late."

Lucifer raises an eyebrow at my lack of empathy. "Tarquin, take some time off and relax. I'm sure Cormal will give you a big bonus for all your trouble."

"I'll send Kavi over with your payment and a bonus. Before you go, how many more Phoenix did you see?" I ask, quickly texting the order to Kavi.

"Thousands," Tarquin replies hoarsely. "They've been living in the old mines on the dark Fae side. Looks like they've been there a long time." On unsteady feet, he leaves.

I wait until Tarquin is out the door. "This isn't something they planned overnight. My guess is they've been waiting for a sign to put it into play. Nyssa's death gave them a golden opportunity."

"Callyx gave me the same assessment," Lucifer admits with a sigh. "To be honest, I can't fault them for it. The aristocratic Fae have mistreated the Lesser Fae for thousands of years. From a governing perspective, they continuously refuse to let them have representation and a say in the laws. In their eyes, Lesser Fae only exist to serve the aristocracy, so they shouldn't need a voice. I'm not sure I could support Meri in a war against them." Intent blue eyes meet mine.

Mentally kicking myself for missing the obvious, I sigh. "When Meri took the crown, my biggest concern was a coup from inside the aristocracy, not the Lesser Fae. I should have realized Nyssa's death would precipitate a grab for power from all sides." For the first time in a long time, I'm feeling outmaneuvered.

"Have you ever met Lord Basilus and Lady Kyra?" I ask, taking a wild chance Lucifer might have met them at a function.

Lucifer pauses, a strange look on his face. "No, but I saw Basilus. Rumor has it he betrayed the Fire Fae, and when he was given their land as a reward, they took their revenge. I don't know if that's true or not, but over three hundred souls arrived on our shores without the proper burial rights, including Basilus and Kyra. All of them had been burned to death."

I nod. Still leaves a lot of questions, but it gives me something solid to go on in my investigation. "Thanks. I need to get to Meri, but I'll keep you in the loop as things progress."

"Callyx will be there in a few days. He's running down a lead for me on another matter," Lucifer informs me.

I wave to indicate I heard him, then slide into a shadow.

MERI'S ASLEEP when I arrive. Silky platinum hair fanned out across the pillow, framing her delectable face. Pink lips begging for a kiss. The perfect picture is ruined by the small line between her brows. Something is disturbing her sleep.

The tiny cami and shorts set she's wearing is driving me to distraction, which isn't a good thing right now. There's a lot of planning to do, and my brain is spinning. I need to figure out how to stop this potential coup before it turns into war. Hooking the sheet with my finger, I slowly pull it over her, allowing myself a few stolen moments to drink in the sight of her.

A small grouping of flowers on her hip catches my eyes. They look like white daisies. Very sweet and completely unlike her. I wonder where she got it. Once she's covered, I can't help but yawn and look longingly at the other side of the bed. My lips curve in a wry smile as I think of her reaction.

Walking over to the small velvet couch by the balcony, I sit and prop my feet on the short table in front of it. Maybe I can rest for a few minutes. I don't have to worry about security, the wards here are similar to the ones in my home. Another yawn escapes.

Bright sun pierces my closed eyes. I've got to stop falling asleep in my office. Yawning, I stretch and force them open.

Meri's beautiful turquoise eyes are staring at me intently. "In all these years, I've never seen you sleeping. That's kind of odd, isn't it? You've seen me asleep countless times, including last night. Is it because you don't sleep much or just not around me?"

Groaning, I hold up a hand. "Can I get a coffee and wake up before I answer?"

She places a mug in my hand. "Here, take mine. I've got to go to training in an hour, and I don't want to throw up."

Interesting. I haven't had time to look into the guard, but with everything I discovered yesterday, he's the least of my concerns. "Do you think he's a good teacher?"

She bites her lip. "I'm not sure there's anything good about him. Is he effective? Yes." Leaning back against the other side of the couch, she slides her toes under my leg like she's done a thousand times. "My feet are cold. What did you find out about Kaius?"

Sensing her reluctance to talk about her training, I move on to bigger topics. "Can you ask the guard at the door to get Kaius and Rivan? We need to talk."

Meri scrambles off the couch and walks over to the door. After making the request, she comes back and sits with her arms looped around her knees. "It's bad, isn't it? You always have this fierce look of determination on your face when things are going sideways."

I sometimes forget how observant she is around me. "It's not good, but Camon's slip-up with Kaius gave us a huge advantage. We have to figure out how to move forward."

Rivan walks in and sits down on the chair beside Meri, who suddenly has a scarf on her head. He looks her up and down. "Feeling better today?"

My eyes dart between the two of them. "What happened yesterday?"

Meri rolls her eyes at my tone. "I let the past get into my head at training. It shook me up." When I continue to stare at her, she leans in close to explain. "It reminded me of The Pit." A tiny shudder racks her petite frame. "Rivan helped me get my equilibrium back."

My eyes meet Rivan's over her head, and he gives me a slight nod to indicate she's okay.

"I see. I'm glad he was here for you. Maybe this training will help you figure out how to move forward from the past and be a badass."

"I'm counting on it," she states firmly. Her voice is full of conviction, something I haven't heard from her in a long time.

Kaius rushes in. "What did you find out?"

Whispering an incantation, I seal the room. "Camon

mentioned Brina in your conversation, so I figured I'd take a look into her background. I took a few men and went to her hometown of Seva," I begin. "As you know, she's Water Fae. Comes from a wealthy Lesser Fae family. We found her family's house. Kavi and I went in to look around and get a better feel of who she was and her relationship with Kaius."

Meri frowns. "Why didn't you just ask Kaius?" She glances from me to him. "What's going on?"

"Let's just say… he isn't Kaius and leave it at that for now," I suggest to her. "He's in disguise."

She gives me a disgruntled look. "You and your secrets. Fine. Continue."

"A little magic led us underground to the person Camon mentioned… Fisk." I pause and look at each of them. "The Lesser Fae are preparing for war."

"Fisk?" Rivan asks hoarsely. "Are you sure?"

I narrow my eyes. "You know him, don't you? Spill."

"Fisk was my father's best friend and unofficial leader of the Water Fae. When he refused to join the Fire Fae Rebellion, it caused a huge rift between them. I can't believe he's now planning his own coup," he says, his mouth twisted in disgust. "My father thought that if they had joined us, we would have won."

Meri reaches out and loops her pinkie around his. He calms a little, which is good, because he's going to hate what I tell him next.

"I need you to hear me without losing your shit," I tell Rivan. "When Meri became queen, I saw an opportunity for you to break free from your agreement. But I knew you wouldn't do it unless you had some motivation, so I sent a hellhound to look for the Phoenix."

"You did what?" he roars, standing to glare down at me. "Why?"

Kaius moves toward the door, but I stop him. "There's a seal on the room. Nobody can hear anything."

Relieved, he comes back and sits across from me.

I return my gaze to Rivan. "I also asked Lucifer if he could lend us Callyx to help. He did." Hopeful eyes turn in my direction, but he remains silent. Almost as if he's afraid to ask. "They found your father."

He drops to the chair. "He's alive? Anyone else? My mother?"

Damn, I really need a drink for this conversation. "I'm not sure about her, but I can ask. Brixton walked into the war room with the hellhound. He thought he was a spy."

Rivan shakes his head in disbelief. "Wait. What are you saying?" His eyes beg me to take it all back, but I can't. "After everything that happened last time, he's going to war? He's aligned with Fisk and the Water Fae?"

"Yes. He is," I answer. "I saw a platoon of elite Phoenix myself. Fire drakes, too." My eyes meet Meri's and silently convey a message. She stands and circles Rivan's finger with hers. "The Phoenix have been replenishing their numbers this whole time. According to Tarquin, the hellhound, there are thousands living on the dark Fae side."

Rivan sways on his feet. "I don't believe you." He points a finger at me. "There must be another explanation. Nyssa told me the phoenix were decimated, and the remaining few left Fae lands." His hands go up to grip his head. "I need to get out of here."

Striding to the door, he slams it open and storms out.

One of the guards peeks his head in and looks for Meri. When he sees her and Kaius, he dips his chin and closes the door.

"Is this because I was crowned queen?" Meri asks in a shaky voice.

Sharing a glance with Kaius, I shake my head. "No. This has been in the works for years. They were simply waiting for the best opportunity to strike. Nyssa was the one thing holding them back. Once she was gone, they must have immediately moved to put the plan into place."

Meri drops her head in her hands. "When you said I'd have to fight for my crown, I didn't think you meant literally." Raising, she looks to me for answers. "What if I gave them rights and land? Do you think that would satisfy them? Or at least open it up for negotiations?"

I can't help but smile at her willingness to give them the respect they deserve. "We're going to try everything but war. Under Nyssa's rule, conditions got worse for them. They are entitled to a lot more than they're getting from the Fae." I stroke the hair back from her cheek. "We'll pull in whoever we have to for advice. You have more support than you realize."

"Don't you have training?" Kaius inserts.

Meri looks at me for the answer.

I nod in agreement. "We know Camon's a spy, but there are others. Since we don't know who they are, you need to keep to your regular schedule. Go to training. We'll stay here. I picked up a lot of troop- and supply information I want to share with Kaius."

Meri moves to the closet and comes out a minute later wearing a troubled expression and workout gear that makes me almost swallow my tongue. This is what she wears for training? Tiny shorts and a cut-off top?

I clear the jealousy clogging my throat. "Keep this between us for now. We'll figure out when to bring in Solandis and the others."

She nods and heads toward the door.

I groan. That trainer better be a damn eunuch.

Kaius grabs a notepad and pencil. "Let's lay it out."

Sealing the room again, I lean forward and take the pencil out of his hand. "You have a problem. Apparently, you—Kaius— was Fisk's grandson and one of the leaders in the rebellion. And twin to Brina, Camon's mate. Fisk knows he's dead and you're an imposter. That puts a huge target on your back."

He scowls. "How the hell does he know?"

I explain what I overheard Fisk tell Camon. "Apparently, this is the form Kaius died in, but it's not his original one."

He nervously runs a hand over his head. "What's his original?"

"I don't know his entire lineage, but his grandfather is top of the fucking food chain," I reveal with a grim smile. "Fisk is a full-blood cirein-croin and one scary old man."

Vargas blanches. "Shit. How do I explain all this to Solandis? She's going to kill me." He stares down at his fingers. "What do you think my original form looks like?"

I hold up a finger. "If you're Brina's twin, maybe blue hair? Hell, I don't know. You need to tell Solandis, but you can't change forms. We have a slim advantage right now. Camon must continue to believe we know nothing about their plans." Five stars on the map. "We have more than one spy in the palace to convince, and since we don't know who it is, we can't afford to tip them off."

CHAPTER NINETEEN

irt flies up when I hit the ground for the hundredth time. Instead of getting up right away, I roll over and glare at Madoc. Apparently, training rooms make for soft soldiers. He snidely informed me that the enemy isn't going to lay a mat down for me to land on. Hence the hard packed dirt under my back. At least we're outside and the sun is shining instead of in a cold, dark dungeon.

He steps forward, and I scramble backward. The first time I went down this morning, I took the hand he offered. Big mistake. He picked me up and threw me fifty yards with a reminder to keep my guard up.

"When are you going to start using your magic?" he asks impatiently. "This is wasting my time."

I stand and give him the evil eye. "I am using magic. What do you call that burned patch of grass at your feet?"

He whips a knife out and throws it at me.

Tracking its swift movement, I turn at the last minute and the small fireball he must have launched behind the knife explodes on my thigh.

"Fuck!" I scream, grabbing my leg.

Tears spring to my eyes, but I blink rapidly, refusing to let them fall. I look down to assess the damage. Skin is hanging off or curling in on itself in several areas. Black edges line raw, bleeding patches. It's nasty and the burnt-flesh smell is clogging my nose. Unable to heal myself, I carefully wrap it in bandages to keep it clean until we get done.

Brows lower into a terrifying scowl. His scarred face twists into a macabre expression, but it's not his face that's worrying me. Whenever he shows emotions, he turns even nastier.

"What?" I demand, although I'm pretty sure he can hear the shaking in my voice.

He launches a full attack. "Shield! How many times do I have to tell you to keep your shield up?" Knives, rocks, and other small missiles fly at me from all directions.

Bracing for impact, I throw up a shield around my entire body. When nothing gets through, I sigh in relief. At least something is working right.

A large branch sways on the tree behind him. It begs to be used against him. Carefully sheering it off, I magically throw the large missile at his head.

Without even looking, he changes the branch into feathers that fall uselessly to the ground.

Huh. I never thought of changing the material.

He scowls and strides forward, tripling the speed of his attack.

Ignoring his advance, I concentrate on changing his missiles into feathers, leaves, and pillows. Anything soft. Faster and faster. When he picks up a nearby boulder and tosses it at me, I change it to snow. It lands like a ton of bricks on top of me, and I go down.

Damn it. Excited at how fast I was countering his magic with mine, I let my shield drop. Again. Angry at myself, I turn snow to water and stand up.

At least my leg stopped burning. Drenched and freaking cold as hell, I wave a hand and dry myself. Glancing at him from the corner of my eye, I see the scowl is gone and his usual emotionless mask is back in place.

The bandage on my thigh slips and I bend over to redress the wound. Carefully unwinding the layers, I peel them back and see nothing but smooth skin underneath. In shock, I pull and poke the healed skin.

"It's gone. The burn. Look."

He gives me a weird look. "Why are you surprised?"

I run my palm down my thigh again. "It used to take days, sometimes weeks, for me to heal. This is amazing." Springing up and down a few times, I laugh. This is a game changer. Some of the fear I've been holding onto fades.

His eyes narrow. "Last time we spoke, you told me you had almost no magic. I didn't believe you. Now you're trying to tell me it took days to heal? It doesn't make any sense. You're Fae. We're born with magic that constantly replenishes itself from the land around us." Crossing his arms, he waits for me to answer.

"I don't know what you want me to say," I grumble. "Until I came to the light Fae kingdom, the little magic I had wasn't mine. When I came in contact with Nyssa at the battle, I could suddenly draw on her powers. When she died, bam. I inherited lots of magic."

"Where were you before here?"

I thought everyone knew. "The Underworld."

He freezes. "Nyssa dumped her daughter in the Underworld?" His tone is incredulous.

Warning signs blink in my head. "She didn't really know I

existed. I lived with my guardian in the Underworld. Are we going to continue training?"

Deep in thought, he doesn't answer, so I walk over to the tree to collect my things.

A meaty fist grabs the back of my tank. "Training isn't over, my queen." He tightens his grip and pulls me backward.

Memories of Leandra doing the same washes over me. Rage rises from the depths of my soul, and everything around me darkens. My hand turns into pure fire, and I spin and grab his arm. Shocked, he immediately releases my shirt. Channeling the power rushing through me, I slam him into the ground so hard it creates a small crater.

Wrapping my shield around me, I jump back and wait for him to attack.

He flips to his feet. "It's about fucking time. Nice trick," he says, eyes lit with satisfaction. "Harness the rage inside you. Use it to fuel your power. But don't bring those emotions into the fight or you'll lose." His lip curls and the scar nearest his mouth pulls tight. "Hope you enjoyed the sunshine."

The rage dissipates, and I swallow, knowing his twisted smile means we're training in the dark tomorrow.

He arrogantly motions to my stuff. "You can leave." A second later, he's gone.

I walk back to my room and fall face down on the soft bed.

SEVERAL HOURS LATER, Cormal and Kaius stride into my room, completely disheveled and worn out. They immediately lean over the map on the table and begin to mark it with x's, lines, and other symbols.

"What are you doing?" I ask, worriedly.

Kaius darts a glance toward me. "Cormal memorized the

map in their war room. We're trying to recreate it, but we have to make sure it's still accurate. We've been slipping in and out of places all day." With a tired sigh, he rolls his shoulders to alleviate some of the tension in them. "I've got to go. I'm taking Solandis on a date tonight."

Cormal stares at him. "You need to tell her."

Kaius scowls fiercely. "I will, damn it. I don't need some pup telling me how to manage my life." He flips him off and strides out the door.

Shaking his head, Cormal turns to me. "Where are you going?"

Watching his reaction, I tell him. "You said to stick to the schedule. I've got a romantic date with Lorn. He's taking me to the botanical gardens to see night plants. Isn't that lovely?" I smooth the black strappy jumpsuit I'm wearing and take one last satisfied look in the mirror. "I'd normally ask Solandis, but since she's not here... What do you think? Does this look good?"

Cormal stands to his full height. "How well do you know Lord Lorn?"

Uneasy, I lift a shoulder. "We've gone on a few dates. I like him. Besides being incredibly handsome, he's funny and considerate. Protective. Cares deeply for his sister. And more importantly, he lacks the arrogance most of the Fae wear like a cloak. Why?"

He walks over to me. "I've been investigating him. Did you know his parents were killed by the Fire Fae?"

That must be the reason they asked for reparations. "I knew something bad had happened in his past. Their past. He told me after his parents died that he and his sister struggled financially. They petitioned Nyssa, and she gave them their inheritance, but he called it reparations."

He tells me how Basilus and Kyra were awarded the land by Nyssa and were massacred two hundred years later.

"Poor Allandra and Lorn. No wonder they don't talk about

their past," I say, empathizing with them. Cormal looks exasperated. "Look. You know I've done a lot of shitty things in my life. Most of them at Leandra's request, but not all. Sometimes I look around here and it baffles me how I ended up queen of the light. But I'm here, and I'm doing everything I can to be a better person. Lorn obviously has a complicated history, but he's also building a new life. I haven't shared all of my past with him, and I'm not sure I ever will. I am choosing to give him the same respect. I appreciate the concern, but we have bigger things on our plate than who I choose to date."

Dark brows come together, and he pulls me closer. "You ask me personal questions all the time."

Ignoring how good it feels to be in his arms, I place my hands on his chest, but instead of drawing him closer like I ache to do, I push back to gain some distance. He allows the inches between us to increase by two, but it's enough. Bright blue eyes stare intently into mine, and for the first time in a long time, I see something in their depths that gives me hope. Internal conflict and jealousy.

"Not that I get any answers," I reply dryly, refusing to let him off the hook. "Every single thing, good or bad, that I've done or that has happened to me is as much a part of your past as it is mine. But it's entirely one-sided. You dole out bits and pieces of yourself like they're unicorn tears. I want more than scraps, and I deserve them. Lorn takes me on dates and gives me little presents. We laugh and talk. He tells me about his sister and their life together. It's wonderful and romantic. I like him."

I pick up my phone and step out of his arms. "As you said, I've got to keep to this schedule of mine. Once I get back, I'd like to go over the map with you to understand it and get your thoughts on the situation." Walking to the door, I glance over my shoulder and find him standing where I left him. "Thank you for doing all this. I'm going to do everything I can to hold on to my crown and this new life of mine."

Kian is waiting outside the door. "Portal?"

I raise a hand to cover my yawn and nod. I'm so tired. The last thing I want to do is go see a bunch of plants, but if I had told Cormal, he would have attributed it to Lorn. I meant what I said, though. I like Lorn. He's handsome and sophisticated, but he's also genuine. And he makes me feel witty and attractive.

Another yawn. Stress is zapping my energy. When I looked at the map earlier, everything felt so imminent and terrifying. Nothing made sense. I haven't even been queen for a month. What do I know about strategy and war? Zilch. Zero. Thankfully, Cormal knows more than most, and I know that regardless of what happens between us, he will stand by me. For a criminal king, he has a high degree of integrity and a fierce need to protect his friends.

Stepping out of the portal, I'm startled to see Lorn, Allandra, and Faris. "Oh. Hello. I didn't realize others would be joining us."

Allandra tucks her hand into Faris' arm. "Lord Faris came over to talk to Lorn about the council meeting tomorrow. I insisted he join us. Three's a crowd, but four is a double date." She giggles and squeezes his arm.

For the first time since I met the weasel, Faris looks uncomfortable. "Queen Merindah."

I flick my eyes to Lorn and notice a tic in his jaw. "Shall we?"

He narrows his eyes on Allandra. "Why don't you two go ahead? We'll catch up."

A tiny line appears between her brow, but Allandra slowly agrees. "Come along, Faris." She quickly maneuvers him to her side and down the path.

Watching Lorn glare at the two of them, I place a hand on his arm. "Is everything okay? I'm not a huge fan of Faris myself, but I don't think he's interested in Allandra."

Lorn stiffens, then releases a sigh. He bends to place a kiss on my cheek. "You smell delicious, and you look utterly divine."

The sensual smell of his cologne wraps around me, along with his arm.

Subtly inhaling, I lick my lips and say, "Thank you, and I loved the candy. It was delicious, but I hate to tell you, it wasn't near as good as the petit chocolate cake."

He laughs. "The cake is a bit otherworldly. Maybe I can bribe some more out of the baker since you love it so much."

I blush. "No, don't. Please."

Intrigued, he eyes me. "I want to. I enjoy giving you presents." He offers me his elegantly clad arm. "Shall we?"

Standing on my tiptoes, I reach up and kiss him lightly on the lips. "Thank you." I take his arm, and we catch up to Allandra and Faris.

The plants are more interesting than I thought, or maybe it's the company. Some glow in the dark, others bloom only at night. One releases a perfume when it's dark to attract its dinner. Lorn explains that this is called a moon garden, and he really wants to add one to his rooftop.

Allandra flirts heavily with Faris all night. Every time she laughs, she looks back at Lorn, but he's too busy explaining the plants to me.

We finally reach the end of the walkway. "This exhibit was wonderful. Thank you for asking me. I brought something for you this time. Here."

He opens the small box and looks at the smoke chocolate. I explain the story behind the candy and urge him to try it and let me know what he thinks. Then, I hand Allandra a small bag. "Here's a candy for you and the sunglasses. They looked better on you."

Her smile is brilliant. "I hope you can forgive me? It was an honest mistake. Although you are right, they look fabulous on me."

All four of us stand there awkwardly looking at each other

for a second. I dip my head at Faris. *See, I can be polite.* Faris bows at me, then excuses himself.

Lorn squeezes my hand. "I'll text you later. Thank you for listening to me talk incessantly all night about the plants."

Disappointed our night is ending so soon, I squeeze his hand. "I had a wonderful time, Lorn, and look forward to seeing you again. Maybe we can make it just the two of us next time."

Guards surround me as we walk over to the portal. When I look back, Lorn and Allandra are having a fierce argument. She abruptly throws my gift on the ground. Lorn bends down to pick it up, but she stomps on it, then walks away. Lorn heads in the opposite direction. I motion for Galen to go back and pick up the gift on the ground. Maybe it's time Lorn and I had a chat.

CHAPTER TWENTY

<u>MERI</u>

Cormal was gone when I returned last night and hasn't been back. So was the map. It's not unusual, but with everything going on, I don't like it. He's not invincible, no matter what he likes to believe.

I take a sip of the dark brew in my hand and contemplate whether I should drink any more. With the council meeting later this afternoon, training will start earlier today. It's all I can do to keep the toast down during our sessions. Maybe just one more sip.

My bedroom door slams and Solandis storms out onto the balcony. "Did you know?" Nearby plants wither and die from the anger and magic she's leaking.

"Did I know what?"

Sparks light up the concrete around me. "Did you know he was Vargas?"

I jump up. "Vargas is back? That's wonderful. Where is he?"

She leans down to stare into my eyes. "Kaius is Vargas."

My eyes widen. "I knew something weird was going on. That's why Cormal trusts him. He trusts maybe ten people in all the realms, and I couldn't figure out why he would trust a Fae guard." I put a hand on my heart. "I swear I didn't know. It wasn't until yesterday that Cormal said he wasn't the real Kaius, but he wouldn't explain what he meant. Then I got sidetracked by the coup the Lesser Fae is planning."

Solandis' blond eyebrows draw together. "What are you talking about?"

I stare at her in dismay. "How far did you two get in your conversation?"

She plops down and picks up my coffee. After taking a long sip, she stares down into its murky depths. "Not far. I thought he was joking at first. Until he changed forms. Even then, I thought it was an elaborate illusion. The Vargas I know would never let me grieve for so long or make a fool of me. It's him, though. He convinced me by telling me things only he would know."

Slamming the cup on the table, she eyes me. "I left him in the middle of a field, hopped around on portals for most of the night, then returned this morning. What else is going on?"

I pick up the cup and motion for her to follow me into the room. Repeating the incantation Cormal said yesterday, I soundproof our conversation, and tell her everything I know.

Her eyes are intent when she asks. "Fisk is involved? Are you sure?"

"Funny. Rivan said the same thing. Who is this guy?"

She blinks. "He's a very old Fae and something of a myth. Most of them died out long ago, although I'm not sure anything really dies here. Things are reborn all the time." Waving her hand, she pops up an image of the Fae in question. "Fisk is a cirein-croin."

A massive blue sea monster. Old and powerful. Lovely. This

just gets better and better. "Brixton is back. He's part of this whole thing, too. Rivan almost lost his mind. Apparently, he thought most of the phoenix dead and the rest scattered to the winds."

"We're coming full circle," Solandis murmurs. "The Fire Fae Rebellion started the first year of Nyssa's reign."

"How long did it last?"

"Two hundred years," she replies. A sad look crosses her face. "But discussions started years before they declared their independence. My father championed the Fire Fae's cause because he felt all Lesser Fae should have a voice and own land. He envisioned a more enlightened Light Fae Kingdom."

She almost never speaks of her parents. "Unfortunately, when my parents were killed by the dark Fae, there wasn't anyone left who believed in his vision. Nyssa didn't, but even if she did, she wouldn't have been able to pick up his cause. With so many contenders, the fight for the crown took all her time and energy, then the rebellion."

This whole thing is bringing up bittersweet memories for her. "You believed in it. Still do. After all, you voted for Camon's initiative." I remind her. "Before I forget, let Camon and the council know we're getting the metals for Meira, but stall them on the weapons."

Solandis agrees. "With the new women joining the council for the first time today, it should give us a bit of a distraction." She reaches for my hand. "What are you going to do?"

"I haven't the first clue, but if I were to follow my gut like Cormal so often suggests… I would give the Lesser Fae the same rights as the rest of the light Fae," I admit softly. "But it's easy for me to say. I'm not sure if it's something we can do. Talk to Kaius. He has a lot more details than I do, including an in-depth knowledge of the map. But don't let him off the hook. You deserve loads of groveling."

Her mouth firms. "Where are you going?"

"To train with Madoc," I call out from the closet. Emerging in workout clothes, I bend down and squeeze her tightly. "If you want me to banish Kaius, just say the word."

Her turquoise eyes look up at me with gratitude. "Thank you. I might. And don't worry. We'll get through this. Together."

Tears spring to my eyes, and I turn away to hide them. "See you at the council meeting. Wear your armor."

On the way to the training center, I can't help but think how lucky I am to have her in my corner. Solandis means everything to me. Her support and love more than makes up for the lack of a mother all these years.

Madoc whisks me away the second I step into the room. When we get to our destination, I can't see a thing in the pitch-black space, but this time, it doesn't smell like a dungeon. Instead, I smell dirt, pine, and a delicious dark combination of amber and musk that must be him. The smell makes me tingle all over.

My feet slide along the floor feeling bumps and sharp points. I'm pretty certain we're outside. Unease and a tinge of fear crawl up my spine to rest at the back of my neck.

An animal snarls nearby. "Am I in the forest?" My heartbeat picks up triple time at the thought. He could leave me here, and nobody would ever find my body.

He places his mouth near my ear. "Does it matter?"

A claw reaches out and swipes my leg, splitting it open.

"Shield!"

Bastard. Why did I have to get a scarred, twisted trainer with a big ass chip on his shoulder?

An animal slams into me, snarling and swiping with its large paws.

"Shield!"

"It's up," I say tersely. Well, it is now.

"Tell me what you hear," he demands.

"Nothing."

"Do you want to go home or not? Sometimes you have to be your own hero," he says harshly. "Listen and tell me what you hear."

Trying to "see" what's in the dark is amping up my emotions and blocking my other senses. Even though it feels counterintuitive, I close my eyes and slow my breathing. Sounds slowly filter in from the darkness. "A snarl. Cat, maybe. Croaking frog. Wind. Branches swaying and leaves vibrating. Twig snapping." Something whistles near my ear, but I don't know what it is. "You. Breathing and grinding your teeth."

He grunts. "Good. I want you to go on the offensive. Listen to everything around you. Hit when the enemy is close. Use all your senses. Let's go."

Releasing my magic, I push it around my body in an attempt to locate my attacker. A ripple in the dark. Not close enough. I continue to scan the area. My gut tingles, and without thinking, I turn my fist to steel and punch into the darkness on my right. A loud yowl tells me I hit the target.

Another ripple. Closer. I move slowly to the right. Alarm bells go off in my head. I duck and punch hard directly in front of me. Bullseye. Another direct hit.

"Good," he offers in a surly voice. "Let's see how you do fighting me. No shield. I want you to fight through the pain. Concentrate on technique."

I barely have time to register what he says when I hear a hit coming straight at me. I slip to the left to avoid it and plow a lead uppercut into his chin. Exhilarated, I grin.

Thank you, Cormal.

He spent hours teaching me how to box and making me practice with his men. Avoiding close contact is best, but it's not always an option. Boxing can help in tight spaces, and it is something most predators don't expect from a female. According to Cormal, the element of surprise will always be the best weapon.

Weaving, I stay light on my feet and listen for his next move. On the right. I duck and slam a hook into each of his sides. Shaking out my aching fists, I dance back to the left and follow it with a jab, but he blocks it. I fake a jab and hit him with a cross. It glances off his cheekbone. Too slow.

Adding magic to my fists, I make sure each hit counts. Faster and faster, we weave and punch, both of us taking hard hits. Blood seeps from the corner of my throbbing lip. I ignore it. Before it can heal, he plows into it again.

Feet and knees get involved, and soon my legs and hips are bruised and hurting. In a lucky shot, I nail him between the legs, and he mutters a filthy word.

"Council meeting. Got to go," I murmur. Breathing heavily, it's all I can manage to say. "Can… take me back?"

Silence. He must have stopped moving, but I don't dare lower my fists yet.

"Not bad. You think too much, but your gut instincts and technique are good. Use your power to amplify your senses not just your fists," he commands me. "Close your eyes."

Nervous, I close them, wondering what torture he's about to unleash, but instead his strong arms wrap tightly around my body.

"We're back," he informs me, his voice tight with some emotion.

Blinking rapidly against the light, I breathe him in while I let my eyes adjust. Once I can see, I drop my fists and move toward the door.

He hits my back with a ball of air. "Shield!" Thundering over to me, he grips my shoulders. Dark eyes full of anger stare down at me. "Keep your shield up. If you think the enemy won't walk into the palace and grab you, you're mistaken. There are no safe places."

True. I open my mouth to tell him about the spies in the palace, but immediately close it.

"Dismissed," he says curtly.

I walk out of the room and down the hall. Reaching into my pocket for my phone, I find nothing and return to the training room. It's lying on the floor. I grab it. A painful grunt fills the air.

Spinning to the left, I see Madoc and a huge guard sparring, shirts off, circling each other on the mat. Madoc's steel-grey eyes never leave his target.

Fascinated, I can't help but follow his every move. Muscles ripple as he makes tiny adjustments to his stance and balance. Every foot is placed with precision. Easily blocking the other guy's hits, he continues to circle and block. Patiently stalking him, he waits for his opening. If I didn't know any better, I'd think he was a shifter by the way he moves. Maybe a panther with his dark looks. In a blink, he pounces and takes his opponent out.

That was seriously hot. Mentally fanning myself, I can't help but clap.

Madoc swivels to face me, and for the first time, I notice a large, puckered wound in the center of his chest. Caved in, it almost looks like someone punched a hole through his ribcage to his heart.

"What happened?" I ask, horrified at the thought.

"This is what enemies do when they catch you but can't kill you," he states harshly, returning to the match. The guard on the ground gets up and taps out, another jumps in to take his place.

Stunned, I wait for him to elaborate, but he doesn't. Not a word. Throwing my hands in the air, I head back to my room.

IN CAMEL-COLORED PANTS, black silk blouse, and the dreaded heels, I stride confidently into the council room. Ansel moves to close the doors, but I stop him.

"We have a few new members joining us today. Solandis, will you introduce the three you are sponsoring?"

She stands tall by the door. "Lady Fiora of Summer."

The smart, petite woman walks in and takes a seat next to a young man whose mouth is open in shock. He whispers furiously to her, but she blissfully ignores him.

"Lady Lain of Night and Lady Isa of the Woods," Solandis adds, smiling at the two ladies walking into the room. She escorts them to their new seats, then finds her own.

Estrella walks in and announces her three. "Lady Brilla of Spring."

The statuesque blond walks in and winks at Camon, her brother, whose face turns red with anger. She lifts her chin and sashays to her spot.

Estrella's voice is full of laughter, but she holds it in. "Lady Talia of Meadows and Lady Marisol of the Sea." Estrella guides the two ladies to their seats, then sits down beside Solandis.

I wonder if Lady Brilla is aware of what her brother is doing. Catching his eye, I wave a hand. "Lord Camon, the floor is yours."

"I..." he sputters. "Start roll call."

The young man sitting next to Lady Fiora jumps up. "Aren't you going to do something?"

Lord Camon narrows his eyes. "There's nothing we can do. The seats were open, and the new members were sponsored by senior council members. Let's get moving."

Fiora tugs the man down to his seat.

After the proper protocols are followed, the floor opens for updates. Solandis stands. "Once Lord Keir sent me the list of metals and quantities, I met with Fallon. While he no longer serves as the Light Elven Prince, he is heading a new coalition for the Elven population who wish to operate independently from the monarchy. They will supply the gold, silver, and copper to us."

Keir beams at his fellow colleagues. "We have a new supplier."

Solandis throws him a dry look. "They can deliver them next week." She sits down.

Camon pushes to the middle of the floor. "What about the weapons we requested?"

Solandis looks at Keir. "I don't recall seeing the specs on the list you sent over."

He sputters. "I'm sure I put them on there." Pulling out his phone, he scrolls down and holds it up. "If you look, it's the last item on the list. Weapons."

"There are no specs. How am I supposed to request something so vague?" she remarks with a look of disdain.

Keir opens his mouth but closes it when Camon makes a gesture. "Get her the specs." He turns to Solandis. "Solandis, make sure we get the weapons next week. We have a possible situation brewing with the Fire Fae and need to supply our soldiers."

Solandis raises an eyebrow. "*Princess* Solandis. Don't forget your place, Lord Camon. I don't answer to you."

I compress my lips together to stop the smile threatening to break out.

Lord Camon grits his teeth but acknowledges her rebuke. "My apologies, Princess Solandis. Moving along. I propose we send a delegation to Lady Estrella's land to address the fire drake situation. We need to determine if we're looking at an uprising or general defiance and resolve it. Who will volunteer to go?"

Faris raises his hand. "I volunteer." He flashes me an innocent look I don't buy for a second. "I would like to ask Lord

Lorn, who is also familiar with the area, to join me. And Lady Estrella, of course."

The red-haired woman narrows her eyes at Faris but agrees with a nod.

Lord Lorn's bright smile flashes, but I can see its brittleness from here. "I've got several matters to attend to here, but, if necessary, I can make other arrangements."

Faris' satisfied smile grates on my last nerve.

Camon holds up his hand. "It's settled. Lord Faris, Lord Lorn, and Lady Estrella will be assigned to this task. I'll join you as the fourth." He looks at Faris. "I'll make arrangements for us."

I hold up a hand. "Let's not be excessive, Lord Camon. Three is plenty. Besides, I have another task for you. I'll send you the details." Ignoring his outrage, I contemplate the handsome but stern man in front of me. He's the last person I thought would join a rebellion. In fact, he looks more like a hero. Maybe we can make him into one.

CHAPTER TWENTY-ONE

<u>CORMAL</u>

F eet propped up on the balcony, Meri stares sightlessly into the garden below. To a casual observer, they might think she was daydreaming, but the small, elegant fingers drumming on the arm of the chair tells me her mind is a whirlwind.

"Penny for your thoughts," I offer softly.

She turns and sweeps me from head to toe. "That's a very human thing to say. Are you slipping in your old age?"

Somebody is upset with me. A dark chuckle escapes. "Like you, I don't age." Her words from last night are still echoing in my mind. She's right to call me out. We can't continue to dance around each other. Her casual acceptance of the growing distance between us terrified me like nothing else.

Taking off my suit jacket, I roll up my sleeves and take the seat next to her. With a thought, a beer appears in my hand, and I take a long drink of the cold brew.

"My father was the first Druid," I begin, watching her fingers stop their dance. "Viridis, a goddess, gave him her blood along with a dose of her powers. She felt the human race needed their own magic to protect themselves against the supernaturals of the world."

A wry smile twists her lips. "Smart of her. Although, I've come to realize power doesn't equate to strength, and humans are surprisingly resilient to the force we've exerted on them."

I proudly reassess the woman changing right in front of my eyes. "True. Like most supernaturals, the Druids became arrogant and kept the power for themselves. As a result, they almost became extinct while humans flourished."

"So, Daddy became a Druid, but you were born a human without powers. Why didn't you inherit his powers at birth?" she asks, subtly prompting me to continue.

I take another swig. "Four of us were born before he received his powers. He gave us his blood in an attempt to make us Druids, too. It backfired. One brother died instantly. My sister, older brother, and I changed into brùid or beasts. Thankfully, Viridis was able to reverse most of the effects and save me and my sister. My older brother was lost forever."

I stare down at the bottle. Bourbon would have been a better drink for this conversation. "Being a beast changed something fundamental in us. My sister and I were Druid, but darker, hungrier than the others. Our never-ending thirst for power took us into the Underworld, where we immersed ourselves in black magic. Ri' was always smarter than me. She discovered a way to get us more magic than we ever dreamed possible. Unfortunately, a demon overheard and kidnapped her. By the time I caught up to them, he had sold her to another. This happened again and again. Every time I chased a lead, it was too late. The last demon sold her to a dark Fae, and the trail went cold. I never found her." I upend the bottle and finish it off.

Meri settles onto my lap and brushes the unruly hair back from my forehead. "Just when I think you don't know how to love, you show me this side of you." She sighs. "I'm so sorry you haven't been able to find her. But you will. You're the most determined man I know. Look at what you did. Facing insurmountable odds, you went from being a human without magic to a powerful immortal running a massive criminal empire with fingers in every pie. Essentially, you extended your life span and expanded your reach. You did that for her. The odds are in your favor. It's only a matter of time, but I truly believe you will find out what happened to her or find her. Honestly, if she's anything like you, she exceeded her original limitations too, and she's still out there."

Her turquoise eyes stare steadily into mine, her belief in me shining in their depths.

"Thank you." They're the only words I can squeeze out of my tight throat.

Crushing her to me, I hold on to the only thing in this world I want more than to find my sister. She feels so tiny and fragile in my arms. Vulnerable. I tighten my grip even further.

Her fingers stroke the back of my neck and run soothingly through my hair until I find the strength to ease back a little.

"You might not know all the details of my life, but you know me."

She stiffens. "In some ways, yes. The way you think, your determination, and the code you fiercely hold on to despite your darkness. But nothing of your past until tonight. And never how you feel about anything." She stops with a sigh and slides off my lap.

Including how I feel about her. She doesn't say it, but she doesn't have to. For a long time, I couldn't say anything. The pact with Leandra prevented it. While it no longer stops me from telling Meri how I feel about her, why would she believe me? All those years of holding her at a distance... She needs to remember the past for it to all make sense. The truth of us from the beginning, not the middle.

But what if she doesn't remember?

The thought terrifies me. I point to her, then me. "You want words? This, between us, will never go away. It's a forever kind of thing. I don't care if you're queen or pauper or if you have ten other lovers, you're mine. And I'm yours. We can't be undone."

Her eyes narrow, and she crosses her arms across her chest. "Why are you telling me this now? Because I'm finally moving on and finding my own way? Because I'm saving myself? Tell me."

"All those reasons and more, damn it. I need you. Us," I say, the words getting caught in my throat.

She takes a deep, shuddering breath. "You want us? Stop holding me at arm's length. Give me more words. Show me how you feel. Stop appearing and disappearing in my life." Her firm voice tells me she's absolutely serious.

A chance. It's more than I thought she would give me. "Deal. But I fucking want it all—the spark I feel when you give me hell, the tension that's constantly between us, and the future we're still figuring out. And, Meri, there's no running away when things get hard," I warn her, watching her tongue slip out and lick her lips. "Most of all, I want you. Meri. Queen or not. I don't give a fuck."

Pulling her into my lap, I lower my head and capture those tantalizing pink lips. Her breath catches, and the little sound makes me rock hard. I've spent years imagining the sounds she'll make for me. The taste of her on my tongue. A feast for a starving man. No morsel too small to savor. Or devour. My hands roam the curves I've ached to touch for so long.

She turns her head and murmurs, "Stop."

I freeze. "What is it?" My voice is husky with need.

A dry laugh. "I can't believe I'm saying this. For years, I've wanted you. Ached for you." She pauses and shakes her head.

"But I need to know you're serious and in this for good. Also, I don't want to fuck it up with sex." Her finger nervously flicks a button on my shirt.

Picking up her hand, I nibble the tips of her fingers. "No sex. How about if I just taste you? All over."

She shifts restlessly in my lap, and I clench my teeth. "We need time."

I give her a pained nod. "How about we agree to take it slow and don't put any parameters on it? Rules aren't something you or I are good at following, and I don't want any regrets. There are enough of those in our past. What do you say?"

She eyes me warily but nods.

Exhaling loudly, I shift her to one side, but keep my arms around her. "Let's just sit here for a few minutes."

She leans her head back on my shoulder, face turned up to the sky. "Council meeting was interesting. Camon suggested we send a delegation to the fire drakes. He assigned himself to it, but I vetoed it on the grounds of having something else for him to do."

Surprised, I glance down at her. I wonder if this is what she was thinking about earlier. "Do you have a job for him?"

"Maybe," she says hesitantly before explaining the request for both metals and weapons from the light Elves. "Camon only concerned himself with two things today… the delegation to the fire drakes and getting weapons in the hands of our soldiers. He could be covering up his involvement with the Lesser Fae, but I can't help thinking he's playing both sides. Hedging his bets."

"He's High Fae of the Spring Court. I doubt he wants to give up that position, no matter his affiliation with the Lesser Fae," I say, agreeing with her. "I didn't realize the council asked for weapons, too. In all the reconnaissance Kaius and I did, you know what we didn't find?"

She turns and looks up at me. "Weapons. What if we set a trap? Give the council information on where and when, then see who shows up? Even if it isn't Camon, it might reveal another spy in the palace." Small white teeth chew on her bottom lip. "But it could also tip the Lesser Fae into a small skirmish."

"We're not prepared for the Lesser Fae to show themselves yet," I state firmly. "What if you give Camon the job of meeting the weapons shipment and securing them for the palace? If he's playing both sides, he won't want to jeopardize his role or the public's perception of him as High Fae. And since the Lesser Fae need a high-ranking spy in the palace, they won't take the weapons from him."

Much to my dismay, she eases off my lap to pace. "Maybe it will give me an opening to ask about the proposal he put together for the Lesser Fae. They vetoed it, but I think we could resurrect a version of it. Living with Leandra taught me to ask for small favors because they were more likely to get approved. Big stuff was automatically denied. If we could get some of the rights approved, it would make him a hero to the Lesser Fae and allow him to keep his prestigious life as High Fae."

"First things first. We need to set up an exchange for the weapons," I remind her.

She agrees. "Fallon has the shipment ready to go. He's waiting on us. Can you and Kaius find a place that can't be ambushed?"

"Yes. It will also need to be a significant distance from any of the weapon depots we saw on their map," I say, thinking about the possibilities. "Good call on having Solandis stall on the weapons."

She laughs. "That one came from you. Never give your enemy a weapon they can use against you."

Chuckling, I stand up and pull her into my arms. "Speaking of enemies, Leandra found an amulet that lets her hide from hers. It's why I can't find her. Nor can anyone else, including the dark Fae king."

"I didn't know you were searching for her." She studies me for a second, then shrugs. "Let's hope she stays in hiding. The last thing I want is for her to pop her head up and join the Lesser Fae against me." Even as she says the words, I hear the lie in her voice. She wants Leandra to come out of hiding. So do I, but I intend to get to her first.

I pull the map out of the shadows and wave a hand to place it on the table inside. "Come. I'll walk you through the map. You're right. I was trying to protect you, but as queen, you need to know all the details." She follows me inside. "And I'm not leaving tonight. Couch or bed, you decide, but I'm staying."

CHAPTER TWENTY-TWO

<u>MERI</u>

Cormal and Kaius are sitting on the balcony eating breakfast when I wake up the next morning. Impatiently waving a hand over myself, I dress and join them a minute later.

"Kaius," I say coolly. But then I can't help but reach down and give him a fierce hug. "I'm glad to know you're not dead and gone, but you picked a hell of a way to come back." I pick up Cormal's coffee and take a sip. "Just so you're aware... I'm on Solandis' side on this one."

He scowls. "Everyone's on her side. Arden is barely speaking to me. Callyx sent me a nasty text. The cadre won't let me visit The Abbey." His gravelly voice is full of bewilderment and emotion.

"Why did you wait so long?" I can't help but ask him.

"I wanted to be sure she would fall for me, even if I didn't look the same, smell the same, or act the same. Would she feel the same about a stranger?" he admits with a heavy sigh. "When I left this world, I lost everything, including my identity. I was the same person for thousands of years. A high-ranking Chaos demon with the respect of the Underworld. Who was I now? Could she love this person as much as she did 'Vargas'?"

"You're an old fool." Solandis' voice comes from the doorway. Spinning on her treacherously high heels, she strides out of the room.

Kaius jumps up, but I grab his hand. "Before your third date, she confessed she felt deeply for this version of you, the same way she did for Vargas, but she was also excited because it was new. Maybe you need to figure out a way to combine the past with the present. You've both changed during this whole thing."

He leans down and places a loud kiss on my cheek. "Thank you."

I watch him rush out the door after her. Taking Kaius' abandoned seat, I turn my attention to the enigmatic man in front of me. "It's hard to believe he's Vargas."

Cormal studies me for a second. "You don't think I would have trusted just anyone with you, do you?" He flips the map around and points to three marks. "I'm going to check these locations today to see if they will work for our delivery."

Sweet words *and* he told me what he was going to do. Exactly what I told him I needed. Why does it feel weird?

"Um, yeah. Thank you. I'm going to talk to Camon, then check in on the delegation to see when they're leaving."

He takes back his coffee, gives me a hard kiss, and disappears into a shadow. I smile. That felt right.

Hurrying out the door, I text Estrella to find out whether she's available. She texts back to say she was heading to Camon's to get a copy of the Lesser Fae proposal. I tap the phone on my chin as I debate whether to go with her.

"Mind if I join you?"

She appears in the hallway not far from where I'm standing,

much to Ansel's irritation. "Oops, sorry. I didn't think." Her eyes meet mine with a plea for help in their depths.

Laughing, I tap Ansel on the arm. "We're going to Lord Camon's. Do you need to call someone to join us?"

While he's busy locating another guard for our trip, I scan the hallway. "How did you get here?"

"The light beams," she replies with a grin. "I'm too impatient to actually walk anywhere." She cocks her head to the side. "Why did you ask to join me?"

"I actually want a copy of the proposal too," I admit with a shrug. "Maybe there are some things we can do immediately for the Lesser Fae. I won't know until I see what's in the proposal. Also, I have a task for Camon. Is the delegation ready to go?"

There's an unusual glint in her eye. "You would champion the rights of the Lesser Fae?"

"Yes, I would," I state firmly, without giving her my reasons.

She nods several times. "Good. And yes, the delegation is ready to go. We leave tomorrow around noon, which should give us enough time to finalize any last-minute details. The meeting will take place on my land tomorrow evening. Everyone should be back a day or two later." Her hand reaches for mine. "It won't resolve anything, but it should give the council concrete evidence of everything I've been saying."

"Maybe we can use it to springboard the changes," I murmur.

Ansel returns with Garren and Galen.

I can't help but grin at the look on Estrella's face when she sees the remarkably handsome twins.

She laughs. "Mmm. We better get going."

When we get to Camon's, he's waiting for us on the front steps of his cream mansion, wearing a huge frown on his face. "Brina's not feeling well. We'll have to make this short."

Estrella gives him a sympathetic look. "When is the baby due?"

He scowls. "A month. Here's a copy of the proposal." He

thrusts it in Estrella's hand. When I open my mouth, he waves a hand and hands me a second copy. "Is that all?"

I motion for him to follow me several yards away. "I want you to meet the weapons coming from Fallon. Can you do that, or do you need to stay here with Brina?"

He stiffens. "When are they coming?"

"In a couple days," I reveal. "I need to know your answer by the end of today. If you can't do it, I'll send someone else or have Fallon deliver them directly to the palace. It might take longer, but I don't want to trust the shipment to the wrong person." Like a spy who wants to supply the other side with weapons.

"I'll do it," he says abruptly. "Send me the details."

No respect. "Thank you, Lord Camon. I appreciate you taking on this additional duty. I'll take a look at the proposal and think about what we should champion first."

He tilts his head. "First? You're not opposed to the idea of giving the Lesser Fae rights? Nyssa was adamantly against it."

With a wry smile, I shake my head. "The light Fae need to move toward a more enlightened path, don't you think?" Thank you, Solandis, for that little soundbite.

He stares at me for a second. "I do."

"Well, I don't want to keep you. Please give my best to your beautiful wife," I tell him, walking over to join Estrella. "Ready?"

When we get back to the palace, I say goodbye to Estrella and text Lorn.

> Meri: Are you around?

I tap my phone against my palm while I wait for him to respond.

> Lorn: Yes. I'm packing for the trip.

> Meri: Do you mind if I stop by for a few minutes?

Lorn: No. I would love to see you.

Meri: Be there in a minute.

I motion to the three guards. "I need to go to Lorn's for a few minutes. I'm not sure all three of you need to go."

Ansel merely folds his arms across his chest.

"Right. Let's move," I say exasperatedly.

When we get there, I ask Ansel to have Galen and Garren step back a bit. I know he won't do it, but I don't want everyone to overhear my conversation.

Lorn bends down and places a sweet kiss on my lips. "Allandra will be upset she missed you."

I tilt my head at him. "Twisting the truth?" When he looks puzzled, I point up. "Can we go up to the rooftop?"

He motions for me to lead the way, but Ansel shakes his head. Heaving an exasperated sigh, Lorn walks in front of me.

There are plants and dirt scattered everywhere. "Are you getting your moon garden set up?"

A breathtaking smile appears. "I am. The botanical gardener gave me a list of plants most suitable for the rooftop. I built a structure to protect them during the day." He leads me over to a large stand with a retractable roof. "What do you think?"

I peer inside and see several familiar plants from our visit the other night and a few new ones. "Very impressive, and the stand is beautiful. I didn't realize you were so handy."

He shuffles uncomfortably. "Allandra tells me I should get someone to build this stuff, but I like to do it."

"Sometimes we don't need to follow convention," I remind him softly. "Speaking of Allandra, I saw the argument you had with her the other night." His face flushes red with embarrassment. "Look, I don't want to come between you and your sister. Is there something I did or said to make her angry with me?"

He grimaces. "She's insecure. The last time we were here,

Nyssa banished us. I think she's afraid something will happen, and we'll have to leave again. I've tried to reassure her, but sometimes she's all emotion." He picks up my hand and places a kiss in the center of my palm. "I'll talk to her after I get back."

Broad shoulders block the setting sun, allowing me to see his every expression. "Does it feel weird to be going back?"

He stiffens in surprise. "You know? Nyssa buried the trail right after it happened. I didn't realize there were enough clues to follow." Sharp purple eyes study me intently.

Most people don't like it when Cormal finds their secrets. "If you know the right people, you can find the past." I drag a finger through the potting soil on the table. "Is that why you called it reparations? Allandra had a weird reaction to one of my guards one day, and once I found out it was likely the Fire Fae who attacked your home, I put two and two together."

A muscle tics in his jaw. "Yes, the fire drake. She told me. Neither of us has a fondness for the Fire Fae. The things we saw that night will live in our memory forever."

"How did you escape?" I ask, unable to stop thinking about it.

He looks out over the city. "One of the staff showed us a tunnel." His eyes dart to mine, and he pulls me into his arms. "We hid for a long time because we feared they would come after us. Not once did we tell anyone what happened. Our family still owned our previous home in the Autumn Court, so Allandra and I went there and stayed for a while. Eventually, the money ran out, and we came here to ask Nyssa for our inheritance. Not for the land, of course. Just the money. She gave it to us on the condition we leave her court."

Placing my hand on his back, I rub up and down. "I'm sorry for the loss of your parents and home. It sounds horrible. How can you bear to return? Why are you going with the delegation?"

"It feels like all this is coming full circle," he admits, eerily echoing Solandis. "For Faris, too. His brother was killed in the war. His father was killed when he visited Estrella's father right after the war ended. He suspects the Fire Fae, although Estrella's family has always denied it."

Interesting. "What do you think about giving rights to the Lesser Fae?"

He stills. "Something needs to be done or they will continue to rebel." With a pivot, he faces me. "I want to spend some time with you when I return. Just the two of us."

My brow furrows. "Talk to Allandra. We'll see."

Firm lips nibble on my own, then he groans. "As delightful as this is, I need to finish packing, but I'll text you when I get back." Determined purple eyes meet mine, but I don't respond one way or another.

Leaving him standing on the roof, we make our way out.

When I get to the palace this time, I dismiss the guards. "I'm not leaving for the rest of the evening. Right now, I'm going to see Rivan."

Kian replaces Ansel and takes a stand in the hallway outside Rivan's room. When I knock, he opens the door and looks at me in surprise.

I laugh. "I seem to be surprising everybody today. Can we talk?"

As I cross the threshold, I automatically cover the crown on my forehead with another scarf. There's a sketch pad lying open on the table, and I can see the portrait of a beautiful dark-haired woman smiling over her shoulder.

"Is that Sima?"

He runs a charcoal smudged thumb over her face. "No. It's my mother. I thought them all gone." Flipping a page, he shows me his sister, Aeris. His father, Brixton, whose portrait now has an angry slash through it. The last image is obviously a human.

"This is Sima."

Sparkling eyes, windswept long hair, and a tall, lithe body. She looks gorgeous and happy in this picture.

"She is stunning. They're all beautiful." Goddess, I hope I get this right. "You should go. See if they're alive."

He rears back. "It's forbidden. I'm not allowed to seek out my family or any Phoenix." With a single finger, he flips the sketch pad shut and puts it away. "Ever since Cormal told me my father was involved with the coup, I haven't been able to think of anything else. It's driving me mad. I made peace with their absence. Now, it's all stirred up again."

"What if I assign you to the delegation as a guard?"

He scrapes his hair back from his face and holds it there. "They'll know. I know little about the guards here except for their faces. They sure as hell know mine."

One face in particular pops into my mind. "I'll send Tiernan with you. As a guard and fire drake, he should be able to blend into both parties. We'll figure out a way to disguise you with a little glamour."

Hope flashes in his gold eyes. "Why are you doing this?"

I raise an eyebrow. "We're friends, remember?"

He studies me. "Will you go somewhere with me?" He strides over to his small balcony and opens his arms.

I don't even think twice.

"Hold on," he murmurs, his cheek nuzzling mine.

With a shiver, my hands slide around his neck, and I clasp them together. In a flash, we're off, but this time, we shoot straight up into the air. Looking down at the palace, I'm surprised to see how tall it is. I really need to explore my new home.

With a sharp turn, we slide between two turrets and set down on a flat section of roof on the highest story. He releases me. The space is full of stuff. A box with art supplies and sketch pads sits in one corner. Binoculars lie next to it. Several pillows and blankets are tucked up under an eave. A flash of water and a box of food is nearby. Tucked between the tall turrets, it's the perfect hideaway.

"Sometimes, my room becomes unbearable," he admits quietly. "This is the one spot not tainted by her. Over time, I've made this my home. It's not much, but it means a lot to me." A flush spreads across his cheeks. "I wanted you to see it."

"It's wonderful. Safe, secluded, comfortable, and has great views," I tell him. "We moved so much; I never found a place to escape to that I could call my own." I'd have poisoned Leandra for a secret hideaway like this one.

He pulls me over to the blankets on the other side, where he has a telescope set up. "Look through the lens."

For the next hour, he sits behind me and positions and repositions the telescope to show me all his favorite places in the night sky. With his arms around me, I can't help but revel in the warm, magical evening.

"This is wonderful," I murmur. Turning my head, I find pouty lips a breath away from mine, and I ache to lean over and kiss them. To explore this tension between us. I flick my eyes to his.

For an eternity, he stares down at me with longing in his eyes. His hand strokes lightly up and down my arm. The quiet surrounding us and the moonlight shining down make this the perfect moment for a kiss. I know he feels the same because his eyes keep drifting to my lips, but anything that happens between us has to come from him. I can't initiate it. Barely breathing, I wait for him to lean down and show me what he's feeling.

His fist clenches, and the moment is lost.

With a disappointed sigh, I lay my hand on top of his.

"Would you mind taking me back to your room? Kian is standing outside your door. He'll escort me back."

Relief and anger war against each other in his eyes, but he

immediately stands and opens his arms. His wings come out in all their glory.

"Do fire drakes have wings?" I ask, curious about them since I've never seen one.

Rivan's look is smug. "Small, leathery looking things. They can barely fly."

Sensing an old argument, I laugh. "Kind of like a wyvern, then." Those were more common in the Underworld.

"Pretty much," he says snidely, suddenly taking off. Lean hands hold me tightly. One thumb slides soothingly back and forth on a patch of skin between my shirt and pants. "We're back."

"Thank you for showing me your place," I murmur. "It's lovely up there." A little heartbreaking, too. "I'll send Tiernan to you after I speak to him. He can get you a uniform and other items for the trip."

He grimaces. "Never thought I'd be wearing the uniform of a light Fae guard unless I was spying on them." Reaching down, he draws me into his arms for a long hug. "Thank you. This means the world to me."

His lean body feels so good against mine. I can't help but wish I could run my hands over the dips and valleys pressing into me.

"You're welcome," I whisper. "By the way, don't say anything to Tiernan you don't want repeated to the Lesser Fae. I think he might be one of their spies."

Shocked, Rivan raises his head and releases me. "He shouldn't be near you if he's a spy. I'm telling Kaius right now."

"Cormal and Kaius both know. Not about you going on this trip, but they know about Tiernan. We haven't proven it, though. So, maybe he isn't, but I've caught him watching me several times," I explain. When his mouth firms and he begins walking to the door, I grab his elbow. "Stop. Tiernan swore an oath to protect me." I explain what happened the night I left here angry. "I'm safer with him than all the other guards. Well, except Kaius. Did you know he was Vargas?"

A wary look crosses his face. "Cormal told me, but I was sworn to secrecy."

All these men need to have their head examined. "It's fine. Solandis might not be okay with you knowing before her, so I wouldn't mention it." I grip his arm. "Be careful. Don't take any unnecessary chances out there, okay?"

He laughs until he sees I'm serious. "I might not be the warrior I once was, but I'm quite capable of taking care of myself. You be careful here, got it?"

CHAPTER TWENTY-THREE

Cormal's waiting in my room when I finally return. "Where have you been?"

"With Rivan," I tell him, taking off my shoes and wiggling my toes. Changing clothes takes little thought, and I walk over to the couch and sit down with a sigh. "Camon agreed to meet the shipment and make sure it gets to the palace. Did you know his wife is pregnant?"

Cormal picks up my foot and begins to massage it. Surprised, I look up, but he's staring off into the distance. Thinking. Always thinking.

"Interesting. I wonder if that's why he's playing both sides. It would explain a lot. So does this." He puts down my foot and holds up a sheath of papers. "His proposal."

"I haven't had a chance to read it. What does it say?" I ask, laying my head on the back of the sofa.

"It's terrifying how few rights the Lesser Fae have if this is the proposal." Cormal's voice is full of anger. "They're not recognized by the law as having any rights. They cannot own land. They are not guaranteed freedom from slavery, nor do they have the right not to be tortured or persecuted. They cannot change locations without permission. They cannot gather or serve in law enforcement. They can be tried without cause by any law enforcement in the land without a trial. The list goes on and on."

He tosses the papers down on the table, and they scatter like the wind. "Lucifer said he couldn't support a fight against them, and I fully understand why. It's atrocious. Everyone talks about how enlightened the light Fae are compared to the rest of the supernatural, but they're not. The Underworld exceeds this kingdom on so many levels."

A startled look crosses his face, then a scowl. "Fuck. I owe Lucifer an apology. I berated him for not giving our citizens what they need, but they have it a hell of a lot better than most of the population here. The Lesser Fae outnumber the aristocratic Fae by at least twenty to one, yet they have almost nothing." He picks up the other foot.

"Solandis said her father thought the same years ago. He was in discussions with the Fire Fae when he and her mother were killed by the dark Fae," I say tiredly.

Yawning, I smile at the fierce look on his face. Few people know this, but Cormal champions the underdog. He hates to see people with little means trod upon or taken advantage of. It's one of the things I like most about him.

"You look tired. Go to bed. I need to go into my office and catch up on stuff. And I want to pull together additional security and a plan for the weapons shipment," he says gruffly, standing.

When he holds out his hand, I take it and get up. "Ok. Let me know what you're thinking on timing and location so I can pass it on to Camon."

Standing next to him, my body instinctively brushes his, needing to be as close as possible. I look up into his blue eyes while I stand on tiptoe to kiss his firm mouth for several long seconds. Slowly releasing his lips, I draw back and wink.

"I'm dying a slow death from the few scraps you're doling out," he drawls. "But I kind of like not rushing. It gives me time to think of all the things I'm going to do when I finally claim every delectable inch of you."

Images flow into my mind, making my eyes widen, and heat pools between my legs. "Cormal..." I swallow. "Words. Feelings. Not sex." I can't even utter a coherent sentence.

He presses up against me. "You don't get to dictate the words I give you and when. Right now, all I want to do is lay you beneath me and fuck you until neither of us can think about anything but each other."

The sound of a throat clearing has me stepping back from temptation. Just in time, too. I was teetering on the edge. "Hello, Eris."

She narrows her eyes at Cormal. "Staying or going? I haven't got all night."

A strangled chuckle emerges from his throat. "Going. Take care of her." He gives me a hard kiss full of intent and slides another image into my brain.

Eris waves him out and sweeps around the room like a whirlwind. The only time I see her pause is when she looks at the stack of papers sitting on the table. An expression of hope crosses her face.

Solandis voice echoes in my mind. *Brownies pretty much run this place.*

"How many brownies are there in the palace?" I ask Eris.

She squints as her mouth moves soundlessly. "One hundred and thirty-seven. Why?"

"And how many Lesser Fae in total?"

"Mixed bloods too?" she asks.

"Any who would be impacted by the proposal on the table," I answer, as it is the only one I think matters.

It takes her a few minutes. "Six hundred and twelve."

My stomach churns, but I have to ask this question. Ever since I heard Cormal mention it, I couldn't think of anything else. "Are any enslaved?"

She shakes her head. "King Arles freed everyone before the Fire Fae Rebellion."

King Arles was Solandis' father.

Thank the goddess.

She sees the relief on my face and makes a correction. "He freed everyone in the palace. Lesser Fae in the palace are treated better than most households in the kingdom. Some are not as lucky as us."

Her words rebound in my head. "I see." That has to be the first thing changed.

"Thank you, Eris, for the information," I tell her. "On a separate note, I need to get money in the morning. Who do I see?"

Hatred glitters in her eyes. "Lord Keir manages the accounts."

"The one on the council?" I ask with a frown, picturing the extremely tall Fae whose face seems to be permanently set in disdain.

She nods.

"Does he have an office here? Is it close?"

Eris waves her tiny hand, and a map appears next to the proposal on the table. "He lives on one of the upper floors. His office is next to his rooms." She whips a hand around and dresses me in my pajamas. "Enough jabbering. I've got things to do."

She disappears.

I didn't even get a chance to give her the chocolate I got for her.

MY BRAIN IS FIRING out a to do list the next morning when Kaius, Solandis, and Cormal arrive. Eris immediately appears with several helpers and more breakfast. She's so quick, even Cormal raises an impressed eyebrow.

I watch Solandis and Kaius for clues they've patched things up. They're silently orbiting around each other and avoiding eye contact. Guess it's going well. Yesterday, they couldn't even be in the same room.

Solandis sits next to me, and I notice she's wearing some type of skintight synthetic jumpsuit. "What is this?"

"Fae armor. Lightweight, with a nearly impenetrable fabric. It protects me against most weapons and some spells. I gave my original suit to Arden, but Kaius showed up with this one today and insisted I wear it," she informs me, rubbing a hand down her arm. She slides a sideways glance at the man and purses her lips.

I hover a hand over her arm, and she nods. Gliding it across the suit, the tight weave of the fabric reminds me of a snake's skin.

"How do I get one?"

"Have Eris order you one," she tells me.

"Where are we going?" I ask, taking a bite of the lightly buttered toast on my plate. "I'll have to let Madoc know I need to postpone. We're supposed to meet for training in an hour."

Cormal digs into his breakfast. "You're going to training. We're meeting Fallon today." He looks up and silently nods at the question in my eyes. "Camon will still accept official delivery tomorrow."

Basically, they're going to take possession of the weapons to safeguard them. Camon will still believe he's officially accepting them. If anything goes wrong, I have an airtight alibi. "Good idea." In the original plan, we were hedging our bets he wouldn't jeopardize his position, but it was risky.

I finish my coffee and kiss Solandis on the cheek. "Be careful." Hurrying to the door, I abruptly stop when Cormal appears in front of me.

"Not worried about my safety?" he asks with a dark chuckle.

I give him a droll look. Most people run when they see him, and his reputation is well earned. "Why? Are you getting soft in your old age?"

"Anything but," he snaps back.

Pulling me to him, he swoops down and takes my lips with his. Hard and demanding, he steals every thought from my head and replaces it with images from his. Drowning in desire, all I want to do is toss caution out the window. I wish I knew how he was doing this. It would be fun to turn the tables on him.

My hands caress the firm chest under the silk button-down shirt. I'd start here, caressing his pecs. A smattering of dark hair covers them, then narrows into a single line below his waist. Cut abs made for drooling, which he maintains the old-fashioned way—fighting in a ring. He once said his father was a warrior. I believe it. The man has impeccable genes.

He tears his mouth from mine in astonishment. "You just mimicked my power. I could see everything you were picturing. The power is still inside you."

Intrigued, I test his theory, picturing my hand sliding down the delectable trail and inside his pants.

He looks down and my eyes follow. Long and hard, he's clearly outlined in the combat pants he's wearing. "You're killing me."

"You started it," I say breathlessly.

Cormal chuckles. "I thought pictures would be better than words."

My whole body is flushed and aroused from our little game. "Oh, it is."

Satisfaction settles on his face. "We should be back in three hours."

"The delegation leaves about an hour after," I remind him. "Be careful."

He moves, and I head to the door again.

When I look back, all three are finishing their breakfast. We almost look like a family. A powerful, dangerous one with a complete disregard for anyone's rules but our own, but I guess everybody has to start somewhere.

I knock on an ornate door fancier than the one leading to my bedroom.

It opens and a small voice greets me. "Your majesty. What an honor."

Following the sound down, I find a beautiful brownie with pink hair. "Hello. What is your name?"

"Vela, don't keep the queen waiting," a harsh voice reprimands her.

She flushes. "Sorry. Please come in."

"Vela is a beautiful name," I say with a smile. Stepping into the office, I have to literally pick my jaw off the floor. It's elaborate and expensive. Half the room is gilded in gold and jewels. "Wow. This is quite the office."

He preens. "Thank you. Have a seat."

"Why don't you stand and show me the respect I deserve as your queen first?" I remark with a pleasant smile pasted on my face. I've met men like him my whole life. Give them an important job and a little power, and they feel entitled to take the rest.

Flustered, he stands and bows. "Your Majesty."

I toy with the idea of sitting in his chair but dismiss it. There isn't time for theatrics. I take a seat in front of his desk. "You may sit." When he does, I launch into the reason I'm here. "I need money."

And there it is. The look of disdain he wears in the council meeting. "Queens don't carry money. Have all bills sent to the palace, and I'll have my staff process them."

"And since I don't want to have to come back here regularly, let's just start with a sack full of gold coins, one of silver, a bag of small diamonds, and one with larger carats too. Or should I get a bag of mixed jewels? You know what… All of it," I state firmly. "Well, what are you waiting for?"

He flashes me a condescending smile. "It's not how it's done. I manage the finances for the palace. Everybody knows to send the bills here."

I look around his office again. "Obviously, there's some misappropriation going on. If the steward of my castle has a better office than mine, it's a clear sign someone is abusing his power."

He jumps up and leans over his desk. "How dare you!"

Tiernan opens the door, sword drawn, and scans the room. "Is everything okay, Queen Merindah?"

"It's fine. We're having a slightly heated argument, but I think Keir's going to understand very quickly who's in charge here," I assure him.

Tiernan closes the door.

"Now, let's get back my request. Money. Now." Power fills the room along with the command to do my bidding.

Outraged, he angrily motions to Vela.

Eyes wide, she hurries to get what I need and deposits it at my feet.

With a wave of my hand, I send it to my bedroom.

"Thank you. It is my understanding that there are six hundred and twelve Lesser Fae here. Is that correct?" I sit back and wait for him to answer my question. He jerks his chin. "Good. What do we pay them?"

It occurred to me when Eris was speaking that she said they had it better than most because they were free.

He sputters. "We give them food, room and board, medical care, and time off."

Honestly, it's not bad. More than most are given in the Underworld, probably in this kingdom too. "Let's add a small weekly wage. Draw up some numbers and present them to me in two days."

His face twists into a puzzled expression. "Why? They can conjure their clothing, bedding, and other stuff."

I stand and lean over his desk. "They might want to save and buy some land. Who cares what they do with it? It will be their money. Also, when you bring me the numbers, let's go over the palace budget and assets. Okay?"

Tired of seeing his face, I dismiss him and head toward the door. Along the way, I swirl a finger at different objects until the office resembles its original, more utilitarian state.

"Sell the things in the hallway. I'm sure they will pay for the first week's wages."

Vela's eyes are a combination of terror and wonder. She curtsies as I pass. "Your Majesty."

An ugly thought occurs to me. "Keir. If you mistreat any of your staff, I will remove you from your position. Do you understand? I've got eyes and ears everywhere." I slam out of the office and down the hallway filled with treasures from his office, Tiernan by my side. "Pompous asshole."

Tiernan coughs. "Thank you for the wage."

I blink. Tiernan is mixed. "I have another job for you. Have you heard about the delegation going to speak with the fire drakes?"

His jaw tightens. "Yes."

I grab the nearest handle and open it to find a small bathroom. "Here." Waving him in, I close it and seal the room. "This is strictly confidential. Got it? I'm sending Rivan with the delegation as a guard. You're going with him. While you are there, I want you to find a way to the lands where the phoenix live. He needs to find out if more of his family is alive, not just his father. You must return with the delegation. Timing will be really tight. Can you do this?"

"What if Rivan doesn't want to return?"

"Unfortunately, due to the nature of the treaty, he has no choice," I state firmly. But now that I think about it, what does it actually say? He believes he has no choice, but who has even looked at the document since it was signed twenty-eight hundred years ago?

I stare at him, waiting for an answer.

He nods slowly. "I'll do it."

Relief makes my knees weak. "Good." I hold my palm out and the bag of gold coins I just received from Keir appears. "Here. You might need to use this for bribes or whatever. He'll need a uniform and a bit of glamour to disguise his face. Oh, and make sure to include a hat to hide his distinctive hair. If you need anything else, let me know before you leave." I glance at my phone. "Let's go. I have two minutes to get to training, and Madoc isn't someone you want to piss off."

He doesn't reply, but by the way he ushers me out the door, he agrees.

CHAPTER TWENTY-FOUR

<u>MERI</u>

"You're late," Madoc snarls in my face. "Save it. I heard. Doling out wages like a fairy godmother." He scoffs. "Next you'll be championing the Lesser Fae." Grey eyes are blank but watchful. A fireball hits the shield around me. "Somebody's making progress."

I stick out my tongue, then pale. *Shit!* Why do I let my impulses lead me astray? Every single time. Peering up at the massive man, I see the tiniest curl to his mouth, and it practically ruins me. I shiver, wanting to see more, then mentally slap myself. Stop ogling the beast. It will pick its teeth with your bones.

"Now that you mention it. I am."

A puzzled expression crosses his face.

"Championing the Lesser Fae."

He tilts his head to the side. "Is this to prevent a coup?"

Surprised to hear the word, I quickly look around to see if anyone's listening. "Are you one of their spies?"

His mouth twists. "Hardly. The shadows whisper to me. Lately, they've been saying all kinds of interesting things."

"At first, I just wanted to stop the coup, but when I found out how little they have, it infuriated me. They're not recognized by the law or government in this kingdom. No rights mean they're at the whimsy of another," I say, infuriated with the Fae's greediness and totalitarian system. "Leandra controlled my life, but the only one holding me back from freedom was me. Well, that and having the power to defend myself."

He reaches over and grasps my arms. "Leandra who?"

Oh, shit. Don't tell me this is another one of her victims.

"Leandra was my guardian. She's an evil bitch sorceress who screwed everyone she met, including me. So, if she did something to you, don't take it out on me," I urge him, staring nervously at the deep scars on his face. I start praying to every goddess I know that it wasn't her who did that to him.

His lip curls. "No, she didn't scar my face. I have my own monsters in my past." He places my palm on his chest exactly where I saw the puckered scar. "She did this to me. Reached in with her power and took something of mine. It's irreplaceable, and I'm going to hunt her down until I get it back."

That sounds familiar. I swallow the hard lump in my throat. "A couple of weeks ago, the dark Fae king sent a messenger to me with almost the exact same message. He's hunting Leandra because she stole something from him. He also threatened to end me if I didn't deliver her to him, but..."

Holding me against the wall, he leans in threateningly. "You know where she is?"

Expanding my shield, I push against him until I can breathe, then use magic to make my knee hard as stone and thrust it up into his dick.

"Shield," I hiss at him, barely able to speak through the anger coursing through me.

He bends over and grunts a few times, clearly in severe pain.

"Nobody knows where she is. Apparently, she traded information to a goddess for an amulet to hide her from her enemies," I snidely inform him. Thoroughly done with jerks today, I shove him to the mat. "I put up with your bullshit in training because it's the only way I'll get good enough to kill Leandra. But don't you ever, ever threaten me again."

Tiernan's round eyes move from Madoc to me. Hurrying to the door, he opens It for me to stride out in my most queenly strut.

"Fucking asshole," I spit out, even though Madoc can't hear me.

Out of nowhere, ice appears beneath my feet, and I slide across the hall. Then, a cloud of ice shards shatters against the shield I have wrapped tight around me. Damn. Madoc was right. The palace isn't safe.

Gliding on air, our enemy moves fast. Feeding the ice beneath our feet until we can barely move, it continues to throw missiles at us. Tiernan uses his fire to melt the ice, but it's a losing battle.

He knows it's going to reach us before we can escape. Concentrating on the ice under my feet, he shouts for me to run and pulls his sword. I glance at the excessively tall deer creature thing-y with claws the size of my hands that is bearing down on us.

"What is it?" I whisper, staring at the horns protruding from its head and the hide barely covering its bones. Dark, fathomless eyes lock on me.

"A wendigo. Fire is the only element that can injure it, but you need faery fire to kill it," he murmurs, lighting his sword with a single word. "Go. Get to safety. Send help back for me."

Really angry, I make two fists and light them up the same

way I did in training that day. Looking at the wendigo, I sneer. "If you're stupid enough to attack me in my palace, come and get me. I'm not easy to kill."

Tiernan runs a bare hand through the fire on my arms. "It's not faery fire, but it will help hold him off."

At full force, it attacks. Tiernan stabs it several times with his flaming sword, but the ugly creature just shrugs it off. While it's occupied watching his sword, Tiernan opens his mouth and a stream of fire spews out of his mouth.

The wendigo shrieks and backs away. Then disappears.

It reappears in front of me. Using magic to build my strength and make my fire extra hot, I use a series of jabs and crosses to punch into his hide. Never letting up, I continue to hit him until he decreases in size and cowers against the wall.

It says something to me. I step closer and hear a shout from Tiernan. The wendigo bares sharp, jagged teeth and rises up three times the size he was a minute ago. *Damn. I thought I had him.* Raising my fists, I stare him in the eye.

"Bring it on, Bones."

A fist reaches out of the shadow and grabs the wendigo around the neck. Eerie blue green fire flows in its mouth and down its throat, burning it from the inside out, until there's nothing but ash. Stepping back from the shadow, I automatically raise my fists, determined not to go down against this new enemy without a fight.

Madoc steps out of the shadow. "Remind me during our next lesson to go over faery fire with you." His eyes scan me from head to toe. Satisfied I'm not harmed, he awkwardly clears his throat. "Sorry about earlier." He pauses. "I'm going to check into something. I'll be back in a few days. Remember your shield." Melting into the shadow behind him, he disappears.

That was a sorry excuse for an apology. I mean, for a man who barely speaks except to yell "Shield!" at me all the damn time, it's kind of a surprise I got that much out of him, but he could have done better.

Tiernan touches my shoulder, and I bring my hands up. He quickly steps back, hands raised.

"Sorry, I'm a little jumpy," I explain. See, that is how you apologize. "Let's go."

Tiernan is really quiet on the way back.

"Everything okay? It's gone, right? It won't come back?" I ask, needing a little reassurance.

He shakes his head a few times. "Sorry. It's gone. Faery fire obliterates most things. I've only seen it a couple of times, mostly when a phoenix resurrects."

"Hmm. I wonder why Madoc thinks I'll have the power?" I muse. Here I thought Cormal was tough. Madoc is a beast.

"All those with royal blood can wield it," he says with a shrug. "Solandis and a few others at court who can trace their lineage to the first Fae king. As Nyssa's daughter, there isn't any reason you wouldn't have it."

Dread fills me. Madoc wields it. He seems to be shrouded in secrecy, knows Leandra, and she stole something invaluable from him. *Shit.* I really need to find a picture of the dark Fae king.

WHEN WE GET BACK to my room, Tiernan reports the attack to Ansel, who listens with a tight lip and fierce expression. "Good job. I'll give Kaius your brief when he returns. Go grab your stuff. The delegation leaves in an hour."

Tiernan subtly dips his chin at me and leaves.

Ansel opens the door with sword drawn to check the room, but it's empty.

"Do you happen to have a picture of the dark Fae king?" I ask him.

His eyes widen. "Why? Do you think the wendigo was sent by him?"

"Well, I didn't, but now I do!" I exclaim with dismay. "Picture?"

"I've never seen him, but I'll find a picture for you," he assures me with a determined look on his face.

"Thanks," I say, entering my bedroom and closing the door. My shaky knees get me to the couch before they give out. Lying there, I stare at the ceiling while I wait for Cormal to return.

Forty-five minutes later, there's a knock at the door. I sit up and stare at the door but can't bring myself to say anything.

"The delegation leaves in fifteen minutes," Ansel reminds me. "Are you almost ready to go?"

Pulling out my phone, I confirm the time. "I'll be ready in five." Where are Cormal, Solandis, and Kaius? They should have been back by now.

CHAPTER TWENTY-FIVE

CORMAL

Fallon and the shipment of weapons arrive at the portal right on time. The dark Elven warrior strides confidently through, along with his right-hand man, Garrett. Both lethal-looking, they scan the horizon to make sure it's safe before the delivery starts. Crates of weapons start sliding into view one at a time. Valerian, massive in his human form, carries the last box with him when he steps into this kingdom.

Clasping arms with Fallon, I eye the number of crates with some worry. "Thanks for delivering early. We're trying to avoid trouble on this end and keep Meri away from the delivery. With her in training right now, it gives her the perfect alibi." I look at Solandis. "Is this the amount you ordered?"

She steps forward to give Fallon and Valerian a hug. "Hello, Garrett." She opens one crate, then another. "This is considerably more than the amount I requested."

Surprised, Fallon shakes his head. "We received a second email from you with an additional order of three more crates."

Solandis frowns and motions to Kaius. "I didn't order more weapons, which means someone has interfered with the shipment count. Could Camon have hacked into my email and ordered extra to give to the Lesser Fae?"

Kaius lifts his shoulder. "Anything's possible. I haven't seen him around lately, though."

Fallon swears loudly. "I should have confirmed it with you by phone. It never occurred to me someone would have added to the order." He shares a look with Valerian. "We asked Arden and the rest of the cadre to come in via a portal about a mile down the road to serve as back-up. If the delivery went smoothly, nobody would know we were here. Looks like it was the right call. We'll escort you and the weapons all the way to the palace."

The back of my neck tingles, and I hold up a finger. "Is there any way to call the cadre to this spot?"

Fallon nods. "I can text Theron. Why?" His eyes dart behind me and he quickly picks up his phone, then stops. "No service."

Kaius takes up position between Solandis and the ridge behind us. "Any other way to reach them? We're going to need back-up."

I swivel around and start reaching into the shadows to gather knives and throwing stars to line my pockets. Looking at the small army coming down the hill, I also grab a pair of xiphos sheathed in their scabbard and sling those around my chest counter to each other.

Fallon unsheathes his sword and tersely calls out to Valerian. "Up to you, big guy." Garrett and he take a stand to the right.

Solandis moves out from behind Vargas to his left. "Look how they move, like well-trained soldiers." She pulls her hood up and over until her entire head and face are covered. "Leader looks to be female. She's mine." Magic sparks along her fingertips.

Kaius gives her a hard look. "Don't take any fucking risks. Hit hard and take them down immediately. You can play another time."

A sultry laugh comes from the hood. "You used to be more fun. Don't die on me. Or I won't forgive you this time."

I choke on her reply. Vargas really can't die anymore. It's a startling thought.

"They're almost here!" I shout, taking a stance.

"Cover your ears!" Fallon shouts a second later.

Using magic to muffle the sound, I hear a massive roar behind me. It echoes across the land for several miles, clearly far enough to be heard by the rest of the cadre. Glancing back, I watch Valerian launch into the sky.

Uncovering my ears, the enemy's shouts to target the dragon with the archers comes in loud and clear. My eyes scan for bows along the ridge. There. Slipping into a shadow, I come out the other side and throw three stars, taking down the archers. Taking their heads eliminates them from the field.

Screams from below filter up the hill to me. I see Valerian's shadow magic strangling men on the ground. Several soldiers immediately change into flying creatures similar to gargoyles and take to the air in squadron formation to fight against him.

Arrows launch into the air from farther along the ridge. Time to go. I step into a shadow and come out near another group of archers. Unfortunately, this time, they're waiting for me. Dodging the knives I throw, two of them pull their swords to advance on me while the other two continue to rain down arrows on the four below.

Gripping the xiphos, I draw them from their sheaths and smoothly spin them around until the weight is perfect. A small incantation adds a healing spell to my shield. I launch myself at them, preferring to attack than defend, and soon we're engaged, swords clashing against each other. Ambidextrous, I slice into one on the left and block his friend's downward blow on the right. The battle is fair and almost evenly matched. Too bad I don't play nice.

I whisper to the shadow on my right to blind my opponent, then swiftly turn to the left to fully concentrate on taking this soldier out. Screams come from behind me, and the soldier in front darts a glance at his friend. It's the last thing he ever sees. I slice through his neck and cut off his head.

The blind soldier behind me swings his sword wildly and catches my side with the tip. Clenching my teeth against the pain, I turn and finish him off. The corner of my eye catches an object moving toward me. I turn.

A hand comes out of nowhere and swipes the arrow from the air. "Need some assistance, Cormal?" Daire flashes his fangs and, in a blink, sinks them into the archer.

The remaining archer stares in horror at the vampire who's suddenly joined the fight, which gives me the perfect opportunity to slip behind him and take his head.

From this vantage point, I see several soldiers circling Solandis. Kaius does, too, but the enemy has him surrounded, and he can't get to her.

Suddenly, a gold lasso of magic captures the soldiers advancing on Solandis and slices them in half. Astor bows with a flourish toward Solandis. He turns and kisses the woman in Fae armor standing beside him, then disappears in a cloud of smoke. He reappears near Kaius and releases his wild magic on those soldiers.

"Arden," Daire explains, a possessive smile curling his lips as his icy blue eyes stare down at the lady Astor just kissed. "Don't get killed." In a blur, he's gone. I see a sword slash a few times, and soldiers fall, but it's hard to follow his vampiric speed.

Theron's dual swords spin in a vicious and intricate dance. Set up within a circle of ice in the center of the field, he takes out the enemy two and three at a time. A light glints on the ridge above him, and I immediately head toward it. Whatever it is, the shining sun bouncing off it tells me it's big.

Riding the shadows, I get there in record time, but it's still too late to stop the weapon from discharging its magic. Big as a cannon, there isn't time to figure out what it does.

"Incoming!" I scream. "Shields!"

The cadre, Kaius, and Solandis throw bubbles up to shield themselves. Magic rains down on top of them, sparking against the outer shells.

When it stops, Astor moves to Arden and covers her with his shield. She slices her hand with a small knife, and her lips begin to move. The second time the cannon goes off, snow rains down on the land.

I grip my xiphos and move to take down the crew manning the cannon. Astor appears next to me blowing dust in their faces. I laugh until I see death staring from their eyes.

"Nice trick. Remind me to ask you for the recipe."

A dark chuckle is all I get in response. "Like you, my secrets are my own. Make up your own recipe."

Once the crew is down, I peel back my shirt and look at the wound. It's healing. Slowly. The Fae magic must be interfering with mine. I'll have to adjust the spell to account for the potential time lapse.

"Have Daire heal you," Astor suggests, dipping his chin at my shirt. Using crackling energy, he dismantles the cannon. "Later." He heads down the hill.

Solandis and the female leader are battling it out in a cloud of elements. All the plant life around them is dead. Both women attack and counter smoothly. Their moves are almost identical, as if they were trained by the same teacher. They're almost evenly matched, but Solandis' royal blood lends an extra level of power to her hits. She catches the leader on the left side in a brutal strike, and I hear her answering scream.

Two soldiers look up at the sound and rush to her. Yelling retreat at the top of their lungs, they grab the leader just as she starts to fall. Soldiers disappear into individual port holes everywhere, leaving their dead behind.

I quickly assess everyone. A few wounds, but nothing major. Garrett's sporting a large gash down his face. Fallon's wearing a couple on his leg. Valerian lands and transforms into his human form. There's not a scratch on him. Astor's grinning. Kaius has the most wounds, but Daire's already healing them.

Arden and Solandis pull down their hoods. They don't have a scratch on them. Impressive armor. I need to make sure Meri gets one of those suits.

Coming out of a shadow at the bottom of the hill, I dodge a line of magic. "It's Cormal."

Arden smirks. "I know. I missed. On purpose."

Fallon strides toward me, full of fury. "What the hell? I thought you said it was secure. If we hadn't thought to bring back-up, we would have been in serious trouble."

Kaius comes to stand next to me. "Only the three of us knew the location and time." He points to Solandis, himself, and me. "Had to be on your end."

"What about Meri?" Arden asks, wrapping her arm around Solandis' waist.

"We were going to secure the weapons first, then give her a second location and time to share with Camon," I inform her, shaking my head. "The whole thing reeks. Extra weapons. A small army. Check things out on your end."

Theron's lip compress. "We will. I don't like the idea of someone spying on us in our own home, and I want to rule it out as soon as possible."

Kaius winks at Solandis.

She pulls back her arm and creates a huge portal directly into the weapons depot at the palace. "We'll store them here."

We quickly work to get the crates inside while Arden stands

watch. Once the last one is in, I create a wall of shadows to hide them. "Nobody will even know they're here."

"Clever," Fallon remarks. He turns to the cadre. "Home?"

Arden hugs Solandis tightly. "Most of us don't get a second chance." She gives her a pointed look, then walks over to Kaius. "I miss your face, old man. And sparring with you. Come for a visit soon and bring Solandis." She wraps him in a fierce hug.

She turns to me and holds her hand to my side. Healing energy knits the wound back together instantly. "Give Meri a hug from me. I've been trying to stay away to let them patch things up." She uses her head to indicate Solandis and Kaius. "If you need us, call."

Moments later, they're gone. I glance at my watch. We're later than we thought by at least an hour. The delegation should be leaving right about now.

CHAPTER TWENTY-SIX

Not wanting to miss the delegation's departure, I quickly change into proper clothes, and leave a note for Cormal to let him know I'll be back soon.

When Ansel and I get to the room, they're all standing together. Lorn, Faris, and Estrella. Camon is giving them last-minute instructions. Ten guards enter and fan out beside them.

Lorn gives me a determined look, then enters the portal with Faris.

Estrella walks slowly into the portal. I frown, wondering what's wrong when I see the slight limp in her left leg.

The guards follow her. Rivan looks back when he enters and meets my eyes. Then he's gone too.

I turn to Camon. "Sorry, I don't have any information on the delivery. Hopefully, I will have the info soon. I did have a chance to look at your proposal. I think we need to tackle slavery first. One right with a huge impact. Everything else is a moot point unless we establish their right to freedom. Plus, we'll need the army to reinforce it. What do you think?"

His bright green eyes blink. "You're right. I was trying to do too much at once. I'll draft up a new proposal that focuses solely on their right to be free."

"Thanks," I murmur.

He turns to leave but stops in the doorway. "I heard you ordered Keir to give the Lesser Fae in the palace a wage. Is that true?"

"It is," I reply firmly. "Why?"

"Watch your back. There are more aristocratic Fae fighting to keep the status quo than there are to change it," he remarks quietly before leaving.

CORMAL, Solandis, and Kaius walk into the room minutes after I return, reeking of magic and sweat. Cormal walks over, drags me into his arms, and kisses the hell out of me. "We were ambushed. Thankfully, Fallon brought back-up. The enemy wasn't prepared to face all of us. Once the leader was hit, the rest fled. We brought the weapons to the palace and hid them."

The blood soaking his shirt has me scrambling to see how bad he's hit, but he stops me. "Arden healed me. For some reason, my spell isn't working very quickly here."

I pull out of his arms and head to Solandis to give her a hug. She squeezes me twice. "One is from Arden." She drops into a nearby chair and takes a long drink of water. "Thankfully, Fallon thought to bring the entire cadre with him, including Arden." She pauses. "I've never seen anything like it. The six of them alone can take out a small army. No wonder they fit so well together. They're all fierce warriors."

"So are you, my love," Kaius tells her. "I always forget how much power you wield until I see you in action." He kisses his fingers. "Magnificent."

She rolls her eyes and turns away from him, but I see the twinkle in her eye.

I move to Kaius, who is covered in dried blood, and gently hug him. "All healed?"

He nods.

"How did they know the location? I didn't even know it," I wonder. Plopping down beside Cormal, I take his bourbon from him and take a sip.

"Somebody must be monitoring the portal alerts," Solandis guesses.

Cormal shakes his head. "I accounted for that in my planning. There wasn't enough time for them to get an army there. It has to be on the cadre's side."

Kaius nods his head in agreement. "Hello." He answers the phone before it finishes the first ring. He rubs his hand over his head while he listens to the person on the other end. When he hangs up, he fills us in. "That was Theron. A Fae female entered The Abbey earlier today. She glamoured herself to look like Maya, the club manager. He's sending over a picture." The phone pings. He looks down and curses, then holds it out to Solandis, not Cormal.

She lifts an eyebrow and takes it from him. Sitting up, she expands the image. "It's Estrella."

"Wait, Estrella glamoured herself to get the information on the delivery?" I question her. When she nods, I wince. "She was limping when she went into the portal earlier."

Solandis lifts her chin. "Left side?" she asks quietly. When I nod, she closes her eyes as if she's in pain. "Estrella must have been the leader I fought. But why? I don't understand. How would she even know the delivery was coming?"

I raise a finger. "Me. I asked Camon to meet the shipment. She was standing nearby. I thought I was far enough away."

"She must have used the light beams to listen," Solandis explains. "As a kid, she used to listen to others' conversations using the light. Looks like she hasn't outgrown that habit." She shakes her head back and forth. "She must have known she was fighting me, but once there, she couldn't back down. I don't understand why she would commit treason. Why does she need the weapons? Do you think the fire drakes have her that scared?"

"Maybe," I say, thinking of her visit to Camon. "Unfortunately, we can't interrupt the delegation. The negotiations are too delicate. We'll have to speak to her when she returns."

Solandis elegantly snorts. "I'm going to interrogate her, not have a polite conversation. Depending on her answers, she could lose everything. The council will strip her of all her assets."

A knock at the door has us all looking at each other. I can't help but laugh. When Cormal sends me a questioning glance, I shrug. It's too long to explain.

Kaius answers the door, then steps out. He comes back with a ferocious scowl on his face. Crossing his arms, he glares at me. "When were you going to tell us you were attacked today?"

Cormal grabs my arm. "What the hell happened?"

I jerk my arm from his.

Kaius launches into the report Ansel just gave him.

"Let me get this straight. You went to training." Cormal asks, looking at me. When I confirm, he continues. "But you had a fight with Madoc, so you left early? Then you were attacked by a Wendigo in the hallway, and Madoc saved you. Is that correct?"

I lift a shoulder. "Pretty much."

Cormal's eyes drill into me. "What was the fight about?"

Squirming, I contemplate whether to tell him. A fierce scowl appears, and he leans closer to me. "I mentioned Leandra's name, and he lost it. Threatened me." Cormal immediately heads toward the door. "Stop. I kicked him in the balls and dropped him on the mat. Then I left." He doesn't even pause. "He's not here. I think he's hunting Leandra."

He stops and gives me an incredulous look.

He didn't know Leandra and I were connected until I told him. *Fuck me.* Here I've been worrying that he was the dark Fae king, but he didn't even know I knew her until I said her name. That was what triggered him. But if he's not the king, then who is he?

Cormal grips my arms. "How did he save you?"

I look at the hands wrapped around my biceps. "I already kneed one man who thought he could demand something from me today. Do you want to be the second?" With a flicker of magic, I light my arms on fire.

"Fuck, Meri!" he roars, slapping his burning hands against his thighs. "Tell me what happened." He grits his teeth. "Please."

"Since you added the please..." I say with an irritated huff. "He came out of the shadows, grabbed the wendigo, and poured faery fire down its throat."

Solandis sits up even straighter. "He's a royal?"

"Tiernan said he had to be to wield faery fire. Apparently, phoenix use faery fire to regenerate, but they can't wield it..." My voice trails off when they all look at me oddly. "I didn't know that, but I guess you all do. Anyway, Madoc told me he would teach me to wield it when he returns. Apparently, I need to learn to save myself instead of relying on others." My mouth twists at the familiar words. Screw them both. My skills weren't great, but I did a pretty damn good job of taking care of myself or I would never have made it this long.

Solandis tilts her head. "Our entire family can wield faery fire because we are descendants of Konnyr, the original Fae King. Before light and dark cleaved us in two, we were one. What I want to know is who Madoc is and why does he have that power? Describe him to me."

"Big. Warrior build. Dark complected. Straight, almost black hair to his shoulders. Steel-grey eyes. Scars all over his body, including a large one in the middle of his chest." I pause, trying to think of his attributes.

Surprisingly plump lips that I don't see very often because he's always compressing them in anger. He has a darkly fascinating way of pushing you to the brink until all you want to do is annihilate him. Or kiss him. *Where the hell did that thought come from?*

"Wields faery fire, rides the shadows, and thinks Leandra punched through his chest and stole something from him."

Solandis points and an image materializes on the wall. "Is that him?"

Suave with dark hair, the man in the image is handsome, but there's a cruel twist to his mouth that makes me not trust him.

"No, why?"

She lowers her arm. "That's the dark Fae king. For a minute, I thought he'd found a way to enter the palace."

That's the dark Fae king, love of Leandra's life, and my father. Lovely.

I silently snort. I'm not impressed. The fact that he knows about me and doesn't care is proof he's not worth my time.

Cormal looks at Kaius. "He rides the shadows."

Kaius nods grimly.

I tap Cormal on the arm. "Tell me."

"We assigned another trainer to you, but someone killed him, remember? The killer used the shadows to enter his room," Cormal reveals, to my astonishment. "Madoc had both the proximity and the skill necessary to do it."

"So?" I state firmly. "Both of you, Callyx, and at least a dozen others have the ability to ride the shadows. Lady Estrella has the ability to ride the light beams. Tell me his motive."

Cormal throws several suggestions out. "He thought you could lead him to Leandra."

Beep. "Wrong. He didn't even know Leandra and I were tied together until this afternoon. Try again."

Cormal gets up and starts pacing. "I don't know, but my gut is churning, and it's never wrong. Nobody hides power without a reason."

Stumped, we all sit there staring at each other.

Reaching behind her, Solandis eases the knot in her shoulder. "My brain is practically mush right now, and with Estrella's betrayal… it's too much. I need to soak and think about everything. Maybe then I'll have some answers." She gets up and walks out.

Kaius stands and stretches. "I'll do some digging into Madoc. Right after I check on Solandis."

When he's gone, I drag Cormal over to the couch with me. "Solandis has the right idea. I don't want to talk. Or kiss. Or anything. For the next hour, I don't even want to think. Right now, I need comforting. Got it?" Closing my eyes, I sigh and snuggle closer to Cormal. "Take a nap. Breathe. Plot the next step in the plan. I don't care. Just hold me and let me take a time out. It's been a bitch of a day. And the wendigo was one of the creepiest damn things I've ever seen."

Cormal makes a soothing sound and wraps his arm tightly around me. For once, he doesn't say a word, merely lets me peacefully drift in and out in the quiet.

Kaius comes back a while later.

"Did you find out anything?" Cormal asks him.

He shrugs. "Madoc came here the day before the soldier was killed. Timing fits. I asked around, but there isn't much information on him. The guards think he's fantastic. He's been training them on advanced techniques for weeks now."

I clasp my hands together tightly. "Let's not assume. Okay?" My eyes dart from one to the other. "Swear."

They grumble, but both of them promise to hold off on any

action until they can prove it. Kaius breaks up our sad little party. "I'm going to Solandis' room. Text if you need me."

I laugh. "Is she speaking to you again?"

He gives me a smug look. "Yes, she said *get out*. It's a start."

"Good luck," I call out. Reaching up, I smooth the lines between Cormal's brows. "Stay with me tonight? I don't want to sleep alone."

I can see how much he wants to leave and chase down Madoc, but I have a feeling he won't find him.

"Fine. Leave. It's what you do best, isn't it? It's been a long day, and I'm going to bed. With or without you," I huff.

Interest sparks in Cormal's blue eyes.

I wave a hand to clean and dress us in fresh clothes.

"Where's the silk camisole and shorts you usually wear to bed?" he asks, with a raised eyebrow.

I glance down at the lounge set I put on. "I need comfort. This is comfortable. Get over it."

He immediately picks me up in his arms. "Don't be so prickly. I happen to love those little pajama sets of yours, but you can wear a fucking sackcloth to bed if you want. I will never turn down an invitation to join you. Got it?" Gently laying me on the bed, he eases over me to the other side and pulls me into his arms. "Sleep. I've got you."

CHAPTER TWENTY-SEVEN

<u>RIVAN</u>

While the council members meet with the fire drakes, I watch the land around us. Shields protect the group but depending on the size of the army surrounding us, they could be shredded if they used enough force. I share a glance with Tiernan, and he nods in return. He feels them too.

Faris starts yelling at the group in front of him, calling them murderers. Tension rises. Guards slip their hands to the swords at their sides. I keep mine perfectly still. Tiernan follows my lead. Slowly, the others release the grips on their pommels. The last thing we need is to start a war we can't finish. My gut tells me the trees are full of warriors, more than the ten of us could handle.

Abruptly, the fire drakes stand. "This meeting is over. It's obvious you have no authority to grant any of our concessions. When you're ready to have a serious discussion, let us know." He smirks and raises his hand with his thumb pointed down.

Stiffening, I wait to see what the army in the forest will do. When nothing happens, I take a deep breath and calm myself.

The fire drakes swagger to the forest to join their friends. Minutes later, the sky fills with fire drakes, phoenix, and other winged Fire Fae. There are at least a hundred of them. If we had reacted, it would have been a massacre.

Estrella starts yelling at Faris. Lord Lorn gets up and walks off, as if he's not the least bit interested in anything, much less mediating. What the hell does Meri see in him? He doesn't seem any different from other Fae I've encountered.

You're jealous.

I ignore the voice in my head and turn toward Tiernan. "I'm going to grab a bottle at the inn. Join me?"

He grins and slaps me on the back. Upon hearing my loud suggestion, the other guards decide to tag along.

"Great. First round is on me."

With a roar, we all head out to get sloshed and pick up a barmaid or two.

Two bottles down, I slip out the back. Tiernan joins me five minutes later. Quietly, we head to the barn to change into the clothes I left earlier. My stomach is in knots, but I don't let myself stop to think about what I'm doing.

"We need to get a few miles out of town first," Tiernan murmurs. "Your phoenix will draw too much attention this close to Lady Estrella's keep." He beckons for me to follow and swiftly takes us into the forest surrounding the field.

"Meri was right. You're one of them, aren't you?"

He tenses. "As a fire drake, I lived here for many years, but my mother left after the war. She didn't want to raise me here. Too many memories." When I stare at him in disbelief, he lowers his brows. "I was one of the children saved when the elite squad sacrificed themselves and you became their prisoner.

My mother knew staying here would lead to nothing good. Since I was also a lord's bastard, I would have better opportunities if I left the fire drake community. As you saw tonight, she was right."

The derisive tone in his voice convinces me to believe only half of what he is saying. "Don't betray me. You won't like the consequences." My wings flare out wide, and I take off into the sky.

"Slow down, damn it. Not all of us were born with speed," he demands, his voice full of irritation. "We cross into the Dark Fae Kingdom in about a mile. Follow me. Quietly. And do not deviate from the path. Got it?"

I look down at the land we're passing over, but none of it looks remotely familiar. The forest has creeped unchecked until it no longer resembles the home I left behind.

"Pay attention," Tiernan whispers urgently.

I dart a quick look around and see we're entering a canyon. Flying low, we twist in and out of each curve, never slowing down. He suddenly stops and dives behind a boulder.

"What is it?" I whisper, settling beside him.

He shakes his head and points down to the canyon floor where a salamander flies by in a ball of fire. When it's gone, he launches into the air, and we continue our harrowing flight.

Emerging from the canyon ten minutes later, he banks sharply right and drops into the nearby valley. This time, the forest forces us to slow our speed in order to avoid hitting the trees and branches in our way.

"Almost there," he whispers on the wind.

We get to the edge of the forest, and he stops. Setting down, he immediately changes back to his human form and holds out his hand. "Put this hat on. We walk the rest of the way."

Bewildered, I take it from him and look around at the empty field in front of us. "Walk where?"

"You'll see," he says enigmatically. In a leisurely stroll, he heads toward the middle with me by his side.

Straining to see through the darkness, I get a strong feeling we're being watched. I lean over to say something, but he throws an arm around me and laughs loudly. "It's the guard tower. Act drunk."

Singing an old phoenix bonfire song, I weave side to side. Eyes peeled, I look for some sign of the guard tower, but don't see anything. And then I do. It's right in front of me. I blink.

"Don't look back," Tiernan hisses. "If you do, they'll know you've never been here. Keep up the act. It's working." He stops and gives a complicated hand signal to the guard. "Wave like a drunk fool."

I do, and the guard in the tower says something to his buddy. They both laugh. "Go on."

When the gate opens, we enter a completely different world. One of fire and earth. Carved into the ground, the old mine shaft is a city filled with shops, houses, and people. Kids and animals are everywhere. The regular noises of a village, except this is much larger than any village we had when I was a kid. This is a massive city.

"Keep quiet. I'll explain anything you want to know later. We don't have much time, and we still have to make the long trek out," Tiernan murmurs. He drops his arm from me and hurries to the left.

I follow, and we come to another area similar to the first except this one has a sign on it. "Phoenix." When I look down, I see a city as large as the first one. This can't all be phoenix, but as I look around, I realize they are my people. Every single one. The hellhound was right. There are thousands of phoenix here. Enough to make an army even without the Water Fae.

My mind is screaming with the weight of it all, but I refuse to give in. Tiernan takes me to a cafe on the fifth floor. We sit and order coffee. He subtly lifts a finger toward the large house tucked into the ring across from us. Only the front of the house is visible. The rest is concealed by the dirt packed around the outside walls.

A little girl comes out, followed by a familiar dark-haired woman. My breath catches. Under the hat I'm wearing, I watch her stop and look around. Expecting to see my mother's beautiful blue eyes, I'm surprised to see amber gold ones sweeping the area. Confused, I study the woman closely and realize her features are slightly different than my mother's. Similar but not the same. My gaze drops to the little girl. *Aeris.* That's not right, though. My sister would be almost three thousand years old. I dart another glance at the woman. That's Aeris.

When they pass by, I hear the little girl call the woman "mommy" as she chatters nonstop about the ice cream she wants after dinner. Aeris laughs, and the sound pierces my heart. It's the exact same tone as our mother's. A few seconds later, they're gone, and it's all I can do to sit here and not chase after them.

I glance desperately at Tiernan, and although he looks sympathetic, he shakes his head and lifts his chin toward the house.

Watching the door, I can't help but think of my sister and her daughter. I'm an uncle. Is she her only child? My father steps out, turns, and kisses… a blond-haired woman. I freeze, staring at the two. When he releases her, I follow him all the way to the stairs. He stops, and I quickly avert my gaze.

A couple of minutes later, I hear his footsteps on the iron staircase. I glance at the door to the house, but it's closed.

"Was that your mother?" Tiernan asks.

"No, it wasn't," I reply. "Do you know if my mother is still alive?"

"I can send word to a friend to ask around, but questions about Brixton and his family can get someone killed. I'm not sure he'll be able to find any information," Tiernan explains.

"That sounds like my father," I reply in a hard voice. "Don't worry about it. He obviously couldn't care less if I'm alive."

Tiernan looks across to me. "Come on. We need to go."

Instead of going out the same gate we entered, he takes us around to a side gate. "Our flight will be longer, but we can't take any chances."

Still thinking of everything I saw; I numbly nod and follow his lead. Nyssa lied. It shouldn't surprise me, but it does. She loved to torment and threaten me. My family would have provided her with the tools to do both. Unless she truly didn't know?

When we get to the forest, he looks back at me. "You can talk now but speak quietly."

"Nyssa didn't know, did she?" Out of all the questions I could have asked, I never thought that would be the first one.

It surprises Tiernan, too. "The dark Fae king took a lot of precautions to hide the Fire Fae on his land. If she had ever visited, all she would have seen were mines, not cities. I don't know what kind of dark magic he found to do it, and honestly, I don't want to know."

I look over at him. "Do they all want war? I know Brixton does. He was never satisfied with the status quo. To be honest, I wasn't either. But the thought of war makes me break out into a cold sweat."

"Most do," Tiernan says, not pulling any punches. "They don't have any rights. I've got a few because my father was a lord, but most of them have nothing beyond what you just saw. Whether you want war or not, it's coming. It would take a miracle to prevent it."

"What if Meri gave us rights?"

He pauses. "I doubt it will be enough, but who knows? Like I said... a miracle." Changing forms, he points to the lightening sky. "We have to hurry."

I transform and follow him back through the winding

canyon to the barn. Quickly changing into our uniforms, we leave the other clothes scattered in the hay.

"Does anyone even remember me?" I ask Tiernan, afraid of the answer.

He hesitates. "The children who were saved think of you. The rest of the Fire Fae… some hold the warrior in high esteem. Others think you gave up fighting to enjoy life in the palace." Placing a hand on my shoulder, he squeezes. "Having watched you for many years, I know what you've endured. But Nyssa is gone now. How you go forward is up to you."

Slipping into the back of the inn, we find our comrades passed out on benches, tables, and even the floor.

Tiernan kicks a few and purposely stumbles into another. "We've got to go, you drunk bastards. It's almost light."

With a groan, we all follow him out the door to the bunkhouse where we catch a couple of hours of sleep. The horn sounds. Bleary-eyed and reeking of whiskey, we stand at attention in the courtyard and wait for the rest of the delegation. A messenger arrives to tell us we're staying one more day. Relieved, the rest of the guards head back to bed, and not wanting Tiernan to get in trouble, I follow.

Lying there, all I can think about is the thousands of years that have gone by. How did I change so much that I don't even recognize who I am anymore? Where is the fire I used to feel?

CHAPTER TWENTY-EIGHT

MERI

Kaius puts us in lockdown. I'm confined to the palace and not allowed to go anywhere outside of my room unless there's at least two guards with me. The delegation put off returning for another day. Apparently, Faris is not stable, and Estrella is concerned about him.

Unable to stand my rooms any longer, I head to the library to read the treaty. Following Solandis' directions, I twist the handle of the main door and open it, revealing a massive room full of books from floor to ceiling. I pause to breathe in the smell of paper and leather. *Mmm.* Rich and musty. People don't always associate books with being rich, but in the Underworld, only the wealthy people like Cormal have libraries.

Besides the clothes in my closet, this is the second time material items have made me feel like a queen. Funny what signifies wealth to someone like me. Power is top of the hierarchy for everyone. Without power, nothing else matters. After power, everything else matters. More clothes than I can wear and more books than I can read tells me I'm rich.

Walking to the ornate gold door in the back, I open it and find a room barely big enough to fit me. Kian and Galen inspect it thoroughly, then station themselves outside the door. Stepping in, I stand facing the back wall and wait. Solandis said the vault will automatically unlock for the queen.

A glow comes from my forehead and shines on the wall in front of me. Seconds later, the illusion disappears, leaving an impressive vault in its place. A tiny thorn protrudes from the center of the door. Tapping it with my finger, it collects a bead of blood, and once absorbed, the door opens soundlessly.

Filled with an assortment of items, the shelves are stacked high with an astonishing number of scrolls, small books, and documents. Magic suspends each piece individually. The pieces are stacked into columns, and each vertical stack represents a century. I find the one from twenty-eight hundred years ago and ask for all historical information on the Fire Fae Rebellion, including the treaty. Several thick documents slide out of the column and float down into my gloved hands. Now I can see why Solandis insisted I wear them.

In the back of the vault is a chair and a table. My head swivels side-to-side as I walk back there with the treaty. Halfway there, I spot a pile of jewels and gold coins. Obviously, Keir knows nothing about this money.

Biting my lip, I contemplate the pile in front of me, and ultimately choose to start with the treaty. Once I've opened it, there's no going back. An image of Rivan's face reminds me of why I'm doing it. I flip open the first page and start reading.

The entire first section of the document is the official surrender by each of the generals, including Rivan and the leaders from each Fire Fae race. Brixton signed for the phoenix.

In the second section, the terms of surrender are listed. I

skim through them—loss of land, congregating or assembly of groups is not allowed, communities were to be disbanded, assets would be seized to make reparations to the families of those killed, and all rights stripped from them. The last one makes me snort. *What rights?*

In turn, the Fire Fae would remain a part of the light or dark Fae realms and would not face persecution for their treason.

The third section lists every Fire Fae child's name whom the monarchy took to end the war. My eyes skim hundreds of name and catch on two. Tiernan and Aerio. After the children, the document lists one hundred thirty-two phoenix willing to give up the power of resurrection to face true death in exchange for the lives of every child listed above.

Rivan's name isn't listed in the elite phoenix squad. Instead, there is an entire fourth section dedicated to serving Queen Nyssa and her court for the rest of his life. It details out how many hours he can fly each week, how far he can go without permission, the tasks he must perform each week for the families of the fallen whom he personally killed, and an extensive list of things forbidden to him, including contacting or searching for his family, living outside the palace, falling in love, and having children. Consequences for breaking the rules would be severe and punishment doled out by Queen Nyssa.

In the fifth section, the Fire Fae land is divided between the light and dark Fae. Nyssa splits her portion and awards it to two lords. Lord Carlen and Lord Basilus.

Interestingly, the last section is a concession to the Fire Fae. Three thousand years from the date the war started, the Fire Fae will be allowed to petition the council for their land to be returned to them. I stare at the date listed. It's ten days away. Full circle indeed.

Waving my hand, I make a copy of the treaty and leave it in the vault. I take the original with me. Next, I skim through the rest of the information. They truly underestimated the time, effort, and lives this rebellion would cost the light Fae.

Turning around, I marvel at the history surrounding me. The Fae have been around for thousands and thousands of years. It's quite intimidating for someone who never felt like they had a heritage. To see it here in front of me makes me want to cry. I'm sure Nyssa knew every document in here, every war, the winners and losers, and the evolution of this remarkable heritage. One which now includes me.

Pondering the idea of learning more, I step out of the vault and tuck the papers in my pocket. The blank wall appears behind me. Not bad for an afternoon of research.

We're halfway back to my wing of the palace when a piercing alarm sounds. Kian immediately pulls me to him, Galen positions himself at my back, and we rush through the hallways until we get to my room.

"What is it?" I ask loudly. Concerned, I push my magic out and through the hallways to look for the disturbance. It's completely empty, but I can't help feeling something is off.

"Portal alarm. Someone unauthorized opened a portal to the palace," Kian explains. He opens the door to my room and quickly scours it for intruders. When he doesn't find any, he motions for me to enter and closes the door.

Three minutes later, the alarm is turned off.

I open the door. "Are we safe?"

A tiny furrow between Kian's brow tells me how worried he is right now. "We were given an all clear."

"That's good, right? So, why are you frowning?" I ask him.

"The last time it happened, we were under threat of war, and Queen Nyssa died," he says, avoiding my eyes. "I was on duty that day."

He feels responsible for not saving Nyssa. "I see." I look down the hallway. "I want to check on Solandis." When he hesitates, I correct myself. "I'm going to check on Solandis. Do you wish to stay here or come with me?" Not waiting for an answer, I sweep out of my room and down the hall.

He snaps to attention and follows me.

We get to Solandis' room, and I knock on the door. It opens, but instead of her maid, it's a huge shadowy male. "Callyx!" I launch myself into his arms and squeeze him tightly. "Cousin. Where have you been? I thought you were going to be here days ago."

His brows lower. "So did I. Bastard is harder to track down than I expected."

Oooh, there aren't many who can elude Callyx. "What did he do?"

Callyx eyes my forehead. "I can't tell you. You're not officially a part of the Underworld anymore." He snorts at the look on my face. "Unofficially, I'm tracking a monster who escaped from Below." He throws an arm around me. "Come in and tell me everything that's been going on."

I know he didn't mean it the way it sounded, but the idea of not being a part of the Underworld breaks my heart. I love the world I grew up in. It's ugly, harsh, and filled with the most unscrupulous races in the world. I miss my home.

"Like the ones in The Pit?"

He sees me shudder and pulls me tightly into his arms. Rubbing my back, he makes odd sounds.

"What are you doing?" I choke out, barely able to contain my laughter.

"I know how The Pit makes you feel," he says, giving me a concerned look. "I was comforting you."

My laughter explodes. "Maybe you need to work on that a bit." His mouth turns down. "Sorry. Thank you. I'm doing better with it, though." Thanks to Madoc. "Tell me what this monster of yours looks like."

"I've never seen him, but Lucifer describes him as a tall, shaggy beast with a brand on his back," Callyx says with a shrug. "He's damn elusive. I've been tracking him all over the place."

I pat his hand. "You'll find him." I look around. "How's Solandis doing?"

Callyx shakes his head. "She says she's not feeling well, but I think Estrella's betrayal hit her hard. They've been friends their entire lives. I'm not sure she can lose another person she calls family."

I stretch up and place a kiss on his cheek. "I hope she feels better soon. It's going to take a lot to get through this betrayal. I'll see you both at dinner." My voice rises to speak over the portal alarm going off. "That's the second time today."

Sword drawn, Callyx opens the door to look outside, but only finds Kian. "Stay alert."

Kian peers around Callyx to find me. "Queen Meri, we need to go back to your room."

With a deeply felt sigh, I kiss Callyx on the cheek and follow Kian down the hall. On the way back, the alarm stops, then starts again a minute later. "Any updates on the alarm?"

"Something keeps triggering it, but no portals have been opened by unauthorized individuals. Security is on high alert. They check every instance," Kian states tersely.

For the rest of the evening, the alarm goes off regularly. It finally stops right before dinner. Callyx sends a note to let me know Solandis isn't feeling well, and he's going to stay with her. Cormal texts to say he and Kaius are running down a lead on Madoc.

Something stirs on the balcony, but when I get up to look, there's nothing there. I turn away, and my magic sparks. I shiver. There is something out there, but whatever it is, it can't get past the wards in my room. I close the curtains and move to the couch. Clasping my arms around my knees, I wait for something to show itself, but nothing happens.

Eris arrives a little later and finds me staring into space.

Unwilling to get in bed, she wraps a blanket around me on the couch and grumbles about queens without any sense.

"Don't forget your truffle," I remind her. "This one is really good. Chocolate raspberry with white chocolate-covered almonds."

CHAPTER TWENTY-NINE

MERI

Cormal steps from the shadows in the corner and immediately looks at the bed. Not seeing me, he scowls and turns toward the door, but stops when he finds me on the couch.

"What are you doing up? Did something happen?"

I tell him about the incident on the balcony and the weird stuff going on with the alarm. "Oh, and Callyx is here. He's staying with Solandis. The Estrella thing hit her hard, and it's going to be worse today when the delegation gets back."

He stalks over to the balcony, pushes back the curtains, and opens the doors. Magic pulses around him in almost visible waves. "I'm definitely picking up a signature. Fae. Too dark to be a light Fae but could be mixed." He eyes me. "You haven't heard from Madoc, have you?"

I raise an eyebrow. "No. What do you think is causing the

alarm to go off? Kian said they haven't registered any portals opening anywhere."

Cormal thinks about it for a minute or two. "The alarm is supposed to go off if someone opens a portal from the outside into the palace. My guess is the spell is being triggered by someone entering the palace, but shutting off when no portal is opened. I would need to examine the spell to see if I'm correct."

"That would explain someone on my balcony," I say with a shiver. "Good thing you reinforced the wards with your own brand of magic."

"If Kaius can find out where the spell has been cast, I'll slip in there and see if I can fix it," Cormal offers. He drops down on the couch. "We didn't find a trace of Madoc, but I've stationed lookouts for both Leandra and him. It's only a matter of time." He yawns and lays his head on the back of the couch. "What's on the agenda today?"

I put the copy of the treaty in his lap. "Can you take a look at this? I think I have a way to release Rivan, but I want your opinion."

He raises his head and stares at me. "You know he won't be able to stay if you release him, right?"

My heart cracks at the thought of him going, but it will break if he stays. "I know."

Cormal takes the copy from me and starts reading through the pages. "Nyssa's arrogance knew no bounds. With the addition of her Prime powers, she probably thought she couldn't be defeated and tied Rivan to her and her court. It's enough to release him. Are you prepared for the fallout from the court?" He hands it back to me.

"It's the right thing to do," I state firmly, avoiding the question. Cormal gives me a pointed look, but I ignore it. "Did you see the last part about the land?"

He rubs a hand over his face. "I did. Because it's written in the treaty, the Fire Fae will have to petition the court for the land. The court will likely refuse to give it back to them, which means war."

"That's a cheerful thought. It's probably what's holding them back from attacking. If the court denies them the land, it will light a fire under all Lesser Fae. A win-win situation," I surmise. His eyes close, and I get up and cover him with the blanket. "Take a nap. I have to get ready. The delegation will be here in an hour, and we have to arrest Estrella."

I slip into a black pantsuit with a platinum silver blouse that perfectly matches my hair, and of course, the power heels. The stranger in the mirror approves. Queen Meri.

Solandis and Kaius are in the portal room along with several guards, and to my surprise, Lord Camon, who is loudly protesting our move to detain Estrella.

Solandis turns around in fury and points to the door. "Do you think it's easy to stand here and arrest my oldest friend? Do you think if there was any doubt, I wouldn't be protesting too? If you can't act like a High Fae, get out. If you think you can conduct yourself with dignity, you may stay."

Camon looks at her, then Kaius, and something ugly twists behind his usually urbane mask. "I'll stay. I want to hear the interrogation."

I move to stand beside Solandis.

Lorn and Faris arrive first. Lorn looks like he's barely holding on to his patience, and Faris is talking nonstop about wiping out the Fire Fae. Lorn glances at me, then leaves.

Estrella arrives next. She, too, throws an irritated glance at Faris before striding forward to stand directly in front of Solandis.

"I knew you would be waiting for me. That last hit to my thigh really messed up my plan to stay incognito," Estrella says with a strained voice. "Unfortunately, the story I tell you isn't going to make things any better."

Solandis coolly studies her friend, then motions to the

guards to escort her to the interrogation room. "I'll see you in a few minutes. I promise, you will have my full attention."

Estrella strides out with her head held high and several guards by her side.

Camon looks on in disbelief. "I don't understand." He turns on me. "You said the weapons weren't coming in until the next day."

Solandis steps in his face. "Queen Merindah knew nothing about the time or location of the delivery. She was waiting for me to pass along the information." She lifts one shoulder in a dismissive shrug. "You gave me the task of ordering the weapons. When Fallon offered to deliver them early, I decided to personally meet him and make sure they were exactly what I ordered. To my surprise, there were three extra crates of ammunition. You don't happen to know anything about the addition to my order, do you?"

Surprise filters across his face. "I assure you, I didn't."

The guards come through the portal one at a time. Tiernan arrives, then Rivan. I turn my head away, not wanting anyone to see the relief in my eyes.

Faris walks over to me and asks for a private moment.

Irritated, I step to the side with him.

"Queen Meri. Your assistant said the first available appointment is in three weeks. That will be too late. I must speak to you in the next few days. It's about the Fire Fae Rebellion treaty," he implores me.

"Is this about the land?" I ask, to his utter surprise.

"Yes. My father wrote that piece," he reveals, which shocks me because it favors the Fire Fae's request. "Unfortunately, he wrote it before he was killed by the Fire Fae. I intend to bring up the treaty at the next council meeting and ask them to vote against it. I've already spoken to most of them and have their full support. The only person who can stop it is you. If you do, you will find most of them withdrawing their vote of confidence in you. I felt it was fair to let you know."

Staring up at the Fae lord, I laugh. "I didn't realize I had anyone's 'vote of confidence' except Solandis', so I will do what I feel is best for the people, including the Fire Fae." He opens his mouth to argue with me, but I hold up a hand. "Please leave. I have something more urgent to take care of right now."

After he leaves, I turn to Solandis and take her hand in mine. "Ready?"

She shakes her head. "No, but a princess never runs away."

We follow Kaius to the lower level, where Estrella is sitting in a room with heavy gold cuffs on her wrists.

"Are those necessary?"

"They nullify her magic," Solandis murmurs, her eyes glued to her friend. She enters the room and takes a seat across the table from Estrella.

I take a position against the wall where I can see everything.

Solandis leans in close to Estrella and whispers, "Tell me why you would betray a kingdom you believe in so greatly? Why would you betray me... your oldest friend and biggest supporter?"

Estrella flinches as if Solandis hurled those questions at her. "You don't remember coming to my house as a child, do you? No? It's because we didn't have one. We lived in the palace with the rest of the court whose homes were destroyed, and their land lost for one reason or another. Land lost in a war as a concession to the enemy, land lost to The Wilds, land lost for some atrocity committed by a Fae ancestor hundreds of years before you were born, and the list goes on and on."

She gives a derisive laugh. "We were aristocratic Fae. Lords and ladies of the Light Fae Kingdom." She scoffs. "It's noble and wonderful for those who have a home and land. For the rest of us, we existed at the mercy of the royals and their court.

"I'm not looking for your sympathy. The reason I'm telling

you is because I want you to understand why my father made the choices he made, the reason I killed him, and the extent I will go to keep my land," she says fervently.

"You killed your father?" Solandis whispers in shock. "You loved him more than anyone."

She eyes Solandis with a knowing glint. "By the time I'm done telling this story, you'll be glad I killed him." The words echo loudly in the small room. "As you know, Nyssa split her half of the Fire Fae land. She divided it between my father and Lorn's father, Lord Basilus."

Solandis nods, wary now that she brought up Nyssa's name and gone so far back in time. "I do."

Estrella's mouth turns down. "She awarded them the land because they betrayed your father, King Arles." When Solandis stands in outrage, Estrella reaches out and grips her hand. "I've had to carry this secret for thousands of years because I was terrified Nyssa would find out I knew and end me. You can damn well sit down and listen to what I have to say."

Solandis slowly sits.

"I'll explain how I found out," Estrella states, nodding to herself. "Faris' father, Lord Dane, came to see my father one morning. When I asked to join them, my father refused. Curious, I couldn't help but eavesdrop. Apparently, my father, Lord Dane, Lord Basilus, and King Arles had been in discussions with the Fire Fae prior to the rebellion to negotiate the release of the land to them."

She stops and looks at Solandis. "Did you know your father wanted to give the Fire Fae the land?"

"It was their land," Solandis replies with a firm nod. "They had lived on it for thousands and thousands of years. My father felt that it was time for us to move to a more enlightened state. Land would be given to the individual races from the monarchy in exchange for their continued allegiance to the Light Fae Kingdom. Essentially, it would be similar to city states governed by an individual people who would still fight and financially support the kingdom."

Estrella nods. "Correct. Unfortunately, only Lord Dane believed in your father's vision. My father and Lord Basilus only pretended to be on board. They went around your father's back to Nyssa. They hoped to gain her support and use the council to fight against him. She refused."

A relieved expression crosses Solandis' face. "I knew she wouldn't go against our father."

Estrella stares at Solandis with pity in her eyes. "She did worse. When your parents left the secret meeting to go home, Basilus and my father provided Nyssa with the route they were taking back to the palace. They never made it home."

Solandis stands up and pounds her fist on the table. "You're lying. My parents were killed by the dark Fae." Sparks light upon the cuffs Estrella's wearing and bounce off.

Estrella stands. "Yes. Dark Fae hired by Nyssa. Lord Dane had proof Basilus betrayed your parents and confessions from the dark Fae. Scared it would all come out and Nyssa would kill him, my father killed Lord Dane. He then sent word to Basilus to let him know what was going on. That night, Basilus and Kyra and all their staff were burned to death and their keep destroyed by the Fire Fae."

Struck speechless, Solandis and I can only stare while her story unravels.

She clenches her fists and swallows hard a few times. "My father knew they would be coming for us next. He ordered my mother and me to start packing. But I refused. I wasn't about to leave the only home I had ever known for something he did two hundred years ago. It hurt like a bitch, but I killed him. Then I dumped his and Lord Dane's bodies on the Fire Fae's doorstep. For months, I prayed it would be enough to appease them. It worked. They never came for us."

Leaning forward, she plants her hands on the table. "I never told a soul until now. If I could have taken this secret to my grave and spared you the hurt, I would have. But in two weeks, the Fire Fae will petition the court for their land. I won't give it to them. Those weapons can help me fight. You think the court will give a shit? They won't see my actions as treason. They'll think me noble for standing up to the Lesser Fae to keep what's mine."

Solandis stands there in shock.

Estrella's right. The council won't condemn her. "Would you accept a compromise? Half of your land?" I ask, knowing the answer but needing to be sure.

"No, I wouldn't give them an inch, much less half," she spits out. "I owe it to my father to keep the land he sacrificed his life to get."

That's a warped way of thinking about it.

Solandis hauls back and punches Estrella hard in the face. "That is for betraying our friendship." She walks over to her. "You're right. I'm glad you killed your father. And you're probably right about the council, too. They'll absolve you. Hell, they'll probably give you the weapons you tried to steal and send you back to defend your land."

Estrella smiles at the thought.

Solandis returns her smile. "Unfortunately, you'll never see victory. Goodbye, Estrella."

I smile. "Do you really think she'll let you live? You denied her right to know the truth about her parents. To seek justice."

She glances at the door and shrugs. "The council will protect me."

Delusional. "I'll see you at the meeting."

Once I'm in the hallway, I hug Solandis tightly, but I don't know what to say or how to help her. "I'm so sorry."

She squeezes back, then eases out of my arms and looks at Kaius. "I don't feel well."

Kaius scoops her up in his arms. "I've got you, love."

CHAPTER THIRTY

Marble floors and golden hallways close in on me. The palace is nothing but a gilded trap full of predators and snakes. It tricks you with its beauty and lulls you into thinking you've got everything when you have nothing. Treaty, pen, and a small sack in hand, I text Rivan to let him know I'm on my way.

He's standing in the doorway to his bedroom when I arrive and steps back to let me pass. "Come in." His eyes dart to Ansel, who swiftly turns his back and positions himself at the entrance.

"We have a lot to talk about, but not here," I say, glancing behind me at the closed door. "Let me change first." Aware of the warm summer day, I opt for shorts, one of my oldest t-shirts, and a hat. Just putting on these clothes gives me comfort, and I'm going to need a lot of it today. "Also, I was wondering if you would tattoo a rune on me?"

Rivan doesn't even question my request, simply grabs the necessary items and places them in a backpack. He holds it open for me to add my small things to it, then hands it to me. Sliding his fingers through mine, he leads me over to the balcony and into his arms. For the briefest of moments, he stands there, holding me without saying a word. He knows.

I touch his arm lightly, and he gives me a single nod.

Wings spread wide behind us and with one movement, we're soaring upward into the sun. Several miles from the palace, he sets us down next to a beautiful waterfall and a small pool of water.

"It's perfect," I assure him. Opening the backpack, I pull out my stuff and set it on the ground. I hold up the small sack. "Eris packed us a lunch. I think she was offended when I asked if it contained enough food. She reassured me that whatever we wanted would be in here."

I hold it open in front of him. "Want to put it to the test? Close your eyes and think of what you want to eat. Now, reach in and pull out the item."

A small smile lifts the corners of his lips, but he plays along. Reaching in, he pulls out a bowl of ice cream. He opens his eyes and laughs. "It worked."

Waving a hand, I create a blanket and lay it on the grass. I sit down and cross my legs. With the sack in front of me, I close my eyes and reach in several times. Every time I pull something out, I hand it to him to set on the blanket around me. Finally done, I open my eyes to see fruit, cheese, crackers, tiny sandwiches, and an assortment of chocolates. And, of course, Rivan's bowl of ice cream.

I laugh at the look on his face. "Some of us need more than a bowl of ice cream, although I applaud your decision to eat dessert first. It's certainly hot enough out here."

With precision, I stack cheese on a cracker and pop it in my mouth. Cheeks full, I enjoy the simplicity of it and the moment. "Mmm."

He leans over and wipes a crumb off the corner of my lip. "You look like a chipmunk." When I raise an eyebrow, he motions to the tree. "They scamper about the trees, building nests and storing nuts. In order to transport large amounts of food, they use pouches in their cheeks to carry it to their den."

"Are you comparing me to a rodent?" I ask, wrinkling my nose at the idea.

"A very cute one," he answers with a laugh. "You didn't have those in the Underworld?"

"There aren't many forests, but if you find yourself in one, don't encourage anything in a tree to come down and be your friend," I reply with a warning. "It's more likely to eat you."

He finishes his bowl of ice cream and reaches for a piece of fruit. "Thank you for letting me go see the phoenix. The hellhound was right. There are thousands of them. Not just phoenix, but other Fire Fae who have replenished their numbers since the war."

I look over and find him staring at the waterfall. "Did you find any answers? Your family?"

A faint smile lifts his lips. "I saw my sister and her daughter. I'm an uncle." He pauses for a second as if this is the first time he's voiced the thought out loud. "My sister looks so much like my mother. It's uncanny. I thought it was her for a second." He chuckles. "And her daughter looks a lot like Aeris did at that age."

"I'm guessing you didn't see your mother?" I ask him.

"No. My father kissed another woman goodbye that night," he states with a catch in his voice. "Tiernan offered to reach out to a friend, but it's too risky. Brixton isn't the kind of man you want to be caught by while spying on him."

He wraps his pinky around mine. "I've spent so many years here. I don't even feel like I exist outside the palace. Seeing the phoenix reminded me of who I used to be. Someone fiery and brave and passionate about everything. I had so many ideas my mind couldn't contain them all. Here… I feel empty."

A tear falls down my cheek. "She took so much from you. I don't understand her hatred of you or the complete disregard she had for anything outside her own ambitions."

His voice is hoarse when she responds. "Her biggest fear was losing her crown and death. Her insecurities would overwhelm her, and she would rage against everyone in the palace. One day, she tore into me until I ceased to exist. It shocked her. Until I regenerated in front of her eyes. In that moment, I became the symbol of her fears."

I slide my hand into his. "This morning we learned from Estrella that Nyssa had her parents assassinated so she could take the crown. It makes sense that those two things became her biggest fears. A demon of envy plays upon people's need for items of status, and their biggest fear is losing the envy of those in the demon community."

He shakes his head. "I thought I knew the worst of Nyssa, but she continues to top herself." His eyes peer into mine. "What is your biggest fear?"

I think back to the day I accepted the crown. "I thought I was a fraud accepting the crown because I knew nothing about being a queen. Or being a Fae, really. How was I going to rule the people? Honestly, I don't think anyone knows. You make one decision, then another, and another. It's like anything else in life."

I stop to look across the water at a tiny, beautiful little creature. One of the gossamer threads inside me pulls tight, and it looks up at me. *Water sprite.* She drops into a curtsy and whirls around in a flurry of light. Flying around the water, she hovers directly in front of me for a second, then zips off. I smile.

I look over at Rivan, who's staring intently at me. "My biggest fear now is not making the right decision." Snatching up the treaty, I hand it to him. "Read sections four, five, and six." While he reads, I pull out a bottle of water from the sack and take a long drink.

He finishes a moment later. "I never thought this day would come." Uncertainty and fear strain his voice. "If you do this, what will happen?"

I adamantly shake my head. "This is the right decision. No matter the consequences. You sacrificed more than anyone. It's time to find yourself again. To find the fire and passion you lost. To fill your head with ideas and hope for the future. To find a love like the one you shared with Sima. I want all that for you, and I have the power to do it."

Why do I so desperately want to be with him on this new journey? To see his face and hear his voice strengthen and fill with his old confidence? To be the love he finds again. I stare at this beautiful man who gave so much and find the resolve to follow a different path… without him.

With the pen, I amend the treaty and release Rivan from all debts and reparations owed to the light Fae, Nyssa, and her court, and return his freedom to him. I make several copies and give one to him. The others I send back to the vault and to my hiding place in the Underworld. Yes, I have severe trust issues.

He stares at it for a long time. "Thank you. This means everything to me. But I can't help but wish we could meet in another life. Far away from here. In a different time." His eyes flick to the hat I'm wearing.

I look at the hope in his eyes. "I can't help who I am, and I don't want to change myself for another. Not even for someone who fits me like you do. We have today. All the tomorrows are yours. Go find yourself again. Even if that means we end up on opposite sides of a war. I will never regret giving you your freedom or calling you my friend. Maybe if we wish hard enough, we will find each other in another place and time."

Tears roll down my cheeks, knowing how much I'm going to miss him.

He pulls my back against his and places his cheek on mine. Wrapping his arms around me, he holds me tight while I let the tears fall. "I'm going to miss you, too." The warmth inherent to his nature seeps into my bones and soothes me.

My fingers intertwine with his, and I capture a memory of our hands clasped tightly together. When have I ever wanted to do something so innocent with another? Yet, being around him, I find myself reaching for his hand every time. A link to connect us both.

I breathe in deeply, imprinting the smells surrounding us. Rivan smells of sun and earth, which pairs perfectly with the nearby honeysuckle and the damp grass. Everything reminds me of the best summer day. The only thing that would make this more perfect is a kiss.

In a husky voice, he tells me he needs to do the rune before we lose the light. "What do you want it for and where?"

"Clarity," I state firmly. "On the palm of my hand. I want to be able to look at it and remind myself of what's important." I think back to the other one. "You can decorate it however you want."

He eases up and gathers his tools from the backpack. Sitting back down beside me, he picks up my hand and places it palm up on his thigh.

While he works, I think about all the things I'm going to have to face soon. Not just the decision to free Rivan, but the Fire Fae land and the rights for the Lesser Fae. The Water Fae army that nobody knows is even forming. I think about Madoc and the revenge I see glittering in his eyes. I think about Solandis and Kaius and the fact that they're going to need to leave soon, preferably before Kaius' current form changes. I've already decided what I'm going to do about Lorn, although I still have to tell him. Cormal remains an open question mark, but if what he says is true, we're stuck with each other. I need clarity for all of it.

His black and red hair falls onto his forehead, and I brush it back. "Thank you."

Gold eyes meet mine with a fierceness I haven't seen in him. "The only time I feel anything is around you. Even at night, I dream of kissing you until the fire rises up and consumes us. I know it will never happen, but the image refuses to leave me. So, I have to believe it's a possibility. Until then, I refuse to say goodbye." A tear rolls down his cheek as he lays my hand in my lap.

On my palm is a tiny red flame with a heart in it. The rune for clarity lies in the center of the heart. I smile and swallow the huge lump in my throat.

"It's perfect. Thank you." I lift the same hand and run my thumb over his lips. "No goodbyes. Take me back. It's time for you to start a new journey."

CHAPTER THIRTY-ONE

<u>MERI</u>

Cormal is gone when I return. No note. I'm glad, though. If I saw him right now, I'd probably start crying about Rivan and be useless for the rest of the day. I stop by to see Solandis, but she's not allowing anyone but Kaius in her room.

Returning to my room, I text Lady Tanith and ask her to send a note to Faris.

Callyx stops by on his way out to hunt down another lead. "I'll be back in a day or two. Watch over Solandis. I've never seen her like this... It's as if all the fight has gone out of her." He spears his finger through his thick blond hair.

I promise to stay close and hug him tightly.

Faris gives him a wide berth in the hallway. With a smug smile on his face, he stops in front of me. "I didn't think you would come around, but I'm glad you did."

"Walk in the garden with me? I have something to tell you," I inform him, ignoring his told-you-so comment.

Galen and Garren follow us out the palace doors. Once we get outside, they drop back a little to allow us some privacy.

"I'm not sure if you're aware, but Lady Estrella was arrested today."

He eyes me with a disapproving frown. "I heard. For trying to steal weapons to defend her land against the Fire Fae. It's despicable that you would allow a member of our aristocracy to be treated with such disrespect."

"Enough," I interject, already tired of his rhetoric. "There are some things that are going to come out in the council meeting tomorrow. I didn't want you to hear about your father's death in front of everyone."

Puzzled, he stops walking. "I know how my father died."

"Actually, you know the lie you were told." I give him a sympathetic look. "Your father received information that Basilus gave King Arles' coordinates to Nyssa, who hired dark Fae to kill her parents so she could take the crown. Estrella's father, Lord Carlen, killed your dad when he confronted him with evidence of Lord Basilus' treason."

I continue. "The reason he killed him is because he was also a traitor. Estrella overheard their conversation. Lord Basilus and his entire keep was destroyed by the Fire Fae that night. In a panic, Carlen tried to flee, but Estrella killed him. Then she dumped your father and hers on the doorstep of the Fire Fae." I hold up a finger. "Stop. You don't have to believe me. Go ask Estrella herself. Or listen to the interrogation."

Disbelief wars with politeness on his face. "I... Thank you for telling me. I guess this means you aren't voting for my proposal to deny the Fire Fae their land?"

"Did you know your father was working with King Arles before the war to turn the land over to the Fire Fae? Him, Basilus, and Carlen. Too bad he was the only true patriot and believer in those talks. Besides King Arles, of course. It's a shame he died fighting for a cause you don't believe in supporting," I say, slipping past him. "He probably had to fight Nyssa pretty hard to add the land clause to the treaty. Such a shame his work is all for nothing. I think his life is worth more than the death he received at the hands of a traitor. I'll see you tomorrow, Faris." I leave him standing in the middle of the garden with the sun setting behind him.

Walking through the halls, I ignore Galen and Garren's repeated requests to go back to the room. I need to walk, and this is my only option. The garden at night has too many memories of the man I'm trying to let go. Murmurs come from the many closed doors I see along the way. I wonder how many of the aristocratic Fae live here like Estrella did when she was younger? Do most of them long for a home, or do they like living in a palace with servants to wait on them hand and foot?

The alarm goes off, and I stop, knowing Galen and Garren are going to force me to go back to my room. "You don't have to say it. I'm going—"

The twins are lying face down on the ground in a pool of blood.

Confused, I look around and find the dark Fae king standing at the end of the hall.

"Denir, how kind of you to come for a visit. Now, I can update you in person. Leandra, lovely bitch that she is, found a way to hide herself from her enemies. An amulet from a goddess. Until she decides to pop her head out of the hole she dug, we won't be able to find her."

The weight of a dagger sliding into my palm makes me look at my hand. It's the Killian Blade. Relieved, I close my fist tightly around it and shift onto the balls of my feet.

Dark power fills the hallway, and he bares his teeth. "I see you know her well. Unfortunately, I don't have eons to wait for her to pop up like a hare. I figure if I take her replacement daughter, she'll find me in record time." The floor begins to vibrate and twist in a macabre way.

Replacement daughter?

I back into the wall to get away from the dark stain growing on the floor.

A hand reaches out and clamps down hard on my mouth. In a panic, I claw at it, but the smell of amber and musk calms me.

"It's Madoc. I'm going to pull you into the shadows. It's going to be disorientating because we're going to be moving fast. Just hold on to my arm and don't let go. Got it?" He looks at the dagger in my hand. "And put that away."

I slowly nod, not wanting dear old dad to see my movements and open my hand to drop the dagger. It disappears before it hits the floor. The last thing I see before darkness covers us are the shaking hands of my father.

Whoosh! Shades of grey, flashes of light, and moments of pitch-black swirl together into one big nauseating ride. I'd do anything to be able to close my eyes, but I need to figure out where he's taking me.

A hand reaches into the dark, and Madoc jerks me to him with a snarl. Suddenly, we're dropping a few hundred feet, only to stop and ride a wave of inky blackness to the left. Maybe. It's hard to tell. We step out of the shadows. Dizzy, I glance around and find we're on my balcony.

Madoc shoves me through the doors of my room and takes off again. I watch from inside as the dark Fae king lands on my balcony. When he sees me, he smiles and steps forward. The wards spark, searing his body in several places. Roaring in pain, he stumbles back.

"You can't hide in there forever. I'll be back to finish our little chat," he spits out, blood dripping down his face.

Cormal bursts into the room with Kaius and Ansel at his heels. "Thank god. We've been looking everywhere for you.

Galen and Garren were supposed to be guarding you, but we found them dead in one of the hallways."

Furious, I burst into tears, which pisses me off even more. I cry like a baby when I'm angry and right now, I'm furious.

"I was there. With them. They wanted to come back here, but I insisted on taking a walk. That bastard showed up and killed them. Madoc saved me."

Cormal grips my face between his hands. "Who showed up, Meri? Tell me."

My eyes dart to Ansel. "The dark Fae King. He's coming in via the shadows. Apparently, his presence is what's tripping the alarm, not a portal." I shiver at the thought of how many times the alarm has gone off over the last few days. "He's been everywhere. Looking for me."

Kaius curses. "I'm calling Astor."

Cormal holds up a hand. "I can fix it. Now that I know who it is, I can ward the palace against him. I may have to call in a huge favor from Oryn to get a sample of his DNA, but he'll do it."

I point to the balcony. "Or you can go scrape up some blood from the balcony. Your wards roasted him." Sniffing, I grab a tissue from the table and wipe my nose. "I'm so sorry about Galen and Garren. It's my fault. I never should have asked them to keep walking."

Ansel stares at me. "You should be able to walk around your own damn palace. I'll go grab Tiernan and Laken to watch over you while I have the palace guards prepare the twins for the funeral pyre." He turns to Kaius. "I'll also find us several more men. We need to double up security with everything that's going on."

Kaius nods and dismisses him. "The wards are weak. Nyssa never upgraded them because she felt she could handle any threat. It needs to be done. Too many people live here to rely on one person's ability to protect it."

My body vibrates with anger. I remember Solandis telling me I can pull power from the people. But how? I get a rush of adrenaline when I'm in a council meeting or at an event with a lot of Fae, but my power level itself stays about the same. I sigh. I would ask Solandis, but I don't want to bother her with trivial stuff right now. Maybe Madoc can teach me.

Cormal comes back in with a test tube of dark liquid. "The wards on this room work. Stay here. Please. I'll fix the spell on the palace and block him. In addition, I'll get my security team in here to upgrade everything." He spears his fingers through my hair to cup the back of my neck and lowers his mouth for a devastating kiss. It's full of anger, worry, and lust.

My body immediately kicks into high gear, and I meet every thrust of his tongue with my own, needing what he's offering.

"Damn it, Meri. You pick your moments. I'll be back." He places one last firm kiss on my lips and strides out.

CHAPTER THIRTY-TWO

<u>MERI</u>

Cormal sent a text in the early morning hours to let me know he was still working on the security. By the terseness of it, I guess it's more of a mess than he thought. Frustrated and anxious about tomorrow's council meeting, I finally drift off to sleep, only to be awoken by the same bizarre dreams that have been plaguing me for weeks.

Except this time, I can clearly see Leandra's fear as she faces me. Me but not the person I am now. It's hard to tell my exact age because my face didn't change much once I hit maturity, but the clothes I'm wearing are what I call relaxed skimpy-ness—a t-shirt over a short skirt with a pair of tennis shoes. A look I favored before I hit a hundred years old.

They're definitely memories, but none I can actively recall. I rub the blank space behind my ear where the rune used to be. Maybe it's all tied together.

Eris arrives, her face solemn, and pulls me out of bed.

"Breakfast. Something more than toast this morning since you won't be going to training." A snap of her fingers and the bed is made. "And I've got just the outfit for the council meeting. Need to look the part today."

It amazes me how she keeps up with every little thing in the palace. "You're incredible, Eris. Thank you." I slip on leggings and a long-sleeved silk t-shirt.

"You couldn't replace me if you wanted." Her eyes dance with her remark.

"Never," I reassure her, before peering out on the balcony.

"Blood is gone, and he's out there waiting for you," she informs me, hustling into the closet.

Cormal's sitting at the table, writing in a leather journal. "Good morning." He tosses it aside and stands up to give me a long, languorous kiss. "I returned two hours ago, and these lips have been tempting me ever since." His finger skims down my cheek. "Bad dreams?"

I stare up into his serious blue eyes. "I think they're memories."

He swallows. "What did you see?"

"Leandra was afraid of me," I say with a strained laugh. "I don't ever remember seeing that look on her face, but it feels too… real not to be memories."

"Anything else?"

"No, not yet, but I think my mind's been trying to release them for weeks," I reply softly. "Maybe it's finally happening because of this." I raise my palm and show him the rune Rivan gave me yesterday. My eyes automatically drift to the garden below. Why does it already feel like he's been gone for ages?

Cormal runs a finger softly over the artwork. "Stunning. Clarity?"

I bite the inside of my cheek as the anxiety rises again. "Hoping it will help me see my way through this mess. I gave

Rivan his freedom yesterday." A dish breaks on the balcony floor, and I swivel to see Eris cleaning it up.

"Don't move. Let me make sure there aren't any stray pieces," she orders me, her voice muffled. Her hand moves in a circle over the floor, and all the dirt and debris lifts and disappears as if it never existed. "There. All done." She looks up at me with her dark brown eyes, and a tear slips down her cheek. "Thank you. For Rivan."

I give her a watery smile of my own. "I'm going to miss him."

She nods briskly and swipes the tear off her face. "I'm not. It's about time he left this drafty old place. Phoenix can't fly in a cage." She sniffs once. "Clothes are on the bed. Call if you need anything."

I blink, and she's gone.

Cormal tugs on my hand and moves me to sit next to him. "Eat. Today's going to be tough, but it's only the beginning. Need to keep your strength up." After he sees me take a few bites, he picks up his journal. "Good move releasing Rivan before the land discussion today. They would have tried to use him as leverage or…"

I breathe in deeply. "Or worse." Lifting the mug, I nod, then take a sip. "He was ready. I secretly sent him with the delegation to see the phoenix and his family with his own eyes. It shocked him how much time had gone by. Living here… it's monotonous and never-ending, and there's no real sense of time passing.

"The hellhound was right. There are thousands of phoenix, and double that amount, if you include the rest of the Fire Fae. They want war," I murmur, barely able to get the words out. "The land is just a catalyst. If we refuse to give them the land, it's war. If we give it to them, they'll take it and go to war over their rights."

"I wonder if the aristocratic Fae are prepared to go to war to keep it," he ponders. "Maybe you should ask them today."

"Maybe I should. I wish you could be there," I say with a sigh. "What are you doing?"

He smudges the ink on the page with his finger and mutters a spell to clean it up. "Trying to get this spell correct. He's entering by the shadows, but if I write it to keep all from using that power, then Kaius, Callyx, and myself will be locked out." He darts a dark look at me. "Your friend, Madoc, too."

"He saved me. If it wasn't for him, I'd be sitting in some dungeon waiting for Leandra to come get me, which we both know wasn't going to happen," I remark with a dark bitterness I only reserve for that bitch. "Denir thinks she will come save her 'replacement daughter.'"

Cormal stops writing. "Replacement daughter. Meaning she had another?"

I look up in surprise. "I guess she did, but how does he know unless... it was his?" Could her hurt be deeper than lost love? "Regardless, he thinks I have something, but he needs her to get it."

"If he needs her, it has to be a spell of some sort," Cormal remarks slowly. "After all this is over, we need to find her before he does and get her to reverse whatever she did to you." His fist slams on the table. "Damn it. I finally think I can kill her, and now I need her alive. Again."

Frustrated, I curse a blue streak. "Funny how that always seems to be the case with her." I tuck a piece of hair behind my ear. "I need to get ready for the council meeting." Bending down to kiss his lips, I pull his bottom one into my mouth for a little nibble. "Meet me back here later?"

He grips my chin and raises my head so he can see into my eyes. "Wouldn't miss it." A carnal smile slides across his face. "Go be queen."

Eris is a gem. Strutting through the halls in my fierce white pantsuit, silk turquoise blouse that pairs perfectly with my eyes, and five-inch heels, I know I look the part. This outfit is a statement. It screams Queen of the Light Fae.

Solandis' lips curve into a satisfied smile when she sees me. "Queen Merindah." Head held high, she struts into the council with an icy glint in her eyes and power crackling at her fingertips. A potent reminder of her place in the Fae hierarchy.

Giving her a moment to work the room, I wave a hand to fetch the folder with the documents I need in it. Strolling into the council meeting at a leisurely pace, I make sure to lock eyes with several key people in the room—Faris, Estrella, Lorn, Camon, and Kier. Once seated, I cross one leg over the other and wait for Camon to open the meeting.

Every single person is in attendance. Good. Maybe we'll be able to see where the lines fall. Camon bows to me and waves his hand at the floor.

"How many of you were here when the Fire Fae Rebellion happened?" My voice rings out in the silent room. "Hands. How many?" I stand and walk to the center of the room.

All but two. "How many were council members?"

Almost none of them. I silently scoff. I bet I know why. "How many lost family members in that war?"

Camon steps forward to protest, but I turn my head. "The floor is mine. Sit down."

Startled at the tone of my voice, he slowly sits.

The crowd nervously shuffles their feet.

"How many lost family members in the rebellion?" I repeat. All of them. "Most of you inherited your council seat from them, correct?" They nod. "Which of your children will inherit your seat when you die in this war?"

Microscopic lines appear in several of their smooth foreheads.

"The Fire Fae numbers are greater now than they were prior

to the rebellion. By double," I reveal to their astonishment. "How many of you are willing to sacrifice yourself for a piece of arid land you've never seen?"

Several hands go up, including Estrella's. Many look at Faris, but his bland face gives nothing away. Somebody learned to play poker in the last twenty-four hours.

"How many of your children are you willing to sacrifice for that land? The previous rebellion lasted two hundred years. This one could last longer, especially if other Lesser Fae join with the Fire Fae. My spies tell me this is a possibility." I slide that last piece of information into their minds and turn to look at Camon.

He gives me a wary look in return.

Pasting a sympathetic smile on my face, I ask him. "Camon, your wife is pregnant with your first child, correct? They should be old enough to fight in fifty years. I wonder if you'll be there to send them off to war?"

"This sounds implausible, right? I assure you, it's not," I remark with a sad smile.

Opening the folder, I pass along copies of the information I got from the documents in the vault. Living in the Underworld taught me that war is an abstract concept unless it's at your door. It means nothing until you lose the things that matter to you.

"If we do not give the land back to the Fire Fae, they will declare war. A lot of you will die. Some of your children will die. Others will inherit your council seats and serve the future of this kingdom. These are the numbers from the last war, including the deaths."

I glance at Solandis, and she gives a firm nod. "Lord Carlen and Lord Basilus inherited the Fire Fae land after the war because Nyssa owed them a debt for betraying their king. They are gone, but their legacy lives on. Lord Basilus and Lady Kyra were murdered by the Fire Fae for their betrayal of King Arles, who had already promised them the land. Lord Carlen murdered Lord Faris' father, Lord Dane, to cover up his betrayal. Lady Estrella murdered her father to keep the land. So much death for an arid piece of land in the middle of the kingdom.

"Lady Estrella has been accused of a crime of theft, and her confession is documented, if any member wants to review it," I tell them, although based on the lack of surprise on their faces, most have already seen it. "I absolve Lady Estrella of attempted theft. Under interrogation, she confessed to another crime, but I believe her father's death is on her conscience and has no bearing on this council." Ready to unleash their indignation on me, the council visibly deflates.

When the whispers start, I hold up a hand for quiet. "Lord Dane, however, was an upstanding citizen of this council and a supporter of King Arles. For his death, I ask that you vote to give Lord Faris the right to seek reparations from Lady Estrella's estate for his life."

"All those in favor?" I ask.

Unsurprising, most of them vote against my proposal. It was a stretch. In their eyes, Lord Carlen killed Lord Dane, not Estrella. My eyes dart to Faris, who's still wearing his poker face. His hands tell a different story. They're clenched in fury.

"I'm sorry, Lord Faris," I offer him. "Lady Estrella, it looks like you're free. However, we're not done discussing the land, so perhaps you want to stay?"

Her triumphant smile fades, and after the guards remove her cuffs, she walks over to take her council seat.

I turn my attention to the crowd. "So, what's it going to be? Shall I declare war, or do we return the land to the Fire Fae? Those are the two options on the table. Choose wisely." Walking over to sit in my chair, I wait for the room to explode.

Furious, several council members jump to their feet. "Why

would we declare war? We should deny them the land and send a delegation to negotiate when the Fire Fae declare war."

"Why would we not? If we declare war, we gain a huge strategic advantage. Not only do we have the element of surprise, which should never be underestimated, but we also pick the time and place of the first battle. They become the defenders," I explain slowly, as if surprised by their question. "Waiting for any reason only gives them more time to prepare and arm their troops. If they declare war, they'll ask for the land and all the rights they've been denied their entire lives."

The entire assembly starts shouting again.

Ignoring them, I dart a glance at Solandis, who's staring at me with the biggest smile on her face.

Camon raises a hand for quiet. "We need time to consider both options, Your Majesty. I'd like to suggest we reconvene this time tomorrow."

A day is better than I expected, but I can't let them off the hook that easily. I heave a disappointed sigh. "Fine. If everyone is in favor, we'll meet on this topic tomorrow." Everyone nods their head. "One day, but Camon, you'll carry the message to the Fire Fae. Land or war."

Camon blanches. "I don't think that's a good idea, Queen Merindah."

Lady Estrella stands up. "Why don't we send Rivan? They aren't likely to kill him."

Camon looks relieved. "That's a fantastic idea, Estrella. Your Majesty?" He looks at me with hope in his eyes.

Too bad I have to crush his rotten little spy heart. "Unfortunately, Rivan is no longer here. When Nyssa wrote the treaty, she tied him to her and her court. She's no longer with us, and you're not her court. You're mine. I could no longer keep him here." I lift a shoulder. "Such a shame she didn't have enough foresight to write the treaty beyond her death. But I took advantage of her lapse. Freeing Rivan right away allowed us to show some good faith to the Fire Fae. After all, we're not monsters."

When they start shouting, I hold up a hand. "A copy of the treaty is in your hands. Read it. I've already amended it."

They start shuffling papers to get to the treaty. Voices loud, they read the terms and the amendment I made releasing Rivan from his gilded prison.

"Since we're not prepared to declare war on the Fire Fae, I need to address the army that has been amassing in another part of this kingdom!" I shout to be heard over their loud protests.

Camon looks ill.

Everyone stops talking and turns their attention to me.

I smile. "Thank you. I abhor shouting. It really shows bad manners," I state with an air I picked up from Solandis. "The Water Fae has amassed an army in Seva with the clear intent to stage a coup." I swallow and pray to every god and goddess listening that this works. "I declare war on the Water Fae and Fisk, the cirein-croin, who is leading the army."

The shouting starts again, but this time, I stick my fingers in my mouth and whistle. Very unqueenly like, but effective. "Enough. The difference between the Fire Fae and Water Fae? I do not have confirmation that the Fire Fae has amassed an army. On the other hand, the Water Fae presents an immediate threat. As queen, it is my right to protect this kingdom. However, I hear your concerns. I will do my best to negotiate with them first. Lord Camon, since Fisk is Brina's grandfather, would you mind acting as intermediary and setting up the meeting between us?"

He stiffly nods.

All eyes turn to Camon, speculation gleaming in their depths.

"Thank you," I say airily. "This meeting is adjourned until tomorrow."

Stopping to pick up Solandis on my way out, I grip her arm

tightly, then we stride out as if the world is at our feet. We don't speak a word until we're in my room.

"Bravo. Well played," she says, clapping her hands. She gives me a hug. "Meri, I've watched you worry and struggle to find yourself here, but you have strengths no other Fae can match. You're a better queen because you didn't grow up in this kingdom. You don't have the prejudices and entitlement of the court. Embrace your background and use your unique experience to find your way like you did today."

I grin. "In the Underworld, you face death on a regular basis. It gives you a completely different perspective on things. I thought the council needed to be reminded of the realities of war. Death isn't something we often face as immortals."

CHAPTER THIRTY-THREE

<u>MERI</u>

Adrenaline high after the council meeting, I prop my heeled shoes on the balcony and sip some of Cormal's expensive bourbon. Normally, I'd advocate for peace, but that's not the reality we're facing. Two very powerful races are bearing down on us. We cannot afford to be caught in the middle. Fisk didn't let the Water Fae join the Fire Fae Rebellion last time. I have to believe there's a much a better chance of achieving peace if I divide and conquer.

"That's a hell of a sight," Cormal rasps from the doorway where he's leaning on the frame. Bright blue eyes are lit with a possessive fire. "A queen celebrating her victory. I take it the council meeting went well?"

"Mmm… for the most part," I reply, holding up the glass for him to take a drink.

Instead of taking the drink, he picks me up and sits down

with me in his lap. Guiding the glass in my hand to his lips, he takes a drink.

"Eris picked one hell of an outfit for today." Strong, dark hands slide down the turquoise silk blouse.

Firm lips skim down the side of my neck. "Tell me about the meeting."

Arching my neck to give him better access, I tell him everything. "I think I'm still in shock. I declared war on the Water Fae. Did I make the right move?"

His mouth stops. "They won't be expecting such a bold move from a new queen, but old Fae like Fisk will respect it. Only time will tell if it's the right one. Do you feel good about it?" He resumes nibbling on my ear.

"I do," I state firmly. "From everything I heard, the Fire Fae isn't going to back down. Fisk is my best shot."

He begins unbuttoning my blouse. "I agree. Goddess, you're beautiful."

I swivel my head to stare into his beautiful blue eyes darkened with lust. "We're outside."

He raises an arrogant brow. "Are you asking me to stop?"

"Definitely not," I say huskily. "Is it safe for us to be out here?"

"The spell is fixed, and security has been upgraded," he assures me, using a bit of magic to remove the rest of my suit until I'm only clad in the turquoise blouse and a bra and panty set the color of my skin.

"You're so fucking beautiful. I can't tell you how long I've been waiting for this moment. Lie back. Let me take care of you," he demands, hands roaming my body.

Staring out into the sun-drenched garden, I gasp when he releases my breasts from the delicate lace and cups them in his warm hands.

"Mm, that feels so good."

His mouth finds the juncture between my neck and shoulder, while his fingers play with my hard nipples. I thrust my breasts into his hands, wanting him to squeeze and play harder with them. Understanding my need, he pushes them together and twists the nipples until I'm writhing on top of him.

"You're so fucking responsive," he breathes out, continuing to play with my breasts. "Ready for more?"

"Yes," I whisper, feeling his hard cock underneath me. "I want it all. All the years you denied us have made me very, very greedy. Tonight, you're going to give me everything. No more holding back. Are you sure you want this?"

"I am. No regrets," he replies harshly. "Show me what you need. Take my hand."

Pulling one of his hands from my breast, I entwine our fingers and slide it down my body and into the wet heat pooled below. I stroke myself using both our hands, reveling in the feel of our hands on my body.

He pulls them out and brings my fingers to his mouth to taste the very essence of me. "An appetizer." His smoky laugh nearly does me in. "Hold on." Draping my hand on the back of his neck, he peers down at my body. Every stitch of clothing disappears, and I'm displayed in all my glory for his eyes to feast upon.

A rough clad knee comes up and parts my legs. Air swirls around my core, and I see his finger moving, directing the magic to all the secret parts of me.

I arch my back. "Cormal." My voice is breathless with need. "Touch me."

"I am," he mocks, tapping his finger rapidly. Small puffs of air pulse around my core, and every muscle tightens in anticipation.

"I want you, not your magic. Touch me," I demand, needing his hands on me.

Fingers plunge into my center, and I can't help moving my

hips to meet their thrusts. His thumb reaches up to stroke the most sensitive part of me. Higher and higher.

"I've waited for you. So long. This is only the beginning, right? You're not leaving after this?"

"After this, I'm going to bend you over the balcony and bury my cock so deep inside, you won't be able to think of anything but how much I fill you up," he responds with a dark laugh.

Spiraling tighter and tighter, I clamp down on his fingers and let my release flow. My body pulses with pleasure, and I ride the wave, but when it's finished, it's not enough. Need batters my body, making my legs shake, but I stand and bend over.

"More."

Hands grip my hips, and he slides into me inch by inch.

I can almost hear him gritting his teeth. "Cormal, so help me goddess, if you don't fuck me right now, I'm going to walk away and find someone else."

"The fuck you will," he snarls, slamming into me.

His cock stretches me, filling every inch, and it's glorious.

Setting a vicious pace, he pounds into me hard, as if he knows exactly what I need in this moment. To be claimed by him. All the years I've ached for him, wondering if I was fooling myself, I need him to show me he wants this too. To mark me as his in a way that can't be reversed.

He swells inside me, and I whimper with pleasure. "Cormal." My voice is barely above a whisper, but he hears it.

"Say it again," he orders me.

"Cormal," I repeat, stronger this time. "Give me the words."

"You're mine, Meri. There is no going back," he replies in a hard voice. "Do you hear me? I'm never fucking leaving, and neither are you."

His words trigger my release, and it comes roaring from the center of my body outward like a gigantic wave. My breath catches. "No, I'm never leaving." Another wave follows the first, and I clamp down hard on him.

He comes silently, but shadows rise up around us as if his magic is responding to his release. Dropping his head on my back, he takes several deep breaths while softly stroking a hand down my hips and over my legs. Lips place tiny kisses on my back before he raises up.

Straightening, I turn to face him. "That was one hell of an appetizer. The main course might knock me out."

He picks up the glass of bourbon and takes my hand, pulling me inside. "You're the main course." The table by the couch is laden with snacks like cheese and crackers, mini burgers, and other snacks.

Somebody has thought of everything. I pick up a cracker and piece of cheese and pop it into my mouth. Eyeing the naked man in front of me, I trace a finger down his chest and encircle him with my hand.

"A feast for the senses. Thank you."

He inhales sharply. "Eat. Then, we'll play."

I laugh. "Why not do both at the same time?" Taking a strawberry from the plate, I lean over him when I take a bite, deliberately letting the juices fall across his cock. "Eat." My tongue licks every red drop from him, then traces around the rim of his tip. "Play." I take him all the way in my mouth and suck a little, then release him. Taking another bite, I wink. "Eat."

This time, I don't stop with a few licks. Teasing and tantalizing him, I drive him to the brink until he curses. I ease up, then start again. This is one of my favorite things to do, but I don't tell him that. Instead, I swirl and taste with my tongue while my hand squeezes and slides up and down until he's practically begging me to finish him.

"Where's the fun in that for me?" I ask, moving to straddle him. Unable to resist his lips, I capture them with mine, while my body slowly rides his.

Hands grip my hips, and he tries to force me into a faster pace, but I zap him with a tiny spark of magic. He shudders and thrusts up hard. *Interesting.* I do it again. Jerking me tight against him, the muscles in his neck strain as he arches back. One more time. I raise a finger.

He grabs it. "I'll lose control." Black seeps into his eyes.

I slowly nod, and he relaxes a fraction of an inch. Feeling him grow bigger inside me, I keep up a steady pace, building the fire between us. My breath shortens. I caress his abs, then slide my hand down to his firm ass. Zap.

The smile he gives me is all teeth, and I shiver in anticipation. His eyes turn completely black, and his body grows bigger, every single inch. He takes full control, never letting up, not when I come once or again. Every time I think my body can't take any more, he manages to coax another release out of me.

"Again," he demands, his voice barely discernible.

I start aching, and the orgasm builds again. My body explodes, and I cry out this time. "How does it keep getting stronger?"

He bites my lip gently. "One more time."

I shake my head back and forth. "I can't."

"You will," he orders me. His body slides in and out, steadily building the friction again. "One more time. Together this time."

Tingles spread down my stomach, pooling in my center. My cheeks burn with heat. My nipples harden, and every time they brush the hair on his chest, a shaft of desire goes straight to my core.

"That's it," he urges me, dark eyes glittering with his own desperate need. His thumb slides down between us and works its magic. My body clamps down on his in response, and he immediately begins to thrust hard, taking us to the edge.

My nails dig into his arms, trying to hold on, but it only makes him wilder. Losing myself, I let go, falling into the heat and darkness swamping my body. I hear a muffled roar as he follows me.

Minutes or hours later, I can't tell, he picks me off the floor and carries me to bed. Snuggling into his side, I sigh.

"I kind of like this brùid of yours."

CHAPTER THIRTY-FOUR

<u>CORMAL</u>

Featherlight strokes across my back wake me instantly. I roll over and see tears sliding down Meri's face. "What is it?" I sit up, prepared to fight whatever is causing her pain.

"Your back. It's you in the memories trying to surface. Leandra caned you. Why?" she asks in a near whisper. "It's because of me, isn't it? I see the fear on her face when she looks at me. Tell me. It's time."

"I can't. I'm tied to a spell," I reveal, at least able to tell her that much. "You're remembering. One day, you'll have all the pieces."

I lie back down and pull her into my arms. Smiling, I marvel at the fact that I'm in her bed again. I grasp her chin with my thumb and finger and pull her eyes up to meet mine. "No regrets?"

She looks surprised. "I don't have any, and you're not

allowed to have them either." Traces of worry cause shadows in her bright eyes.

Capturing her lips with mine, I roll her over and slide into her. "My only regret this morning is that we have limited time to enjoy one another." She raises her legs and locks them around my back, and on the next thrust, I slip in deeper. "Every morning should start with you wrapped around me."

Her nails slip down my back to grip me and pull me in tighter. "Harder."

"What was that? Slower?" I ask, hooking my arms around her legs to push in just a little farther.

"Cormal," she drawls. "Eris is going to appear in this room in ten minutes. Get a move on. Harder." Face flushed; she arches her back.

Changing the pace, I speed up and slip my hand between her legs to stroke her until her body begins to shake. A breathless moan escapes, and the sound triggers my own release. Breathing hard, I lie between her legs and kiss her pink, pouty lips, savoring the feel of her in my arms for a few more minutes.

"Besides the council meeting, what else is on your agenda today?" I ask her.

She looks up at me with a defiant look in her eyes. "Finding Madoc. Look. I need him to teach me how to wield faery fire. Solandis didn't look well when she left yesterday afternoon, so I don't want to bother her. Plus, I want to talk to him about Leandra."

"Two guards," I order her. "It's non-negotiable. There's too much going on right now. I'm going to secretly check in on the enemy. I want to see what kind of impact your declaration of war had on the Water Fae." I place a finger on her protesting lips. "In and out."

"Kavi goes with you," she demands in return. "I mean it."

I can't help the smile that spreads across my face. She does care for me. "Agreed." I tap her on the nose and slide out of her body. Groaning at the feel, I stand and wave a hand to dress and clean us both.

She looks down and raises an eyebrow. "Good try." With a laugh, she changes the baggy sweatshirt and pants for leggings and a crop top. "I'm famished." Her eyes dance with suggestive innuendo.

I slide my thumb into her mouth. "I'll give you—"

Ahem.

"Good morning, Eris," I greet the brownie with laughter in my voice.

"Breakfast is on the balcony. Chop, chop," she replies, as she looks over the food we left out last night.

Waving a hand, I make it all disappear. "Only your queen. I can clean up after myself."

Brown eyes soften. "Always my queen. I'll pick out an outfit for today's council meeting." She disappears into the closet.

"Look at you. Making friends in your old age," I say with a laugh.

Meri narrows her eyes and flips me off. She sashays to the balcony and picks up her coffee. "Today will be interesting."

Her eyes are full of worry.

I give her a firm kiss. "One thing at a time. Eat now. Play later, remember?"

With a groan, she picks up a piece of toast and sits down.

THIS TIME, Kavi and I slip into one of the tunnels instead of the backyard. Riding the shadows, we make our way to Fisk's war room. Hundreds of people are slipping in and out of the room. Fisk is yelling orders right and left. Too bad the light Fae don't allow full-blooded Lesser Fae to serve. He's one hell of a general.

His phone rings, and he barks out a hello.

"She wants what? A meeting? With me? Why?" He listens for a minute, then hangs up. "I'll be damned." He thinks for a few minutes, then points at a young man in the corner. "Find the kraken. Probably in one of the pubs. Pull him out and get him sober," he orders him.

The young man blanches. Fisk sees his reaction and sighs.

"Tell him it's an order from me. Take at least a dozen men with you. Whatever you do, don't threaten him."

Clearly afraid of the task given to him, the man still straightens his shoulders, nods firmly, and hurries out. That action shows a lot of respect for Fisk.

Rivan comes walking in and stops in front of the old man. "Fisk."

Uneasy, several of the Fae pull weapons out of thin air.

Rivan holds up his hands. "I'm unarmed. Only here to chat with an old friend about a new queen." He leans against one of the desks. "What do you say, Fisk? Or are you going to ban me, too?"

Fisk motions for the men to lower their weapons. "For fuck's sake, I'm a cirein-croin and quite capable of handling one phoenix. Besides, this one is out of shape. Hasn't fought in years."

"Pulling no punches, I see," Rivan remarks with a wry smile. "You're right. I haven't touched a sword since the rebellion ended almost three thousand years ago." He leans over and whispers loudly. "But I'm still a hell of a lot faster than you."

Fisk laughs and the tension eases. "Did you know she declared war on the Water Fae?"

"I heard. Did you hear she wants to meet with you to negotiate a treaty?" Rivan asks, his eyes intent.

"Camon just called," Fisk replies.

That bastard waited all night. What the hell is he up to? I throw a furious look at Kavi, and he nods in agreement.

Rivan scratches his chin. "Funny. She ordered him to set it up yesterday. Are you sure he's on your side?" Deep gold eyes watch Fisk carefully.

Nice, Rivan.

He rubs a hand over his head. "You can never be sure with the High Fae, but I'll take precautions." His eyes meet Rivan's. "It was a pretty bold move. Declaring war, then arranging a meeting. Does it mean what I think it does?"

"Sometimes a treaty is the only way to get things done without going through the council," Rivan states with a nonchalant shrug, but his intense eyes convey more to the old man. "Why team up with Brixton? I thought you were always against his methods."

"Nyssa is gone. The situation is untenable for the Lesser Fae. We deserve more," he states simply, but emphatically. "Are you going to join up with your father?"

Rivan shakes his head. "I went to see him. He feels my presence would only be a reminder of the defeat the Fire Fae suffered the last time." He chuckles, but it's a bitter sound. "Maybe it's time for me to look beyond the Fae kingdoms. The human world is a fascinating mixture of supernaturals. I doubt anyone would even notice a phoenix in the mix."

Fisk reaches out and grabs Rivan's arm. "You're right. I don't trust Camon. Not fully. Stay. Go to this meeting with me. I need someone who can see the middle path."

Rivan hesitates. "You should know… I care for Meri. She's my friend. I'm not sure I can be the neutral soundboard you need."

Fisk considers his words. "You care about both sides. Even better." He points to the map. "I want to be close to the water to draw on its strength, but I doubt she'll be comfortable on a ship. What do you think about Stib's Cliffs?"

Rivan studies the map. "I doubt Cormal will let her hold a meeting with her enemy on top of a cliff."

"Underworld Cormal?" Fisk asks cautiously.

I hear the concern in his voice, and I laugh silently in the shadows. *That's right, old man. Meri's protected by me.*

He nods and flashes Fisk a sardonic smile. Rivan's finger slides along the map to a large body of water farther inland. "Here. You can pull from the lake. It's on flat ground, allowing both of you to see your enemies coming. The two sides can portal in at the exact same time." He pauses. "I wouldn't give Camon the coordinates until the last possible minute. And I would limit the number of people on each side to five."

Fisk beams at him. "You might not have picked up a sword in a while, but you sure as hell remember how to think like a warrior. I agree. With one condition." His smile disappears. "I want Kaius to join her."

Rivan studies him. "You know he isn't your grandson."

"I never got to say goodbye, and it haunts me," Fisk murmurs.

Rivan hesitates, and it's apparent he thinks Fisk is up to something, but he can't figure out a way to say no. "Add the condition. She won't deny the request. But Fisk, the man wearing Kaius' shell isn't one you want to fuck with, or literal hell will rain down on you. Underworld hell."

Fisk gives him a sharp nod. "I understand, and I'll wait to call Camon in the morning." He nods toward a tunnel. "Go get something to eat and rest. You look like you need it."

Rivan thanks him and heads out the same way he entered.

"Do you trust him?" A fierce looking, blue-skinned merman asks Fisk.

"Not sure, but he's never been able to lie worth a damn," Fisk tells him. "Brixton used to think it was a weakness, but his men followed him because he was full of truth and honor. The words mean something to him." He claps the man on the shoulder. "You'll be in charge while I'm gone. Don't let Brixton pull you into anything the Fire Fae plans. I have a feeling we have different ideas on how to reach our goals."

The man dips his chin. "Don't worry. I won't."

Kavi and I listen for another hour. It's apparent Fisk is preparing for war. Whether they move forward hinges on Meri's ability to negotiate.

Once we're outside Seva, I give Kavi a slew of orders to carry out while I'm gone. The Underworld will have to continue to do without me for another day or two. Besides, I like to drop in unannounced and see what my men are up to. I grin and send a text to Lucifer to update him on Meri's plans. I also ask for any information he can share about the current dark Fae king. With him skulking around Meri, I need to arm myself with as much information as possible. You never know what you'll uncover.

CHAPTER THIRTY-FIVE

<u>MERI</u>

Solandis eyes the red power suit and black blouse I'm wearing. "Eris is really stepping up her game. She must approve of what you're doing."

"I know, right?" I say with a spin. Solandis is wearing a cream and camel ensemble that is supremely elegant, but the dark area under her eyes tells me she still isn't feeling well. "You don't have to attend, you know. They will decide or pay the consequences."

She clasps my hand and opens her mouth but shuts it when she sees Camon nearby. "We'll talk later." Leaving me to deal with him, she strolls into the council room and takes her seat.

Camon steps up to me. "I don't appreciate you dragging my mate into the council meeting's discussion yesterday. They didn't need to be reminded of her relationship with Fisk." Green eyes flare with anger. "I called Fisk. He'll meet with you tomorrow. I'm waiting to hear back from him on the details."

I turn and face him. "You're responsible for putting her in the middle. That's what happens when you play both sides."

He rears back. "Who's telling you these lies?"

"I was standing ten feet away when you confronted Kaius and heard every word," I murmur, keeping the smile on my face for everyone passing by. "Someone followed you after you left him. All the way to Seva and Fisk. To the war room." I lean in close. "I have spies too." With a wave, I motion for him to enter the council room.

Furious, he moves forward and takes his seat.

I stroll in behind him and the council reconvenes. "What is your decision?"

Faris takes the floor. "I would like to negotiate with the Fire Fae on our behalf."

"I don't believe this was one of the choices," I drawl, looking at the rest of the council members. By the look on their faces, they're set on this course. "Granted. They have the right to petition for the land in seven days. You have three. If you're not back on the fourth day, I will make the decision."

The council moves restlessly.

I stand. "This meeting is over."

Solandis looks relieved when I walk over. "Let's go."

She asks to go back to my room with me. When we get there, Kaius, Cormal, and Callyx are all there.

"What's going on?" I ask, staring at the three of them.

Cormal seals the room and explains what he overheard in the war room.

"You can have five join you. One of them has to be Kaius. Me," Cormal says, pointing to himself. "Two guards."

"Ansel and Tiernan," I state firmly. Ansel will do what's right for the crown, and Tiernan will honor his oath to me. "Who's going to be the fifth?"

"That's what we were discussing when you came in," Cormal

informs me. "Solandis can't go. If Kaius is required, Callyx will need to stay here with her."

Kaius walks over and takes Solandis' hand. "I'm sorry, love. This is my fault for choosing this body."

She waves a hand. "You worry too much. I'm a princess with considerable power of my own. I can handle your absence for a day or two."

He chuckles. "Two days? Are you sure?"

"Please. You used to be gone a lot longer when hunting for Lucifer's enemies," she reminds him. "Besides, I'll enjoy having Callyx to myself."

"Madoc," I interject. "I'll ask him. He's a fierce warrior and could come in handy."

Kaius looks at Cormal. "She's right. We need back-up who can fight."

Instead of looking angry, Cormal bares his teeth in a semblance of a smile. "I've been wanting to meet the bastard. This will give me time to observe him."

I glance at my phone. "If I can find him," I remind them. "I'm hoping he'll go to the training room with the same idea." Walking into the closet, I change into a crop top and shorts.

"That's what you let her wear when she's training with him?" Callyx asks Cormal, with laughter in his voice. "Brave man."

Cormal sends a poisonous snake flying at Callyx. "Shut up." He strides over to me and gives me a long, hard kiss. "Now you can go find Madoc."

I chuckle. "Jealousy looks good on your face." He once told me something similar when we saw Evren for the first time.

A wicked smile appears on his face. "Touché."

Laken and Kian are waiting for me in the hall. "When is the funeral for Galen and Garren?"

Kian glances down at me. "Today. Sunset. In the back garden."

"Thank you," I say softly.

When we get to the training room, Madoc isn't there. I send Kian to find his room, but when we get there, it's empty of any personal belongings. Stumped, I try to think where he could be. If I were hiding in this drafty place, where would I not go? Grimacing, I look at Kian.

"Take me to the dungeon."

When we get there, I make Kian and Laken wait outside in the hall. "Madoc. I know you're here."

He appears in front of me. "Look who's suddenly braving the dungeon. Don't you know there are monsters down here?"

"I'm well aware," I reply drily. "Unfortunately, I've got bigger monsters to worry about today. Real ones. I'm supposed to meet with Fisk tomorrow."

His eyebrows shoot up. "Fisk, huh? Why? You think you can talk him into not declaring war?"

I laugh. "Your spies are letting you down. I declared war on the Water Fae yesterday. Tomorrow's meeting is to negotiate a treaty." I bite my lip; absolutely certain this was a bad idea. "I thought you could help me learn faery fire. Or to walk in the shadows. Or pull power from a group of light Fae. Something a little more badass than my current bag of tricks."

"You can't learn all those things in a day," he says with a harsh laugh.

"Which is the easier one?" I ask, an idea popping into my head.

He thinks about it. "Shadow traveling is probably easier than faery fire, but you still can't learn it in a day."

"I might not have to learn it," I tell him. Explaining about my ability to mimic, I tell him how I can pick up on others' powers. "The only thing is you have to be there for me to pick up the powers. Will you come?"

He rubs his face. "You know he's going to have his best fighter challenge you, don't you?"

When a look of panic crosses my face, he sighs. "Treaty talks always open with a challenge of power. You have to be a worthy opponent for them to sit down and negotiate with you."

"Why the hell didn't anyone tell me?" I cry out. "Do you think I'm going to have to fight a cirein-croin?"

He chuckles. "No, Fisk is the last of his kind. It will be his best fighter, though."

The worst of the worst from the Underworld flashes in my brain. "This is bad. Really bad."

He nods. "It's not great. You're going to have to embrace who you are, but I'll be there in the shadows to coach you. You might have a few advantages."

A hysterical laugh rises up. "Like what?"

"You can draw on power reserves from your subjects… even Fisk. It's why they limited the number of people, but I can teach you the basics of how to do it. You think differently than the Fae, more like someone from the Underworld. And, apparently, you have the ability to mimic other's powers," he says, listing them out.

Shuffling sounds come from the corner, and I peer into the darkness. "Who's there?"

"Rats," he says with a scowl. "Huge rats."

"You know, you don't have to stay down here. Cormal fixed the alarm."

He takes me by the arm. "We're going to travel through the shadows. Slowly. I want you to get a feel for the twists and turns along the way. Picture the training room in your head. Step forward."

I take a step, and it's like I stepped off a cliff. There is nothing but air under my feet, yet my body hovers above an invisible road. Kian and Laken's face slide by. "Wait. I need to tell them to go to the training room."

He stops.

Popping my head out of the shadows, I tell them, "Meet me at the training room in five minutes."

I step back into the shadows and grab Madoc's hand. It's rough and full of the kind of callouses you get from fighting. A lot. I rub my thumb over it, and he clamps down on my hand.

"Sorry."

He stares down at me. "Don't do it again."

"You're such a touchy bastard," I say without thinking. "Sorry. I suffer from foot in mouth disease." He snorts. "Oh, benevolent one. What do we do now?"

He shows me how to "see" the shadows and the ribbons extending from one shadow to another. I learn how to use the darkness to step in and out of the real world, slide down the hall, and take a leap to a different destination.

I can feel the power inside me pick up the ability. Exhilarated, I beg him to let me try. He does, and I realize it's harder than it looks. Sometimes I lose the ribbon. Other times, I'm distracted by his closeness and forget where I'm going, which really pisses him off.

Next, we practice pulling power from individuals. The training room is full of guards when we step inside, including Kian and Laken. My adrenaline spikes and a tingling buzz courses through my blood.

"It always feels like I'm having a heart attack."

He dismisses it. "Good. It means the power is available to you. Close your eyes. Let your power loose. Seek out the most powerful person in the room. Do you have him?"

"Yes," I tell him excitedly, turning to face to the left. "Now what?"

He steps up behind me to whisper in my ear. "Picture a thread running from you to that person. Pull gently on it. Bring it inside your body and wrap it around the core of power inside you. Do you feel how it increased the ball of power?"

"Yes!" I exclaim. "There is… more magic available to me."

"Good. When you're done, unwrap it and release it," he directs me.

"It's infinitely more difficult with large groups because the power can overwhelm you, but that is the basic idea," he says, with his hands on my shoulders. "What made you think of declaring war?" Large hands slide down my arms, then release me.

I shrug and tell him my reasoning. "I needed a way to negotiate without having to go through the council."

"You better win the challenge," he advises. "Or Fisk won't be able to negotiate with you. Turn around." He stares down at me with an inscrutable expression. "You have what it takes to be powerful, Meri. Don't be afraid to take risks."

I stare into his grey eyes. "I won't. I promise."

He opens his mouth to say something else, but my phone pings, interrupting the moment.

"I have to go to the funeral. I'll see you tomorrow at the portal?"

"You'll see me, but everyone else won't," he reminds me. "Don't tell anyone I'm there."

GALEN AND GARREN'S funeral is heartbreaking. In their prime and struck down so fast they didn't even have a chance to defend themselves. This is on me. I own this one. They tried to get me to go back, but I wanted to wallow. Taking the torch from Kaius, I walk forward and light each pyre.

"May the keepers bless them on their journey to the other side."

And may the keepers give me the strength to take down their murderers.

I consider Leandra just as culpable as the dark Fae king. Where is she hiding?

CHAPTER THIRTY-SIX

<u>MERI</u>

Cormal, Ansel, Tiernan, Kaius, and I are standing by the portal the next morning. Camon too, but he doesn't count as one of my five since he's the intermediary. My eyes drift to the shadows, but I don't see Madoc anywhere. Not a surprise. He's paranoid about anyone besides the guards seeing him. Most would think it's because of his scars, but Madoc isn't vain. Just secretive.

Camon's phone rings. He answers with a terse hello, listens, hangs up, then shares the coordinates. Cormal didn't like the idea of anyone outside our tight little circle controlling the portal, and I agreed with him. Camon isn't to be trusted.

We arrive at our destination in seconds. As we step out, so does the group across from us. I suck in a breath. Rivan. My eyes devour every inch of him. He already looks better, as if a massive weight has been lifted off him. His shoulders are back, and there's a spark in his eyes that was missing. I drag my eyes from him to the Fae next to him. Dark blue hair, light blue eyes, and standing only comes up to Rivan's shoulder. His wrinkled face tells me he's old. This must be Fisk.

I move from him to a younger and significantly more massive Fae. Bald with a shaggy beard and black, fathomless eyes, he assesses our group closely. His eyes find mine, and he sneers. I chuckle. He reminds me of Madoc.

The remaining two men are obviously guards, based on their stance and the alert way they're standing, hands hovering over the hilts of their weapons.

We meet in the center. Old blue-haired eyes me up and down. "You're a tiny thing, aren't you? Are you sure you're old enough to be queen?" He barks out a hoarse laugh. "I'm Fisk."

"You're not exactly the tallest one out here," I reply drily. "I'm Meri, and don't worry, I assure you I'm old enough to be queen. I guess young people always look like babes when you're as old as the Devil."

The hulking man next to him laughs. "I don't know, Fisk. I kind of like her. Doesn't mean I won't kill her, but I might feel a tinge of regret when I do."

Cormal steps forward. "Fisk. Rivan. Whoever the fuck you are."

Fisk slaps an arm across the chest of the big guy. "Stand down. Cormal looks human, but he's deadly. Don't fuck with him." He gestures to the man. "This is Hyne. Please excuse him. He isn't known for his manners."

I turn my attention to Rivan. "I didn't expect to see you so soon. You look good." My voice trails off, but my eyes stay glued to his.

Fisk clears his throat. "Per our customs, we challenge you to a fight, and if you win, we'll sit down and talk. If not, it's war."

Swallowing, I nod. "Understood. Who am I fighting?" Please don't let it be Rivan. Please. Please. Please.

He gestures to Hyne. "He's our best fighter."

Relieved, I smile. "Great. When?"

Fisk looks taken aback by my response, especially my smile. "Never had anyone react to Hyne that way. Five minutes."

I wink at the giant man. "See you in five. Bring your A game."

A deep laugh shakes his body. "Aren't you confident."

The group walks away and Cormal grabs my arm. "What has gotten into you?"

"Stop grabbing me," I warn him. "Nothing. I'm just glad I don't have to fight Rivan. Why?"

"Hyne is a Kraken," he says with an incredulous look. "He's brutal in a fight. Incredibly strong, fast, and very agile. Multiple arms."

"Sounds like Madoc," I say with a laugh. "Well, except the multiple arms."

Cormal grips my arms. "Whatever happens, don't let him take you into the water. It's his domain, and he'll dominate. Take him out quickly." He runs a hand through his dark hair. "I wish I could fight him for you."

I lay a hand on his arm. "Cormal, if I can't fight him and win, I don't deserve to call myself queen. Besides, you used to throw me in the ring with every crazy demon you could find. Have some faith. I'm trying to." Placing a sweet kiss on his lips, I change into a crop top, sports bra, and shorts. Last, I oil up my skin. It was a trick I learned in the ring.

Walking to the center, I feel a presence nearby.

"I'm here." Madoc whispers. "Remember your shield. Cormal was right. Take him out quickly. He won't tire easily."

Is it wrong to get turned on when he whispers in my ear like a dark predator stalking my every move? Blushing, I glance around, but don't see him.

Quietly finding the threads nearby, I wrap them around the core of power inside me. Buzzing high, I clench my teeth together to keep the extra boost under my control.

Hyne cracks his knuckles and saunters to the middle of the field to meet me. He reminds me of the demons back home for some reason. Maybe it's his less-than-civilized, bordering on neanderthal manner. The Fae are always so damn proper, I constantly worry I'm committing some damn faux pas.

Hyne reaches his hand out for me to shake, but I refuse to fall for that trick. Instead, I flip him off.

"Stop flirting with me. I can't let you win," he admonishes me. His eyes are gleaming with challenge. Fighting the queen is an honor. He'll give it everything he's got.

Fisk raises a hand. "This is not a fight to the death. Do you hear me, Hyne?" He waits until he gets a grunt for an answer. "Match is over when one of you cries 'mercy.' Go!"

With a roar, Hyne charges straight toward me. I watch him for a second to pick up the timing in my head, then I run straight toward him. Surprise lights his face, but it's quickly replaced by determination. Just as we're about to meet in the middle, his arms open wide, and I fuse an extra dose of power in my right hand.

At the last second, I slide between his legs. He tries to close them, but the oil on my skin helps me keep my momentum. Power punching him right in the crotch, I spring up on the other side.

A tentacle wraps around my ankle, and I conjure a knife out of ice and slice it off. I do the same to the next one that reaches for me. When the first one regenerates, I realize this is futile and get rid of the sword. My feet slosh around, and I look down to see the tentacles are secreting water.

Missiles hit my shield and bounce off. I look up to see a windmill of tentacles throwing rocks, trees, and everything else at me.

Safe for a second, I build a circle of fire next to me. Then, I begin to siphon the water from the ground around us, the air, and his tentacles, and stream it across the fire. The liquid evaporates, leaving only steam behind. He roars. Tentacles drop to the ground like wrinkled husks. Dehydration is a bitch. I smile.

A huge whirlpool appears between us, and it starts sucking me toward the middle. Panicking, I look around for a tree or something to hold on to, but the field is barren now. The edge is about two feet away. If my body touches it, I won't have the power to pull myself out.

"Fly," Madoc whispers urgently. "Pull from the bird."

Bird? I glance around and see Rivan. My feet move another foot closer to the whirlpool's edge. Closing my eyes for a brief second, I picture flying with Rivan and the movement and magic he deployed. Air caresses my face, and I open my eyes. I'm not exactly flying, more like hovering a couple of inches above the ground, but the whirlpool has lost its grip on me. Wobbling, I hold my arms out for balance. This needs practice.

A splatter of something hits my shield. Smoke rises, and a burning sensation starts crawling over my skin.

"Fuck. Acid," Madoc curses. "You need to rinse it off with water. Quickly."

I look around at the arid dryness around us. Shit. The only thing with water is the whirlpool, and since I don't know where that goes, there's no way in hell I'm jumping in it. I glare at Hyne, who is laughing with glee and pointing at the lake. His domain.

Another splatter hits the shield, a huge hole appears, and the acid drips onto my arm. Burning like fire, I grit my teeth and race to the lake, Hyne on my heels. As I get close, a huge wave rises up. He crashes into me and closes his arms and tentacles around my body. The wave scoops us up and carries us down into the deep.

My skin instantly stops burning, but my lungs are getting tighter and tighter. I look around for a weapon but find something worse. His tentacles are releasing an ink cloud. Soon I won't be able to see anything. It will be utter darkness. Fear rises, and I try to swim for the surface, but I can't get away from him. Remembering the forest, I close my eyes. My panic recedes, and I smile. I know what to do.

The second it's pitch black, I throw my arms around Hyne and jerk him into the darkness. This is trickier than riding the shadows because there isn't even a modicum of light, but I think it will work. I use Cormal's power to open a portal directly to The Pit.

Upon our arrival, terrifying sounds greet us. I drop him in the middle. "Try not to die while you're here."

Seeing one of the monsters move toward us, I take the portal back to the lake and swim up to the surface. Everyone is on the shore, peering down into the lake, except for Rivan, who's flying above the surface. I swim to the edge and walk out.

Fisk's face is priceless. "Where's Hyne?"

"In The Pit," I tell him.

His eyes widen. Guess he knows what it is.

Waving a hand, I dry my clothes. "Let's give him a few minutes to get acquainted with his new friends."

Cormal laughs and so does Madoc, although it appears no one can hear him but me. How is he staying so hidden?

After thirty minutes has passed, I open a portal back to The Pit. Hyne's surrounded by the worst of the worst, and they're sucking all the power out of him. He's on his knees, but surprisingly, he's still fighting.

"Time to go." I crawl under one of the monsters, grab him, and drag him over to the portal. Good thing they aren't exactly quick.

He lands on the ground, fists still flailing. "Mercy, mercy." His voice is hoarse, as if he's been screaming it for a while.

"Hyne, you're back. Safe," I tell him. Regret fills me.

Eyes black, he stands and reaches for me, but Fisk stops him with one hand. "Challenge is over. Queen Merindah is the winner."

"She won by default," he stubbornly insists. "I bet if you dumped her there, she wouldn't last five minutes. How is this a sign of strength?"

Cormal steps forward. "Actually, she lasted three days... with no magic or power to fight back. Could you do the same? Want to test it?" He bares his teeth in a feral grin. "I'll be happy to take you back and pick you up."

Hyne looks me over. "Three days?"

"All I had was my immortality and a stubborn desire to live," I confirm with a nod. "But every single second was hell. I still have nightmares, and unexpected things trigger me. Prepare yourself."

He nods at Fisk. "She wins." With a shudder, he stalks into the lake and submerges himself.

I hated to do it, but the kraken is tough, and it was the worst place I could think of in that moment.

Fisk sweeps his arm toward the field. "I knew this challenge was going to be different when you ran straight at the hulking giant instead of using your magic first. Never expected it to end like this, though." He eyes the water where Hyne disappeared.

"Are we ready to negotiate?" I ask Fisk, thoroughly exhausted.

"Almost," he remarks, his eyes darting to Kaius. "I want to speak to him first."

CHAPTER THIRTY-SEVEN

MERI

Fisk eyes the man masquerading as his grandson. "I know you're not Kaius. Who are you?"

Kaius looks at Camon, who's standing about twenty feet away. "Vargas," he murmurs, not wanting the High Fae to hear. "I died and needed a body. My mate was returning with Meri to the Light Fae Kingdom. I saw this one. It—Kaius— offered me a chance to be light Fae. It wasn't until later that I realized he was a chameleon."

A sad expression appears on Fisk's face. "Kaius is only one of the disguises he wore. His true appearance is more like mine. He's one-fourth cirein-croin, you know." He pauses. "He must have died on that last mission. Only four people knew about it, and I trust all of them. So, either we have a mole or one of them betrayed me. Neither of those are options I care to think about right now."

He places a wrinkled hand on Kaius' face. "Did he remember

anything?"

"A flash of light," he replies. "Like a beautiful fire."

Fisk stills. "Thank you." He studies Kaius. "I wonder if my DNA will live on through you? I can't say I'd be disappointed to see another warrior with my blood in him."

Kaius' face whitens. "Time will tell."

Fisk takes one last lingering look at Kaius, then turns to me. "Let's negotiate." He claps his hands together and food appears on a long table. "We eat and talk."

"What do you hope to accomplish from these talks?" Fisk asks me bluntly, tearing into the bread at the table.

"I hope to change the path of the Lesser Fae," I tell him quietly. "Do I think everything can be accomplished in an instant after thousands and thousands of years of repression? No. But a treaty allows us to plan out a progression of rights with absolute deadlines. The council refuses to consider any proposals for Lesser Fae rights, but they have to comply with a treaty."

"Why shouldn't I attack? Demand all the rights when we win?" he asks with a hard look in his eye.

"Are you willing to wait hundreds of years to get them? You have a great-grandchild who is going to be born to a High Fae. Don't you want him or her to have their full rights? Or do you want them to have to go to war for them?" I ask, glancing at Camon.

"If war comes, who's to say any of you will survive? Who are the next leaders to pick up the cause? Will they let power go to their head or will they be responsible and fight for the cause?" I shake my head. "There are so many uncertainties. Why not negotiate with me now and avoid a lot of unnecessary deaths and time lost?"

"You certainly don't think like the Fae, especially an aristocratic, entitled one," Fisk says. "Sorry, Camon." He eyes me for a minute. "What exactly do you have in mind?"

"Essentially, I want to help the Lesser Fae establish their rights as citizens and all that it entails. Immediate rights would include freedom from slavery and the right not to be tortured or persecuted," I begin slowly, figuring things out as I speak. "Given the land situation with the Fire Fae, the other immediate change would need to be the right to own land."

Fisk adds one. "If the Lesser Fae are free and have the right to own land, they must be able to change locations without permission."

Cormal conjures up a piece of paper and starts writing everything down. I'd given him the last treaty to use as a template for this one. I would hate for something to get caught because of a stupid Fae technicality.

"With those rights established, the right to require a trial, equality, vote, gather in groups, serve in the army or government, and get an education can be spaced out. It might take ten or twenty years to get all the rights, but it's better than a war that will last hundreds of years." I look into Fisk's unnerving, light blue eyes. "Don't you agree?"

"I do," he agrees. "I never wanted war. Not because I'm afraid of it, but because it would decimate our land and fracture our people. And there are no guarantees we can win. There are too many variables. A treaty is a better solution."

Everyone takes part in the negotiation. Camon gives us the High Fae and council viewpoints. Fisk and Rivan provide examples of how rights can be implemented to suit both parties. Cormal's knowledge of the steps the Underworld is taking to address the lack of education and basics for their people is helpful in determining how to do the same for the Fae.

For the rest of the night, we eat and hash out the details of the treaty. We consider the time it will take to execute each step. It's not a simple declaration of freedom and suddenly everyone complies.

The sun rises, and we each complete one final read through

of the draft to make sure there are no mistakes, and all the terms are clear. Once we confirm, we all sign it. Fisk for the Water Fae, myself for the Light Fae Kingdom, and the others as witnesses.

We make a copy for each person, including the witnesses, and one extra one for the council. I pick up the blade on the table, slice my thumb, then add my print to each of the copies. Fisk does the same. Blood is indisputable and lends the treaty authenticity.

Hyne ambles up to us, dripping water and mud, and sits down next to me. Cormal tenses on the other side, but I take his hand to reassure him.

"I don't want to die," he confesses to me. "I did. Before last night. I lost my mate, and there didn't seem any point to it all. The last few years I've done everything I could to drink myself to death, but every morning, I woke with the sun." He tilts his head toward me. "In The Pit, I fought to survive when I could have easily just given up. Everything became so crystal clear in that instant. Thank you."

"Clarity is a rare thing," I state softly, looking across the table at Rivan. "Sometimes we need help to see it for ourselves."

Rivan's slow smile is breathtaking. "It's a rare person who helps others stand."

Fisk stretches and yawns loudly. "Been a long time since I stayed up all night. Now I remember why. I'm too damn old." He looks at Camon. "Tell Brina I love and miss her. I'll be glad when this baby comes, and she can come visit."

Camon inclines his head respectfully. "I will."

We make our way to the portals.

Hyne holds his hand out to shake, but I refuse with a laugh. "Still not falling for that trick, but if you dry off, I'll gladly give you a hug."

In an instant, he's dry. With Cormal muttering something obscene in the background, I reach up and hug the kraken.

"When you tell this story, make sure you get the details right or I'll find you and challenge you again." I crook a finger to make him bend down. "There are worse things than The Pit. Callyx just told me about the Below."

Someone chokes behind me, but when I turn, they're all staring at me with an incredulous look on their faces. Kaius, especially. "Damn it. He has no right to be telling people about the Below. Lucifer will have his hide."

Now I really want to know what it is. I wink at Hyne, but he backs away with his hands up in the air.

Fisk laughs and holds his hand out to shake, and I take it.

"I wasn't sure what to think about a queen who knew nothing about the light Fae, but you might be the best thing that's happened to us in thousands of years," he states gruffly. "Only time will tell if I'm right."

"I'm just glad I picked the right person to declare war on," I say, only half joking. "I'm sure the council will meet within the next day or two. I'll send word."

Rivan comes and stands in front of me. "I'm leaving the Fae realm. There's nothing for me here."

Pain sears my lungs, and I can't breathe for a second. "Where are you going?"

An optimistic smile spreads across his face. "I'm going to the human world. With the mix of supernaturals, I won't stand out, and maybe I can build a new life. Something to call my own."

I wish I could go with him.

"Go to Arden," I urge him. "She'll help you get settled, and it will be good to have people you know nearby."

He smiles. "I will. No goodbyes." His gold eyes stare into mine.

"No goodbyes," I murmur to him, although this sure as hell feels like one. I step back.

Cormal opens the portal, and we all leave.

Once we return, I send my copy of the official treaty to the vault, along with the council's copy, and I make a secret copy without the blood and stash it in the Underworld.

My phone buzzes with several text messages. All from Lorn. I stare down at it, tempted to wait, but I can't keep avoiding him.

Cormal looks over my shoulder. "Lorn?" When I nod, he looks at me. "Go. You haven't seen him in days. I'll go check on things in the Underworld."

"If I ask him to be a part of my life, are you going to be okay with that decision?" I ask, needing to know his answer.

"We are never-ending. Lorn or no Lorn," he assures me. "If he makes you happy, I'll learn to live with him." He kisses me hard on the lips. "You were amazing last night but stop throwing out challenges like they're candy. I can't take the stress."

Knowing he deals with things way more stressful than this little challenge; I laugh. When he doesn't join me, I realize he's serious.

"Not too long ago, you told me to save myself," I remind him with a touch of bitterness in my voice. "Why are you suddenly worried? Do you think I can't do it?" When he says nothing, I throw up my hands. "Go. I'll see you later."

With an irritated growl, he stares down at me. "Stop. I'm not quite used to this new badass who seems willing to take on all her enemies at once." He thrusts a hand through his hair. "I hear you. I do. Do you want to talk about this now?" His blue eyes are serious as he waits for my answer.

"No, but this is only a temporary reprieve. Got it?" I ask, narrowing my eyes on him.

He gives me a short nod and a firm kiss. "I'll be back later."

After he's gone, I head to my room to switch clothes and guards.

Meri: Sorry, I've been gone the last couple of days. Do you have time to meet now?

Lorn: Yes. Botanical gardens?

Not quite what I had in mind.

Meri: How about the little restaurant where we first had lunch?

Lorn: We need somewhere where we won't be overheard. Botanical gardens. Fifteen minutes.

Irritated, I debate canceling, but I know it's more procrastination on my part than any desire to avoid the gardens.

Meri: See you there.

Ten minutes later, I arrive with Kian and Laken. Lorn is already waiting for me at the entrance. This time, there is no bright smile or kiss on the cheek.

I frown. "Is everything okay?"

"Let's walk," he replies, looking at my guards. He bends his head and lowers his voice. "I had a visitor a couple of days ago. She told me your father is the dark Fae King. At first, I laughed, but later, I remembered the creature in the alley."

I tilt my head. "The boy?"

He gives me a derisive smile. "It wasn't a boy, but yes, the one with the message from Denir." His dark purple eyes study me closely. "She was telling the truth, wasn't she? Your father is Denir, the dark Fae king."

The only woman who knows outside of close friends and family is Leandra. "Did this female tell you her name?"

He shrugs. "Leandra. You didn't answer my question."

Not liking the tone of his voice, I step away from him. "I wasn't sure when I came here today whether I still wanted to see you, but this conversation has helped convince me we should just remain friends. And the answer to your question… it's none of your business."

"Oh, but it is," he states firmly. "You see, Basilus wasn't King Arles' cousin, he was his half-brother. The Fae love their secrets, remember? Royal blood ran in his veins, which means it runs in Allandra's too."

Not liking where this conversation is going, I look around for my guards, but we're in a back corner, hidden from view. "So?"

"The light Fae deserve a queen worthy of their lineage, not some half-breed who carries dark Fae in her blood," Lorn sneers. "I've called for an emergency council meeting. I will ask for your crown and present Allandra as a worthy alternative."

"Why not yourself?" I say flippantly, even though I'm beyond furious right now.

"I'm not Lord Basilus' child," he reveals, to my astonishment. "Lady Kyra stole me. She lost their baby, but didn't want to tell Basilus, so she brought me home and presented me as his son and heir. I didn't find out until many years later when I fell in love with Allandra. My mate."

What the hell?

Shocked, I stand there and stare at him. "No wonder she was so jealous."

He laughs. "It was her idea. She thought if I got close to you, we would find a way to get rid of you, and it worked. Although she did get a little jealous when I admitted I enjoyed spending time with you." He peers earnestly at me. "I do, you know. I genuinely like you, and you like me too."

I stumble backward only to come up against Laken. Lorn's dark purple eyes flash with something dangerous. "Liked. Past tense. I'm going home. See you at the council meeting. Lorn."

CHAPTER THIRTY-EIGHT

<u>MERI</u>

The council decides to delay the meeting for another day to give Faris time to finish his discussions with the Fire Fae. Lorn sends a message to all the council members with details on my background and asks them for a vote of no confidence.

Weary, I drop into bed, pull the covers over my head, and sleep for hours.

When I wake, the world is in an uproar. Eris bustles in at her usual time and informs me that Lady Estrella's keep was burned to the ground.

"Fire Fae?" I ask, dreading her answer.

"Lord Faris," she responds gleefully. "He awarded the land to the Fire Fae, then burned her keep to eliminate any contention between them."

Shit. He certainly took the opportunity I gave him and made the most of it.

She stares at me. "It's not all good news. The Water Fae are assembling not far from here. They'll launch an attack on the palace within a week."

What the hell?

I scramble into the navy-blue pinstripe suit Eris is laying out for the council meeting. "I don't understand. Fisk and I have a treaty."

Cormal steps from the shadows. "Rumor is Fisk is dead."

"When?" I pick up my phone and text Rivan.

"Shortly after they returned from the negotiations," he says tersely.

Kaius bursts into the room, followed by Callyx. "My sources say Fisk was murdered."

A tear slips down my cheek at the loss of such an old and honorable Fae. "Any information on Rivan? He isn't answering my texts."

"He disappeared," Callyx informs me. "Sources saw him in the vicinity. Some are trying to pin this on him."

"That's not the only thing going on." I tell them about Faris and his deeds and follow it up with my conversation with Lorn. "Our enemies are attacking us from all sides. It's going to be one hell of a council meeting today."

Putting my head in my hands, I try to think of what to do next. The Fire Fae situation will cause an uproar, but the council gave Faris the right to negotiate. The crown will, of course, provide reparations to Lady Estrella for the loss of her keep and land. Lorn. He'll do his best to sway the council with his potent charm. Frowning, I immediately text Laken.

"Fisk thought he had a mole, remember? Only a few knew about Kaius' mission," I remind them. "Camon was one of them. Maybe the High Fae isn't playing both sides. Maybe he's playing the long game." I look at Kaius. "Too bad you can't access Kaius' real memories."

I know I'm grasping at straws, but I don't even know how to unravel this mess.

Cormal squats down in front of me. "Breathe. That's it. Go to the council meeting. I'll look for Rivan. If I can't find him, I'll see if I can find out what happened to Fisk. Whatever you do… don't give them your crown. They can't take it from you."

He wraps his hands around both sides of my head and brings me close for a long, tender kiss. "There are always going to be problems, Meri. Granted, these are pretty bad, but you're strong and intelligent. You'll find a way."

I stare at him. "I needed to hear those words. Thank you." I kiss him again. "Be careful."

Standing, I straighten my suit. Sharp, powerful. "Thank you, Eris." I leave Callyx and Kaius looking at a map of the palace and the land around it and stride out the door. Ansel and Tiernan immediately follow me.

Solandis is standing at the council room doors, but she looks worse than ever.

"This is about more than Estrella's betrayal. You're sick. Have you seen a healer?" I ask her, waving at Ansel to shut the council doors so we won't be overheard. Crossing my arms, I wait for her to answer.

She looks at me and laughs. "You sound like Arden." Leaning close, she raises a finger to her lips and whispers, "I'm pregnant."

My mouth drops open. "What?! Seriously?" I smile broadly.

She raises a finger to her mouth again and tilts her head toward the doors. "A council meeting isn't going to kill me. Although this one is going to be rough. Are you ready?"

I beam at her, anyway. "I'm so excited." I can tell she is, too, but now is not the time to celebrate.

Throwing my shoulders back, I lift my chin. "Didn't you hear? I won against a kraken. I can handle a bunch of council members."

The room is in an uproar, and unlike previous times, it

doesn't stop when I enter. If anything, it gets worse. Lifting a hand, I mute every one of them except Solandis.

"We will conduct this meeting in a civilized manner, or I will postpone it until next week," I warn them. "Call the roster and read the minutes."

Taking my seat, I release my hold, but the second one of them opens their mouth, I immediately mute them.

"Lord Camon."

"Lord Camon."

I look at where he usually sits, only to find the seat empty. That's unusual. Maybe he's hiding out until all this is over.

Everyone else is here.

"Lord Faris, take the floor and give us an update," I order him.

He bows deeply to me. "You were right. If the Fire Fae didn't get their land, they were going to declare war. Nothing I said could deter them. I felt it was in the best interests of the light Fae to grant them the land."

The council erupts, and I stand. "We will have order. If you wish to speak, stand, and I will call on you."

"Lady Estrella," I call out when she stands. Might as well hear her first.

She points at Faris. "I want him arrested. He stole my land and burned my keep. There is nothing left."

"The council gave Faris the right to negotiate on our behalf. Just because you don't like the outcome doesn't mean he has committed a crime," I state with an elegant shrug. "There is plenty of land available. Pick out a spot and the crown will grant it to you, along with reparations to build a new keep."

She throws up her hands. "I want my land back."

"Was it your land?" I ask her. "Technically, the treaty gave Nyssa the land. She granted it to your father and Basilus. Both are gone. Wouldn't that mean the land should have automatically reverted back to the crown?" She opens her mouth, but I hold a hand up. "We could argue semantics all day. It is within your rights to take this to court, or you can accept the crown's very generous offer."

Faris' eyes gleam with personal satisfaction. He bows and takes his seat.

"Next agenda item," I call out.

Lorn stands and flashes his bright smile at the crowd, but instead of the usual fawning, he gets small smiles and a few fluttering lashes.

I look over and give a subtle nod to Laken, who is standing in the corner. Winter Fae. I had him lower the temperature in the room by ten degrees. I wasn't sure the tactic would work, but the nymphs often complained when it was cold.

He clears his throat, and his smile vanishes. "It has come to my attention that Merindah, the Queen of the Light Fae, is half dark Fae. Her father is the worst of them—the Dark Fae King, Denir."

The crowd looks at me but remains silent.

Lorn steps down to the floor. "I ask you to render a vote of no confidence. We have a better option for our queen. My sister, Allandra. She carries the royal blood of the light Fae. Basilus was King Arles' half-brother, not his cousin, like everyone believes."

Whispers rise.

Solandis stands and regards Lorn with disdain. "Whether your story is true or not, I don't know, but it doesn't matter. There are quite a few individuals here with royal blood. The crown chose Merindah to be our queen. A vote of no confidence in a council meeting means nothing. If she wasn't the right queen for us, the sacred throne and crown would have rejected her. It didn't. There is no law against having dark Fae blood. You have no authority to ask for her crown." She sits down.

Lorn looks around at the council. Most of them turn away from him. Instead of sitting back in his seat, he storms out.

"It is my understanding that Fisk was assassinated after our negotiations," I tell the council, tackling the elephant in the room head on. "We're currently investigating the situation. Once I have more information, I'll share it with both the Water Fae and council." I hold out my hand for the vault copy, but nothing appears. "We have a treaty. I'll share copies of it with everyone once we have answers about what's happening."

Keir stands. "We deserve to know what's in the treaty, especially with the Water Fae beating down our door." He slaps a fake smile on his face, but I can see the glee in his eyes.

"Here's a copy of the original agreement. It will have to do for now," I tell him, pulling my extra copy from the Underworld. I quickly make copies for them, then put it back. "Read the terms at your leisure. We can discuss them at the next council meeting. Dismissed."

I stand and escort Solandis out of the meeting and back to her rooms. Once there, I try to call my copy from the vault again. Nothing. "I put my original copy in the vault. It has my blood and Fisk's on it to show its authenticity. I keep trying to call it, but nothing is happening. I need to go look for it."

Solandis stops me. "Be careful. If it's not coming to you, it may not be there anymore. If it's not, take a look at Keir. He's the only other person who can access the vault, but to do so, he would need a senior member of the council to give him permission." She raises an eyebrow. "I noticed Lord Camon wasn't there today. Perhaps he gave him permission."

"If he did, he likely destroyed or hid his own copy of the treaty," I surmise with a grimace. "Thanks." I look around. "Cormal strengthened the wards on this room, too, didn't he?" She nods. "Stay here. Don't leave for any reason. I'm sure Kaius or Callyx will be back soon."

I head straight to the vault. When I get there, it's in shambles. Papers are everywhere, and the stack of jewels and gold I saw the last time are gone. Robbery or Keir?

Madoc slides into the room and presses a finger to his lips. "They're monitoring your every move."

"Who is?" I whisper. "And where have you been?" I can't help but scan him for new scars.

"Taking care of a friend of mine," he informs me coolly. "I don't report to you."

Rearing back, I put a hand on my hip and glare at him. Asshole. "The treaty is missing. Fisk is dead. Rivan isn't answering my texts, and I haven't seen or heard from you since the challenge. Forgive me for being worried. I won't do it again." I brush past him and enter the hallway.

Shit. I forgot to get an answer about who is monitoring me. Forget it. If he really wants to help, he's going to have to step out of the shadows. I don't have time to play tag.

Cormal's waiting for me when I get back to the room. He immediately pulls me into his arms and seals the room. "Fisk is dead. Rivan's in hiding. I can't find him. Word on the street is that the Lesser Fae revolution has started."

I fist my hands in his jacket and hold on to him. "The original treaty is missing. I gave a copy to the council but without the official ones with the blood, there is nothing to prove they aren't fake. Everything I did was for nothing. War is here."

CHAPTER THIRTY-NINE

<u>MERI</u>

Callyx arrives via the shadows. "The portals aren't working. I was going to bring in back-up, but if I have to do it via the shadows, it will take all night."

Cormal fills him in. "Where's Kaius?"

Worry crosses Callyx's face. "He went to assess the Water Fae army, but he should have been back ages ago. I'll go check on Solandis."

"Bring her back here, if she'll come," I tell him. We need to stay together.

Minutes later, Callyx walks back in via a shadow with an unconscious Kaius in his arms. He lays him down on the couch. "Solandis has been taken. There's a note in my pocket." The gravelly tone of his voice tells me his demon is close to the surface.

Cormal pulls out the note. "Give up the crown or she's dead. Coronation hall tomorrow morning at sunrise."

Callyx splashes some water on Kaius. "Come on, old man. Wake up."

He doesn't even move.

"How did they take him down? I doubt they snuck up on him," I ask with a frown. Walking over, I feel for any lumps on the back of his head and neck, just to be sure. "Nothing." As I roll his head from side to side, the glittery yellow dust in his hair catches the light.

Where have I seen this before?

I dab a tiny bit on my thumb and hold it up to the light. "Lorn's rooftop. It was in the soil he'd spilled on the table. It must have come from one of his plants."

Cormal and Callyx look at each other. "Stay here. Watch Kaius. We'll check it out."

They disappear into the shadows.

I run to the door. "I need you to send one of the guards to the botanical gardens. Ask for the gardener or person in charge of the night plants. Tell them the queen needs information on the plant that emits a glittery gold dust like this. It's an emergency. Some of it got on Kaius, and we can't get him awake." I transfer it from my finger to Ansel's. "Hurry."

Ansel looks at Kian. "Stay here. I'm going to send Tiernan to join you." He takes off running.

I close the door. Turning back to Kaius, I grab a glass of water. Maybe if I get some water down him and clean off the dust, it will help.

A hand clamps around my mouth, and I drop the glass.

I don't even think, simply twist my hip, and pull the person over my shoulder. He slams into the floor in front of me.

Kian pops up to his feet. "Nice move, but you need more than that to take me out."

He pulls his sword and swings.

I jump backward and press myself against the wall.

He stares at me, a zealous look in his eye. "The crown shall not be tainted with the blood of the dark Fae." Advancing on me, he raises his sword.

I slide to the right and into the corner.

He flashes a triumphant smile.

I step into the shadow behind me and follow the ribbon to the corner on the opposite side of the room. When I step out, he's facing away from me. At least now I have the space to maneuver. Palm out, I conjure a fireball and send it flying at his back.

He ducks and swings around to face me. "You have to do better than that to catch me." In a blink, he stands by the couch, his sword over Kaius. "Traitor. He knew about your father and did nothing." He pushes the tip into his neck.

Kaius can't die, but right now, we don't have the months it will take for him to find another body and make his way here.

"That's because he isn't Fae," I say abruptly, trying to buy some time. "I mean, his DNA might be Fae, but nobody knows for sure. The real Kaius was Fae. In fact, he was part cireincroin. Can you believe it? I thought they were long gone. Myths."

He stares down at him with his head cocked to the side. "Who is he?"

"Vargas Karth," I reveal, to his shock. "What are you going to do when Lucifer comes after you? There isn't a place in any of the realms where he won't find you. Or Callyx, Lucifer's assassin and Vargas' son. Or Solandis, his mate."

"Solandis is being detained," Kian says gleefully. "Once I kill him and you, I'm going to join Lorn in his campaign to put a new queen on the throne."

His smile is still on his face when his head rolls off his shoulders and on to the floor.

I take in a deep breath and hold it. "Thank you, Tiernan."

He sheaths his sword. "My pleasure." Spitting on the body, he heads to the door.

"You should leave," I tell him. "I don't know what's going to happen to the palace when the Water Fae gets here. The aristocratic Fae who live here full time have enough power and provisions to keep anyone from entering for years. Or leaving. If they find out you're a spy, they'll tear you to pieces."

He stops and turns toward me. "How long have you known?"

"For a while now," I reply. "It's why I sent you on the delegation with Rivan. He needed someone who could be honest with him about both sides." I smile. "If I didn't have your oath, I probably would have turned you in, but as you've just shown, the gamble was worth it."

Tiernan studies me. "Thank you. I'll leave once Ansel returns." He pauses. "You're not a bad queen, you know? You're the one we needed after King Arles died to carry out his vision, but it's too late now." He slips out and closes the door.

I send Kian's body out to the balcony and set it on fire. Then I clean up the glass of water I dropped when he grabbed me. Getting a fresh glass, I take it over to Kaius and pour a sip down his throat. With a wave of my hand, I remove all the yellow dust. He doesn't stir.

I lean close. "We don't have time for you to die. Do you hear me? They took Solandis. Fight this so we can save her."

Nothing. I drop my head into my hands with a weary sigh. The door opens, and I jump up with a fireball in my hand.

"It's just me," Ansel says, holding up a paper bag. "The gardener told me to grind this leaf up and put it under his tongue. He should wake a few minutes later."

"Thank you, Ansel," I say, taking it from him. A thought occurs to me. "Where does your oath fall?"

He looks me directly in the eye. "With the crown. Always. The sacred one you're wearing." Looking around, he comes back to me. "Why?"

"No reason," I say nonchalantly, unsure of whether Tiernan

said anything about Kian. "I might need to leave in a bit. Who's on duty?"

"Tiernan and myself," he informs me. "Kian switched with him."

"I see. Thank you," I reply with a smile. Tiernan must have felt it was better he didn't know about Kian. "I'll stick my head out when I'm ready to go. Thank you for getting this back to me so quickly."

He straightens and dips his chin. "Queen Merindah." Striding to the door, he steps outside.

I contemplate the bag in my hand. Do I trust Ansel?

Callyx and Cormal return. "The entire home is in shambles, and there's nobody there. We did find the plant on the roof," Callyx says with a growl. He plops the plant down on the table. "Any changes?"

I tell them about Kian, then hold up the bag. "What do you think? Should we take a chance?"

"The worst-case scenario is he dies and comes back later, right?" Callyx says, his voice filled with uncertainty. "Best case, it works, and we save Solandis. Do it."

Crushing it with the bottom of the glass in my hand, I keep twisting it until it's completely pulverized, then pick up the mushy mass and put it under his tongue.

A few minutes later, he shoots up into a sitting position and grabs me by the throat. Cormal immediately grabs his wrist and hits a pressure point in his shoulder. He releases me with a look of confusion.

Kaius puts a hand on his head. "What the hell?"

Callyx steps up beside him and gets him standing. "Someone took Solandis."

Anger builds in Kaius' face until suddenly, it's not Kaius anymore. Vargas stares back at us, but with eerie and very familiar looking light blue eyes instead of his dark ones.

Cormal pulls me up and pushes me behind him. "Easy. We're

not the enemy." Smoke curls out of his fingers as he stares at this version of Vargas.

Lines appear between Vargas' brows. "I know who the hell you are. What's wrong with you?" He tries to peer behind Cormal to me. "Sorry, Meri. I didn't mean to grab you."

"Look in the mirror," I urge him, gripping the back of Cormal's shirt.

When he does, he reaches out a hand to touch the glass. "I guess the old man was right. There is some of his DNA in me." His face whitens. "Which means It's also in our child."

Callyx stares at him. "What child?"

"You're having a brother or sister," Vargas replies harshly, his smile deadly. "Once I get my mate back." He whips around to look at me. "It was Lorn."

Sensing he's back to a somewhat normal state, I step out from behind Cormal and explain everything that's happened since we found him.

"You don't think he took her back to the Autumn Court house, do you?" I ask, remembering he lived there after the Fire Fae destroyed everything.

They all three shake their heads.

"Too far," Cormal states confidently. "Sunrise is only two hours from now. With the portals down, we don't even have enough time to get the cadre in here. Not all of them."

Something crashes onto the balcony. Cormal immediately moves in front of me. Callyx and Vargas head outside to look. They hurry back in a minute later with Rivan held up between them. They lay him on the couch.

Rushing over, I sweep the hair back from his bloody face and wave a hand to clean him up. "Thank the goddess. What happened? Do we need to get a healer?"

He shoves something into my hands. "My body will repair itself. Give it a minute. My father happened." His eyes move to

Vargas. "Something you said made Fisk believe it was my father who killed his grandson, Kaius."

Vargas frowns. "He asked me about Kaius' memories, but the only thing I could recall was a flash of light and a beautiful fire. Why?"

Understanding dawns in Rivan's eyes. "When phoenix regenerate, they emit faery fire. It's blue-green light. Very bright. Fisk only told four people. Your description gave him his answer."

I look at the paper in my hand. "Is this Fisk's copy or yours?"

"It's mine. I'm going to leave here and take Fisk's copy to the Water Fae. With both his blood and scent on it, it will give them enough proof of its authenticity," he tells me. "Then I'm going to hunt down Camon. He's the only one who knew where to find my father. Hyne and I tried to stop Fisk from going until we could get back-up, but we turned around and they were gone."

"Bastard," Cormal spits out.

Rivan's body finishes healing, and I look at him sadly, not wanting him to leave.

He sees the look on my face and sweeps my hair behind my ear. "I'm coming back," he reassures me, pushing up from the couch. My face must tell him more than I realize because he suddenly pauses. "What is it? Is something else going on?"

I clutch the treaty tightly in my hand and force a smile. "I'll fill you in later. We need you to get Fisk's copy to the Water Fae or the palace will be under siege. Go. No goodbyes, remember?" My voice is tight with emotion as I silently say goodbye.

He pulls me into his arms and hugs me tightly. "No good-byes." Flashing a strained smile, he steps back, checks to make sure the other treaty is in his vest, then walks out to the balcony and shoots up into the sky.

Callyx gives me a furious look. "Why didn't you tell him? We could have used his help to save Solandis!"

I turn to my cousin. "Do you think Solandis would want him

to save her or the light Fae? He's the only one who can get the treaty to the Water Fae. I'm still queen, and I promised to protect the light Fae against all threats. This is me fulfilling that promise the best way I can. Besides, we're going to save Solandis."

He throws up his arms. "How?"

"I'm going to give up my crown," I say quietly but firmly. "She is worth everything to me. Do you honestly think I wouldn't give it up for her? The tricky part will be giving up the crown and getting us all out of there in one piece. Aren't you three supposed to be good at planning battles? Get to it."

CHAPTER FORTY

MERI

Grey filters into the black, and the sky lightens. Not long now. I turn my attention back to the mirror and trace the crown on my forehead. It feels like forever since I stood here, feeling overwhelmed and completely inadequate for the role of Queen of the Light Fae. If it hadn't been for Cormal, I probably would have run away. He sure knows which buttons to push.

I look across at him. The crown might be lost, but I've gained so much more here. Not him. He's just a bonus. Me. I found the person I've always wanted to be, and crown or no crown, I refuse to let her go.

My biggest fear is whether I will have any power when this is done. I quite like having some juice to back up my sass. Without it, I couldn't have taken down the kraken. Something I intend to own until the day I cease to exist. I chuckle. Cormal. My eyes find his across the room. He raises an eyebrow to silently ask if I'm okay, and I nod. Maybe I'll persuade him to share his trade secret—the way he gained all his powers and made himself immortal. After all, I'm going to need some serious magic to take down Leandra. Magic or no magic. That's one goal I refuse to give up.

Wailing comes from outside the balcony doors, followed by mournful sound. I turn to go look.

"It's the cry of the banshee," Eris says softly. "They foreworn the living of the death that's coming. This one only cries for members of the royal family."

I walk over and stare out into the garden. A beautiful, ethereal woman cries in the garden below, sending her message to the inhabitants of the castle. *Does she cry for me or another?* Goddess, please don't let it be Solandis. We all need her.

"I'm glad you stopped by," I remark with a smile, turning away from the wailing woman. "Thank you for everything. I couldn't have done this without you." Sitting on the floor, I pull a box out from under the couch. "This is for you."

She looks at me with sad brown eyes. "It's not your fault. This has been coming for a long, long time. Nyssa's rule destroyed all the good in this land. Everything disconnected a long time ago, but she couldn't feel it through the haze of power."

"I wonder if that is why there is a dark hole inside me instead of the information Solandis said would eventually fill me," I ponder.

Eris' wise face nods in agreement. "There's nothing you could have done to stop this, although many, including myself, will remember you tried your best. Save Solandis and yourself." She darts a glance at the three men. "Your scary men, too. This isn't your fight. It's ours. The Lesser Fae revolution will charter a new path for us."

She opens the box, and her mouth drops open.

"Surely you're not speechless over a few jewels and coins," I tease her. She tries to hand it back to me, but I toss my head at Cormal. "He can afford to keep me in whatever style I wish. Take it. It's a pittance, but hopefully, it will help you and the Lesser Fae of the palace find a new home."

"Thank you."

Little arms wrap around my neck, then in a flash of magic, she's gone.

I sniff and wipe the tears on my cheeks. I'm going to miss having her saucy mouth wake me in the morning and take care of everything. I wonder if there are any brownies in the Underworld.

Pink streaks through the grey. Cormal wraps his arms tightly around me. "It's almost time to go. Are you ready?" Blue eyes filled with pride look down at me. "You don't have to wear a crown to be noble. In your short time as queen, you did more for the Lesser Fae than any before you. The treaty will live on long after you're gone. It's an incredible legacy."

I smile at the thought. "Do you think I'll lose all my power?" I bite my lip when I voice my biggest fear out loud.

He tucks a platinum curl behind my ear. "I don't know, but you won't stay that way for long. I promise. Besides, you already have the greatest power. The ability to mimic." His eyes stare intently into mine as if he's trying to convey something, but I don't understand his silent message.

Bending down, he captures my lips in a kiss that makes every one of my toes curl. He finally pulls away and presses his forehead to mine. "Whatever you do today, don't sacrifice yourself. Trust me to save you. I know it's hard given our past, but I promise, you are my priority. Kaius and Callyx will focus on getting Solandis out of there. Can you do that for me?"

"Yes," I promise him. Orange joins the pink and grey outside. "It's time."

"We decided to have Vargas walk in with you. Not only will the shock factor give us an edge, but it will remind the aristocratic Fae that you have powerful ties to the Under-world. Very few want to fuck with demons or Lucifer," he divulges.

"Or you," I add.

His chuckle is full of darkness. "Or me."

With a wave of my hand, I dress in a sleek black suit with nothing underneath. I laugh at the look on Cormal's face. "Held together by a wing and a prayer. Might as well go out in style."

His eyes fill with heat. "Definitely one hell of a statement." His lips find mine one more time. "Go. I'll see you there."

Vargas' face is grim when he holds out his arm for me to take.

"Just a second." I look around at the beautiful room that was mine for a moment, then turn my back on it. "Let's go."

This is a very different walk than the one I took weeks ago. Last time I couldn't imagine being queen. This time I know I am queen. Am I going to regret giving up my crown? Never. I will miss it though. Maybe I'll find my own empire to rule like Cormal. I chuckle at the idea.

I hope Rivan got the treaty to the Water Fae. My fingers lightly twirl the one in my hand as if it's not the most important thing in my possession right now. When the tall doors appear, I use a little magic to tuck it in my pocket.

Vargas stops. "I don't know how I'm ever going to thank you for doing this. Quite frankly, it sucks. But I'm so damn thank-ful." He looks down at me with his heart in his eyes. "She means everything to me."

I lean in and whisper, "She means everything to me, too. I never knew a woman could be so kind and loving and giving before her. A crown is nothing."

The doors open, and I straighten. "Put on your 'don't fuck with me face.' Things are about to get real."

He chuckles at my order.

Striding into the hall with Vargas on my arm, I walk straight to the dais and sit on my throne. That's right. The one that accepted me.

"Outsiders aren't allowed in the coronation hall," Lord Camon sneers to my right.

My nails lengthen with the need to claw his eyes out. "Well, when the light Fae kidnap the mate of the commanding general of Lucifer's army, it becomes a multi-realm incident. In other words, it's a big fucking deal."

He freezes. "Solandis is his mate?"

"You don't recognize Vargas?" I say snidely. Looking up at the fierce man beside me, I shake my head. "It must be the eyes." I turn my attention to Camon. "He picked up a little cirein-croin DNA while he was in disguise."

Brina whispers furiously to him.

"Speaking of Fisk, the cirein-croin who tragically lost his life avenging his grandson's death," I begin, but stop to let the crowd catch up. "Yes, the leader of the Water Fae army. Apparently, Brixton, the leader of the Fire Fae, killed Kaius, then Fisk. He's not a good person. If you see him, run the other way."

I tap a finger on my chin. "Where was I? Oh, yes, that's right. The treaty with the Light Fae. Where's Faris?"

The Fae in question saunters forward, wearing his best poker face. "Here, Your Majesty." He bows.

Cheeky. I can't believe I ended up liking him, of all people. "Since I don't know who to trust with this when I'm gone, I'm going to give it to you." I reach into my pocket and pull out the treaty and hand it to him. "It's the treaty. The Water Fae have Fisk's copy. Both have been authenticated with our blood. Word of caution… don't store it in the vault. Keir has a key."

The crowd noise rises considerably. Several people move away from Lord Keir, who's standing not too far from Camon.

"I may not be on the throne, but this treaty will live on without me. Whoever inherits this crown will have to honor it. Consider it my gift to the light Fae. All the light Fae." Okay, I might be the tiniest bit bitter that I won't be here to see the Lesser Fae get their rights.

Allandra claps loudly when she steps forward. "Congratulations. Although, there are many ways to twist the truth and honor an agreement. The Lesser Fae will find that out when they deal with me."

"Getting a little ahead of yourself, aren't you? In a recent council meeting, Solandis said several light Fae have royal blood." I look to my right. "Lord Camon, for instance, is probably third in line behind me and Solandis. What makes you think the crown will choose you?"

She looks uncertainly behind her.

Lorn steps up with Solandis, a large dagger at her throat.

Vargas snarls and walks over to them. "Are you okay, my love? Did he hit you?"

Her eyes are filled with fear and anger. "No, but he isn't what he seems." A bead of blood trickles down her throat.

"Shh," he admonishes her. "Don't spill my secrets. Or you and your baby won't make it out of here alive."

The crowd goes utterly silent when they hear his words. If there's one thing the light Fae cherish, it's children. There are so few of them born to the aristocratic Fae. Several glare furiously at Allandra and Lorn.

I once asked Lorn about the magnetism he seemed to wield against men and women so effortlessly, and he glibly replied something about an ancestor, but I can't help but wonder if his ancestor is something darker than the light Fae.

"The crown," Allandra orders me.

I peer down at her and tap the crown that is literally branded on my forehead. "Instructions, please."

She looks confused.

"It's not a physical crown. How. Do. I. Take. It. Off?" I grit my teeth to stop myself from calling her an idiot.

Brina pushes Camon forward. "Tell her."

Hmm, I guess there's more than one person who wants this crown.

"You renounce the crown and kingdom. When the power starts to flow out of you, the crown will allow you to grab it and pull it off," he grimaces.

Dread fills me. "In other words, this is going to hurt like hell. Lovely."

More blood trickles down Solandis' throat.

"Stop hurting her," I growl at Lorn.

Vargas clamps a hand down on his wrist.

Closing my eyes, I search for the gossamer threads inside me and the black hole at my center, and tug on them. They shift a little.

Keepers, hear my plea. I gladly give up this throne and crown to save another, but I beg you to examine all the contenders to find the best ruler among them. Not the one with the most royal blood, or the best lineage, but the one who will have the people of the Light Fae Kingdom in their heart. The aristocratic Fae and Lesser Fae. Not one or the other, but both.

With those words, I cut the gossamer threads. Excruciating pain swallows me whole, and I lock my jaw together. Muscles tighten, and my back bows. I grip the arms of the throne to keep my body in the seat. I accepted this crown without a whimper, and I'll give it up the same way. Power flows out of me piece by piece, along with my ties to the kingdom. My heart breaks at the loss.

The pain eases, and when I look inside, it's all gone. Except the knowledge. A gift? Or is it harder to take away knowledge than power?

I reach up and grasp the crown and rip it away from my forehead. Gasping, I double over with pain, but a soothing coolness swipes my brow, and the pain recedes.

Thank you to whoever just did that.

Standing tall, I hold the crown in my hand for one last time, then hold it up for everyone to see it in all its glory.

I look at Lorn. "Release her."

He hesitates, but Allandra gestures at him furiously.

Green scales appear across both of Lorn's arms as he stubbornly shakes his head. "No. Give Allandra the crown first."

Vargas takes a firm hold of Solandis.

Lorn tightens his grip, and she cries out in pain.

Furious, I hold the crown out to Allandra, but when she reaches for it, I toss it high into the air, hoping to give Vargas the distraction he needs.

Everyone's eyes follow its path.

Guards pour into the room and surround Callyx and Vargas. Callyx immediately pulls his sword in defense. Vargas reluctantly releases Solandis to join Callyx.

I look up. The crown is near the top of the ceiling, suspended in air as if held by a string. It spins one way, then another, as if looking for someone. Suddenly, it begins to spin furiously around and around. Light bursts from it. Camon steps forward and holds out his hands. Allandra glances at him, then does the same. Others follow.

I step down from the dais.

"Why won't it choose?" Brina cries frantically.

Allandra grabs my arm, her nails puncturing my skin. "What did you do? I know you did something."

"I told it to pick the best ruler," I state truthfully.

Power surges through her and into me. "Tell it to pick me."

"The crown chooses the ruler," I force out through clenched teeth. "Why don't you ask it to pick you?"

Her eyes gleam and she looks up at the crown. "Pick me." Nothing happens. She waits another minute. Furious, she sends more power through me. "It's not working."

Camon laughs at her feeble demands. "I'm a High Fae with royal blood on two sides. It will choose me."

Brina grips her husband's arm tightly. "Call it to you."

"I'm trying," he mutters.

The pain is so crippling, I fall to my knees. "Let go of me."

Faery fire erupts from the tips of her fingers. "Maybe it can't choose another unless you're dead."

The smooth hilt of a familiar dagger slips into my palm. Gripping it tightly, I wait for the right moment, knowing I have no other choice.

She raises her arm.

Cormal erupts from the shadows a foot away, but it's too late. For Allandra. I plunge the dagger into her heart. She steps back and looks down with a laugh, then crumples to the floor, her eyes staring sightlessly at the ceiling.

Lorn roars in pain and immediately erupts into a huge green beast. He shoves Solandis to the floor, then charges toward me, every step thunderous in the golden hall. Cormal smoothly slides between us and raises his hands. Dark magic flows from his fingertips into the beast, slowing it immediately.

I look at Vargas and Callyx. They've taken out the guards around them.

Vargas picks up Solandis and steps into a shadow.

A brilliant golden light fills the room. Shading my eyes, I look up and watch as the crown suddenly disappears.

I step closer to Cormal. "Solandis is safe, but we need to go. Wrap it up."

Incantations slip from his mouth. The floor beneath the beast opens into a dark, endless tunnel. It drops into the massive black hole, roaring the entire way down. Cormal closes the floor and grabs my hand.

With the threat gone, Callyx steps into a shadow to follow Vargas and Solandis.

A sharp point presses against my chest and I jerk Cormal to a stop.

While I was distracted by everything else, Brina pulled the Killian Blade from Allandra's chest and now holds the tip of it against my heart. One prick, and I'm dead.

Cormal blinks. The only indication of his surprise. None of us thought to watch Brina.

"Where did the crown go?" she asks me furiously.

"How the hell should I know?" I ask with an incredulous look. "It's an ancient artifact. I don't control it."

Furious, she raises her arm and stabs... straight into Cormal's heart.

He staggers, and I grab him. The weight of him takes me to my knees.

"Fuck!" He roars.

Brina reaches down and yanks the blade from his chest, causing a fresh spate of cursing from Cormal.

Pressing my hands against the wound to stop the flow of blood, I realize Cormal needs a few seconds to catch his breath. I look up and glare at Brina. "You missed."

She gestures toward Cormal and smirks. "Looks dead center to me, but don't worry, you won't have to watch him suffer."

Forcing a laugh, I sneer at her. "Don't you know anything? It's a Killian Blade."

She looks down at the dagger in her hand, her face puzzled.

I deliberately heave an exasperated sigh and roll my eyes. "It was created to kill Fae, not other immortals. All you did was piss Cormal off."

Cormal throws up a hand and sends Brina flying into the marble column. Her neck breaks, and she slides to the floor. Not dead but incapacitated for a few minutes.

Camon hurries over, but instead of checking on his mate, he picks up the Killian Blade and turns toward us.

Cormal holds up his hand, but Camon's a High Fae, and he's powerful. He counters every spell Cormal throws at him.

Only a few feet away, I hold up a hand, hoping the blade will come to me, but Camon tightens his grip on the hilt.

"Good try," he taunts.

Suddenly, a swirl of black shadows erupts from the floor, a

thin wire wraps around Camon's neck, and his head drops to the floor beside Allandra's body.

Faery fire erupts across both bodies turning them to ash. The crowd instantly backs away from this new threat.

"Madoc," I say with a hysterical laugh.

The beautifully scarred man strides over and helps us stand.

I look up at him. "Your timing is impeccable."

Madoc looks around at the light Fae with a sneer on his face, then turns to me. "I was worried about you."

My lips twitch at his admission, knowing he's only repeating my words. I look at Cormal. "Where?"

"The Abbey," he says, gritting his teeth. He glares at the tall Fae beside us. "I suppose he's coming too?"

I hold out my hand to Madoc. "Join us?"

Madoc's steel-grey eyes assess Cormal, then move to me. "Yes. Until we find Leandra, I go where you go." A large strong hand grasps mine, and the three of us slide into the shadows.

THANK YOU!

Thank you for continuing to follow this series! For a long time, Meri's story only came to me in bits and pieces until wham! It was suddenly there in all its glory. I thoroughly enjoyed writing this book and I can't wait for you to see what comes next! I'd love to hear your thoughts. Whether it's "give me more," or "I want to see a book with…" reviews help me write the next story. Please consider leaving one for this book.

*If you find an error, email me at Stellabrie@stellabrie.com.

*If you see the ebook anywhere besides Amazon KU, please send me an email (see address above) or contact me on social media. Pirating can have severe consequences, preventing authors from creating new stories.

To get a free eBook copy of my first book, My Salvation, just subscribe to my newsletter.

Website: https://www.stellabrie.com/my-salvation

AWESOME PEOPLE

Huge thanks to everyone who make my books possible!

To my readers, friends, and fans! Thanks for all the wonderful words of encouragement, friendship, and love for my books! And for participating in my shenanigans and all the other weird things I post. You guys rock! I couldn't do it without you!!!

My awesome beta readers. They catch so many big and little things, help me with names, show me such amazing friendship, encouragement, and excitement, and they can't even share it with anyone! My books are a thousand times better because of their feedback. Thank you, Nia, Bianca, Iliana, Melissa, Rachel, Sandi, and Debbie for everything!

My ARC team who gives me so much support and enthusiasm even though I drop things on them at the last minute. Ooh, look, cover reveal! Book's launching in a week! Seriously, I appreciate all of you!!

My biggest supporters—my husband and mom. I'm so lucky to have you both! Love you!

And always... a special thanks to all the wonderful authors in the writing community who support each other day in and out. Writing would be a lonely and weird world without you. It would be me and my characters sitting around chatting (drinking) while we plot the next book. Your friendship and support mean a lot to me!

ABOUT THE AUTHOR

Stella Brie lives outside of Nashville, TN, with her husband. After mentioning her desire to write a book a million times to her husband, he challenged her to sit down one day and write a paragraph. Instead, she wrote her first book, *My Salvation*.

She traded in her career in digital marketing, working on big brands, for this wildly creative one. Armed with a notebook crammod full of ideas, she's constantly thinking about bold heroines, sexy men, and HEAs. Whether it's a paranormal book full of creatures and magic or a contemporary romance full of heat and drama, she's always thinking about how she can bring her books to life.

Facebook Group: Stella's Stalkers

Instagram: @stellabrie_author

TikTok: @stellabrie_author - Signed paperbacks!

Etsy: https://stellabrieauthor.etsy.com - Signed paperbacks & swag

YouTube: https://www.youtube.com/@authorstellabrie - Playlists for each book

Website: Stellabrie.com - Exclusive sneak peeks, cover reveals, giveaways, and more!

BOOKS BY STELLA BRIE

PARANORMAL WHY CHOOSE

KILLIAN BLADE SERIES

The Rowan (1)

The Rowan's Stone (2)

The Rowan's Destiny (3)

The Light Falls (4) - Meri's story

The Dark Rises (5) - Meri's story

Spin-offs:

Wicked Savior - Lucifer's story (MF Romance) - Book 3.5

CONTEMPORARY WHY CHOOSE

THE SAVAGES SERIES

Savage Traitor (1)

Savage Ruin (2)

Spin-off:

Lethal Vengeance (Standalone)

My Salvation (Standalone)

To get a free eBook copy of my first book, My Salvation, just subscribe to my newsletter.

Website: https://www.stellabrie.com/my-salvation

www.ingramcontent.com/pod-product-compliance
Lightning Source LLC
Chambersburg PA
CBHW021246190726
48289CB00005B/1514